*A Bowl of*

# A BOWL OF CHERRIES

*Anna King*

**ROWAN**

A ROWAN BOOK

Published by Arrow Books Limited
20 Vauxhall Bridge Road, London SW1V 2SA

An imprint of the Random Century Group

London Melbourne Sydney Auckland Johannesburg
and agencies throughout the world

First published in Great Britain
by Barrie & Jenkins 1990
Rowan edition 1991

Printed and bound in Great Britain by
Courier International Ltd, Tiptree, Essex

ISBN 0 09 975630 7

My parents, Peggy and Bill Masterson.
My brothers and sisters.
Last but by no means least, my husband Dave and my Children,
Tony and Victoria.

To all the doctors and nurses at St. Bartholomews Hospital, especially Dr. Anthony Dawson to who I owe a huge debt of gratitude. My sister Maggi Deere for her valuable help in correction my numerous spelling mistakes.
Special thanks to David Grossman who believed in me.

# Chapter One

The man walked slowly, a suitcase in each hand. When he reached the corner of Well Street he stopped for a moment taking in the scene before him. It was not yet seven o'clock on this cold November morning but, being Saturday, already both sides of the long road were lined with stalls, the overhead green and brown canvas canopies blowing in the bitter wind. The stallholders shouted to each other as they loaded up their stalls.

"'Ow did you get on with that bird last night, Pete – any luck?"

"Naw, but I'm taking her out again tonight. Think I might be on a promise."

This last remark was greeted by loud laughter and ribald comments from the East End market traders. Listening to the light-hearted exchange the man with the suitcases felt a pang of envy that he couldn't join in the camaraderie that was part and parcel of the East End markets. He was a "fly-pitcher", a trader who travelled from market to market in search of a space between stalls where he could lay his cases and sell his wares while keeping a wary eye out for the local bobby. At best he would be moved on with a warning; at worst he could be nicked on the spot. Stepping carefully over a crate of ripe red tomatoes that lay on the ground by the fruit and veg stall he stepped sharply into a vacant gap putting his battered cases down onto the frosty ground.

"Oi, you can't set up there. That pitch belongs to Tiny Dodd. I'd 'ave it away on your toes, mate. 'Ere 'e comes now." The fruit and veg man was standing by his side, his cold breath billowing out a cloud of vapour that swarmed like smoke in front of his face.

The fly-pitcher looked to where a huge giant of a man pulling a stall already laden with tinned goods and housewares was bearing down on him, a ferocious look on his weatherbeaten face. Hastily he picked up his suitcases and moved swiftly to the middle of the road.

"Bloody fly-pitchers! Why don't you get a licence like the rest of us instead of trying to nick our pitches. Go on, sod off!" Tiny shouted, his big fist held in front of him lending weight to the verbal warning.

"Oh, come on, Tiny", the trader from the fruit stall said lightly trying to ease the tension, "we all started that way. I 'ad to fly pitch for months before I got me licence." Turning back to the fly-pitcher he pushed his woolly cap to the back of his head and said kindly, "Look, see over there, between the sweet stall and the bloke selling toys?" He pointed over the other side of the road, his hand wearing the fingerless gloves essential in the cold weather for handling money. "The bloke who usually works there 'as just bought a shop up Mare Street. All right for some, ain't it? Anyhow, I'd get over there a bit sharpish just in case another of your mob gets the same idea."

The fly-pitcher thanked the man and watched him turn back to his stall, his hands trying the navy canvas money belt around his waist, the hall-mark of all market traders. Stamping his feet against the cold he walked over to the space between the stalls, put his cases down and waited. When no one challenged him he breathed a sigh of relief and opened one of his suitcases displaying rows of watches and lighters. As he bent to open the second case two women walked past him chattering happily, their extra-large shopping bags clasped firmly in their gloved hands, their arrival proclaiming the market open for business.

"Nice pair of kippers for the old man's tea, darling?" The fishmonger stood behind his stall, his white coat smeared with the blood of the dead fish that stared sightlessly into space. Peggy Cowley carefully averted her gaze as she hurried past, the smell of the fish making her gag. As the crowds closed around her she experienced a moment of fear. Her head seemed about to explode, and for one terrifying moment she thought she was going to faint. Taking a deep breath, she surged forward almost knocking over a carton of eggs. Ignoring the trader's shout of protest, she stumbled on, her apologies lost amidst the noise of traders and customers. Angry cries followed her as she weaved through the crowded street, her heavy bags knocking against the legs of the women who crowded around the stalls, and made her way out of the mêlée into a small side street. Heading straight for a nearby bench, she thankfully lowered her two bags of shopping onto the ground, while at the same time easing herself onto the long bench. As she sighed with relief, she looked down at her swollen ankles, her eyes travelling upwards towards her even more swollen stomach. Minutes passed before she attempted to rise, only to sink back down again. She felt tired; no – not tired, weary – there was a world of difference. Closing her eyes, she leaned her head back against the wall behind her, grateful for the opportunity of a few moments solitude.

"Are you alright, Peggy?"

Startled, she opened her eyes to find Joan Brown, her neighbour, staring down at her anxiously.

"Yes, yes, I'm fine, thank you."

Hastily, she rose to her feet, using the arm of the bench to steady herself. As she bent to pick up her shopping she was alarmed to find that her hands were trembling, as was her entire body.

Seeing her friend's distress, Joan put her arm around Peggy's shoulders saying, "Look, you stay here, I'll go and fetch Bill."

Fighting back a wave of nausea, Peggy smiled. "No, I'm fine now. Really."

Her looks belying the words, she picked up her shopping. Quickly now, Joan took one of the heavy bags from Peggy's hand. Ignoring her friend's protest, she linked her other arm through Peggy's and began walking her home. The East End in the sixties was a mixture of old and new houses. Called a new "urban region" most of the East Enders had been rehoused in less crowded, if rather drab, three-storey council and private semi-detached "dwellings". They were comfortable but lacked originality. Those less fortunate had to make do with the new high-rise flats, the designs showing a lack of sensitivity on the part of the architects.

Peggy and Joan were two of the luckier ones, having been allotted one of the newer type of two-storey flats grandly named maisonettes. Then of course there were still the old pre-war habitats – ugly small terraced houses usually standing in a row of six or eight, their occupants elderly, stubbornly clinging to the past and refusing the council's offers of re-housing, not knowing that soon they would be forced to move and make way for the bulldozers. The sites were needed for yet another block of flats to house the ever-growing number of people desperate for accommodation.

It was down such a road that Peggy and Joan made their way home. Barnabas Street stuck out in sharp contrast amidst the new flats. On one side of the road stood four drab little houses, once a whole row, the ends on either side of the row having been demolished, the exposed walls still bearing scraps of wallpaper, the former occupants having long gone to newer homes. On the other side stood the row of shops that were a godsend to Peggy, Joan and the rest of the community, for these were the shops that gave tick. On Monday, Tuesday and Wednesday, when money was scarce and the market was closed, the small parade of shops did a thriving business with customers buying their goods on these days and not having to pay until Friday, the day when the men brought home their wage packets.

Today, like most Saturdays, the shops stood empty, their owners knowing their customers would be down the large, sprawling market buying their shopping, some haggling and bargaining with the traders, all with good-natured camaraderie. Meeting friends and neighbours, the women held up the throng of customers as they stood and gossiped, their heavy bags laid down for a minute while people tripped over them, cursing. The market served an additional purpose as a meeting place for those not able to afford the pubs and clubs that littered the East End.

As they approached the first shop, both women glanced quickly in and hurried on, fearful that the grocer Danny would see them with their bags of shopping and berate them for their desertion. It was all done good-naturedly, the shop keepers knowing that Saturday was the day for bargains. They were quite happy with the trade they did during the week. The second two shops were owned by husband and wife, Maud and Pete Fisher. Maud ran the sweet shop while her husband attended the greengrocer's adjoining it. Both were surly individuals and neither Peggy nor Joan ever went into either of the shops unless they were desperate. The last shop was the only one that did any trade during market days. Kosseff's, the baker's, had the advantage of supplying the only goods that couldn't be found among the traders: fresh bread and appetizing cakes.

As they passed the bakery a small, dark-haired woman stepped from the doorway, the cold sunlight glinting on her enormous earrings. "Good morning, Peggy," she called out, her face breaking into a smile at the sight of them. "So, when is the baby due?"

"Sooner than expected if she doesn't take more rest like she was told to," Joan replied before Peggy could answer.

Smiling faintly at her friend, Peggy turned to the woman who had enquired after her.

"Take no notice of her, Sadie. None of my children have ever come early; I don't suppose this one will be any different."

Anxious to get home, Peggy lifted her hand in a wave and began to walk on.

"Send some of the children down about five," Sadie called after her. "Business is terrible today, such a waste of good bread and cakes. Maybe you can take it off my hands?" As Peggy started to protest, Sadie threw up her hands as if warding off any arguments. "So, I should feed it to the birds when it could go into the children's bellies? Go, get home and rest, and don't forget to send the children down." And then she was gone, back into the bakery, giving Peggy no chance to refuse the kind offer. Not that she would have – pride was a luxury she couldn't afford.

"Not far now," Joan urged her on, anxious now to get her friend home and off her feet.

The sudden sound of drunken voices caused the two women to quicken their steps as a group of men staggered from the large red-brick pub that stood on the corner of the street. The morning drinking session was ending and the men would now be making their way home to their long-suffering wives, expecting their dinner to be ready on the table, after which they would probably fall asleep on the settee until tea-time. Most of them would be back in the pub by evening. Peggy said a silent prayer of thanks that her Bill didn't drink, an unusual trait in an Irishman.

"Here we are, just another couple of minutes and we'll be home," Joan said cheerfully. Glancing at Peggy, she noticed the tired lines around her eyes and felt a pang of pity for her friend.

She could remember the day the Cowley family had moved into No. 5 Seagrave House. Together with Mrs Masters from upstairs she had watched in horror the seemingly never-ending stream of children alighting from the back of the large white removal. Laughing and shouting to each other, they had run onto the small square courtyard while a slenderly built man had tried to maintain some kind of order over them. It had been the sound of his voice that had caused Mrs Masters' eyebrows to rise even further.

Turning to Joan she had said just one word "Irish".

The single word had spoken volumes, and the two women had exchanged a knowing glance before returning to their respective homes. The residents of Seagrave House had had Irish families living in the block before and they weren't too happy about having another lot take their place; but as the weeks went by, it had become evident that this was not the usual type of Irish family. There were no disturbances, the children were polite and bore no trace of their parents' Irish brogue, their accents being undeniably cockney. But the biggest surprise of all had been the discovery that Bill Cowley didn't drink, swear or gamble.

Three weeks after their arrival, Joan had knocked on Peggy's door to welcome her and the family to the community. Peggy had been delighted to see her and had accepted the hand of friendship, gracefully ignoring the fact that it had

14

been a little late in coming. Over a cup of tea in a spotlessly clean, if sparsely furnished kitchen, the two women had talked for hours, and when Joan had finally left she knew she had found a friend.

As they neared their homes, Peggy cut into Joan's thoughts by saying, "Would you like to come in for a cup of tea?"

Shaking her head, Joan answered, "No, thank you, Peg, I'd better get in." Jerking her head towards her front door, she added, "They'll be wanting their tea."

Stopping outside her own front door, Peggy took her shopping bag from Joan, thanking her once again as she did so.

"If you get time tomorrow, pop in for a cup of tea and a natter," Joan offered, then added, "And it wouldn't hurt one of your lot to get the shopping now and then. They're not all babies." So saying, she raised her hand and knocked on her front door.

Peggy rang her own doorbell and waited. She heard Joan's door close, and still she waited. Losing her patience, Peggy lifted her hand and began to bang on the kitchen window. Suddenly the door was flung open by her daughter, Ellen. At eight years of age she was what Peggy often called "a little madam". Her small frame was bursting with indignation, the long blonde hair falling over her blue eyes trying to hide her childish resentment at having to leave the television to open the door.

"What took you so long?" Peggy demanded angrily.

Shrugging her shoulders, Ellen began to walk away.

"Just a minute, young lady," Peggy shouted after her. "How about giving me a hand with this shopping?"

"Oh, Mum, I'm watching the telly."

"Never mind the telly, get hold of one of these bags and put it in the kitchen." Tutting and blowing, Ellen pulled one of the bags into the hall. Then, making a great show of exertion, she set the bag down on the small kitchen's floor.

"There," she said. "Can I go back to the telly now?"

Resisting the impulse to smack her face, Peggy put her hand on Ellen's shoulder, and none too gently pushed her

15

from the room, calling after her, "Tell your father I'm home."

Going into the kitchen, she went over to the small table. Sitting down for a minute she rested her head in her hands, then, hearing the sitting room door open, she got to her feet and began to put the shopping away.

"Give me a hand, Bill," she said over her shoulder.

Bill Cowley came into the kitchen clutching a newspaper in his hand. He was a small man of five-foot eight; his weight of nine stone had never altered in all the years that Peggy had known him, and this in spite of the enormous dinners he consumed. Whereas Peggy, as she was wont to say, only had to look at a cake and she put on pounds. Then again, seeing as she was permanently pregnant, it didn't seem to matter very much.

"What do you want me to do, dear?" he asked.

"Use your eyes", she snapped at him, "or do you expect me to climb on a chair and put this lot away myself?"

Recognising the warning signs, Bill quickly put down his newspaper and set to work. They were both silent for a few minutes, then, with all the groceries put away, Peggy once more sat down at the table.

"Are you all right, dear?" Bill asked, looking at Peggy's pale face. Without waiting for an answer he went on, "You know, you shouldn't carry all that shopping at once, it's too much for you."

Peggy looked up at him, a warm feeling going through her, a feeling that quickly vanished as he added, "If you were to get up earlier, you could make two trips."

Looking up at her husband's serious face, Peggy didn't know whether to laugh or throw something at him. The situation was saved by their eldest son. Bobby was a very sensible child for his age, and, hearing the tail end of the conversation, had decided to rescue his father.

"Hello, Mum, want any help?" he asked, his voice cheerful.

Seizing his opportunity, Bill backed away into the hall saying, "I'll be away out from under your feet, dear."

Watching the retreating figure of her husband, Peggy turned her attention to her son. At eleven years of age, he was a good child, never giving her any worry, unlike some of her children. He was a handsome boy, with dark curly hair and blue eyes, slim but sturdy with a pleasant disposition. Now he stood in front of her waiting to be told what to do. When no orders came, he used his own initiative. Going over to the cooker, he lifted the copper kettle over to the sink and proceeded to fill it with water.

"I'll make you a nice cup of tea, all right, Mum?"

Watching him struggle with the heavy kettle, Peggy went over to him and lifted it out of his hands, saying quietly, "It's all right, love. If you want to help you can lay the table." Always pleased to help his mother, he ran to the drawer where the cutlery was kept and began putting the knives and forks on the small formica table. This done, he watched his mother light the gas under the big pan of bacon stew she had prepared before going to the market. With nothing more to do, he sat with his elbows on the table, his hands cupping his face, his eyes following Peggy as she walked around the room.

She was pretty, his mum. Her long dark hair which fell to her shoulders was shiny, her face was smooth with blue eyes that matched his own. Lowering his eyes he looked at her stomach. He knew all about babies, and although he got on well with his brothers and sisters, he wished his mum would stop having any more. She always looked tired, and since a friend at school had told him that some women could die having babies, he had been constantly fearful for her.

He remembered the night he had found out she was going to have another baby. He had woken up with a toothache and had come downstairs to find her. The angry voices coming from the sitting room had stopped him in his tracks. He hadn't been able to hear properly, but his mother had been crying, saying over and over again, "I don't want any more, I've had enough, I don't want any more." Bobby had crept back to bed, but he hadn't slept that night. Lost in his thoughts, he jumped when Peggy spoke to him.

"Get down now, love, I'll call you when dinner's ready."

"Can't I help you, Mum?" he pleaded.

"No, thank you, love, I can manage, go on now." As Bobby reluctantly left, two small figures came bounding into the kitchen, nearly knocking him over.

"Mind out, you," he shouted at his younger brother, Jimmy.

"Ignoring Bobby, Jimmy clambered up to the table. "Is dinner ready yet, Mum? I'm starving."

"You're always starving, now get down from that table," Peggy yelled at him.

Five-year-old Vicky, who had followed her little brother to the table, stopped suddenly and stared at her mother, then quickly backed away, her blue eyes wide with surprise.

Jimmy, however, one year her junior, grinned back at Peggy and cheerfully helped himself to some bread and butter.

"You in a bad mood, Mum?" he mumbled through a mouthful of food. Exasperated, Peggy stared at her youngest son. Whereas the rest of her children, and indeed Bill, would avoid her when she was in a mood, Jimmy would just slant his eyes towards her and grin. He didn't seem to know the meaning of fear. He would always be able to look after himself. Peggy found herself smiling back at him.

Reassured by her mother's change of mood, Vicky edged her way back to the table, only to scramble down again, as she watched Jimmy being grabbed by the scruff of the neck and deposited firmly onto the floor.

Vicky fled, her small legs running down the passage, when suddenly she fell and immediately set up a loud wailing. Sighing, Peggy picked her up and, taking a handkerchief from her pocket, she wiped her eyes and smoothed back her blonde curls from her forehead, murmuring all the while, "It's all right. It's all right." Holding Vicky's hand, she led her into the sitting room where the rest of the children were staring fixedly at the small black and white screen that stood in the corner of the room.

Ellen and Andy sat crosslegged on the floor, Bobby was sprawled on his stomach, while Patti sat next to Bill in the small armchair. Marie, of course, was curled up in the other armchair; she liked her comfort.

Setting Vicky on the floor, Peggy said, "Dinner's ready, Bill."

Back in the kitchen, she began to dish up a plateful of stew. As she set it onto the table, she felt her foot come into contact with something underneath. Looking down, she saw Jimmy happily demolishing the last of the bread and butter that she had left on the table. With a cry, she pulled him out and delivered a hefty smack to his backside.

Jimmy looked up at her reproachfully, his normally happy face crumpling for an instant. For a moment Peggy thought he was about to burst into tears, but, drawing himself up to his full height of two foot, he marched with dignity from the room, his back straight.

Biting on her lip, Peggy resisted the impulse to run after him. Picking up her plate, she sat down to eat.

"Is that all you're having?" asked Bill, as he looked at her meagre portion. Getting no answer, he turned to his own dinner and began to eat. When he had finished he sat for a while, then, after making the sign of the cross three times, as he did after everything he ate whether it was a dinner or a sandwich, he stood up.

"Will I send them in now?" he enquired. Peggy nodded.

As she set about dishing up the dinners, Marie, Bobby, Ellen and Andy trooped into the room, followed by Jimmy, all rancour forgotten.

Quickly now, Peggy laid their plates in front of them saying, "Now, don't dawdle, Vicki and Patti have got to have theirs yet."

It was a source of irritation to her that the family had to take their meals in shifts, the small table not being big enough to seat them all at once. She would have liked one of those new tables that could be extended, then she would be able to serve the meals at one sitting. That was one little luxury she would have to wait for, among other things; money was scarce.

"Hurry up, Marie," she said to her eldest daughter who was pushing her food around her plate listlessly. "Have you got a stomach ache again?"

Marie shook her head and began spooning peas into her mouth, forcing herself to swallow the small morsel of food. Looking over to where her mother stood by the sink, her back towards the table, Marie quickly speared two potatoes with her fork and deposited them onto a delighted Jimmy's plate. Putting her finger to her lips, she looked at her brothers and sister willing them not to give her away, praying that her mother wouldn't look over at the table until they had all finished their dinner. Five minutes later Peggy put the pan on the draining board to dry and, wiping her hands on a teacloth, she walked over to the kitchen table.

"Have you all finished?" Picking up their empty plates, she carried them over to the sink, pleased that Marie had eaten all her dinner for a change. Half an hour later, after Vicky and Patti had had their meal, Peggy went into the sitting room to watch the television while Bill tidied the kitchen. It was a long-standing arrangement. She cooked and fed the family, Bill cleaned up after them. Easing herself into the comfortable armchair, she was able to rest her legs on the small stool by the fireplace. The children were scattered about the room, some watching the television, others playing or fighting. She let the noise wash over her; she was used to it.

"Did you get any cakes from Sadie for tea, Mum?"

Opening her eyes, she stared into Bobby's face only inches from her own. She had nearly forgotten about Sadie's kind offer.

"No, I didn't. I couldn't afford to buy any today." Seeing the crestfallen look on her son's face, she quickly added, "But she said that if you go down about five she might have some left over for you." As she watched his face light up she said quietly, "Don't go getting your hopes up, Bobby; she may have sold out by five."

Grinning back at his mother, Bobby gave a small laugh. "Sadie always saves us some cakes, Mum, you know she does."

"Yes, thought Peggy, she always does. The small Jewish woman was yet another kind East Ender who had taken her under her wing.

There was Joan, of course, and Mrs Masters from upstairs, both of whom had offered to look after the children while she was in hospital. She had thanked them both but had explained that her mother was going to come in to keep an eye on them while Bill was at work.

Then there was Marie, her eldest. She was fourteen now, she could help get the shopping and do a bit of cooking if necessary. Marie wouldn't like that, Peggy reflected wryly, but it was too bad. May, her mother, couldn't be expected to do it all. Anyway, she shouldn't be away for too long.

At ten to five Bobby came to her side, Jimmy in tow, both of them hopping from one foot to the other, impatient to get down to the bakers before it closed.

"Not you, Jimmy," she chided him gently, "you're too young to be crossing roads."

"But, Mum," Jimmy protested, "I'll hold Bobby's hand, honest I will."

Looking at his earnest face, Peggy relented. Seeing his mother weaken, Jimmy let out a whoop of delight, then dashed from the room before she could change her mind.

"Hold Bobby's hand, do you hear me?" she shouted after them, but they had already gone, the front door banging noisily behind them.

Hand in hand the two boys ran down Cooper Road and into Barnabas Street, fearful they would be too late. Rushing into the baker's, they saw the broad figure of Sadie bending over the large, heavy baking trays. Their hearts sank; all the trays were empty. Hearing them come in, Sadie stopped what she was doing and turned to face them, smiling when she saw who it was.

"Yes, boys, and what can I do for you?" she asked them, trying to keep the smile from her face. The boys stood in front of the counter, both red in the face from running, their feet shuffling on the wooden floor. Bobby faced her awkwardly; he had come to this shop often, but he always felt embarrassed at having to ask for the leftover bread and cakes that made Saturday night tea so special.

21

Jimmy, however, had no such scruples. "Got any cakes for us, Sadie?" he asked, trying to peer behind her back.

Holding out her arms, Sadie waved them round the empty shop. "You can see cakes, Jimmy; such a day I've had. I could have sold twice as much."

Jimmy's face fell; they were too late. Now he would have to have beans on toast for tea. He felt Bobby take hold of his hand and lead him from the shop.

"What's this I've found?" Sadie's voice followed them. Looking back, they saw she was holding a large brown paper bag, her face wreathed in smiles.

Bobby put out his hand and took the proffered bag, thanking her profusely. Jimmy showed his appreciation by throwing his arms around the small, stout body. His short arms, unable to encompass Sadie's waist, held tightly to her sides. Gazing down at the curly black hair, Sadie felt a lump come into her throat. The memories of other small boys swam before her eyes. Children who had died before they'd known life.

Sadie had fled her native country over twenty years ago. Her husband Joseph, dead now these past five years, had realised the danger to all Jews living in Poland, long before the Germans invaded the country and began the persecution of their fellow countrymen. In vain he had tried to warn their family and friends, but they had laughed, calling him an hysterical fool. Sadie had complete faith in her husband, and so she had joined her voice to his, pleading with her two brothers to leave with them before it was too late, but it had been no use. No one was prepared to leave their homes and businesses on the strength of Joseph's premonition.

And so they alone had left the place that had been home to them, left the people they had loved and sailed to England with their baby daughter and opened the bakery with their small savings. It had been over a year before they had received any word about the family they had left behind, and then one day a woman had come into the bakery, a woman from Sadie's village who had escaped from the horror with the help of a young Polish couple.

Sadie had impatiently waved the details of her neighbour's escape aside. All that concerned her was the fate of her family, and when the reluctant woman told Sadie what had happened to them, the shock was so great that Sadie collapsed. Joseph had been called to look after his wife, and as he'd gently sponged her face with cold water he had listened gravely to the woman's story. Sadie's two brothers and their wives and small children had been taken by force from their homes, their precious possessions confiscated and they themselves herded like cattle onto a packed train heading for one of the notorious death camps.

Sadie forced her mind back to the present, her eyes resting on the two boys in front of her, boys the same age her nephews had been before their young lives had been cruelly ended in a concentration camp. Swallowing the lump in her throat, she said kindly, "Off with you, get home to your mother and be good boys to her."

"Course we will," answered Jimmy indignantly. "She's our mum."

"Bye, Sadie, thank you," Bobby shouted over his shoulder, eager to get home and start on the delicacies that were hidden in the paper bag.

Slapping Jimmy's hand away from the cakes, he ran off, only to come back and grab his little brother's hand to steer him safely across the road. Sadie watched them go, a feeling of sadness stealing over her. She would be leaving this shop soon, as her daughter, Rose, had found a new house in Barking and was urging Sadie to come and live with her. She would miss the East End, especially the children, but she wasn't getting any younger, and she needed someone to be there when she came home. Sighing deeply, she returned to the counter and began sweeping the floor.

The children had a feast that night, for Sadie had been extra generous. When Peggy had seen the cream cakes and iced buns that had fallen from the bag and watched the children's faces light up, she had felt the familiar tightening in her throat when faced with kindness. While Bill cleared away the tea things, Peggy and the children retired to the sitting

23

room. There they watched television for a while, until seven o'clock, whereupon Peggy rose and switched the TV set off. Ignoring the protests that started every night at this time, she herded them all into the kitchen again, this time for their nightly wash. Filling up the plastic bowl, she lined them up. Patti was first, holding onto Vicky's hand, followed by Andy and Ellen; Jimmy came last. Bobby and Marie saw to their own wash in the bathroom.

Rolling up her sleeves, Peggy proceeded to wash their faces and hands, after which they were passed over to Bill who dried them. Then back to Peggy who got them into their pyjamas and nighties. With a quick brush of their hair, and a reminder to brush their teeth in the bathroom, they each in turn kissed her goodnight. As the last one disappeared from view, she made her way back into the sitting room and, with a deep sigh of relief, she sank down in one of the armchairs. She'd give them five minutes, then check to make sure they were all in bed.

Marie and Bobby came quietly into the room and sat down. Being older, they were allowed to stay up later, until nine. Peggy felt her eyes begin to droop. Shaking her head, she tried to concentrate on the small screen in the corner, but it was no use, she was too tired. Her head dropped slowly to her shoulders and within minutes she was asleep. Bill, watching her, was undecided whether to wake her or not. *Hawaii Five-O* was about to start and it was her favourite programme.

He need not have worried – at the first strains of the opening music, Peggy opened her eyes. For the next couple of hours, the four of them watched the television in comparative silence. Then, at nine o'clock, Bobby rose without being told and said goodnight. Half an hour later, Marie too rose, and bid them both goodbye.

"Fancy a cup of tea, dear?" Bill asked.

"All right," Peggy said, getting up slowly. "I'll just check on the children."

Climbing the stairs, Peggy reached the top out of breath. Going first to the boys' room, she carefully picked her way round the small beds that were set side by side. This room, like the rest, was hardly big enough to swing a cat in. Covering up Jimmy who had thrown his covers off, she checked Bobby and Andy before going to the girls' room.

This room was furnished with one double bed which Marie, Ellen and Vicky shared, and a small cot for Patti. They were all fast asleep. Stopping by the double bed for a moment, she looked down at Marie. She'd gone to sleep quickly. Peggy frowned as she looked down at her daughter. There was something wrong there: Marie hadn't been eating properly for weeks now, maybe longer. When Peggy had tackled her about it, Marie had denied being ill, but Peggy was still worried. Tomorrow she would make an appointment to take Marie to see Dr Downey, their family doctor. It was probably something and nothing, but better get it seen to. Casting one last look over the sleeping figures, she quietly closed the door.

As the door closed behind Peggy, Marie opened her eyes. Trying to ignore the pain that had started once again in her stomach, she turned onto her side biting her lip. What was happening to her? she asked herself silently. She was only fourteen. Nobody got seriously ill at her age; did they?

Looking back at her schooldays, she remembered the time she had suffered from eczema. None of the children in her class would play with her, fearful of catching the unsightly skin ailment. She had been five years old, a vulnerable age. Playtime had been a nightmare for her, and she had constantly sought the protection of the playground teacher from the jeers and torment of her classmates.

It hadn't become any easier as she had got older, for then she had contracted asthma. Her schooldays had continued on much the same lines, the only difference being that the insults had become crueller, often accompanied by physical onslaughts. Many a time Marie had been deliberately chased and tormented by the girls in her class until she had collapsed, sobbing, unable to catch her breath. She soon learnt that the only way to ward off the attacks was to make the girls laugh. Always ready to put herself down, she fast became an expert at making fun of herself, thus preventing anyone else from doing so. She would spend hours dreaming up stories to keep them amused. That there was very rarely any truth in these didn't matter. As long as she made them laugh, they left her alone.

Although she was always in the midst of things at school, she had no real friends. Often she would hear them discussing plans for a party, but she was never invited. In school, she was good for a laugh, but once outside the gates, she was soon forgotten.

A stabbing pain brought Marie quickly back to the present. With an anguished cry she pulled her legs up to her chin in an effort to ease the pain. Then, as another vicious pain tore through her stomach, she stumbled from the bed, leaving behind the warmth of her sisters' bodies.

Ellen heard and felt her sister getting out of bed but made no offer to help her. At eight years of age she had her own troubles. That day in class she had broken the lead in her pencil. The punishment for this offence was a penny fine. She lay awake staring into the darkness wondering what she was going to do. It was no use asking her mum for the penny: as young as she was, Ellen knew that money was scarce. Had Peggy known of Ellen's predicament, she would immediately have given her the penny, but Ellen didn't know this. She only knew that on arrival at school in the morning, if no penny was forthcoming, she would be caned.

Wiping away a tear of self-pity from her cheek, she thought of her teacher, Miss Brown, who was the only teacher in the school to enforce this rule, and she, Ellen, had the misfortune to be in her class. She finally fell asleep, only to be woken by Marie climbing back into bed. About to make a protest, she suddenly remembered what the morning had in store for her, and her slight body trembled. As she turned her head into the pillow to stifle her sobs, she was unaware that beside her, her sister, for different reasons, was doing the same.

"Marie, wait a minute, love, I want a word with you."

Hearing Peggy's voice, Marie stopped in the act of opening the front door. She turned to where Peggy was coming out of the kitchen, with Vicky as usual hanging onto her skirt, while Patti struggled to get down from her mother's arms.

"What is it, Mum?" she asked in a bored voice.

The smile slipped from Peggy's face at the sound of Marie's voice. "Don't you dare speak to me like that, young lady!" she shouted angrily. "You can keep that attitude for your friends."

Marie, realising she was on dangerous ground, changed her tactics. "I'm late, Mum," she said apologetically "I didn't sleep well last night."

Turning around to where Vicky still clung to her skirt, Peggy gently eased the small fingers loose and said, "Go and play, love, Mummy's busy." Reluctantly, Vicky let go of her mother's skirts. Peggy watched her walk into the sitting-room before turning back to Marie.

"What's the matter, love?" she asked gently. "I know you're not well."

Bowing her head, Marie mumbled, "Nothing. Why do you keep on? I've told you, nothing's the matter."

Peggy closed her eyes and swallowed before answering. "All right, if that's the way you want it." Her voice sounded tired.

Thinking her mother had finished, Marie opened the front door, but as she was about to leave the house, Peggy's voice stopped her. "I'm making an appointment for the doctor's, I'll take you after school tomorrow."

"No, Mum," Marie whispered, "I don't want to go, please."

Ignoring the plea in Marie's voice, Peggy turned her back on her and repeated, "Tomorrow."

Unable to make any reply, Marie sent one last beseeching look at Peggy's back, then, seeing that her mother wasn't going to relent, she bent her head and walked slowly through the open doorway into the street.

Peggy stood for some moments in the hallway before returning to the kitchen. Going over to the window, she lifted the net curtain and watched Marie as she walked dejectedly down the road. She saw as if for the first time the thinness of her arms and legs, and saw also the lank, greasy brown hair that hadn't been washed for over a week. Letting the curtain fall, she walked back to the table and sat down on one of the chrome chairs. For the first time she felt fear – fear for her daughter. She hadn't realised Marie was so ill.

Peggy felt the tears starting; she cried so easily these days, she tried to hold them back but it was no use. The first tear fell, then another. Patti, too young to realise that something was wrong, happily tried to prise her mother's eyes out, while at the same time she clutched a handful of Peggy's hair.

Vicky came wandering into the room looking for something to eat. At the sight of her mother crying, she stopped in her tracks. Her own lips started to tremble, and without knowing why, she threw herself onto her mother's lap, while Patti played happily on.

# Chapter Two

Deep in thought, Marie hardly noticed the cold November wind. The fear that had taken hold of her obliterated all else from her mind. As she walked along the road that led to her school she tried to pinpoint the time when the pains had first started. She had been all right before her granddad had died. As if she had conjured him up, he seemed to appear in front of her eyes.

"Oh, Granddad," she whispered, "why did you have to die?"

Unbidden memories of summer mornings after Mass appeared in her mind. On the occasions when she had stayed overnight at the weekend, she would always refuse to accompany her nan, Teresa and Pauline to the nine o'clock Mass, preferring to wait and go with her granddad at the later time of eleven-thirty.

She would sit beside him on the hard wooden benches, listening to Father Dodd's sermon, in the blue taffeta dress that had lasted her two summers, and her granddad dressed in his grey three piece suit, white shirt and navy tie, his thin red hair combed and parted neatly in the middle. Together they would follow the service; kneeling, standing and sitting at the appropriate times. Then came the collection, where the round wooden plate covered in the middle with green baize would pass under her nose and she would proudly drop the threepenny piece her granddad had given her into it. He in turn would hold the ten shilling note in his hand for a moment as if giving the people in the other pews time to make note of his offering before placing it gently into the silver- and copper-filled plate.

Sometimes they would take Communion together, kneeling side by side on the padded pew before the altar, waiting for the priest to stand before them holding the Holy Sacrament in front of their faces and making the sign of the cross with the small sliver of bread before gently placing it on their tongues. Marie had always felt nervous at this point, afraid she would somehow drop the holy bread onto the floor, and was grateful for the foresight of whoever it was that had thought of placing an altar boy beside the priest to hold a silver plate underneath the supplicant's chin in case of just such an accident.

After Mass her granddad would always stop and chat with Father Dodd for a while, and then they would walk hand in hand to the pub at the corner of the street. As they walked he would already be undoing his waistcoat buttons and loosening his tie, his weathered face breaking into a look of relief at being freed from restriction. Once they had reached the pub he would leave her outside with the strict instruction not to wander off, and would disappear inside the pub. She would sit happily outside, feeling the warmth of the pub step seeping through her cotton knickers, until he reappeared with a bottle of orangeade and a bag of crisps for her. While he drank his beer and chatted to friends in the bar, she would open the packet, take out the blue paper bag of salt and sprinkle it liberally over the large golden crisps, washing them down with the orangeade, the bottle held firmly between her lips. After she had finished her treat, she would sit and wait patiently for him to finish his beer and take her back to the house for dinner. She remembered these things clearly, but most of all she remembered how happy she had been.

Her nose prickled and tears formed in her eyes as she thought back to the last time she had seen him. It had only been a few months ago. Her mum and nan hadn't wanted her to see him, it was only the fact that he had so little time left that had made them relent. She would never forget that day.

With her mum and nan flanking her on both sides, they had made their way up the sloping hill into Homerton High Road. Marie had gazed up at the sprawling, archaic hospital building, a sick feeling gripping her insides. The front part where they were entering was situated in Homerton High Street, and the rest of the building wound round into Bradstock Road. This part was mainly used for the nurses' quarters. Walking down the winding corridor, Marie had felt her stomach lurch as the smell of antiseptic and ether hit her in the face. Knowing if she said she felt ill her mother would take her straight back home, she had gritted her teeth and marched on.

When they had arrived outside the entrance to the ward, her mother had once again asked her if she still wanted to see her granddad, saying gently that it might be best if she remembered him the way he used to be. Grimly Marie had shaken her head, determined to see him. And then they were pushing their way through the heavy plastic swing doors and walking down the aisle that separated the single beds, each one covered in a drab green coverlet, the starched white sheets folded over neatly, while the patients sat up in their beds looking as if they too had been washed and starched, their faces eagerly scanning the visitors as they walked down the ward searching for a familiar face. Marie had walked on, her eyes darting from one bed to another looking for her granddad. Feeling a tug at her arm, she had stopped at the foot of the metal-framed bed. Her eyes had widened in disbelief as her mother had led her to the side of the bed. There, propped up by a mountain of pillows, lay her granddad, a tremulous smile on his lips, his eyes brightening at the sight of her.

Swallowing hard, Marie had walked slowly to his side and stared down at him. The cancer had taken its toll. The once full cheeks had caved in, making his eyes sink into their sockets. The strong hands that had lifted her and swung her in the air, making her squeal with delight, were now bony and weak. She had wanted to run, run from this apparition, but he had been so pleased to see her, and so she had sat on the side of his bed holding his hand in hers and silently wept. When the time had come to leave, Marie had kissed his cheeks for the last time, and as he'd raised himself on the pillows his face had contorted in pain. At the ward entrance she had turned back towards him, and as his hand had come up in a farewell wave his gold wristwatch had slid down his wrist, coming to rest just below his elbow.

He had died two days later. She never saw him again.

Brushing away a tear at the memory, she accepted that what had happened had been for the best. He had been in so much pain.

Pain, was it pain like she was feeling? The thought brought Marie to an abrupt halt. No, it couldn't be. Granddad had had cancer; only old people got cancer, didn't they? Fear clutched at her belly, starting the pain again. Leaning against a wall, she tried to push the unbidden thought from her mind. Through a mist of pain she heard her name being called and looked up. Two girls from her class were coming towards her. A smile sprang to her lips and the pain eased. Within minutes, her fears were forgotten as she launched into a tale, made up of course. With the first opening words, the two girls had started laughing. Marie felt exalted. She didn't know from where this talent sprang, but she was forever grateful for it. She joined in with the girls' laughter as they entered the school gates.

"Marie," a small voice said beside her.

Looking round she saw Ellen; she was obviously in great distress.

"What's the matter?" she asked, alarmed.

Stumbling over her words, Ellen told her about the pencil. "She'll give me the cane," she sobbed. "I couldn't help it, Marie, I didn't do it on purpose."

Marie gathered her young sister into her arms, feeling her small body shaking. A cold anger rose in her. She too had suffered at the hands of Miss Brown when in her junior class.

"Don't worry," she said, "I won't let her hurt you."

Having made this foolish promise, she wondered how she was going to carry it out. Just at that moment the focus of their fears bore down on them.

"Ellen Cowley," she boomed in a voice that made them both tremble. "Have you brought the penny fine?" The look on her face conveyed the hope that her young charge hadn't, thus giving her the excuse to exercise the punishment she loved handing out.

As she stretched out her hand towards Ellen, Marie, in a rare moment of bravery brought on by the feel of her sister's tight hold on her hand, actually slapped Miss Brown's hand away, crying, "Let go of her, you. Let go of my sister you horrible old witch."

The brief moment of boldness soon passed as she looked into Miss Brown's eyes, the steely gaze completely unnerving her. Pushing Marie contemptuously to one side, the teacher reached out and wrenched Ellen from her grasp.

"Marie, Marie!" Ellen screamed in terror as Miss Brown carried her off. Glancing once more at Ellen's terrified, tearstained face, Marie turned and ran from the corridor. The only thought filling her mind was the need to get home. Legs aching and heart pounding, she headed for home, to her mother, to safety.

Peggy was in the process of making the beds when she heard the frantic hammering on the front door. For a moment she froze, then, holding onto the bannister, she half walked, half ran down the stairs. Her mind started ticking over. One of the children hurt, maybe an accident; or was it Bill? Reaching the front door, she flung it open. Marie rushed into her arms, shaking and crying, stumbling over her words.

"Miss Brown's going to hurt Ellen, Mum. She's going to hurt her because she didn't bring the penny fine for breaking her pencil. I tried to stop her, Mum, I did really, but she pushed me out of the way, and Ellen's crying and screaming. Oh, please, Mum, you've got to come quick, please."

Peggy's face settled into a grim mask as she heard Marie sob out the story. She had heard about Miss Brown's tactics, but up till now she hadn't used them on any of Peggy's children, and what was all this about a penny fine? Surely to God Ellen hadn't been frightened to ask her for a penny? All of the children knew money was scarce, but they surely knew that she would find it for them if the need were great.

Untangling Marie's arms, Peggy took off her apron and donned her coat and scarf. Placid by nature, Peggy rarely lost her temper, but iike any mother when her child is threatened, she was transformed into a raging virago. Stopping only to ask Joan to keep an eye on Vicky, Patti and Jimmy, she stormed off down the road, dragging Marie behind her. No word was spoken between them on the short journey, then as the school gates loomed up in front of her, she squared her shoulders, took a deep breath, and sailed forth to do battle.

After Marie had fled for help, Miss Brown had pushed Ellen before her, slapping her up and down the corridor as she steered her towards the classroom. Now Ellen stared down at the book before her, trying to make out the words through tear-filled eyes, her body still shuddering with fright. Slowly, she became aware of the other children staring, their work laid down on their desks Following their gaze, she felt her stomach lurch at the sight of Miss Brown bearing down on her, the dreaded long wicker cane held in her hand. Jumping up, Ellen made to run, and felt a hand turn her round, then bend her over her desk. Screwing up her eyes, Ellen determined not to cry any more; clenching her hands by her sides she waited for the cane to fall.

Peggy hurried down the corridor, Marie by her side. Coming to a stop outside a classroom, Peggy looked through the window, her eyes widening at the sight before her. Ellen was sprawled across a desk, her dress pulled up to her waist exposing her pink cotton knickers, and bending over her, a cane held high in her hand, stood Miss Brown, her large, plain face suffused with rage. So great was her concentration, she didn't hear Peggy approach until the cane was pulled forcefully from her grasp, accompanied by a push that sent her spinning away from her young victim.

Ellen dashed to her mother's side, her body trembling with relief as she felt Peggy's arm go around her shoulder. The room was deathly quiet, the children sitting still at their desks not knowing how to deal with the situation. They had seen irate parents come to the classroom often; they usually left with their tails between their legs. The two women faced each other, one old, plain and embittered, the other young and attractive, a child on each side of her and one in her belly.

For the first time since she'd become a teacher Miss Brown was at a disadvantage. Trying desperately to retain some kind of authority, she turned to her class, fixing them all with a steely glance. With one accord the children's heads dropped at once, only to pop up again as soon as their teacher had passed, her steps taking her towards Ellen's mum.

"I think we should step out into the corridor, Mrs Cowley. I don't want my class further disrupted than it is now." Miss Brown had assumed the role of the injured party, determined that this common Irishwoman wouldn't get the better of her. Flinging her arm out, she gestured towards the door, but Peggy, ignoring the outstretched arm, stood her ground for a moment and then said quietly, her soft Irish voice quivering with suppressed anger, "I have never brawled in public, Miss Brown, and I don't intend to start now. But if you ever frighten my child unnecessarily again, I'll come back and finish what I started." And, so saying, she took hold of Ellen's arms and steered her from the silent room, leaving Miss Brown staring after them, her mouth agape.

Marie and Ellen walked on either side of their mother, their timid natures rendering them silent after the incident they had just witnessed. Stopping outside the headmaster's door, Peggy raised her hand and knocked loudly. Her blood was up, her Irish temper flaring. If she hadn't been pregnant she would have floored the woman. Without waiting for an answer to her knock, she flung open the door. Mr Preedy the headmaster looked up startled as the woman burst into his study accompanied by two young girls he recognised as the Cowley girls, both of them with their heads hung low as if fearful of meeting his eye. Getting to his feet, he came out from behind his desk and said, "Good morning, Mrs Cowley; what seems to be the trouble?"

The answer came back sharply, "Miss Brown."

Hearing the teacher's name, he gave a deep sigh. Not again, he thought; this will make six complaints in as many months. Forcing a smile to his lips, he said quietly, "Won't

35

you sit down, Mrs Cowley? I'm sure we can sort this out amicably."

Marie stood in the corridor staring after the backs of her mum and Ellen, a piece of white paper in her hand. She looked down at it in disgust. It was a letter from the head-master to her teacher explaining why she was so late for school. She had been certain of a day off in view of her bravery. Hadn't she risked life and limb to save her little sister from the claws of old dragon Brown? Dragging her feet, she made her way towards her classroom. Still, it would be playtime soon, and she would have a large audience today. A smile lit up her face in anticipation. Hurrying now eager to get to her classmates, her mind was already in overdrive as to how she would tell the story.

"Well, go on, what happened then?"

Back home once more, Peggy was drinking a much needed cup of tea and telling Joan all that had happened, while her friend sat opposite her waiting impatiently for Peggy to continue her story.

Putting her cup down, Peggy sighed dramatically – she was enjoying herself. "Nothing much really, I just told the head what had happened. He wasn't surprised; apparently it's happened before. He said he'd have a word with her, and told me to take Ellen home with me for the day. She's still very upset."

Joan nodded, her face grim. "The poor little mite, it tore at my heart to see the state she was in. That woman should be given a taste of her own medicine. It's not right she should get away with it." Leaning forward now, she said excitedly, her eyes gleaming, "And you threatened to punch her on the nose? Oh, I wish I'd been there, I didn't think you had it in you."

Peggy had the grace to blush as she said hurriedly, "Well now, I didn't say that exactly, but she knew what I meant," while at the same time cursing her vivid Irish imagination. It was always running away with her. Marie was exactly the same.

Marie – with all the excitement about Ellen, she had forgotten all about her eldest daughter. Walking Joan to the door, she once again thanked her for looking after the three children.

"Oh, it was no bother, Peg," Joan said, smiling. "Any time."

Closing the door after her friend, Peggy went up to see if Ellen was awake. Opening the bedroom door, she peered into the room. Ellen was on her back, arms flung wide, her slight body still shuddering, even in sleep. Peggy gently sat down on the side of the bed, watching her sleep. Reassured that she was none the worse for her ordeal, Peggy switched her thoughts back to the morning's events. She remembered the faces of the children in Ellen's class. They had, as one body, stared at her with eager eyes, willing her to deal out retribution on their behalf. The disappointment on their faces as she had walked away had been comical to see.

Then there was Marie. The smile left Peggy's face as she contemplated the problem of Marie's mysterious ailment. Who would have believed that the sullen, unresponsive child of this morning and the frightened little girl who had come running for her mum were one and the same person? No doubt things would revert to normal in the morning when the drama was over. And there was still the matter of the visit to the doctor's. Sighing, Peggy gave Ellen one last look before leaving the bedroom. There'd be tantrums and tears tomorrow, and she wasn't looking forward to it, but Marie was still only a child; this morning had proved that. She would do as she was told.

"I don't want to go to the doctor, you can't make me," Marie stood by the kitchen door, glaring at her mother. The argument had raged since she had come home from school. Her thin body shook with an emotion she didn't fully understand, but her eyes blazed defiantly. Peggy, too, was in high dudgeon. Her arms folded over her raised stomach, she glared back at her daughter, the silence in the small kitchen broken only by the ticking of the small carriage clock. They stood facing each other, like combatants waiting for the other

37

to give ground; both angry, but it was an anger brought on by fear. As Peggy began to speak once more, she was suddenly gripped by a contraction. Grabbing behind her for a chair, she sat down heavily, her hand gripping the table for support. "What's the matter, Mum?" cried Marie, running forward.

"It's all right, just a twinge," Peggy answered, trying to calm herself. Marie watched her, her face ashen. It was all her fault, she had made her mother ill. Listening to Peggy's laboured breathing, Marie felt the familiar tightening in her stomach, as if a giant hand was twisting her innards, making the sweat stand out on her forehead.

"Shall I get Joan, Mum?" she gasped, desperately trying to ignore her own pain.

"No, love, just help me up the stairs. I'll lie down for a while." Getting clumsily to her feet, Peggy looked at her daughter. Marie looked worse than she herself felt. A smile crossed her lips as she realised the absurdity of the situation. It was a case of the blind leading the blind. At that moment the door was pulled open and Bill stood in front of them, his face a picture of fright at the sight of the pair of them, each trying to hold the other up.

"Is it the baby, dear?" he whispered, embarrassed to be asking the question in front of Marie.

"What do you think it is – wind?" Peggy snapped at him, apprehension making her irritable. Even though she had been through labour many times, it never got any easier, and she was afraid.

Turning to where Marie stood watching them, Peggy said, "Go and keep an eye on your brothers and sisters. I'm just going to rest awhile. Oh, one more thing," she added, as Marie pushed past her, "we'll continue this little conversation later, I haven't forgotten."

There was no argument from Marie this time, she just bent her head before escaping into the front room. Peggy slowly walked up the narrow stairs, Bill behind her. In silence they entered the bedroom they shared. Once she was settled on the big double bed, Peggy started giving Bill his orders.

"Now," she began, "it's not time yet, I've got a few more hours before going to the hospital. I've got my bag packed.

Marie and Bobby can get Ellen and Andy ready for school and take them with them. Joan will look after Vicky, Jimmy and Patti until Mum gets here. I should only be away a few days; a week at the most. Marie and Bobby will get the shopping. I've told them what to get, but you'll have to help with the cooking, all right?"

Throughout the long soliloquy, Bill had just nodded, aware that no answer was required – his wife had a habit of asking and answering questions to herself. He felt, though, that he should make some contribution to the conversation, and so he said, "Now look, dear, I've looked after them before, haven't I? Now you just rest and I'll bring you a cup of tea about six, all right?"

Without waiting for an answer, he closed the door behind him.

Peggy watched him go, then slowly swung her swollen legs over the side of the bed and made her way to the old dressing table by the wall.

Sitting down on the small stool, she picked up her hair brush and began to pile her hair up into a bun. When she had fixed it to her liking at the front, she turned the two side mirrors inwards so that she could check the back. It was a bit untidy, but her arms ached from brushing her long hair up into the latest style. Putting the hairbrush down on one of the pink doilies, she started to take off the blue smock that she had worn all day. Another contraction caught her as she lifted the dress over her head, causing her to flinch.

Carefully now, she eased the dress off her shoulders, trying not to disturb her hair. Out of breath from this simple exertion, she sat down for a minute on the bed. After a short rest she again got to her feet. Ten minutes later she was ready. She had put a clean dress on, a pink one this time, checked the battered old suitcase that she had bought when expecting Marie, and taken one last look around the bedroom before descending the stairs.

"What are you doing up?" asked Bill, surprised to see her so soon.

"Putting her case down, she came into the room saying, "I wouldn't mind that cup of tea."

Bobby jumped up straight away, crying, "I'll make it, Mum."

Nobody else had moved, engrossed in the television. Most of the children were unaware of her presence. Seeing that her favourite programme was about to start, she sat down to watch *77, Sunset Strip*.

Two hours and three cups of tea later Peggy was standing by the front door, her small case packed and ready. Joan, who had come in to keep an eye on the children until Bill got back, remarked that it would save some time if Peggy kept it permanently packed. Standing on the doorstep, she waved her friend off, then returned to the sitting room where she could hear a fight breaking out.

It had started to rain as they made their way up the hill. Peggy paused to catch her breath while Bill urged her on, fearful she might give birth in the street. The thought so horrified him that he resisted the urge to pick her up and carry her the rest of the way.

As the Hackney Hospital loomed up in front of them, Bill began to breathe more easily. Peggy walked the short distance to the maternity ward, calling out a greeting to various nurses as she passed them. She knew most of them by sight and quite a few by name. With the exception of Barbara and Patti she had had all her children in this hospital, and it was in this same hospital that her father had died such a short time ago.

As she thought of Barbara the familiar feeling of pain passed through her. Poor dear Barbara, her fourth child, had been born a spastic. She'd had her at home and there had been complications. By the time the midwife had delivered Barbara the damage had been done. Peggy remembered clearly the midwife handing her the tiny bundle before going over to the window, there to weep silent tears for the beautiful blonde child who would never know a normal life.

The following years had been hard. Pregnant once again with Andy, she had been advised by her G.P. Dr Downey to have an abortion. The very word had horrified her and

40

she'd left his surgery in rage and fear. The next day she'd found herself back in the surgery, the tears running down her face. She'd sobbed in anguish and despair. She could never agree to an abortion, it was against all the teachings of the Catholic church. But it was more than that, something deep inside her shied away from taking a human life. What else could she do? Every night Marie woke screaming, driven mad with pain from her eczema-covered body. Then there was Barbara crying night after night. She'd been torn in two as she'd gone from bed to cot trying to pacify the two girls while Bobby and Bill had slept peacefully on. Finally, after much soul searching, she had agreed to go to the hospital to arrange the abortion.

Despite the letter from Dr Downey explaining the reason for this drastic step, she had been met with hostility from the Catholic doctor to whom she'd been referred. She had been left crying in an empty cubicle, her arms wrapped around her waist as if trying to explain to her unborn child why she couldn't give it life.

Then the priest had come; not to comfort but to berate her for what she was about to do. "Murder," he had shouted, "that's what you're attempting to do, commit murder!"

At that moment Peggy had forgotten her life's teachings, forgotten this man was a priest, just one step down from God. Standing straight, she had confronted him, shouting back, asking him if he had ever had to walk the floor at night with two screaming children and then get up at the same time the next day and do a full day's work. On and on she'd shouted, her voice bordering on the verge of hysteria. She remembered seeing the look of shock on his face. Catholics didn't answer a priest back, they did as they were told.

She had left the hospital as she'd come, alone. She hadn't wanted company and Bill had been only too relieved to be spared any unpleasantness. No, she thought, looking back, she hadn't been alone. She'd had her child still intact in her womb. All the way home she had spoken softly to the unborn child, reassuring it that it was all right, it was safe.

"Hello, Mrs Cowley, back again?" the blue-clad figure of the ward sister came towards her, breaking into her thoughts. Stretching out her hand, she took Peggy's case from her.

"You know the drill don't you, Peggy?" the sister smiled at her. "You should do, you've been here enough times."

"Good evening, Sister Ruth." Peggy was pleased that this particular sister was on duty. She had been at the birth of five of her children, and it was a comfort to see a friendly face. Once she was safely settled in the hard hospital bed, Bill stood awkwardly by the side of the wooden locker, anxious to be off. He threw a grateful look at the ward nurse when she ordered him out. Bending over Peggy, he gave her a perfunctory kiss on the cheek before he left the ward at great speed, his footsteps clicking on the polished floor.

Watching him go, Peggy lay back on the pillows, her mind drifting back into the past once more. After she'd made up her mind to keep Andy (although there had never been any real doubt) an appointment had been made to take Barbara for an assessment test at County Hall in London. There Barbara, now three years old, had been examined by a panel of doctors and then presented with a few simple tasks to complete.

Her blue eyes had looked up at Peggy in bewilderment, unable to understand what was expected of her. Things had happened quickly after that. With Barbara on her lap and Bill by her side, they had been driven to Tooting Hill Hospital where Barbara had been taken from her. On the verge of collapse, Peggy had been led from the hospital by Bill, the screams of her daughter ringing in her ears as she'd frantically tried to wriggle from the nurse's arms, her blonde head flopping on her shoulders as she'd tried to see where her mum and dad had gone.

"Stop it, stop it!" Peggy thrashed about on the bed, trying to let go of the painful memory, and of Bill who had walked around in a daze for weeks afterwards, unable to take in what had happened. Turning onto her side, she whispered into the pillow, "I couldn't help it, Barbara, love. I had no choice. God help me, I had no choice."

"Hey, what's all this. Peggy, what's the matter?"

Opening her eyes, Peggy saw Sister Ruth bending over her, her face concerned. Haltingly Peggy told her, her hand going out to take hold of the sister's hand for comfort. Sister Ruth listened, her eyes filled with sympathy. She knew all about Barbara; she had been here the day Peggy had gone for the priest and had watched with admiration as the proud Irishwoman had walked from the ward with her head held high, only her dignity and her self-respect keeping her on her feet.

"You've got to let go, dear," she whispered. "You did all you could. It was a a straight choice between your son or your daughter, and – be honest – she's much better where she is, isn't she?"

How many times had Peggy heard those words? But was it true? Who knew what went on in her daughter's confused mind, how could anyone know? Barbara could neither walk nor talk, she still couldn't hold her head up straight. Turning her head to one side, Peggy waited for the sobs to quieten down. She and Bill still saw her of course, they went as often as they could, but Peggy could never leave the nursing home without that feeling of guilt. Not for the first time the unbidden thought came to her mind that maybe it would have been better if Barbara had died at birth, as had her second child, Pamela. But shaking her head, she dismissed the thought; everyone had the right to life. Wasn't that the reason she had had Barbara admitted to the home, so that Andy could have his?

The sister watched her patient, wondering whether to call the doctor or not. For a fleeting moment she felt a deep anger at the woman's husband, and indeed at men in general. There should be a law that prevented men from fathering more than three children. After all they didn't have to carry and give birth to them; if they did the population would drop overnight. Leaning over the now still form, she saw with relief that Peggy had cried herself to sleep. Patting the covers round Peggy's neck, she let her sleep on. She would need all the rest she could get before the night was out.

Half an hour later, Peggy was on the way to the labour ward. The short nap had done her good and she was able

43

to talk and joke with the young staff nurse as she walked alongside the stretchered trolley. Soon she was being lifted onto the delivery table. With all the worry about the impending birth and her guilt-ridden thoughts about Barbara, she had forgotten about Marie. Just as her mind was switching to the problem of her eldest child, the nurse broke into her thoughts by asking, "What are you hoping for, dear, a boy or a girl?"

Peggy looked at her for a moment before bursting into laughter. The moment was short-lived as a strong contraction brought her knees up to her chin, and all thoughts were blotted from her mind as she gave herself up to the painful business of bringing a new life into the world.

John was born just before midnight. Looking down at the small, wrinkled face, Peggy marvelled at how all her children had looked the same at birth. Always the same features, only the hair colouring was different. Dark hair for the boys, blonde hair for the girls. Only Marie had been born without any hair at all. Sensing a presence by her side, Peggy looked up to see Sister Ruth standing by the bed.

"Why do all your children look as if they've just come off an assembly line?" she asked, at the same time taking in the expression on Peggy's face, pleased and relieved to see that the earlier outburst had been forgotten. No, she shook her head, this woman would never forget, but she had the strength of character to live with the memories, however painful they may be. Taking the child from Peggy's arms, she walked with him to the nursery adjoining the ward, saying softly over her shoulder so as not to disturb the other patients, "Get some sleep; it might be the last chance you get for a long time."

Gratefully Peggy snuggled down under the covers. She was sore and tired but a good night's sleep could work wonders, at least that's what she told herself. Her ever-active mind started to form a thought, but she was so tired, the moment she closed her eyes she was asleep.

*

A week later Peggy was waiting for Bill to bring her clothes in so she could get dressed and go home. She'd meant to pack them herself, but had only brought with her her night things and a towel and flannel, and of course a shawl for the baby. She was sorry that Sister Ruth wasn't on duty today, she would have liked to say goodbye; and it *would* be goodbye this time.

Oh, yes, she thought grimly, her mouth settling into a tight line. Tapping her fingers impatiently on the coverlet, she looked at the ward clock and wondered what could be keeping him. "Your husband's late, isn't he?" The staff nurse had come up beside her, the starched white apron crackling as she walked.

Peggy relaxed her mouth into a smile as she nodded in agreement.

"Sister Ruth asked me to give you her regards," the staff nurse continued, "and she also said that although she thinks you're a very nice person," here she nudged Peggy, giving a wink, "she said she hopes she doesn't see you again; at least not in here."

"Don't worry, she won't," Peggy replied, her lips settling into a grim line once more. By God she won't, she added silently. The staff nurse said goodbye and walked off.

Getting up from the bed, Peggy walked to the small crib where John lay sleeping peacefully. She had debated about having him at home but had decided against it. Not because of what had happened to Barbara; that might have happened anyway. No, she had opted for hospital just to get a little rest, something she wouldn't have got at home. A sudden laugh escaped her lips as she remembered Patti's birth. About an hour after the delivery Bill had appeared in the bedroom doorway carrying a bowl of potatoes. "I thought you might be bored with nothing to do," he had said in all seriousness, "so I've brought you some potatoes to peel for dinner." The irate midwife had, to put it mildly, put her toe in his backside and chased him from the room, along with a few choice words. Peggy never knew whether to laugh or cry at some of the things Bill did. Just then the object of her thoughts came hurrying down the ward. Any thought that he was hurrying to see her quickly faded as he came to an abrupt halt by the bed.

"Hurry up, Peggy, I've only got a couple of hours off work."

Pushing a carrier bag containing her clothes towards her, he stared at her impatiently until she snatched the bag from his hand and stormed off. No flowers, no special card, not even a box of chocolates. She hadn't really expected it, but it would have made all the difference. Still, she mused to herself, if he had brought her a present, the shock might have set her back another week.

Peggy hurried into the bathroom to change, but as she unpacked the case he had brought she felt the tears well up in her eyes. Looking down she surveyed the contents. No underwear, just a dress, her old coat, and a pair of worn-down shoes he had meant to throw away. Not even a pair of stockings, and it was mid-winter. Brushing back the tears, she put on the clothes, washed her face and slowly emerged from the bathroom to find Bill pacing up and down the ward looking at his watch.

Catching sight of her, he strode over and took her arm, hurrying her along, his eyes going to his watch once again. Biting back the harsh words that rose within her, Peggy went to the cot and lifted John out. Wrapping him up well, she said her goodbyes to the nurses, ignoring the impatient looks Bill was sending her.

As they came out of the warm building, the icy cold hit her at once. Her arms tightened protectively around the small bundle. When they walked along the street, she could feel the icy wind blowing up her dress. Her privates felt as blue as the air was going to be once she got him home. But what she might have said she never knew, for as soon as they were inside the house he made a cup of tea for her, kissed her lightly on the forehead, and before she could say a word he had disappeared back to work.

Peggy sat for a long time in the cold kitchen feeling numb, in more ways than one. The sound of the baby waking up roused her from the stupor she had been in. Bustling about now, she quickly lit the fire, noting the fact that there was plenty of coal. Sitting in the front room before a blazing fire, she began to feel better. Looking at the clock, she realised the children would be in in a few hours' time. She hoped Bill had remembered to get something for dinner. For the next hour she gave herself up to the child in her arms. Once he was fed and changed, she put him down into the small basket that had held quite a few of his predecessors. Leaving him safely away from the fire, she went back into the kitchen to see if there was anything for dinner.

On the workshop table was a big bowl of potatoes, ready peeled and submerged in water. Beside them was a packet of collar bacon and a pound of sausages along with a note from May saying she would be round later after she'd finished work. It would have been nice to come home to find her mother waiting for her. May could have given up work years ago, but as she was always saying, she preferred to keep busy.

As she set about making the bacon stew, Peggy's mind went to the new addition to the family. Well, it would be the last one, she'd made up her mind about that while she had lain in bed recovering from the birth.

Even if it meant going against the church's ruling on birth control, she for one was closing up shop. She'd had enough. Her family was complete.

# Chapter Three

Marie hurried along, her feet taking her towards Cheapside and the shop where her new coat was waiting for her. Coming to a stop outside Chelsea Girl, she closed her eyes for a moment. Oh, please let it still be there, she prayed silently. Opening her eyes, her lips widened into a smile. There it was – her coat. She had first seen it over two weeks ago and had fallen in love with it, but even though it had been marked down in a sale, she still hadn't been able to afford it. Her mum would have helped, but Marie was well aware that money was as tight now as it had always been. The fact that she was now working and able to help out a little filled her with pride, but oh, how she wanted that coat. Yesterday her Uncle Tommy had popped in for an hour and, as he'd left, he had slid a ten shilling note into her hand. Luck seemed to be with her today. She'd been given an hour's tea-break because there was no work in the office at the moment. Opening her large black patent handbag she searched around in the jumbled collection of tissues, sweets, make-up and other assorted rubbish. Her face became anxious as she fumbled round for her purse, then she breathed a sigh of relief as her fingers closed around it. Taking it out of the bag, she quickly checked once again that she had the correct money and then pushed open the double glass doors.

The saleswoman looked at the skinny young girl as she stood in front of the long display mirror admiring herself in the huge black and white checked coat that she had despaired of ever selling. Forcing a smile to her lips, she went through the sales patter, telling the girl how nice it looked on her, how much it suited her, and then swiftly steered her to the counter and the cash register before the girl changed her mind about buying it. Taking Marie's money, she quickly wrote out the customary receipt, folded the coat and dropped it into one of the shiny carrier bags that bore the name Chelsea Girl, glad that the offending article was now hidden from sight; it had been making her feel quite bilious. As she handed the bag over the counter to the smiling girl she suddenly felt a pang of guilt. She should have told her that the coat didn't suit her, that she looked like a walking draughtboard in it.

"Thank you," the young girl was saying, her face alight with happiness. "I was frightened that someone else would have bought it before I'd saved enough. It must be my lucky day." And then she walked from the shop, the carrier bag held proudly in her hand.

Marie went quickly back to work, her face wreathed in smiles. As she approached the building where she worked she stopped for a moment, then looking round to see if anyone was watching her, she quickly drew the new coat from its shiny bag and put it on; her old blazer she discarded into the empty carrier. Shaky with the prospect of what the girls would say when they saw her in her new finery, she hurried through the entrance door and ran up the stairs.

A wave of disappointment ran through her as she entered the empty office. Where could they all be? Then she saw them at the far end of the office, all crammed into Mr Trivett's office. She could see two of the senior girls talking and by the look on their faces an animated discussion was taking place. Taking her coat off, she hung it on the coatstand she shared with her colleagues, and made her way to the desk where she carried out her clerical work. Sitting down, she glanced towards Mr Trivett's office wondering what was going on. Catching the eye of one of the girls Marie felt her stomach lurch as the girl deliberately averted her gaze.

Marie felt her mouth drop open in surprise; they were talking about *her*. That was why she had been allowed an extended tea-break. Her hands trembling, she picked up a sheaf of invoices pretending to study them; she felt hot and sick with worry. The sudden opening of Mr Trivett's office door made her jump. She watched as her workmates studiously avoided looking at her as they scuttled back to their desks with alarming agility.

"Marie, could I have a word with you please?"

Mr Trivett stood in his office doorway looking decidedly uncomfortable.

Without a word, Marie rose from her desk and followed him into the small office, her head bowed in shame – she knew what was coming.

"Sit down, Marie, make yourself comfortable."

Still silent, she did as she was bade. Mr Trivett looked at her bowed head and felt a stab of guilt at what he was about to do. Clearing his throat he said, "It's come to my attention that you've not been very well lately, so I suggest you take a few weeks' leave. You know, get yourself back on your feet again." He laughed heartily, as if he had made some great witticism. Getting no response, he looked helplessly at the pathetic figure in front of him and sighed, his florid face taking on a deeper hue in his embarrassment.

Lord, he thought, this is awful. He had been stunned this morning when Pat the senior girl in the outside office had requested that Marie should be given an extended tea-break so that a delegation could make a formal complaint against her. With Marie out of the way the rest of the girls had trooped into his office. They hadn't actually put into words what their grievance was, there had been a lot of humming and hawing, but he had got the gist. Marie had a personal problem. From what he had managed to read between the lines, after she had used the toilet no one else could go in, and she was unable to control her wind. Clearly the complaint hadn't been made out of spite, or they would have made it months ago.

Unable to stand the silence any longer, he got to his feet. "Well then," he said briskly, "I'm glad we've got that sorted out, eh?" Not waiting for a reply, he strode over to the door and opened it for her, anxious for the interview to be over.

"Take as much time off as you need; your job will be waiting for you when you're well again." He felt a qualm of guilt as he ushered her out of the room. He wouldn't be able to keep her job open for long, but he lacked the moral courage to tell her so. A letter would be enclosed with her wages and sent to her. Yes, he nodded to himself; it was the best way.

50

Gathering the last shreds of her pride around her, Marie walked slowly from the office. Looking straight ahead, she made for the coatstand and took down from its peg the coat she had bought so proudly less than an hour ago and put it on. Acting as if there was nothing wrong and ignoring the lump in her throat that threatened to choke her, she sailed out of the office as if she hadn't a care in the world.

Pausing outside the glass door, she heard the typewriters stop one by one. A screech of laughter rang out making her wince, then the babel of voices began. Her defences down, she let the tears flow as she raced down the stairs and into the street.

Sitting on the top of the bus, she thought back on the past year.

It was almost a year to the day when she had had the row with her mum about going to the doctor's. It had only been the imminent arrival of John that had saved her. Strangely enough, she had begun to get better after that night – it was as if the worry about Mum and looking after the children had taken her mind off it. Of course her nan had done most of the work, but she had helped. Then she had got the job at Staple & Sons as a junior clerk; the first six months had been wonderful, then the pain had started again.

Shrugging her shoulders as if throwing off the memory, Marie stared out of the window, her breath steaming up the glass. Pulling her coat tighter around her, she shivered; she hated the winter, especially November. As she neared her stop, she stood up and rang the bell. Holding onto the rail, she made her way down the curving stairway and onto the platform. When the bus stopped she jumped onto the pavement, then stood in the bus shelter undecided what to do. She didn't feel like facing her mum just yet, but it was so cold, she couldn't walk about for long, she'd be frozen. There was nothing else for it but to go home and face the music. Reluctantly she began the short walk home. Maybe her mum wouldn't be in. Well, she could hope, couldn't she?

Arriving home, Marie put her hand through the letter box and withdrew the key attached to a piece of string. Letting herself in, she called out, "You home, Mum?"

Getting no answer, Marie brightened up. Humming under her breath, she ran up the stairs to her bedroom. Her mum must have gone round to see Nan. Taking her coat off, she wandered aimlessly round the room, coming to a stop before the large mirror on the wardrobe. Surveying herself, she saw a small, underweight girl clad in a dress which was too big for her, one that had fitted her only a few months ago. It was bright red, woolly and soft, with long sleeves and navy buttons down the front. Moving her gaze downwards, she looked at her legs; they were so thin they resembled two pieces of thread hanging from her drawers. On her feet she wore the new fashion in shoes: lace-up clogs, thick and clumsy. If she were to be unlucky enough to fall into a river while wearing them, the weight on her feet would make her sink without trace.

Lastly, she let her eyes travel up to her face, something she didn't often do. She saw a small face almost obscured by an enormous pair of wooden glasses, hiding the blue eyes that could be seen staring out of any one of the Cowley children. Her eyes were the only thing she had in common with her brothers and sisters; whereas they possessed good looks, she was painfully plain by comparison. Even her hair was different. The boys all had dark hair and the girls' hair was blonde and curly – Marie's was mousy brown and lank. She had tried curling it, but there was no body in it, and after a few hours the curls would fall out, leaving it straggly. All in all, she wasn't a pretty sight.

Sighing, she left the bedroom and went down to the kitchen. Making herself a cup of tea she carried it over to the table, picking up the *Daily Mirror* from the worktop.

The sudden bang of the front door made her jump.

"Marie, are you up there?" her mother shouted up the stairs.

"No, Mum, I'm in the kitchen," she replied and, bracing herself, she walked out into the hallway. Peggy was busily divesting John, Jimmy and Patti of their outdoor clothing. Part of her mind was wondering why Marie was home so early, the other part was counting the dwindling number of children she still had at home. Vicky had started school in

September and Jimmy was due to start next year, that would leave her with just John and Patti. Once they were at school she could . . .

"Joan said she'd seen you come in. What's wrong?"

About to tell a lie, Marie stopped. She was tired; suddenly her body slumped as if all the life had been drained from her. She hadn't realised until this minute just how weary she was.

Following Peggy into the front room, she sat down on the settee and, amidst the noise of the children playing, she recounted what had happened. Peggy listened silently until she'd finished. Nodding her head, she got up from the settee and said, "I thought so. It was bound to happen sooner or later. Maybe now you'll see sense."

"What do you mean?" Marie asked fearfully.

"I mean I'm going to do what I should have done last year – I'm taking you to the doctor's, and no arguing."

Two hours later, while Peggy was dishing up the dinner, Marie crept out of the house. Walking quickly up Hasset Road, she crossed over into Cassland Road and began walking towards the park. She stayed on the path, avoiding the grass that was still wet from last night's downpour. Looking longingly at the wooden benches, she resisted the urge to sit down and rest a while. She was anxious to get to her nan's. On she walked, a lonely figure in the almost deserted park. Underneath a large oak tree she cursed as a large drop of rainwater splashed on her head – she hoped it was just rainwater. Gingerly she touched her hair, relieved to find she hadn't been the victim of a passing pigeon. Cutting through a side turning that bordered on the edge of the park, she found herself in Victoria Park Road. A few minutes later she was standing outside her nan's house. A tall, three-storey Victorian building, it stood in the middle of a long row of its contemporaries. Further down, at the end of the row, stood a newly built, four-storey block of flats, its presence spoiling the otherwise beautiful tree-lined road.

Marie stood outside for a few minutes, wondering what she was going to say to her nan. Then, shrugging her shoulders, she stepped forward; she would think of something.

Standing on the porch, flanked by two large white pillars, she rang the doorbell. The house had been divided into three flats. Her nan lived on the top floor.

While she waited for May to answer the door, she thought back on the many times she had stayed in this house.

When her nan and granddad had moved here ten years ago, after their previous house had been demolished, it had been bulging at the seams. Her four uncles, Peter, Robin, Jimmy and Tommy, had somehow managed to share a room and her four aunts, Lucy, Mona, Teresa and Pauline, shared another, her grandparents having the privilege of a room to themselves. Just a year after they'd moved in, Robin had married and moved to Aylesbury, and shortly after him Peter had also married and moved to Basildon. Jimmy and his new wife had lived with May and Paddy for a while, but soon they too had found a place of their own and now they lived in Loughton. Lucy and Mona had married within a year of each other. Lucy and her husband had moved to Basingstoke and Mona and Ron had settled in Essex. Marie knew that Mona and Ron preferred the East End, but Ron's firm had relocated to Essex and in order to keep his job they had reluctantly moved house. Maybe they would come back some day – Marie hoped so. They had been very good to her when she'd been a child, taking her to the seaside with them and on a few holidays. She was very fond of them.

Walking away from the door, she stared up at the window that until two years ago had been the bedroom of her two younger aunts, Teresa and Pauline. Marie had been one of Teresa's bridesmaids when she'd married just over two years ago. The day had been a mixture of happiness for her aunt and a little sadness at the knowledge that Marie would be seeing her less often in the future. Even Pauline had deserted her. She had married six months after Teresa and had moved with her husband Tommy to Northampton. At least Teresa hadn't moved too far, Marie consoled herself. Gant's Hill was only a half-hour journey by car and Teresa's husband Vic often picked her up from home to take her to stay with them for the weekend.

Her nan was taking her time answering the door; maybe she was out. Marie's heart sank. Standing on tiptoe she peered through the stained blue and red glass window that formed the top half of the front door. Pressing her thumb into the bell, she rang again. Just as she was about to walk away the door opened. May Flannagan stood in the doorway surprised to see her granddaughter standing there.

"Hello, love, this is a surprise. Are you not at work today?" Although May had lived in England for over twenty years, her brogue had hardly altered since the day she'd left Ireland. Marie followed her up the wide stairway which gave out onto a large square landing. There were six rooms, all told, in the flat. The bedroom that had once belonged to her aunts faced the top of the stairs, next to which was her Uncle Tommy's. Along the wall on the left of the square was May's room, next to the toilet. Over to the right side lay the kitchen and bathroom. Alongside in the far corner was Marie's favourite room. The large sitting room was set back from the other rooms. The big picture window always let in plenty of light. In the corner stood the television set, the green three piece suite arranged around it. On a table by the window stood the red Dansen record player. Before Teresa and Pauline had married, Marie had come round every weekend to stay, and the three of them would play the latest record, dancing round the room until their boyfriends arrived to take them out. Finally her gaze rested on the old brown piano which took up nearly all of the main wall. She would have liked to sit in here a while, but she knew her nan was expecting her to come into the kitchen.

"Ah, there you are," said May and, turning from the sink where she was busy peeling potatoes, she added, "Put the kettle on, there's a good girl, then we'll have a little chat."

Marie complied, then, going back to the wooden table, she sat down and waited for May to finish what she was doing.

As she put the last potato in a bowl of water, May was silently wondering what Marie was doing here in the middle of the day, but she said nothing, biding her time.

May Flannagan was sixty years old. She had lived twenty of those years in England, but still talked about Ireland as her home. She had never really settled. She and her large family had come to England soon after the war had ended. Both her husband, Paddy, and her eldest son, Robin, had flown with the R.A.F. during the last half of the war and had been unable to settle back in Ireland after their demob. A year after her men had returned to their native land, May had found herself on a ship bound for England. Her children surrounding her, she had watched through tear-filled eyes as her beloved Ireland had faded from sight. A small woman, barely five foot, she had given birth to sixteen children of whom only nine had survived. Eight had married, leaving only her youngest son, Tommy, still living at home. Peggy, her eldest, seemed to be trying to beat her record in bearing children.

"Well now, and to what do I owe the pleasure of a visit from my favourite grandchild?"

Marie had been waiting for the opportunity to tell May her fears, had even rehearsed what she would say. But now, sitting here in the old familiar kitchen, she knew she couldn't. As much as she loved her nan, there was only one person in whom she could really confide, the one person to whom she never had to pretend, unless it suited her: her mum.

Lifting her head, she said a little too quickly, "I've got a day's holiday."

The lie stuck in her throat and it was with relief that she heard the front door opening downstairs, preventing her from having to continue in the deception. When she heard the voice of her uncle she smiled broadly. Running out onto the landing she shouted over the banisters, "Hello, Tommy," the rest of her greeting cut off by the sight of the two men coming up the stairs behind him.

Tommy Flannagan looked up quickly and, seeing the thin legs almost blending in with the banister rails, he smiled. Reaching the top of the stairs, he lifted Marie high in the air, ignoring her protests. He was a big man, stocky in build. Startling blue eyes stared out of rugged face, eyes emphasised by his red hair. He had the kind of character that could be described by the saying, "easy in his skin". Marie didn't quite know what this meant; it was a saying her mum often used to describe him – that, and other things.

The two men had reached the landing and, looking over his shoulder, Tommy said, "Go in the front room, I'll be in in a minute."

Still not talking, the two men went quietly into the front room, closing the door behind them. May came out from the kitchen wiping her hands on her apron.

"I told you not to bring them here again," she said angrily. "I want no teeves in this house."

"What's a teeve, Mum?" Tommy said, laughing.

"You know what I mean," May shouted. "They'd steal the eyes out of your head and come back for the eyelashes. Now I'm telling you – no more."

"I think I'll be off now, Nan."

"There now, you see what you've done, frightening the child half to death."

"Mum, Mum, give it a rest," pleaded Tommy, hands in the air as if in surrender. "We'll be leaving in half an hour. We just stopped off for a cup of tea then we'll be off."

"Well, see that you do," May retorted, going back into the kitchen, "and I'll be checking to see nothing's missing before they leave."

The parting shot made Tommy and Marie smile at each other then, putting his hand in his pocket, he pulled out some silver.

"No, Tommy. Thank you, but I'm working now you know," Marie said, proudly forgetting for a minute the events of this morning.

"I keep forgetting you're a big girl now." Rumpling her hair, he added, "You don't look very big. Probably take after your dad, he never gets any fatter either." Nodding to her in farewell, he walked over to the front room. Before entering he said, "Get yourself the new record by that long haired group of yobs, what are they called? The Spiders."

57

Laughing back at him, Marie answered, "It's the Beatles and thank you Tommy," indicating the ten shilling note he had put in her hand.

"Take care, love," he said, soberly now as he went into the sitting room, closing the door behind him.

"Are you off then, love?" May said, coming from the kitchen. "Won't you stay for a cup of tea?"

"No, thanks, Nan. I only stopped off on the way to the park. I'm meeting a friend," Marie said, a little scared at the ease with which she could lie.

"It's not those two frightening you off, is it?" May asked, nodding towards the closed door. Leaning towards Marie, she whispered, "I'll be going in there with the hoover in a minute, that'll get shot of them."

Smiling at the thought, Marie shook her head. "No, Nan, really, I've got go."

"All right then, love, I'll see you soon."

When she heard the front door slam, May quickly walked over to the sitting room. Opening the door, she walked past Tommy and the brothers, their heads together in a conversation which stopped on seeing her. Walking over to the large window, she looked out onto the street. Seeing Marie walking in the opposite direction to the park, she shook her head, a worried expression on her face. Letting the curtain fall, she walked passed the three men completely ignoring their presence, wrapped up in her thoughts.

"Any chance of a cup of tea, Mum?" Tommy's voice brought her out of her reverie.

"About as much chance as those two getting an honest job."

With that parting shot she left the room, slamming the door behind her.

Peggy sat in the kitchen drumming her fingers on the table, her mouth set in a grim line. The little cow, she thought to herself, probably gone round to Mum's to complain about me. She had been furious when she had found Marie gone. Getting up, she moved restlessly round the room, her anger building inside her. Bill and the children had wisely left her alone, each one glad that they weren't the recipient of her anger. Out of the corner of her eye, Peggy saw Marie pass the window and, moving quickly, she wrenched open the front door and pulled Marie into the hall. The angry words died in her throat at the sight of the tear-stained face in front of her. Marie looked up at her mother, and completely uncharacteristically she threw her arms around Peggy's waist and sobbed uncontrollably.

"Come on now, come on," Peggy soothed, all anger forgotten.

"What will he do to me, Mum?" she sobbed. "Will I have to have an internal?"

Amazed, Peggy looked down at her and, shaking her head, she led her into the kitchen and gently took her in her arms.

"What in God's name put that into your head?" she asked in bewilderment.

Almost incoherent, Marie stumbled over the words. "One of the girls said they put things up you."

"Oh, love, love," Peggy cried, horrified. "Why didn't you tell me that's what you've been frightened of?"

"Do they, Mum?" Marie sobbed. "Do they?"

"No, no, of course not. The doctor will probably just ask you some questions, he won't put anything up you."

God forgive me for lying, she prayed silently. "Come on now, dry your eyes, we'll go and see what he says."

Putting her head round the front room door, she said, "I won't be long, I'm just taking Marie to the doctor's."

As she closed the door she couldn't help hearing the audible sigh of relief that followed her.

Holding hands tightly, they set off.

"Where did you go?"

"Round to Nan's," sniffed Marie as she searched in her pocket for a hanky.

"I thought so. What did she say?"

Looking at the ground, Marie answered quietly, "I didn't tell her, I said I had a day's holiday. Tommy was there with his friends. You know – the brothers."

"Did they speak to you?" Peggy demanded, pulling her to a stop.

"No, Mum, they didn't say anything. Nan was annoyed with Tommy."

Walking on, Peggy muttered under her breath, "Good."

Ten minutes later they were outside the doctor's office. Peggy tightened her hold on Marie's hand and led her through the surgery doors. Once inside the waiting-room Peggy quickly counted the people sitting on the wooden chairs. Only five, thank goodness; they shouldn't have too long to wait. With no appointment system, surgery time could become fraught with patients arguing as to whose turn it was, especially when the waiting-room was packed solid. Marie cast a disparaging look at an elderly man who was coughing and sneezing with gusto. Picking a seat as far away from him as possible, she sat down, Peggy beside her. Peggy picked up a magazine from the oblong table that stood in the middle of the room. Flicking through the pages she found she was unable to concentrate and after a few minutes she put it down. After what seemed to be an interminable wait it was their turn. Squeezing Marie's hand, Peggy walked with her into the surgery.

Dr Downey looked at the thin young girl in front of him. He knew all about her from her mother. Noting the trembling hands in her lap, he tried to put her at her ease.

"I'm not going to eat you, you know," he said kindly. "Now then, how long have you been feeling ill?"

Her voice quivering, Marie told him all about the pain, the running to the toilet, not being able to eat. As she talked, she felt a weight lifting from her shoulders. It was such a relief to be able to talk about it without having to lie or pretend it wasn't too bad. It was bloody awful, and she told him so, unreservedly. When she had finished, she leant back in the chair feeling drained. Peggy looked at her daughter in disbelief. She'd had no idea it was that bad.

Pulling a pad towards him, Dr Downey began to write. Looking up at her, he said, "I want you to take this letter to the out-patients at Bethnal Green Hospital. They'll soon have you jumping about again."

Getting to their feet, both Peggy and Marie shook hands with him, so relieved that the first step had been taken. As they walked home Marie felt a lightness she hadn't felt for a long time. Beside her Peggy was feeling apprehensive. Remembering the doctor's words on the phone that afternoon when she had called him, she shivered slightly. It was more than likely that Marie would have to undergo some unpleasant tests. Shrugging off the thought, she slipped her arm through Marie's. The hardest part was over. They would go on from here.

# Chapter Four

1964.

Peggy bounced around the kitchen, banging cups and plates down at random. Watching her sister working herself up into a temper, Teresa flinched. She had only dropped in for a cup of tea and a chat; she was now fervently wishing she hadn't bothered.

"Anaemia!" Peggy shouted, making her jump. "That bloody doctor should be struck off. He wouldn't recognise a dead man if he fell over one."

Running out of breath for a moment, Peggy stopped.

Seizing the opportunity, Teresa said quietly, "Be fair, Peg, he can't do much if she won't have the tests done."

About to make a sharp retort, Peggy stopped. Teresa was right. She cast her mind back to last year. She remembered her joy when she had walked out of the doctor's surgery with Marie, her belief that everything would be all right.

They had set off to keep the appointment at the out-patients' department a week later. There, a young doctor had examined Marie and had taken a sample of her blood. This had shown her to be anaemic but hadn't explained the pain. A request for further tests to be carried out, made by the same doctor on a subsequent visit, was met with a blank refusal by Marie. Since that time, she had found herself another job, having received her cards from her previous employer, and had seemed to be coping well, until yesterday. She had been sent home from work with a letter from the firm's nurse, advising Peggy to take Marie to see a doctor. Shaking her head, Peggy rose from her chair and appealed to Teresa.

"She's upstairs in her room. Will you have a word with her? She might listen to you."

Nodding mutely, Teresa left the kitchen, avoiding looking at her sister's strained face. Mounting the stairs, she knocked on Marie's door. Marie, lying on the bed, scowled as she heard the knock. It was her mother again. Why couldn't she leave her alone? Her face lost its surly expression when she saw who it was.

"Teresa, what are you doing here? Oh, I am glad to see you," she exclaimed happily.

Coming into the room, Teresa picked her way round the clothes and comics on the floor to where Marie was sitting in the large double bed. "Don't you ever tidy up?" she asked smiling.

Marie looked at her aunt, taking in the smartness of her clothes, her brown hair neatly in place in the latest cottage loaf fashion, but most of all the air of calm, steady confidence that exuded from her. Teresa was everything that she, Marie, would like to be. "Oh, it's not all mine," she said, returning the smile, "most of it belongs to Ellen."

Ignoring the blatant lie, Teresa cleared her throat preparatory to what she was about to say. "I came down for the day to see your nan and I just popped in on the way home." Clearing her throat, she continued. "Your mum asked me to have a word with you."

Knowing what was coming next, Marie quickly interrupted her. "Can I come down for the weekend, Teresa? Vic can pick me up, he doesn't mind."

Ignoring the pleading look on her niece's face, Teresa plunged on. "Don't you think there's somewhere more important for you to go?" she asked gently. Tearing her gaze from Teresa's face, Marie threw herself down on her pillows and wept.

Twenty minutes later, Teresa was back in the kitchen talking to Peggy. "She said she'll go to the hospital again, Peg, as long as it's the Bethnal Green and not the Hackney. I think she's frightened of the Hackney Hospital because of what happened to Dad. Or maybe she said that just to get rid of me. She's very frightened you know."

Peggy came back at her sister in a loud voice, crying, "And you think I'm not? Do you think I'm not frightened?"

63

Sitting down abruptly, Peggy appealed to Teresa. "Why does she have to be so bloody awkward? You'd think the whole thing was my fault. If you could hear the way she talks to me sometimes, it's all I can do to keep my hands off her."

Putting her arms round Peggy's shoulders, Teresa said softly, "She's scared, Peg – all that bravado and meanness is just a front to hide her fears. I know she can be a cow to you, but she loves you very much."

"I wish I could believe that, Teresa."

Walking her to the door, Peggy kissed her sister goodbye, before returning to the kitchen deep in thought.

Marie sat in the small whitewashed room holding tightly onto her mother's hand. They were in the waiting-room of the Bethnal Green Hospital and had come to find out the results of the blood tests she had had done last week. She no longer cared if they had found anything or not. The thought that she might have cancer no longer frightened her, only the uncertainty of how long she would have to suffer before she died. She stole a quick glance at her mum, who looked tired and drawn; the whole business had aged her.

The sound of a door opening made Marie's stomach contract painfully.

"Mrs Cowley?" enquired the young nurse. Peggy nodded her head in acquiescence. Smiling, the nurse beckoned to an open door and said, "The doctor will see you now. Would you come this way, please?" Pushing Marie before her, they entered the surgery. A middle-aged man garbed in the obligatory white coat of all hospital doctors rose to greet them.

"Please take a seat," he said, gesturing to two uncomfortable chairs. Thanking him, Peggy sat down and, after a moment's pause, Marie also sat.

"Now then," he began, shuffling the papers in front of him.

Peggy and Marie remained silent as he continued to read the notes before him.

Finally he lifted his head and smiled at them. "Well now, young lady, you seem to have been having a rough time of it lately."

Receiving no answer, he looked at Peggy.

"Have you found out anything yet, Doctor?" Peggy asked anxiously.

"No, I'm afraid not, Mrs Cowley, but," he went on, seeing the look of despair on her face, "I'm sure that once all the tests are out of the way we'll find what's causing the pain." As a look of fear crossed Marie's face he hurried on. "I think it would be best if you came into hospital for a few days. There's nothing to be alarmed about, but rather than have you coming back and forth to the hospital, it would save time to have you on the ward where the nurses can keep you under observation. Also of course all the facilities for the various tests needed will be close at hand. It really is the best possible thing for you right now."

He looked at the girl's white, drawn face. According to her notes she had suffered from asthma and eczema as a child and as these illnesses were often a result of a nervous disposition he wondered if perhaps the symptoms she was displaying were psychosomatic.

"Look, you go to the Admissions Office and give them this letter," he handed Peggy the note he had scribbled, "and see when we can fit you in. We're very popular here you know," he finished, smiling broadly.

Peggy managed a tremulous smile back, but Marie still sat as if she had been turned to stone. She didn't appear to have reacted to anything that had been said, apart from that fleeting look of fright at the mention of hospital. The truth was she just didn't care any more.

Standing up, the doctor ushered them to the door, calling to the nurse as he did so, "Nurse, show Mrs Cowley to Admissions, will you please?"

He shook Peggy's proffered hand. "I know it's easy to say, but please don't worry."

"Thank you, Doctor." Putting her arm around Marie's shoulders, Peggy nodded her head slightly at the doctor and led the still silent Marie from the room.

Marie lay in the small, hard bed and watched as her mum and dad left the ward, their daily visit over. She had nothing to look forward to now except a long lonely night. Turning onto her side, she looked at the tube that was taped to her arm, and then raised her eyes upwards to see how much fluid was left in the large plastic bag that perched atop the tall metal stand by her bed. It was nearly empty; soon a nurse would stop by the bed and either change it for a full one or take the whole contraption away leaving her with freedom of movement for the rest of the day. Turning her eyes away from the hateful sight, she recalled the doctor who had admitted her. A few days he'd said; she had been here for nearly four weeks.

Every night before she went to sleep she prayed she wouldn't wake up, and every morning that she did, she cried. When she had first come into this ward she had been scheduled for a multitude of tests, but after the ward consultant had examined her, it had been decided she was as yet too weak to undergo the more strenuous tests. She had greeted this news with relief.

The doctors had converged at the foot of her bed, their voices lowered to a whisper as they'd discussed barium meals, barium enemas, and other kinds of test she couldn't even pronounce. She had never heard of any of them, but they didn't sound too choice.

And so the business of building her up had begun, starting with the drip she was currently attached to. This, it had been explained to her, would provide the vitamins and minerals she was lacking due to her inability to eat properly. Then there were the daily iron injections she had to endure, also designed to build her up. When she had protested that they weren't doing her any good, she had been told that without them she would certainly feel much worse than she did now.

She remembered that day crying out, "How, how can I feel worse than I do now? It's not possible," but the doctor had just smiled and patted her hand before walking on to his next patient.

Hearing a click of heels, she looked round and groaned as she saw the small, white-coated woman holding a box of glass tubes heading her way. When she stopped by her bed, Marie dutifully held out her free arm and waited for the sharp pain as the large needle sank into her vein.

"Just a little prick," the woman said cheerfully, the same words she said every day to every patient she visited. Marie wondered if she uttered the same inane comment when she did the men's ward. As the woman was labelling the glass vial that now contained a goodly sample of Marie's blood the ward sister appeared.

"I think we can have this down now," she said as she checked the empty plastic bag. Marie gritted her teeth as the tape was pulled from her arm and the needle withdrawn and once again felt the tears fill her eyes at the futility of it all. Tomorrow it would begin all over again. How much more could she take?

Closing her eyes, she recalled her two suicide attempts. The first time she had tried to drown herself in the bath. As her head had gone under, she had taken one mouthful of water and had shot up quicker than she had moved in months.

The second attempt had been even more pathetic. She had carefully saved the sleeping pill the nurse gave her every night by hiding it under her tongue. By this method she had accumulated five. The night she took them, she had written several notes; one to her mum and dad, one to her nan, and one to Bobby. When she had finished that she had second thoughts for a moment until a pain had gripped her; there had been no more hesitation after that. She had quickly swallowed them before she could change her mind. Before she had lain down to die, she had carefully combed her hair and even went so far as to put some lipstick on. Then she had arranged herself on her back so as not to spoil her last efforts, but within minutes the pain had forced her onto her side. She remembered the last thoughts had been of relief that the nightmare would soon be over. She had expected to go out like a light, but it had taken quite some time before they had taken effect. Instead of arriving at the pearly gates, she had been rudely awakened by the tea-lady shaking her shoulder as the woman put down the warm cup of tea on her bedside locker. She had quickly destroyed the notes and, much to her surprise, had felt a surge of relief.

Then just two weeks ago she had been awake early having been unable to sleep for the pain and, unable to bear it any longer, had gone looking for the night sister. On her way to the end of the ward she had stopped by the fire escape and, without stopping to think, she had opened the green wooden door and stepped out onto the cold iron balcony. Pausing for a second she had then proceeded to climb down the stairway not with any real plan in mind, just a feeling of desperation to get away. She had only taken a few steps when the chill of the stairs on her bare feet had sent her hopping and jumping over the ice cold steps back to the warmth of her bed.

For a moment Marie came out of the well of depression that she had sunk into over the last few months – she found it easier to cope if she didn't feel. But now, recalling the memory of her abortive attempts to kill herself, she found herself actually smiling. She hadn't smiled for a long time. Sighing, she lay staring up at the ceiling, letting her mind go blank, which wasn't difficult. There she went again, trying to be funny. Tutting impatiently to herself, she turned over onto her side. She didn't want to be funny ever again, she wanted the deep oblivion she had found where there was no pain and no feeling. It was easier to cope that way. She closed her eyes and forced herself to think of the colour black. Darker and darker the blackness covered her mind; she felt herself slipping down into the realms of semi-consciousness. It was peaceful there, everything was shut out, the fears damped down. Then, suddenly, unbidden, the face of May, her nan, swam before her.

"No," she cried silently, she didn't want to think about her nan, it was too painful. But the images kept coming, forcing her up out of the darkness.

It had happened the day after her admittance to hospital, but it was still as vivid in her mind as if it were yesterday. It had been snowing for days and she hadn't expected to see anyone during the day visits, so it was some surprise that she had looked up the ward to see her nan hobbling down the corridor towards her, a smile lighting up her face. May

68

had broken her hip a few months back, and still found it very difficult to walk, yet here she was easing herself painfully down onto the hard wooden visitor's chair.

"Hello, love," she said, putting out her cold hand to cover Marie's. "Goodness, it's like a sheet of ice out there. I'm lucky I didn't fall and break the other hip," she said, still smiling.

"Well, no one asked you to come, did they?" The words were out before she could stop them. The smile slipped from May's face for a moment.

Swallowing hard, she tried again. "I missed you, love, and it wasn't far to walk. How do you feel?" Looking at the sullen face of her beloved grandchild, May wanted to cry. It was going to be one of those visits. She wished now that she hadn't come. She was cold and tired and her leg pained her, but none of that would have matter if only Marie would show some sign of being pleased to see her.

After twenty minutes of idle chatter May could suddenly no longer stand the strain. If she didn't get away soon she would break down. "Well now, love," she said, rising painfully to her feet, clutching at the bedclothes for support, "I'd better get away and let you get some rest." Leaning over the small form she attempted to kiss Marie goodbye and flinched when she felt her draw back from her.

Unable to hide her tears any longer, May turned from the bed and began to make her way slowly down the ward. She felt sick. She couldn't believe Marie could be so cruel.

Watching her go, Marie stared at the back of her nan as she made her way towards the swing doors at the end of the ward. Even at this distance she could see May's shoulders shaking and knew she was crying. Feeling tears spring to her own eyes, she cried out silently to the retreating back, "Don't, don't cry over me, I'm not worth it." Why couldn't anyone understand why she acted as she did? She didn't want their love, she wanted them to hate her so that when she died they wouldn't mourn for her, but it wasn't working. No matter how hard she tried, her mum and dad and her nan kept loving her.

"Nan, Nan, don't go." She was out of bed, running, stumbling after May. "I'm sorry, I didn't mean it, please don't go." The words were pouring from her lips as she held out her arms.

Quicker than she would have thought possible, May was by her side, and then they were laughing and holding onto one another as May helped Marie back onto her bed. She stayed for an hour longer, and when she left she was smiling.

Whenever over the past month the painful scene had come unbidden to Marie's mind, she had only been able to see the hurt on May's face, never the laughter, and she prayed now as she had then, "Thank you, God, for making me go after her."

She knew that even if she hadn't her nan would still have gone on loving her and would have forgiven her, but she would never have been able to forgive herself – never. Thinking back on that day, Marie wondered why she had bothered trying to kill herself. There must be at least a half a dozen people who would be willing to do the job for her.

Swinging her legs over the side of the bed, she felt around for her slippers and made her way to the day–room. Her hopes of finding it empty vanished as she pushed open the door and saw the two women sitting by the television. Not wanting to engage in conversation, she nodded at them and, keeping her head down to discourage any attempt at talking, she walked to the back of the room. Placing herself on the armchair, she laid back and closed her eyes. The two women had stopped talking on her entrance and now they looked at each other and shrugged. Unaware of them Marie was trying to escape once more into the comforting darkness of her mind. She felt herself drifting, sinking deeper and deeper into the inky black darkness that was relief. The sudden blast of music made her start.

"Oh, I didn't know this was on today!" exclaimed one of the women.

With an impatient shake of her shoulders Marie was once more forced back into reality. She felt like screaming. This was the worst part, no privacy, nowhere to go to be alone except in the confines of her mind, and now the stupid women had broken her train of concentration once again. They were both looking at her now, smiling. She knew if she attempted to walk out they would try to engage her in conversation, so she stayed were she was, her eyes firmly fixed upon the small television screen.

She recognised the film at once. It was *Showboat*. She had seen it before and enjoyed it, but now the music and songs bounced off her. The woman spoke again, "Oh, this is my favourite."

Absently Marie nodded at her. It was no use, she wasn't going to get any peace here, she would have to wait for night before she could be by herself. Glancing up at the screen once more, she saw that it was the scene on the river with the coloured man singing. What was his name, she couldn't remember. The music drifted over her when suddenly she felt a tingle at the base of her spine. The music was coming through. Against her will she started to listen to the words of the song.

"*You and me work all day, bodies all aching and racked with pain.*" The feeling was moving up to her stomach now, sending a strange sensation into her chest. She wanted to move, but found herself transfixed by the sounds coming from the screen.

"*Tote that barge and lift that bale, you get a little drunk and you land in jail.*" Her mind was screaming out for him to stop singing . . .

"*I get weary and sick of trying.*" No, no, the feeling had moved up into her throat. She felt as if she was choking.

"*I'm tired of living.*" Tears were in her eyes now, spurting out, running down her cheeks.

"*And scared of dying,*" Her shoulders hunched, she felt the sobs rack her body. "*But ole man river . . .*" She knew the darkness had gone for ever, she was back in the land of the living, until it ended.

"*He just keeps rolling, aaaaaaah long.*"

71

# Chapter Five

1965.

Peggy and Bill walked from the dark hospital into the bright sunlight in silence, the sight of their daughter hooked up to drips and wasting away before their eyes etched deeply in their minds. They were just approaching Victoria Park when Peggy spoke.

"Look, Bill," she started anxiously, searching for the right words, "she's dying, and it's no use you burying your head in the sand."

At the sight of Bill's bowed head she went on, "We've got to face up it."

Without a word Bill walked away, his steps taking him towards a nearby park bench. Peggy watched him go, a feeling of anger and frustration coursing through her body. Taking a deep breath, she followed him over to the bench and sat down beside him. His body was slumped over, his head in his hands. Peggy watched him and fought against the desire to scream at him. It was too much, she shouldn't have to cope on her own. Forcing herself to be calm, she reached over and took one of his hands from his face, forcing him to look at her. Her voice soft now, she said gently, "You've got to help me, Bill, I want her home where we can look after her, make her last days more comfortable." Getting no response, she felt the anger rising again.

"It's not fair, Bill. I need your help in coping with this, I can't do it on my own any more." She felt him wrench his hand away then get up from the bench. As he walked away she screamed after him, "Go on then, pretend there's nothing wrong; go down to the church and say your three Hail Marys and two Our Fathers. That's all you've been doing for the past few months and it hasn't helped has it?"

Bill heard Peggy shouting after him and stopped abruptly. She was right. Marie was dying and there was nothing he or anyone else could do. The doctors had been trying for weeks and she was still no better. When they had left the hospital she had been connected to a feed drip. She couldn't even eat the small bits and pieces she had been surviving on for so long any more. Her weight had dropped to four and a half stone. When he had held her hand it had felt as if he were holding a lifeless object. Peggy thought that he was refusing to see just how ill Marie was, but the truth was he *did* know, he just didn't want to admit it, even to himself. People were selfish, he reflected tiredly. When someone they love, was ill they held onto them, refusing to let them go, while the object of that same love was suffering and would rather be at peace.

He turned to see Peggy standing behind him. She was crying. "It's the only way, Bill," she said, her voice quiet. "At least she'll be with people who love her."

He stood still for a few moments longer, then slowly he bent his head and nodded.

Sitting in the consultant's office, Peggy and Bill sat holding hands, listening to the doctor trying to dissuade them from taking Marie home.

"I can't stop you from taking your daughter home, Mrs Cowley," he said, directing his gaze at Peggy, "but I strongly advise against it."

"We know you've done your best, Doctor," Peggy answered quietly, "but she's not getting any better and we want her home with us."

Dr Jones sat in silence for a few moments, wondering what he could say to make them change their minds.

"Look," he began, "I know that the sight of your daughter looking so ill is frightening, but you must remember that she was ill for a long time before she finally came into hospital. Her body has taken a terrible beating from the pain she's suffered. That's why we have postponed the tests we originally planned until she is a bit stronger."

He looked from Peggy to Bill, willing them to understand what he was trying to tell them. "Your daughter isn't going to die. If she had contracted some fatal disease, there's no way she could have lasted as long as she has."

Peggy and Bill looked at each other, then Peggy turned to Dr Jones again. "Couldn't we take her home and I'll bring her up for the tests in the out-patients?"

Dr Jones sighed deeply. It was no good, they obviously didn't believe him. He wondered now if he should have ordered the barium tests when the girl had first been admitted, then he shook his head. The barium meal was an unpleasant ordeal in the best of circumstances; in the Cowley girl's case, there was no way she would be able to retain the thick liquid long enough for the test to be completed – but there was something he could try.

"All right, Mrs Cowley," he said gravely, still not happy about letting the girl go home, "but I'd like her back here in a couple of days time. A letter will be sent to you from the X-ray department, giving you an appointment. You will keep it, won't you?" he asked, his face anxious.

Peggy nodded, and said she would bring her back one more time. Standing up, she extended her hand to the doctor and watched Bill do the same. As the door closed behind them, Dr Jones shook his head and looked down at Marie's medical notes. Rubbing his hand wearily over his forehead, he sighed deeply before picking up the notes and returning them to the filing cabinet.

The nurse had just finished taking down the saline drip and was about to put a new bag on the long metal rod when Marie looked up and saw her father put his head round the ward door. She stared in disbelief – her father never came to see her in the daytime, he wouldn't take the time off work. For a moment her heart missed a beat, something must be wrong, then she saw her mother standing behind him, a strained smiled on her face.

"We've come to take you home, love," Bill said, sitting down on the bed. "That's if it's all right with you."

Marie couldn't speak for a moment, then she was holding out her arms towards them and suddenly they were both there, one on either side of her, and they were all laughing and crying at the same time.

"I'll get it," Peggy shouted, as she went to answer the phone. "Hello," she said into the mouthpiece. Her face became set as she listened in silence to the voice at the other end of the line. Minutes later she replaced the receiver and stood for a moment rubbing her hands together pulling, at her wedding ring something she always did when she was nervous or agitated.

"Who was it, Mum?"

Startled, Peggy looked up the stairs to see Marie staring down at her. It had been a week since she'd come home, and in that time she'd seemed to pick up a bit. Before they'd left the hospital the doctor had told Peggy that the change in environment could cause Marie to enter into a remission for a time, during which she would probably appear to be getting better. He'd also warned her that it wouldn't last. Now looking up at her daughter's small pinched face, the look of apprehension that clouded it, Peggy felt her stomach contract.

"It was the hospital, love. They've got the result of that test you had on Tuesday and they want us to go up there now."

Coming down the stairs slowly, Marie tried to form the words she desperately wanted to say, but found she couldn't speak.

Without giving either of them time to think, Peggy quickly pulled her coat off the metal peg in the hall, at the same time handing Marie her jacket. Shrugging her arms into her coat, Peggy went towards the sitting room. Flinging open the door. she shouted to Bill, "That was the hospital. They want to see us about that test Marie had. We won't be long."

Before anyone could answer she grabbed Marie by the arm and marched her quickly out of the door, careful to avert her eyes from Marie's face for fear she'd see the rising panic that was engulfing her body.

\*

Peggy glanced at her watch; they had been waiting for over an hour. Tutting loudly, she turned to the woman sitting next to her and said wryly, "By the time you get seen to, you've either forgotten what you've come for, or you're cured."

Before the woman could answer the nurse came into the waiting-room and called out, "Marie Cowley?"

Hearing her name called after such a long wait caught Marie unawares. Gripping Peggy's hand tightly, she stood up and followed the nurse. Stopping outside a white door, the nurse knocked once then ushered Peggy and Marie into the room.

Dr Jones stood up to greet them, the smile on his face indicating he had good news to impart.

"Hello, Marie, Mrs Cowley", he nodded at both of them, "sit down, won't you?"

He watched as the mother and daughter sat down, their hands tightly entwined.

"Well now," he started, "I've some good news for you." Pulling himself forward in his chair, he rested his hands on the large wooden desk. "Remember that test you had on Tuesday?" he asked, his gaze directed at Marie. Dumbly she nodded, her mouth too dry to speak. She remembered all right. She had been taken to a small operating theatre where a doctor had strapped two tennis balls to her stomach and then injected an inky blue substance into her arm. Then the table on which she had been lying had started to revolve up, down and around. She had half expected an Indian to appear out of nowhere and start throwing knives at her.

"Well, that was a test designed to check your kidneys," Dr Jones continued, "but look, I'll show you."

Warming to his theme, he got up from his desk and walked over to the X-ray screen. Picking up an X-ray from the table beneath it, he placed it over the white plate and flicked on a light. Then, with a long pencil, he began to point at the black and white mass that was Marie's insides.

"These," he indicated what looked to Peggy and Marie like a couple of ink blobs, "are your kidneys, which are perfectly healthy by the way. "But look behind, see that lighter area, just there?"

Peggy and Marie leaned forward in their chairs trying to look intelligent. Then Peggy, her nerves stretched to breaking point said, "Doctor, that may make perfect sense to you, but to me it just looks like someone's dropped a pot of ink. Would you please tell me in plain English what exactly is wrong with my daughter?"

"Of course, Mrs Cowley, I'm sorry." Switching off the light, he pulled the X-ray from the small machine and came back to his desk.

When he was seated once more he looked straight at Marie and said kindly, "You have an inflammation of the bowel. It's called Chron's disease. The stomach pains, lack of appetite, tiredness and diarrhoea are all classic symptoms of Chron's disease. Now, what I propose to do is put you on a course of tablets called prednisolone. It's a steroid drug that will keep the inflammation under control. I'll start you off on a high dose and then decrease the amount over a period of time. I'll also prescribe some antibiotics to fight any infection you may encounter in view of your weak state."

Picking up a prescription pad, he began to scribble, his hand seeming to fly over the paper. Watching him, Peggy felt her body slump with relief. And then remembering something he had said earlier she felt a slow, burning rage engulf her. She turned her head and glanced at Marie who had sat through the entire consultation without uttering a word, her face white and pinched-looking. Giving her hand a comforting squeeze, Peggy turned back to the doctor. "Tell me, Doctor," she said, trying to keep the anger from her voice, "if all my daughter's symptoms are classic to this disease, then why the bloody hell didn't you find out what it was sooner?"

Dr Jones slowly laid down his pen, his expression resigned as if he'd expected this onslaught. "You have every right to be angry, Mrs Cowley," he said, picking his words carefully, "but Chron's disease isn't a common illness; it's not rare, but it isn't something we automatically look for. I know that sounds like a poor excuse, and I can only offer my heartfelt apologies for making Marie suffer longer than was necessary."

Looking at his genuinely contrite face, Peggy felt her anger seep away. What if it had taken a long time to diagnose, they had found the cause and now, God willing, the nightmare was over. Reaching into her handbag for a handkerchief, she began to dab at her eyes, catching the tears before they fell to her cheeks. Turning once more to Marie, she said gently, her voice shaking with emotion, "Are you not going to say anything, love? Didn't you hear the doctor? You're going to get well again. It's all over now, you won't have to suffer any more."

Running her tongue around her lips to try and ease the dryness, Marie tried to answer but found she couldn't. She had dreamed of this moment for so long, the moment when a doctor would tell her that she would be well again, but now it had come too late. She felt dead inside. She couldn't remember what it was like to feel well, to be without pain, and she didn't believe that a simple course of tablets would bring about such a miracle, and so she bowed her head once again and retreated back into her private shell of misery and despair.

Peggy could only guess what Marie was going through and decided not to try and force her to speak. Maybe later when she had time to digest what had happened . . .

"How long will she have to take the tablets for, Doctor?" she asked, a tremulous smile on her lips.

Dr Jones looked at her across the desk, and when he spoke his voice was steady. "Chron's disease can't be cured – at least not at this moment in time. Your daughter will have to take these tablets for the rest of her life."

"I don't understand," Peggy said, her voice breaking.

Folding his arms on the table, he looked straight into the vivid blue eyes suddenly anxious to take the fear from them.

"It can't be cured – no – but it can be kept under control by the steroids. There may also be times in the future when your daughter will have to be re-admitted for further treatment, but on the whole she'll be able to lead a normal life."

Moving his gaze to Marie, he felt a surge of sympathy for the young girl who hadn't spoken a word since they'd come in. She looked no more than twelve years old; until you looked into her eyes, eyes that looked too old to be in such a young face.

Picking up his pen once more, he finished writing. Handing over the small piece of white paper to Peggy, he said gently, "I'd like you to come back in two weeks, by which time we should all see a marked improvement." He wondered if he should warn the mother about the side effects that would occur and then decided against it.

It was only with prolonged use that the girl's bones would become brittle causing her to bruise easily. There was no use in telling her that now; it wasn't dangerous and they had both had enough shocks for one day. The puffiness that would soon be evident in her face would be taken for a sign of health. He would explain at a later date that steroids taken on a high dose cause the face to swell, giving a moon-like appearance. Again that was nothing serious; as the tablets were decreased so would the swelling abate. Getting to his feet, he held out the prescription. With a trembling hand, Peggy took if from him, at the same time thanking him, then rose unsteadily to her feet. As if woken from a dream Marie also stood up, and then her sight became blurred, black dots danced before her eyes, and then she was falling, her legs buckling under her as she came to rest at Peggy's feet.

For the first week on the steroids, Marie didn't notice any difference and she began to think that maybe the doctors had made a mistake. But by the second week she was eating anything that wasn't nailed down. Peggy could only look at her and marvel.

So well did Marie feel that ten days after she'd begun taking the tablets she announced that she was going to visit her friends at work. Ignoring her mother's protests that she was still too weak to go out on her own, she left the house one morning and set off down the road to the bus stop. While she waited for the bus that would take her to the firm's gates, she began to rehearse the stories she would tell them when she got there, with the aid of a bit of imagination of course.

Oh, here was her bus, she had nearly missed it with her daydreaming. It pulled into the stop and Marie got on – at least half of her did. As she put her second leg onto the platform, her knees buckled under her and she crashed to her knees.

The next fifteen minutes were a nightmare. Holding onto the pole with one hand and the rail with the other, she went tearing down the road at thirty miles an hour. Desperately she tried to raise herself to a standing position, but the months spent in a hospital bed had weakened her legs to such an extent that she could no longer put any weight upon them. As Marie tried once more to rise she cursed herself for her stupidity; she couldn't even get up the stairs at home without holding onto the handrail. Holding on for dear life, she waited for the next stop so she could get off and go home.

Luck was against her. It being late in the morning there wasn't anyone at the next stop or the one after. On and on the bus went, turning corners at what seemed like breakneck speed. The lovely beehive hairdo she had spent half the morning creating was swept to one side by the wind and was standing out like the hand of a drowning woman going down in water for the third time.

Two women standing gossiping stopped in mid-sentence as they caught sight of the bus flying by and the figure of a young girl kneeling as if in prayer, her legs dangling over the edge of the platform. Marie was indeed praying, at every chance she got she uttered a feeble "Help," but there were no other people on the bus and the conductor was upstairs.

"Help!" she cried once more, at the same time wondering what people passing in the street thought as she sped past them, kneeling on the platform, holding on for dear life. Probably thought she was trying to dodge her fare. If she was ever to see such a sight, she would wet herself laughing. After what seemed to be an eternity the bus finally began to slow down and came to a stop. They hadn't hit one red light all the way there.

The bus conductor came down the stairs whistling. He stopped halfway through *Danny Boy* and stared at her in amazement.

"I thought I heard someone get on a while back," he said, startled.

Carefully backing off the platform onto the safety of the pavement, Marie looked up at him and said simply, "I've been ill."

He stared at her for a long moment before ringing the bell. They continued to stare at each other until the bus turned the next corner. Weakly, Marie propped herself against a nearby wall. At least he hadn't asked for her fare. Then she started to laugh. It could only happen to me, she thought wildly, and what was worse, when I tell this story no one will believe me . . .

# Chapter Six

1966.

"Isn't it your day for the hospital?" asked Pam as she passed Marie's desk. About to answer, Marie suddenly changed her mind.

"No," she lied, not looking at her friend, "not till next week."

When Pam moved away from her desk, Marie carried on with her work. It *was* her day for her monthly check-up at the hospital, but she wasn't going – in fact she wasn't going back there ever again. The sudden decision made her stop work for a moment, then her fingers once again returned to the large I.B.M. punch machine before her.

Her mind racing, she began to make plans. She knew that she had to have medical supervision, probably for the rest of her life, but there must be another hospital, one better than the Bethnal Green. Alright, alright, she told herself, they'd found the cause of her trouble and had made her well for a while, but the last few months had seen the return of the pain and misery. She knew she'd have to go into hospital again but not in that grey, dreary place. The obvious solution was to find somewhere better – but where?

The sudden arrival of the tea-lady put an end to Marie's thoughts and plans for the moment. As she went to collect her cup of tea, she resolved to visit Dr Downey tonight – he'd know what to do. Having made her decision, she immediately felt better. Sitting round the large table that was used for lunches and tea breaks, Marie took out her sandwiches and settled down to the usual twenty minutes of gossip and laughter with her friends.

Dr Downey listened in silence as Marie told him of her decision. Privately, he agreed with her about the conditions and the gloomy atmosphere that pervaded the old hospital, but he kept his opinions to himself. Promising her that he would arrange something, he was rewarded by the happy smile that lit her face. After the door closed behind her he returned to his desk. Pulling a well-thumbed book towards him, he began to look up the doctor he had in mind, then he reached for his pen and began to make notes.

Two weeks later Marie, received a letter from the out-patients' department at St Bartholomew's Hospital asking her to attend the clinic in a week's time.

Showing Peggy the letter, she moaned, "Bart's is a long way to go, Mum."

Well, you asked to be transferred, and what other hospital is there round here? Only the ear, nose and throat, and that wouldn't be much use to you, would it"?

Looking at her mother, Marie smiled and said, "No, I don't suppose it would – wrong end isn't it?"

"Oh, you," Peggy said, pushing her lightly on the shoulder before going into the kitchen to start the tea.

Marie looked after her mother smiling to herself, it was good to see her happy; she had been through so much because of her. She'd have to make sure she didn't cause her mother any more pain.

A week later Marie and Peggy were standing waiting at the bus stop in Wick Road. Scrambling on board, they pushed their way down to the front of the bus, only to be beaten to the last empty seat by a large lady who sat down quickly, with an air of triumph. Such was her girth that she took up the entire seat and neither of them felt brave enough to ask her to move along to make room – not that there would have been much room anyway. Peggy reached up for the leather strap attached to the roof, telling Marie to do the same. Twenty minutes later they alighted from the bus, and while Peggy went to queue for the tickets, Marie bought a magazine from the newsagent's stall and began flicking through the glossy pages.

"All right, love?" Peggy came up behind her.

Marie folded up the magazine and put it into her shoulder bag, then linking arms with her mother she answered, "Yes, I'm fine." Remembering the daily journey she'd made to get to her first job in the city she said cheerfully, "By the way, Mum, have you ever been on the tube in the rush hour?"

"No", Peggy replied, a puzzled look on her face.

Pulling her towards the escalator, Marie laughed. "You've got a treat in store for you then."

Half an hour later they emerged from the crowded compartment.

"Holy Mary," Peggy gasped as she staggered towards a nearby bench. For the past twenty minutes she had been pushed, shoved, dug in the back and touched twice in a familiar way – whether by accident or design she didn't know – and all the while her face had been flattened up against the tube window.

When she got her breath back she declared, "Never again. We'll get the bus home. No, no," she said as if warding off any argument in the matter, "I know it takes longer but I'd rather walk than go through that experience again. How," she asked in amazement, "do people travel like that every day?"

"You get used to it."

"No," Peggy answered, shaking her head violently, "never in a million years would I ever get used to that cattle train."

"Mum, we're going to be late."

"All right, all right, I'm coming. I don't know about you seeing a doctor, I think I could do with seeing one myself."

Leading Peggy out of the station at St Paul's, Marie paused for a minute to get their bearings. To the right of them stood the cathedral, but it was further down the road that they saw the statue of the scales of justice on top of the Old Bailey.

"Teresa said the hospital was over the road from the Old Bailey," Marie said, starting to walk on. After asking a policeman the exact directions they now stood in front of the wrought-iron gates of Bart's.

Marie felt a sinking feeling in the pit of her stomach. The building was old and dirty-looking; it was nothing like she had expected. Although she had worked just around the corner from the hospital for nearly a year in her first ill-fated job, she had never had occasion to study it closely. Her stomach was churning and she felt sick with fear; maybe she should have stayed where she was. Sensing her thoughts, Peggy grabbed her by the arm and none to gently propelled Marie through the heavy green plastic doors that led to the out-patients' department.

"You know the old saying, when one door closes . . ."

"Yes," Marie answered her, "another one slams in your face."

Fighting down the rising panic, Marie allowed Peggy to lead her further into the building. There was no going back now.

Two hours later Peggy emerged from the hospital alone. Marie had been kept in.

She sat up in the all-too-familiar hospital bed. It might be a different hospital but the beds were universally hard and uncomfortable.

Marie was still in a state of shock. Nothing had turned out as she'd expected. She had assumed that her notes from the Bethnal Green Hospital would have been transferred here, and the doctors would treat her accordingly, but, as she'd been told, every hospital likes to make its own tests. It wasn't fair, she thought childishly, and quick on the heels of this thought came another – I want my mum . . .

Then followed weeks of examinations and tests that left Marie both physically and mentally exhausted.

When Marie had first come onto the ward and the tests had begun she had railed against the indignities that had been perpetrated upon her frail body. The first test had been a barium meal and she had gagged as she'd been forced to swallow the thick, sickly substance while a doctor had pushed and probed her already tender stomach.

Two days later when she had once again been taken down to the X-ray department for a barium enema, she had some-how found the strength and courage to scream and kick out in fear as the doctor had explained gently what he was about to do. After it was over she had been taken back to the ward in a wheelchair and helped into bed, where she'd lain for hours shuddering with revulsion at what had been done to her.

There had followed a quick succession of tests whereby instruments had been put down her and up her. The fear she felt every time she saw a doctor approach her bed had brought her temporarily out of her enforced apathy. Now she no longer protested or cried; it did no good and she no longer had the strength to fight. She hadn't realised how ill she had actually been. The disease had flared up again long before Marie had been admitted, but the ordeal she had gone through had exacerbated it.

Now the tests had all been completed she could relax a little, but she wouldn't feel completely at ease until she was back in her own bed at home. Plumping up her half a dozen pillows, she sat upright and looked down the ward to where Dr Lawson was making his ward rounds. It was Friday, the day you were discharged if you were one of the lucky ones. Feeling a little more optimistic, Marie settled herself more comfortably on the pillows.

Letting her gaze wander round the ward, she had grudgingly to admit that this was indeed a much better hospital. The ward was bright and cheery and the consultant, Dr Lawson, was terrific. She had walked into his consulting room fearing the worst, but had been immediately put at ease by the slim-built man with light brown hair and kindly grey eyes partly hidden by a pair of half-moon glasses. She had judged him to be in his early forties, still old by her standards, but a lot younger than the other doctors she had been used to. He also possessed that special quality that drew people to him, making them like and trust him as Marie now did. Every Tuesday and Friday when he did his ward rounds he always took the time to sit by her and talk, doing his best to allay her fears.

She heard him talking to the woman in the next bed and then, after what seemed an eternity, it was her turn. Any hopes she had of going home were immediately dashed as he sat down on her bed, taking her hand as he did so. She felt her tears start to fall as she tried to listen to what he was saying.

"You're still very ill, my dear," he said gently, his eyes soft with concern.

"But I thought I could go home once the tests were finished," Marie sobbed.

Seeing her distress, he motioned the students away from the bed and, with the ward sister standing on the other side of her, he tried to explain why she was being kept in: "You're still in the early stages of the disease. The steroids help to keep it under control, but you also need antibiotics and iron. Even more importantly, you need to get some flesh on your bones," he added, smiling at her. Getting no response, he looked to the sister for help, then turned back to Marie. Squeezing her hand, he said quietly, "It's for the best, dear. Be patient."

Pulling her hand free, Marie turned her head into the pillow, her sobs racking her body. Dr Lawson looked down at the slight figure in concern, wishing he could think of something to say. Slowly rising from the bed, he gave Marie a gentle pat on the shoulder before continuing his rounds. Left alone once more, Marie beat her small fists into the pillow, all the while muttering, "It's not fair. It's not bloody fair," until, finally exhausted, she fell asleep.

There followed weeks of pleading with her mother to take her home. All the good resolutions she'd had about not upsetting her mum again went flying out the window. She felt desperate and trapped, but gradually as the days turned into weeks she felt herself getting stronger.

She was still very thin – but what could you expect with the sort of food they gave you in hospital? Up until a few weeks ago she had eaten her meals on a tray in her bed. She never ate the food, but sneaked it into a sick bag and later smuggled it out to the toilet, where she would dispose of it in the bin. The only food she ate was the treats her mum brought with her when she visited every day.

She'd been found out two weeks ago when she'd persuaded Bobby on one of his visits to take the food out of the ward with him. He'd protested strongly when she'd handed him the soggy bag of roast potatoes and stringy meat dripping with gravy, but because he'd felt sorry for her he had agreed to dispose of it. The trouble had started when, on his way out, the paper bag had broken and two roast potatoes had rolled across the floor to land at the ward sister's feet.

Bobby had stood rooted to the floor with embarrassment before taking to his heels. Since then he'd refused to take out any more – not that he could have done. The sister had insisted on Marie taking her meals at the table from that day. Now meal-times were a nightmare. It was like being back at school. One of the nurses would stand over her while she ate. It didn't matter how she cried and pleaded. A few times she'd been sick and now they were talking about putting her on a special diet. Then came the day the dietician visited her and wrote down all the things she liked to eat, telling her that Dr Lawson had sent her to the ward, causing him to go up another notch in Marie's estimation.

From that day on life became more bearable. She had to suffer the looks of envy on the other patients' faces when she sat down to chicken and ham while they tried to guess what was on their plates, but she found she could live with that.

As her health improved, so did her mind, and she soon became bored sitting in bed most of the day. When she had first come into the ward, a few of the patients had tried to talk to her but she had rebuffed them, wanting only to be left in peace. Now, on this early Sunday morning, without any diversions to look forward to until visiting time, she felt restless and wished she'd made more of an effort to make friends with the other women on the ward. Looking up from the Agatha Christie book she was reading, she saw three of the women walking down the ward chattering happily as if they were in a supermarket instead of a hospital. Seeing they had their dressing gowns on, she guessed they were going for a walk in the grounds and without stopping to think Marie called out hopefully, "Can I come with you?"

The women stopped talking and stared at her for a moment before the youngest of them smiled and said, "We're only going down to the grounds, but you'll have to ask Sister if you can go."

Quickly Marie was out of bed. Getting the necessary permission, she donned her candy-striped dressing gown and walked happily from the ward.

The next few days passed quickly. Together with her new-found friends she went down to the library, browsed around the hospital paper- and sweet-shop and strolled in the large grounds when the weather was fine.

The day finally came when Dr Lawson sat on the side of the bed and said the magic words, "Well, my dear, I suppose you'd like to go home."

With a cry of happiness Marie sat up in bed and just re-strained herself from throwing her arms around his neck.

"I want to see you in out-patients' in a fortnight's time. Get your mother to phone the hospital for an appointment. Alright?"

"Oh, thank you, Doctor, I will. Can I go *now*?" Marie asked, her voice breathless, as if fearful he might change his mind.

Giving her one last smile, he patted her hand and continued on his way. She watched him go, wondering how it was he could bring comfort to those he cared for simply by his presence.

"*I can go home,*" she whispered excitedly to the new patient in the next bed. Completely uninterested, the woman merely smiled faintly and went back to reading her book. Unperturbed Marie jumped out of bed and, getting into her dressing gown, hurried down the hall to the pay phone. She couldn't wait to tell her mum and dad to come and get her.

"I'm going home, I'm going home," she sang as she made her way down the corridor.

As she left the ward with Peggy on one side and Bill on the other, Marie had a feeling of *déjà vu*. But this wasn't like the last time. She felt happy and confident and couldn't seem to stop smiling. Shaking hands with the ward sister, she thanked her for her care, forgetting all the times she had called her an old cow under her breath of course. As they approached the exit gates, Marie noticed that although her mum had been talking practically non-stop, her dad had hardly said a word. The truth was that Bill didn't know what to say and if he had done he would have found it hard to get a word in. Once Peggy was in full swing there was no stopping her.

"You all right, Dad, you've not said a word?"

Bill thought for a moment then said, "Henry Cooper lost to Ali in the sixth round. I thought he was going to win."

"Jesus, you silly sod, she doesn't want to hear about a boxing match", Peggy broke in irritably "Can't you think of anything more interesting to talk about?"

Completely unruffled by his wife's outburst, Bill rubbed his hand over his face as he thought for something to say. "Ronald Reagan – you know, the actor – he's been elected Governor of California. He might be President one day."

Unable to contain herself Peggy burst out, "Ronald Reagan, President of the United States, God help us." She turned to Marie as if making an appeal, "Can you imagine it; your father really thinks a B-picture actor is going to be President one day." Turning to Bill she exclaimed, "You're getting worse you are – you'll believe anything you read in the newspapers."

"I do read the newspapers, Dad," Marie broke in quickly. "I've been in hospital, not solitary confinement."

"Of course you do, love, take no notice of him."

The familiar bickering went over Marie's head; she was used to it. It didn't mean anything. Her mum moaned, her dad listened; in one ear and out the other. All she could think of was that she was free, that's what it felt like. She'd just said she hadn't been in solitary confinement, but for a long time it had felt just like that. As they went through the hospital gates Marie stopped to take in the sights around her. Even watching the buses go by and seeing the men and women rushing to their places of work fascinated her. She took a deep breath. She was seventeen years old and out of the last two years she had spent a total of ten months in and out of hospital, but it didn't matter – nothing mattered – she was going home.

# Chapter Seven

1967.

"Can we go round to see Nan?" Marie asked as she sat happily eating her tea. She had been home for only a day, but she was missing her nan.

"Oi, you, you've already had a cake, greedy pig." Marie hit out at six-year-old Jimmy's hand as he tried to take the last iced bun from the large plate in the middle of the table. Undaunted, he poked his tongue out at her. Nudging five-year-old Patti, he pointed to the ceiling and as she looked up he deftly swiped the half-eaten cake from her plate.

"Mum, Mum, Jimmy's taken my cake," Patti wailed, bursting into tears.

Peggy bustled over to the table to restore order. "Now come on, all of you. Marie's just come home from hospital, and she needs peace and quiet. You, Jimmy, give Patti back her cake and go into the sitting room."

As the two children got slowly down from the table Peggy shouted after them, "And take John with you." Patti had already left the room, still moaning that Jimmy had eaten most of her cake. Jimmy came back to the table and took his little brother's hand, careful to avert his face from his mum lest she should see his mouth still crammed with his ill-gotten gains. Peggy heaved a sigh of relief as they left the room; maybe now she could have a bit of peace in which to have her own tea – and to answer Marie's question.

Putting off the evil moment for a while longer, she said brightly, "Well, isn't it nice having your sister back home?"

She looked round the table at the underwhelming reaction her question had evoked. She would be the first to admit that her eldest daughter wasn't always the most lovable person in the world but, apart from Jimmy, who was an affectionate child by nature and had given Marie a hug when he'd come home from school, then spoilt it by asking her for his pocket money, Bobby was the only one who seemed glad to have her home. Ellen was put out at the prospect of having to share her bed again, she didn't think Andy had even noticed she'd gone, and Vicky and the younger children had assumed Marie was at her nan's.

Peggy sighed heavily. In a way it was Marie's own fault. When she was at home she either spent all her time in her bedroom, or continually moaned at the children for making too much noise when they ate, or when they played; it was small wonder they hadn't missed her overmuch.

Still, she told herself, that had been when Marie had been ill; and she had been very ill. Now that she was receiving the proper care, perhaps she would become a happier person.

"Come on, you three. I want to talk to Marie."

"See you later, Marie," Bobby said, smiling as he left the table.

"Can I go and play out for a while, Mum?" Ellen asked hopefully. Peggy waved them away, she wasn't looking forward to what she had to tell Marie, but she couldn't put it off much longer.

"All right, but only for an hour and don't go away from the door." She watched as they left the room, then Vicky, who hadn't said anything, came over to Marie and shyly leant up on tiptoe and kissed Marie on the cheek.

"I'm glad you're better now, Marie," she said quietly before she too left the room.

Bill had been standing by the sink and now he caught Peggy's eye and mouthed the words, "You'd better tell her."

"When can we go round to Nan's, Mum?" Marie asked again, looking happier than Peggy had seen her in a long time.

When she received no answer she looked up from her cup of tea just in time to see the look that passed between her mum and dad. Her heart skipped a beat.

"What's wrong?" she asked, her voice rising with an unknown fear.

"In a minute, love; finish your tea."

"Something's wrong – tell me." Marie was getting really scared now. It must be her nan. Of course she would have been round by now if she'd been able.

"Your nan's on holiday; you know she went away with the church." Peggy said, hating herself for the lie. Marie watched as her mum walked calmly to the sink where she deposited the dirty plates into the hot water, humming all the while to herself.

Marie looked at her dad and then got up from her chair and walked over to where Peggy was standing, her arms deep in soapy water.

"Nan went on holiday over a month ago, Mum. She must be back by now."

Swallowing painfully, Peggy turned to face her daughter, the look on her face causing Marie to take a step backwards.

"She's not dead, is she, Mum?" she asked fearfully. Her throat felt constricted and her head swam as she tried to fight down the panic that was engulfing her entire body.

"No, no, love, she's not dead," Peggy said quickly, "but she's not very well at the moment, she's in a sort of hospital."

Marie looked at her mother stupidly. "A sort of hospital? What do you mean, a sort of hospital?"

"Sit down." Peggy led Marie back to the table, noticing that Bill had done his usual disappearing act. When they were both seated Peggy took hold of Marie's hands and said gently, "There's no easy way to tell you," and taking a deep breath she added, "Your nan's had a nervous breakdown."

The room swam for a moment as Marie tried to digest this startling news.

Raising her head Marie looked straight into her mother's eyes. "When you say a 'sort of hospital', you mean a mental hospital don't you?"

Holding on tightly to Marie's hands, Peggy went on, "It happened on holiday; no one knows why. Father Bailey told me that she was sitting quietly one minute and the next she had picked up a chair and hurled it through a window. She was lucky she wasn't cut by flying glass."

Dumbly Marie looked at her mother. "But why?" she asked, confused.

"I don't know, love, but she's getting good care. I promise I'll take you to see her as soon as the doctors think it's advisable."

Standing up slowly, Marie turned and walked from the room, her head whirling. Yesterday she had been so happy – now this. It wasn't fair, she thought fiercely, her Nan had never done anyone any harm, she didn't deserve this.

Watching her go, Peggy bit on her lip. If Marie found out it was partly her fault, she would never forgive herself. Peggy hadn't told her the whole truth. Part of the cause of May's breakdown had been the traumatic years of seeing her granddaughter suffering, and now, her mind broken, May thought Marie was dead.

What can I do? Peggy thought helplessly. If seeing Marie would help her mother she would take Marie to the hospital right this minute, but the doctors had told her that, in May's confused state of mind, seeing Marie might make matters worse.

"Why did this have to happen?" she said aloud to the empty kitchen. Echoing Marie's earlier thoughts, she cried to herself, It isn't fair – but then nobody said that life was fair. May had told her that many years ago. As Peggy felt the tears slip down her face she didn't know who she was crying for – Marie, her mother, or herself.

She didn't hear Bobby come into the kitchen; she wasn't aware of his presence until he gripped her hand. Bobby watched his mother crying and his young mind searched for something comforting to say, but instead he could only watch helplessly at his mother's grief.

The hospital was set in beautiful large grounds. It looked more like a stately home than a mental institution. Marie clutched Peggy's hand fearfully as she gazed around her in wonder. She didn't know what she had expected, but it certainly wasn't this. Taking advantage of Marie's preoccupation, Peggy gently guided her towards the entrance to the day-room.

"You sit there," Peggy said, indicating the wrought-iron bench, "while I go and fetch Nan."

94

As Peggy went to disentangle her hand Marie tightened her hold. "I'm frightened, Mum."

Peggy sighed; it was a mistake, she should never have agreed to bring her here. When she had talked to the doctor on the phone he had been apprehensive about the visit and warned her that at the slightest sign of agitation from May they would have to leave. Gently freeing her hand, she pushed Marie down onto the bench and with a muttered, "Wait here," she left her. Marie kept her eyes fixed firmly on the ground, fearful to raise them up lest she should catch the attention of one of the inmates. She'd thought it bad enough in an ordinary hospital, but at least she hadn't been afraid of being attacked. After all, she told herself, they must be a bit doolally or they wouldn't be in here.

Strangely enough she didn't apply this description to her nan – that was different, her nan was just a bit run down, she wasn't mental.

She didn't hear them approaching until she heard her mother's voice gently telling May to sit down. Looking up slowly, she stared into the face of her beloved nan, but before she could say anything she caught sight of her mother's face and the slight shake of her head as if warning her against saying anything. Her nan was staring down at her, smiling in a puzzled way; there was no sign of recognition on her face. Marie felt the first flutter of real fear as she realised that her nan didn't know her. She was smiling, yes, but in the same way she would smile at a stranger.

"Move along, love, and let the lady sit down." Jumping at the sound of Peggy's voice, Marie complied with her request. When they were seated an uneasy silence fell over them. May seemed unaware of the atmosphere and gazed serenely in front of her. When she finally spoke, both Marie and Peggy jumped.

Addressing herself to Marie, May said quietly, "I had a granddaughter the same age as you once. Her name was Marie. What's your name, dear?"

Completely unnerved now Marie looked frantically at her mum for guidance. When she saw the slight almost imperceptible shake of her mother's head she remained silent. Not that she would have been able to speak; her throat was so con-stricted with fear she felt sick. And then May started talking to herself. She talked about all the things Marie had done as a child, how much she had loved her and all the while Marie bit down the desire to scream.

This isn't happening, she thought wildly. Even in her darkest days and nights she had never been as frightened as she was now.

Before Peggy could stop her, Marie had thrown herself into May's arms sobbing. "I'm here, Nan," she shrieked, her voice rising, touching on the edge of hysteria, "I'm here. It's me, Nan – it's me, Marie. I'm not dead, I'm alive. Oh, Nan, please, I'm not dead!"

When she felt the arms pushing at her Marie held on tightly until she felt herself being shoved so violently that she fell to the ground. Her body shuddering with sobs, she looked up at her nan through tear-filled eyes, and when she saw the look on May's face it chilled her whole body. Her nan was a stranger – and when she thrust an arm out towards her, Marie flinched, as if bracing herself for a physical attack. May was screaming now; a nurse came running followed by a doctor.

When Marie saw them grab May's arms, trying to restrain her, she jumped forward crying, "Leave her alone, leave my nan alone!" She lunged at the nurse, clawing at her arm, all the while screaming at them to let May go. Now Peggy was holding Marie's arms, pulling her away. As the doctor and nurse led May away, Peggy tried to hold onto Marie in a vain attempt to calm the small demented body. She cursed herself for the stupidity she had shown in bringing her here. If she wasn't careful her daughter would be joining her mother. The more Marie struggled, the tighter Peggy's hold became, until gradually she felt the small body quieten. When she was sure Marie's passion was spent, Peggy re-leased her hold and gently gathered her daughter into her arms. As she led Marie away from the grounds her mind was racing at the damage they had done and, although Marie was wailing loudly, all Peggy could hear was the sound of her mother's voice as she screamed, "Take her away, take the silly little cow away. My granddaughter's dead, dead, dead, dead . . ."

The nurse held May's arm as the doctor plunged the hypodermic into her vein. Within seconds she had calmed down and began to drift into sleep.

"Poor old thing," said the nurse. "I suppose this will put her back weeks, doctor; do you think . . . ?" She broke off in mid- sentence as May tried to speak. "What is it, dear?" the nurse asked, bending over her.

Receiving no answer, she straightened up and looking at the doctor said, "It's a bloody shame," to which the doctor replied, "I agree with you, nurse. It's a bloody shame."

May heard them leave, their footsteps echoing on the polished floor. She tried to ward off the darkness that was descending over her mind. "Marie, was it really you?" she whispered thickly. "Marie." And then the darkness fell.

For a long time after the disastrous visit to see May, Peggy feared for Marie's sanity. Her fears were proved groundless, as Marie had soon reverted to her former self; moody one minute and sweetness and light the next, although her better moods were reserved strictly for friends. For a while she and Peggy had been close, but now the "keep out" sign was up again.

But what did it matter? Peggy chided herself. Marie's health had never been better; the change in hospitals had worked wonders and it was mainly due to the influence of Dr Lawson. Peggy had been favourably impressed the first time she'd met him, and on further aquaintance the feeling had grown. He had worked wonders with Marie; it was only a pity he couldn't do something about her disposition.

Taking a pile of woollens from the kitchen table, she walked over to the sink and began to submerge them into the soapy water. She was up to her elbows in suds when the doorbell rang.

"Blast, isn't it always the way?" she muttered to herself, then shouted, "Get the door somebody."

The bell rang again. Where was everyone? Out playing or watching the television most likely, each one hoping someone else would answer the door. Giving an exaggerated sigh, Peggy grabbed a tea-cloth and walked out into the hallway, rubbing her arms dry as she went.

"Sadie, what a lovely surprise. Come in," she said, her face alight with pleasure at seeing her old friend.

"Are you sure, Peggy?" Sadie asked, her lined face anxious. She stood away from the door, her attitude suggesting uncertainty at arriving unannounced, for fear that she would not be welcome. "If you're busy, I can always come back another time."

"Will you away in and stop your nonsense," Peggy laughed, her hand going out to the older woman's arm in a gesture of friendship. "Go through into the kitchen, Sadie. You arrived just in time. I was about to make myself a cup of tea," Peggy lied. "Go on, sit, make yourself at home."

Peggy watched happily as Sadie squeezed her ample body onto the kitchen chair, the anxious look disappearing from her face. While she waited for the kettle to boil Peggy got the cups and saucers from the cupboard and began putting milk in the two cups.

"Do you take milk, Sadie, and sugar?"

"A little milk, no sugar, thank you, Peggy." Settling herself more comfortably on the chair, Sadie looked around the large tidy kitchen. "It's a nice place you have here, Peggy. I only wish mine was as big. A cat to swing in it you couldn't."

"Are you not happy, Sadie? Didn't you go to live with your daughter?"

Spreading her hands wide, Sadie nodded. "My Rose is a good girl, kind like her father was, but she's out all day working, the children are at school, I have no one to talk to. It gets very lonely, Peggy. That's why I decided to come and see the market. I was happy here in the East End. I miss it. Then when I met Joan down the market I asked after you and the children, and she told me you were still here, so here I am. I hope you don't mind."

"Don't start that nonsense again. I've told you, you're more than welcome." Setting the tea cups on the table, she was

98

about to speak again when Jimmy burst into the room, only to come to an abrupt halt as he saw the large woman with enormous earrings sitting in his favourite place.

"Is this Jimmy?" Sadie asked in mock surprise. "Such a big boy you are now."

"Where are your manners, Jimmy? Say hello nicely."

Jimmy looked at his mum, then back to the lady, his fore-head wrinkled in an effort of concentration. A sad look came over Sadie's face as she realised the boy didn't know her. But what had she expected? The child hadn't seen her for over a year. He had probably forgotten her within the first few weeks after she'd left the baker's. Picking up her tea, she shook her head trying to hide her disappointment.

Jimmy noted the movement, caught the glint of gold as the thick, ring-shaped earrings swung back and forth, and suddenly recognition dawned. The frown disappeared from his forehead, and with a cry of delight he rushed forward. "Sadie, where have you been? I've missed you!" He was on her lap, his arms trying to encircle her large waistline as he beamed up into her face.

"Mum, Mum," Bobby came running into the room, his face alight with laughter. As Peggy put out her hand to steady him, she found herself smiling back at him. At thirteen years of age he was growing into a fine lad.

"Never mind that, Bobby. Look who's come to see us."

Bobby turned slowly, his face like Jimmy's lighting up at the sight of the woman who had been so kind to them. "Hello, Sadie," he said shyly.

"Hello, Bobby. And what is it you've just seen?"

Shuffling his feet, he looked from Sadie to his mother then blurted out, "A man with long hair, right down to his shoulders. Like a girl, honest, Mum." He stared at her as if frightened of being disbelieved. He had been down the market with two of his friends when they had first set eyes on this phenomenon. Tommy Fisher had run after the man calling him a poof, upon which the man had turned around and chased them all the way up Well Street. He'd been fright-ened, not that he would have admitted that, but the thought that was nagging at him came out in a rush.

"What's a poof, Mum?"

Dumbfounded, Peggy looked at him, then catching hold of his arm she shook him none too gently. "Where did you hear that word?" she demanded.

"It wasn't me, Mum," he spluttered, anxious to put the blame squarely where it belonged. "It was Tommy Fisher, he said it, he called the man with the long hair a poof. What does it mean? Is it a bad word?"

Letting go of his arm, Peggy looked over to Sadie, her eyes asking the older woman for assistance, but Sadie, who was trying hard not to laugh, had her eyes firmly fixed on Jimmy's dark curls. Seeing that she would get no help from her old friend, Peggy walked over to the sink and began to rinse out the soapy garments, trying to think of how best to deal with the situation. She too had seen a few young men sporting the new fashion and thought they looked ridiculous.

As her neighbour Joan had commented, "Some poor sod's going to get a fright when they try to grab a handful." Peggy laughed to herself. Joan was coarse at times, but she couldn't help but like her.

Bobby was still waiting for an answer.

"Never mind what it means, I don't want to hear you saying it again."

"Don't you know, Mum?"

Peggy reflected for a moment before answering, "Go and ask your dad when he gets home from work. No, wait a minute." She grabbed him as he made to run from the room. She didn't want to risk Bill having a heart attack the minute he walked in the door. So, reverting to the age-old answer when dealing with children, she said, "I'll tell you when you're older. Now – out. You too, Jimmy, I want to talk to Sadie in peace."

Ignoring the "Oh, mum, do we have to?" she ushered them from the kitchen. Leaning against the door, she looked at Sadie and within a couple of minutes they were laughing like a couple of young girls.

Wiping her eyes, Sadie gasped, "Oh, Peggy, I'm so glad I plucked up the courage to knock on your door. I haven't laughed like that in a long time."

Hearing the wistful note in Sadie's voice, Peggy felt a moment of sadness. Reaching out for the plump hand, she held it tightly for a minute before saying, "You'll always be welcome in this house, Sadie." The two women were quiet for a moment, enjoying the peacefulness of companionship. Sadie was the first to break the silence.

"So, Peggy," she said briskly, "how are the rest of the family?"

Always ready to talk, Peggy told her about May. Her mother had been in that place for nearly three months, but thank God she was fully recovered now and back home.

Sadie listened carefully, genuinely interested. She nodded sympathetically as Peggy told of the nightmare of the last few months. From May, Peggy went on to tell her about Marie, and again Sadie nodded in sympathy as she heard all about the girl's illness, and then Peggy's concern about her eldest daughter's social life.

"She's going down to my sister Teresa for the weekend, and then the following week she's going down to Northampton to spend a few days with my younger sister Pauline. Don't get me wrong, Sadie, I'm glad she gets on so well with her aunts, but I wish she'd start going out with friends her own age. She's only eighteen, but she has the makings of an old maid."

Sadie gave a deep sigh, sad that her friend had so much worry, wishing she could help and knowing she couldn't.

"So, Peggy, she's young, she's been through a lot. Give her time, you'll see, she'll turn out to be a credit to you."

Peggy looked doubtful, then a loud cry from upstairs broke into her thoughts.

"That's John," she said to Sadie by way of explanation. Then, she looking up at the kitchen clock gave a start of surprise. "Lord above, will you look at the time, and me sitting here talking when I should be getting the tea ready. It always puts me out when the children are on their school holiday. Excuse me a minute, Sadie."

Sadie watched Peggy leave the room and began to gather her shopping together. Her visit was over, and she worried whether she had overstayed her welcome. As soon as Peggy returned she would pick up her shopping, thank her for the tea and the chat, and leave immediately. As she waited she thought of the lonely flat she called home. She had let Peggy believe she was still living with her daughter, but the truth was that Rose and her husband had moved to Cornwall six months ago, and Sadie hadn't been asked to go with them. But she would keep the truth to herself, she didn't want anyone's pity.

"Here he is, the latest Cowley, and the last." Peggy came back into the room carrying a plump, blue-eyed blond-haired child whom Sadie judged to be about fifteen months. Behind her walked Jimmy who immediately made for Sadie's side.

"You're not going, are you, Sadie?" he asked, noting the way she was standing, a shopping bag in each hand. "Why don't you stay for tea? She can, can't she, Mum?"

"Yes of course she can," Peggy told the flustered Sadie, seeing the pink tinge that had come to her cheeks.

"No, Peggy. You don't have enough to feed? You have to ask strangers?" Her voice came out on a high note.

Gently Peggy pressed Sadie back onto the chair.

"Will your daughter be expecting you home?"

"No, she's not expecting me home," Sadie said truthfully, "I told her I might be late."

"Well then," Peggy said, putting John onto Sadie's lap, "that's settled."


"Going anywhere tonight, Marie?" asked one of her workmates.

"Only to see my aunt," replied Marie, getting into her coat.

"Don't you ever go dancing or to the pictures?"

Shrugging, Marie replied, "I don't fancy it."

"Goodnight then, see you tomorrow."

As Marie walked home, she reflected on the girl's remark. How could she explain why she never went out? She was afraid. She didn't know why, but she was afraid to mix with boys for fear of being rejected. One of her favourite daydreams was having a boyfriend and being able to join in the conversation on a Monday morning when all the other girls said what they had done over the weekend. But when it came to Sandra from the typing pool, Marie wondered which of them had the more vivid imagination. Some of the stories she told were hair-raising, but she always listened avidly. Hearing accounts of their love lives was the closest she was going to get to one of her own.

Moodily Marie walked on, trying to pinpoint the real reason why she was so reluctant to go out. What was she afraid of? It wasn't as if she had no one to go out with. There was Carol who lived four doors away from her. She was always stopping her in the street and asking her to come out with her and her friends. An image of Carol appeared in her mind; a tall slender girl with enormous blue eyes and golden blonde hair that hung down to her waist. As the image appeared so did the answer to her question. How could she go out with a girl like that? A girl who would be picked up the moment she set foot inside a dance hall. She could see herself standing alone and humiliated while Carol was whirled round a dance floor by some handsome bloke and then having to face the lonely walk home in the dark by herself. Giving a tremendous sigh, she carried on walking, feeling thoroughly sorry for herself. She stopped suddenly as she heard someone calling her name. Turning round, she saw Carol running towards her, a happy smile on her face.

"Hello, Marie, you walk fast for a little one. I've been trying to catch you up for the last ten minutes." Walking side by side, they made their way home chatting about the sort of week they'd had, while Marie prayed Carol wouldn't ask her to go out with her this weekend as she normally did whenever she saw her.

They reached Carol's house first and as she fished around in her bag for her door key she asked, "I don't suppose there's any use in asking you if you want to come out with me and my friend tonight, is there?"

Marie was about to refuse and then stopped. There was an air of finality about the question, as if this was the last time Carol was going to ask her, and suddenly, instead of being relieved, Marie felt afraid.

Before she had time to analyse her feelings she said, "All right, where you going?"

She saw the look of surprise that crossed Carol's face and felt a moment of panic.

"Great," Carol said, looking genuinely pleased. "We're going to try the Adam and Eve pub, it's supposed to be good."

"Do you think they'll let me in?" Marie asked worriedly. At eighteen years of age she could easily have passed for thirteen. She didn't want to suffer the humiliation of being refused entry.

"Course they'll let you in, you'll be with us. You're not going to change your mind, are you?" Carol asked anxiously. She was fond of this skinny girl, but she had to admit she did look young for her age and for a moment she felt a twinge of doubt. "Don't worry, if they don't we'll go somewhere else, but they'll let you in, you wait and see."

"You can't come in here."

Marie made to slink back into the night but Carol caught hold of her arm. "Why not?" she demanded fiercely, picking up the gauntlet on Marie's behalf.

In answer to Carol's question, the bouncer pushed her out of his way to enable a couple to pass by him into the hallowed portals of the pub. When Carol continued her verbal onslaught, he lost his patience.

"Now look, I'm not going to stand here explaining myself," he shouted, glaring behind Carol to where Marie was standing, wishing the ground would open up and swallow her. In an effort to appear older she had carefully piled her hair into a bun at the back of her head and, after much deliberation, had chosen to wear her sleeveless pink laced dress with a silk turtle neck, determined to look her best on this her first venture into the unknown.

The bouncer's voice came to her, making her cringe. "She's too young, can't be more than fourteen. If I let her in I'll lose my job. Now," he moved forward threateningly, "on your way."

Marie had already gone. She was wobbling painfully along the road in her new four-inch patent shoes when she heard

Carol shouting after her. Reluctantly she slowed down and waited for her friend.

"Why did you run off like that?" Carol asked, panting slightly from her exertions.

"I'm going home, Carol," Marie replied miserably. All she wanted to do now was reach the safety of her room. Then she thought with dismay of her mum and how disappointed she'd be if she came back early. She'd been so happy to see her going out you'd have thought she'd announced her forthcoming marriage. She couldn't go home yet. Apart from not wanting to face her mum, Carol's friend had let her down, so if she went home now, Carol would miss out on her evening. With sinking heart Marie wondered what was going to happen next.

"Look," Carol was saying, "there's a small dance floor round the back of the pub. The bouncer said we could try in there as long as you don't drink. But don't worry," she winked, "I'll get you one."

With feet like lead, Marie reluctantly followed her friend back to the pub. To her surprise they were allowed entry without any trouble. She gazed in wonder at the psychedelic lights whirling overhead. It was the first time she'd ever been in a dance hall and she wasn't sure that she liked it. Everyone seemed so confident, as if they belonged here. Even with Carol to back her up, Marie still felt uneasy. Putting on a brave face for Carol's sake, she followed her across the small dance floor and waited in a corner while Carol got the drinks. After what seemed an age she returned and handed Marie a small glass with a greeny coloured drink in it.

"What's this?" Marie asked suspiciously. Raising the glass, she sniffed at it the way a dog sniffs a bone, but without the enthusiasm. It smelt of lime. Taking a tentative mouthful, she sipped the drink carefully and then made a face. "Ugh!" she spluttered, and repeated the question. "What is it?"

"Vodka and lime," Carol said gleefully. "Go on, it won't kill you."

Not wanting to appear a killjoy, Marie took another swallow and found that it was quite pleasant after the third swallow, by which time the glass was empty. As the sounds of *A Whiter*

*Shade of Pale* drifted over her, she felt herself relaxing and wondering why she'd never come out with Carol before. After the third drink she was positively mellow. Carol was off dancing with some fellow; he was the third one she'd danced with in an hour. Marie now knew the true meaning of the term "wallflower".

There had been one instance a little while ago. A nice-looking lad had come over to the table where she was sitting. As he'd bent over her, she'd thought he was going to ask her to dance. She was just about to accept when he'd picked up his drink from the table behind her and walked off without a backward glance. She'd felt her face burn with embarrassment but had continued smiling and waving at Carol whenever she floated by.

The Kinks were singing *Waterloo Sunset* and Marie tapped her feet to the sounds of the music while sipping nonchalantly at her fourth drink. She was feeling decidedly woozy by now and hoped that Carol wasn't going to go home with the boy she was dancing with – she didn't think she could make it on her own. When the record finished she watched as Carol and the boy stood heads together deep in conversation. Marie felt her heart skip a beat. Was he asking if he could walk her home? Her face anxious, she continued watching them, wishing she could hear what was being said.

"Yeah, I'd love to come to a party," Carol was saying, "but I'd have to bring my mate, I can't leave her on her own."

"Sure, no problem, there's plenty of drink for everyone. Hang on a second, there's a mate of mine. Hey, Alan, here a minute," he called out to a passing young man. Alan turned at the sound of his name, then made his way through the crowd to reach his friend.

"All right, Tom?" he said, his eyes on Carol.

"Yeah fine. Listen, we're going to a party round at Graham's house. Fancy coming?"

Not taking his eyes from Carol, Alan answered, "Okay, I've got nothing better to do."

Noticing the way his friend was looking at Carol, Tom decided to put the record straight. Telling Carol he'd be over to their table in a minute, he waited till she was out of earshot then said, "Listen, mate, that's my bird for the evening; you can take her friend."

Shrugging his shoulders, Alan turned and watched as Carol stopped to talk to a small skinny girl, her face almost obscured by a pair of oversized glasses, and waited for her to move on to her friend, wherever she was. When Carol moved round the table and sat down beside the girl his jaw dropped.

"Do me a favour, Tom, I like a bird with something to get hold of – see ya."

As he went to walk away Tom grabbed his arm. "Come on, mate," he pleaded, "I really fancy my bird, but she won't come to the party unless her mate comes and I don't want her hanging round us all night. Please."

Alan looked at his friend's earnest face, and then over at the girl again.

"All right" he sighed, "but you owe me one."

"Great, thanks a lot, Alan, I'll make it up to you. Come on, let's ask them to dance."


"Here they come," Carol said excitedly. "Now don't worry. I'll stay with you at the party, and we won't stay late, I promise. I have to be in by twelve same as you."

Marie watched the boys approaching and felt her arms and legs go weak with fear. What could she say? Fighting down a feeling of panic, she picked her drink up for support, then quickly put it down as the liquid began to jump around in the glass.

"Fancy a dance, Carol?", the nice-looking boy was saying. Marie looked on as Carol jumped up and walked off with her date.

"How about you?" came the surly request from the spotty, fair-haired boy standing in front of her, a bored look on his face.

Ignoring the insult, Marie rose unsteadily to her feet and followed his retreating figure onto the dance floor. Not knowing what to do next, she stood in front of him waiting for him to take the lead. Impatiently he reached out and grabbed her round the waist, pulling her close to him. As she felt his body press against hers she jerked away, causing him to lose his balance and cannon into a couple dancing next to them. She felt a rush of blood to her face and muttering an apology she stumbled away from him and back to her chair. Shamefaced she sat and waited for Carol to return so she could tell her she was going home.

Carol had witnessed Marie's headlong dash across the floor and groaned. It had been a mistake bringing her here, and even more of a mistake trying to arrange a date for her. Making her apologies to Tom, she walked back to Marie. Bending over her, she said quietly, "Come on, Marie, let's go home."

Marie looked up, her eyes brimming with tears of mortification, then defiantly she shook her head and a voice she didn't recognise as her own said, "No, we've got a party to go to."

So now here she was in a darkened room, hardly able to see a hand in front of her face. If Peggy had seen the entwined couples that were laying on the floor and holding up the walls, she'd have been horrified. Gloomily she stared into the dimness. Carol had disappeared soon after they'd arrived despite her promise not to leave her. The only consolation was that Alan had also left and she'd been glad to see him go. He had made it perfectly obvious he'd only brought her here as a favour to his friend, and she wouldn't have minded so much, but he wasn't much to look at himself – she'd seen children suffering with measles with fewer spots than him.

Looking around once more, Marie sighed deeply. Apart from making a dash for it, there was nothing else to do but stay and hope the party would finish early and end her nightmare. Stepping over a couple on the floor, she sat herself down on a chair she'd retrieved from the hallway. She had started off by sitting by the wall, but as the couples began falling like flies onto the floor, she found herself being edged into the centre of the room. And there she sat, looking like the last survivor in a game of musical chairs. She'd acquired a pineapple juice from the kitchen, not being able to face another vodka, and as she sipped her drink she was painfully aware of how pathetic she must look sitting in the middle of the floor surrounded by snogging couples. Her shoes were killing her but she didn't dare take them off or she'd never get them on again. Also the pink mini dress she was wearing, much against her mum's advice – "Not with your legs, love" – kept riding up her thighs.

She was brought out of her reverie by a figure lurching against her. It was her date.

"Got a light, darling?" he said drunkenly.

With a look of disdain Marie answered, "No, I don't smoke."

Whereupon he grabbed her legs and, rubbing them briskly together, said, "Never mind, should get a spark off of these."

Seething with rage now, she attempted to rise but he pulled her back down.

"Nothing else going," he slurred, "suppose you'll have to do."

Marie could feel her anger building and, with a superhuman effort, she shoved him off her. Feeling a surge of satisfaction, she watched him fall to the floor, then, bending over him, she said sweetly, "Have you got a pencil or pen handy?"

She watched the smug, self-satisfied smile come to his face. "Want me phone number, do you?"

"No," she smiled at him, "I just wondered what sort of picture I'd get if I joined up all the spots on your face."

His smile vanished. Angrily he tried to get up from the floor but slipped down again. Taking her chance, Marie made a beeline for the door. She would have liked to have made a dignified exit, but with the problem of the upwardly mobile dress and her feet almost crippled by her new shoes, she was denied this luxury. Her mind raged with mixed emotions to such an extent that she forgot her fear of being out on the streets on her own, and it wasn't until she'd reached her front door safely that she realised she was home.

As she was about to put her key in the lock she suddenly saw the funny side of the evening. Why had she ever been afraid to be out on her own after dark? She knew now that her chances of being attacked and ravished were highly remote.

Good Lord, she couldn't even get molested in a room full of drunken men. Then the vision of herself sitting on that chair in the middle of the room primly sipping a pineapple juice swam before her eyes. What a prat she must have looked. Feeling the laughter bubbling to the surface, she let herself in. Leaning against the front door for a moment, she savoured the feeling of security these four walls always afforded her. Nothing would ever hurt her here. Then, pushing herself away from the door, she went to find her mum.

Peggy was sitting on the much-coveted sofa wondering if God would forgive her if she missed church tomorrow and stayed home to watch *The Forsyte Saga*. She always went to evening Mass, not being able to go in the mornings, she was always too busy then.

When the door burst open and Marie danced in she was surprised at the look of happiness on her face. She must have had a good time. And such was the evidence of the good mood she was in, she ventured to ask what the party had been like. Sitting down beside her mother, Marie regaled her with stories of the evening. As she listened, Peggy felt a lump come to her throat – she must have felt awful and yet here she was laughing about it and seemingly not a bit put out. Not for the first time, Peggy marvelled at the changes in character her daughter was capable of. When she had left her earlier, she had looked as if she'd swallowed a bee. She would never understand her. But what matter? – she'd always love Marie, come what may.

# Chapter Eight

After that disastrous night, Marie retreated into her shell even more. Carol was going steady with Tom so she hadn't been round much, much to Marie's relief. If she never went out again, she wouldn't mind. Her quiet nights were soon shattered when a tearful Carol appeared on her doorstep one night declaring that her boyfriend hadn't shown up when he was supposed to, and before Marie knew what was happening she had agreed to go to the pictures with Carol the following night.

They made their way to the Regal, not knowing what the film was, just that it was a "U". Marie didn't want to risk being refused entry, she wanted to rest her bruised ego for a while. They'd only been in their seats for twenty minutes when Marie noticed out of the corner of her eye a young man making his way down their aisle towards the empty seat beside Carol.

Well, she's not going to be on her own for long, Marie thought with relief. She was happily envisioning cosy nights in her bedroom with a supply of library books, when she felt someone sit in the seat next to her. Without turning her head she raised her eyes to see who it was. Just her luck it would be a dirty old man plus raincoat. But, no, it was another young man. A coincidence was ruled out when they leaned over Marie and Carol and started talking. Having established that they were together, the men sat back and enjoyed the film.

Marie couldn't concentrate on the screen, she was too aware of the man's presence – every time he moved his leg she jumped. Then there was Carol on the other side of her who kept nudging her gleefully. She seems to have got over her lost love quickly, Marie thought with annoyance.

When the first film ended and the lights came on she made a big pretence of looking in her bag. As it only contained a hairbrush and her purse she was unable to pursue this line of defence long. Carol was chatting to the young man beside her as if she'd known him all her life, but Marie felt so awkward and uncomfortable that she could only sit still, keeping her eyes firmly on the blank screen.

By his silence her unwanted companion was obviously sharing her feelings, but it was of small comfort to Marie. She wanted to go home. She could hear the young man and Carol talking animatedly. When the fellow on her side stood up and started to make his way towards the aisle, his friend followed, making Marie sigh with relief. A relief that was short-lived as Carol said, "They've just gone to get us some chocolates, they'll be right back. I hope," she added as an afterthought.

"What do you mean they're coming back?" Marie squealed in alarm.

"Don't panic," Carol said, putting her hand on Marie's arm, "if you don't like him, I'll help you dump him later. What's he like anyhow?"

Impatiently Marie shrugged Carol's hand off. "I don't know, I haven't looked."

As the lights dimmed she prayed they wouldn't come back while Carol was craning her neck anxiously trying to spot them. Was there ever such an unlikely combination of two friends? There was Marie, who would be perfectly happy to sit at home to watch television and read, and Carol who was never happy unless she had a boyfriend.

"Here they come."

Marie groaned and slumped down in her seat, determined not to look at the young man who was stumbling around beside her trying to get his seat down. When the box of Milk Tray was pushed under her nose she hesitated for a moment before muttering an awkward "Thank you" as she took the unwanted gift. With the unopened box in her lap they sat in silence throughout the main film. Marie felt trapped, pinned down, her mind searching frantically for a way to escape. All too soon the picture finished and when the lights came on she stood up too quickly and stumbled. The boy's hand came out to steady her and for the first time she looked up into his face and saw a pair of gentle brown eyes below a mop of curly brown hair.

When she saw that he was as apprehensive as she was, she felt slightly better. They left the cinema in a silence that lasted all the way home. In front of them Carol and her new boyfriend walked along talking and laughing.

It was as they were turning into her street that he spoke. "My name's Brian, what's yours?"

"Marie," she answered tersely. Oh God, this is awful, she thought as the silence descended upon them once more. No more, she vowed silently. After tonight I'll stay at home and when the others have all married and moved out I'll get a small flat and live the rest of my life in peace.

"I hope you don't think I'm rude," he said suddenly, "but I'm not very good at chatting up girls. Pete," he jerked his head in the direction of his friend, "he usually does all the talking."

"That's all right, I'm a bit shy myself."

Taking a better look at him, she discovered that he was quite pleasant. His manner was awkward but he seemed kind enough. He wasn't as nice-looking as Carol's boy, but then hers never were. And at least he didn't have any spots. Maybe it'll be all right this time, she thought optimistically. As they reached her front door she had forgotten all about being an old maid. Already she could see herself walking down the aisle. In fact by the time they'd stopped at her door she had already chosen her bridesmaids. It was a pity about the old beige duffel coat he had on, but perhaps he had come straight from work.

After some awkward humming and hawing he said, "Would you like to come out for a meal tomorrow night? Maybe we could take in some sights as well."

Visions of a candlelit meal and a walk along the Embankment came to Marie's mind. Smiling now, all fear gone, she answered, "Thanks, I'd like that."

The next minute she found herself shrinking back in fright as he leant towards her. The moment was saved by the door opening and the appearance of her dad. Before he could make any comment she said a quick goodnight and pushed her dad back into the hallway.

"Who was that?" Bill asked.

"Who was who, Bill?" Her mum was coming from the sitting room. "Hello, love, have a nice night?"

"All right," Marie answered grumpily as she started up the stairs ignoring her mother's enquiring glance.

When Peggy heard Marie's bedroom door shut she shook her head sadly before returning to the sitting room. Her daughter had snubbed her once again. She should be used to it by now but she wasn't. It hurt, and while Marie continued to put up this wall between them it always would.

"I can't go, Carol. I've changed my mind."

"They'll be here in a minute, don't be silly," Carol said, exasperatedly. "What do you think he's going to do to you?"

"He's not going to get the chance to do anything because I'm not going."

They were in Carol's bedroom. Marie was done up to the nines. She had on a new navy dress with a white panel down the front that she had bought this morning and she had enjoyed getting ready, but now the moment was drawing nearer to her first date she had lost her nerve.

"You've just got cold feet," Carol said, tilting her head to one side in front of her mirror, making sure her blonde hair was looking its best.

"Cold feet," Marie replied in a shaky voice, "more like a severe case of frostbite."

When Carol didn't respond to her feeble joke, Marie shuffled about on the bed. She didn't know how to deal with the situation and, what was worse, she was in real danger of losing Carol as a friend. Feeling sick and miserable, she hung her head in despair. Why had she ever agreed to this date? That awful coat he had been wearing when she'd met him. Her mum was always saying that it was the person who was important not the clothes, but even knowing this was true it didn't serve to make her any happier. The sudden ring at the front door brought her to her feet.

"They're here, Carol," Mrs Lewis called up the stairs.

Clutching Carol by the arm, Marie pleaded, "Please, Carol, tell him I'm ill, tell him anything. I can't go, I just can't."

The genuine panic in her voice brought Carol's eyes upon her. Seeing the obvious distress on her friend's face, Carol softened her attitude. Gently extricating Marie's arm, she said, "All right, calm down, I'll see what I can do, but you're being silly, you've got to start somewhere." So saying, she ran from the room and down the stairs.

Marie could hear her voice talking to the two boys but she couldn't hear what was being said. After what seemed an eternity Carol returned, shouting over her shoulder, "I'm just getting my coat."

"I told him you were ill in bed." Seeing Marie's body slump with relief, she added reluctantly, "He's gone down to your house to leave a message with your mum."

Marie's head shot up, her eyes filled with alarm.

"Well, I didn't know he was going to do that, did I?" Carol said defensively. "I was trying to help you out."

Getting no response, Carol cast one last furious look at Marie before leaving the room. Marie sat back down on the bed, her whole body shaking. Her mum would kill her – he must be there by now, what would she tell him?

Time passed slowly; after about twenty minutes she heard her mum's voice coming from her house a few doors away. The street was quiet and her voice carried clearly.

"I'm sorry she wasn't in, love, she's probably at a friend's house and forgotten the time. I'll tell her you'll see her tomorrow."

Marie heard his footsteps coming towards her and shrank back against the curtains. There was a last shout of "Goodnight" from her mum before she heard the distant slam of her own front door.

Peeping out carefully, she could see Brian pass by under the window, and with some surprise she saw that he wasn't wearing the scruffy duffel coat he'd worn the night before but he was gone before she could have a proper look.

Quietly descending the stairs, Marie called out to Carol's mum that she was going and ran the rest of the way down the hall and out the door. Her footsteps dragging, she walked slowly towards home, her mind ticking over, frantically trying to find some excuse that would pacify her mum. Taking her key from her bag, she gently inserted it into the lock, but before she could turn it, the door was pulled open with such force that she was dragged forward, her hand still holding onto the key in the lock. Standing before her was her mother, looking more angry than she'd ever seen her.

"Mum," she spluttered, which was as far as she got. Peggy's hand came out and grabbed her by the front of her dress, pulling her off her feet and into the hall. The resounding crash of the front door echoed in Marie's ears as it slammed behind her.

"You little cow, you've been hiding down at Carol's, haven't you?"

Without waiting for an answer Peggy let go of Marie's dress, and with her other hand smacked her sharply on the side of the head.

"Ow, that hurt!" Marie put her hand to her ringing ear; it felt red hot. But it wasn't the pain that worried her, it was the fact that her mum had actually hit her; she'd never done that before, and there had been plenty of times Marie had deserved it more than she did now. And she'd sworn.

Peggy looked at the surprised Marie and refused to feel sorry at having hit her. She'd been building up to it for a long time. Besides, it had felt good. When she thought of that poor young chap . . .

"Now, listen, my girl, I don't know what you thought you were playing at, saying you'd go out with that young man and then showing him up in front of Carol and his friend, but I've told him you'll be here on Monday at seven. He wanted to come back tomorrow but I put him off. You're not setting one foot out of this house until Tuesday morning, so don't try sneaking off to Carol's."

Marie gaped at her mum. She couldn't understand why she was taking it so personally. She'd expected a telling-off, but not a clout round the ear and not being allowed out until Tuesday. She had planned to get down to Carol's first thing tomorrow to find out what had happened, but now she'd have to wait to find out what had been said. She glanced up at her mum, wondering if she dared try to get past her and escape upstairs, then decided against it.

"Now then," Peggy was speaking again, calmer now but still angry, "you'll be here ready on Monday night, or down at Carol's, but I'll be watching to make sure you don't play the same trick twice. It was a cruel thing to do, Marie, nasty in fact. It would serve you right if he didn't show up on Monday, but then I don't suppose you'd care, would you?"

Marie stared back, wanting to defend herself against what she saw as an unwarranted attack. She wanted to explain, but before she could say anything her mother turned her back on her and walked from the room.

She was back in Carol's bedroom, but this time there would be no backing out.

"You should have come on Saturday," Carol was saying. "He looked really nice. He had on a blue three piece suit and a white shirt and tie. I could have fancied him myself."

Biting back the retort that sprang to her lips, Marie smiled. She had to go so she might as well make the best of it. Maybe it wouldn't be so bad after all and, as Carol had said, she had to start sometime.

"Where are we going, do you know?" she asked.

"Pete said something about seeing some sights, then going for a meal. He phoned me at work today."

"Did he say anything about me not turning up on Saturday?" Marie asked, wondering what Brian's reaction would be to her after being stood up. And what would she say if he queried the two different accounts of her absence? Oh, what the hell, she'd play it by ear and see what happened.

"No, he didn't mention it," replied Carol as she put the finishing touches to her make-up. The sound of the door bell rang through the house making Marie's stomach lurch. Carol looked at her, a worried expression on her face.

Marie smiled weakly at her. "It's all right, I'm not going to do a runner this time. My mum's watching from her bedroom window, if I don't come out of here with you she'll be down here quicker than you can say knife."

Taking a deep breath, she followed Carol down the stairs and out of the house.

From her vantage point at her bedroom window, Peggy watched the four figures walking down the street and nodded to herself.

"Really nice, eh? Three piece suit, eh? Well, where is it now?"

When Marie had first gone down to meet him at the door she had concocted a reasonable excuse for her behaviour in standing him up, but one look at the old duffel coat he was wearing had changed her mind so she'd decided not to bother. He looked the same as when she'd first met him, and she'd had her hair done specially. What a waste of money.

"I told you, he works for a tailor's and he borrowed the suit I told you about. He couldn't take the chance of borrowing it again, he'd get the sack if he got caught," said Carol, telling Marie for the second time that evening.

"And," said Marie refusing to be pacified, "where are the sights we were going to take in, and the meal we were promised? We've been walking for over an hour and the only sights I've seen are the corporation dump and the poxy canal. My feet are killing me."

Looking down at Marie's black patent high heels, Carol answered in a tired voice, "You shouldn't have worn those shoes; you can't walk properly in them at the best of times."

"I didn't know we were going on a bleeding hike, did I?"

Thoroughly fed up by now, Carol rounded on her, "I wish you hadn't come now," she said angrily. "You've done nothing but moan since we came out, you're getting on my nerves."

They stood glaring at each other. It was the first row they'd had.

Before Marie could answer, thus ending their friendship once and for all, Pete's voice called out to them, "Come on, you two. What are you talking about? Hope it's not us."

"Just coming," Carol answered as she walked off leaving Marie staring after her. Slowly she walked towards where Brian was waiting. Falling into step beside him, she kept her eyes firmly on the pavement.

As if he guessed what was going on in her mind, he cleared

his throat self-consciously before saying, "Were you upset about Elvis Presley getting married?"

Not realising that the poor lad was just trying to make conversation Marie looked at him as if he were an idiot. "Why should I have been?" she snapped at him "I wasn't going out with him at the time."

Now it was his turn to take umbrage. Staring hard at her for a moment, he thrust his hands in his pockets. "By the way, how are you feeling? Better I hope," he sneered, the placid features twisted in suppressed anger. "You must have made a quick recovery to be able to go to a friend's house two minutes after Carol told me you were laid up in a bed in agony."

The sudden verbal attack stunned Marie; she hadn't expected him to argue back. He had turned the tables on her, leaving her at a disadvantage. She watched as he thrust his hands deeper into his coat pockets and walked on, leaving her standing alone on the pavement. After a moment's hesitation she reluctantly hobbled after him. They continued in silence until they reached a row of brightly lit shops.

Marie breathed a sigh of relief. Now they could have the meal they'd been promised, and maybe while they all sat together in the restaurant the conversation between Carol and Pete would ease the tension between herself and Brian.

Carol was standing outside Woolworth's on her own. As Marie came level with her she tried to say something, but Carol ignored her.

Looking past her to where Brian was standing, she said, "Pete's gone over there," indicating a spot behind her by nodding her head.

With a quiet word of thanks, Brian followed her directions and they were left alone.

Looking at Carol's stony face, Marie tried again. "I'm sorry, Carol," she whispered humbly.

Before Carol could answer, Pete's voice came to them. "Here you are, girls, fresh out of the pan. Get stuck in." Marie looked on in amazement as he began to share out the portions of chips. So this was the meal they had been promised, and after an hour's walk; what a tight pair of sods.

119

She was about to make a comment when she caught sight of Carol's face and immediately clamped her mouth shut. Silence descended once again as they ate their meal. When they had finished Pete suggested they make their way to the bus stop in case they missed the last one home.

What a night out, Marie thought miserably as she trailed behind Carol and Pete.

"If you're trying to think up an excuse not to go out with me again, don't bother," Brian said, his voice bitter. "I wish I hadn't told your mum I'd come back for you tonight. I must have been mad to waste my money on you."

Marie stopped dead in her tracks, her mouth agape. "Waste your money," she spluttered. "Sixpenn'orth of chips you've bought me; I'd hardly call that chucking your money about."

They faced each other in the street, their faces dark with anger, then turning on his heel sharply he walked off, Marie following angrily behind.

As they neared the bus stop they saw a bus coming and had to make a run for it. Pete got there first and held the rail until the rest of them had caught up. Putting his hand under Carol's arm, he helped her onto the platform before following her. Marie was about to board when she felt herself being pushed aside as Brian got on before her. Controlling her anger, she made her way down the length of the bus to sit behind Carol and Pete. Brian was sitting on the opposite side but by now Marie couldn't have cared less.

The ticket collector came along and stopped at Brian first.

"One to the Wick, please," he said, holding out the right fare.

"One? Don't you mean two, son?" said the conductor, looking over to where Marie sat on her own. She felt her face start to burn. What was she going to do? She didn't have any money on her. She had thought that after the party nothing could happen that could possibly be worse, but she was wrong. The humiliation she was feeling now was indescribable.

Luckily Pete noticed what was going on and, calling the conductor over, he paid her fare. She smiled at him gratefully then sank back and stared out of the window for the remainder of the journey home.

120

Leaning against the railings outside her house, she was acutely aware of the hostility coming from the angry young man next to her. When they'd got off the bus she had made an effort to rectify the evening's events, knowing full well it was all her fault, but it was no good, the situation had gone too far. Well, she wasn't going to stand here all night; best say goodnight and chalk it up to experience. Pushing herself from the railings, she turned to face him.

"Goodnight then."

No answer. Shrugging her shoulders, she started to walk away, relief that the evening was finally over making her body slacken. The next thing she knew she was sprawled out on the pavement. He had tripped her up. Marie couldn't believe it at first, but he had definitely put his foot out as she'd made to pass him. As she made to get up, he calmly stepped over her and walked off into the night. Stunned, she sat there on the cold pavement not quite believing what had happened.

Her first experience with a boy had resulted in her being left sitting on a chair in a room full of snogging couples, and now this, her first date, had ended with her lying flat out on the pavement. Shaking her head in bewilderment, she got to her feet and let herself quietly into the house.

"You mean he actually tripped you up?" Carol asked incredulously.

"Yes, I've told you twice, he put his foot out and tripped me up. It was deliberate."

Silence reigned for a moment in the small bedroom then, looking at each other, they suddenly burst out laughing. When finally they got their breath back, Carol spoke first. Wiping away a tear from the corner of her eye, she said in a choked voice "Haven't been very lucky so far, have you?" whereupon they both burst out laughing again.

Carol sat up on the bed wondering whether to broach the subject of another date for her friend. Twisting a crumpled tissue in her hand, she said quickly, "Pete wants to know if you fancy going on a blind date with one of his mates from work."

121

"No, thank you very much," Marie answered, jumping up from the bed.

Carol sighed. "I thought that's what you'd say."

A glutton for punishment, Marie agreed to go out with Carol and Pete one last time. All she knew about her date was his name. Frank. At the last minute Carol had come down with a heavy cold and had been put to bed by her mum. Unable to get in touch with Pete, Marie had agreed to go on her own to the Regal to meet the two men and explain what had happened. Standing outside the picture house, she searched the street for any sign of them. It was with relief that she saw Pete's familiar figure coming towards her.

But who was that with him? Not her date, surely. He must weigh seventeen stone at least, she thought in horror as the heavy figure lumbered towards her. Averting her eyes from him, she directed her attention to Pete. Within minutes of hearing about Carol's illness he had left at a run, anxious to see Carol and make sure she was all right. Hardly daring to look beside her, she was startled when she felt her arm being firmly grasped, and before she knew what was happening she found herself inside the foyer while Frank bought the tickets.

"Please God, let this be a nightmare. Let me wake up in a minute and find myself at home in bed."

"I've got seats for the balcony, all right?"

Raising her eyes, Marie looked at the huge figure that seemed to be oozing out of his suit. She had actually started to make for the exit when she once again found herself being grasped firmly by the arm and then she was being propelled up the stairs to the gallery.

She never remembered afterwards what the film was, she was too busy trying to keep Frank's hand from going up her skirt. When the credits started to roll she stood up. "I'm just going to the loo," she told him, trying to keep a straight face.

"Good idea, I could do with going myself." That's it, I've had enough, she told herself firmly, no more excuses, I'm going home.

Bracing herself for a row, she watched him trying to get out of the plush red seat. His face, the colour of the chair, deepened as he tried in vain to rise. He was firmly wedged in his seat. Not waiting any longer she took to her heels and was out of the building and in the street heading for home within minutes.

Carol lay back on her pillow weak with laughter.

"No more blind dates, Carol, or I'll end up needing a guide dog."

Reaching across the bed, Carol patted Marie's hand. "I wish I had your sense of humour," she said. "If any of this had happened to me I'd be crying my eyes out."

And so do I, when I go to bed at night, thought Marie as she smiled back at her friend. That was her secret.

# Chapter Nine

1968.

There had been rumours for quite some time that a merger was being discussed between Marie's firm and another much larger one. Marie had hoped fervently that the rumour was false. She had been working here for over four years and she loved it. The girls she worked with were good friends; even the supervisor was fun to be around, providing you got on with your work and didn't take liberties. Then there was Matthew. He was a computer programmer. She seemed to be drawn to tall men as Matthew stood well over six foot. She closed her eyes and conjured him up. Dark brown hair cut in the Beatles fashion, with a pencil thin moustache, always wearing the latest clothes. He was kind, often stopping to talk to her, unaware of the way her heart would start racing as he looked down at her with his greeny-blue eyes. He had mentioned once that he would never go out with anyone he worked with, and when she'd asked why, he'd told her that at his previous job he had taken a typist out for a meal and the evening had been a disaster; they'd had nothing in common. The girl in question had made his life a misery after that night, telling lies about what had happened on their date, sniggering with her friends whenever he walked into their office, until he had finally had enough and given up a perfectly good job in order to get away from the girl.

Flopping onto her stomach, she gazed at the window. She had been re-admitted three times to the hospital in the four years she had worked here. They had been bad times, but the girls from the office had always come to visit her she'd been lucky to find such good friends. And now it was all coming to an end. Pam, the supervisor, Irene and Jenny the computer operators were to stay on in their prefabricated building, while Marie and the rest of the punch girls were to join the girls from the other firm in another building. Rather than work under a new supervisor, Marie had this morning given in her notice. Getting up from the bed, she walked to the window. Only a fortnight left – just two more happy weeks, working with people she knew and liked, the anticipation of seeing Matthew and feeling her heart and stomach do flip flops when he smiled at her. She felt the tears roll down her cheeks and angrily brushed them away. She had made such a song and dance about refusing to be pushed around, not working under someone she didn't know, there was no way she could withdraw her notice without losing face.

"Damn, damn, damn," she cried, her whole body bent with misery, unaware that something was about to happen that would make the sorrow about leaving her job pale into insignificance.


As Marie let herself into her nan's house she could hear her raised voice. She smiled to herself. Some unlucky sod was getting a tongue-lashing. As she reached the top step she saw her Uncle Tommy edging his way closer to the stairs, obviously trying to find a way of escape from his mother's tirade.

"Hello, Tommy," she said, smiling at her red-headed uncle. He was the black sheep of the family, but to her he was just Uncle Tommy.

"Never mind, 'hello Tommy'," shouted her nan. "I've told him and told him, but it's like talking to a brick wall."

Her uncle turned round and winked at her. May was momentarily distracted from her son as she looked in disbelief at her granddaughter.

"Holy Mary," she cried, "what in the world have you got on?"

Marie was dressed in a bright red hot-pants suit and although the craze for flower power had died out somewhat, she still wore a chain with a bell around her neck.

"It's the fashion, Nan," she said defensively.

"Fashion be blowed; I've never seen anyone else dressed like that. You look like a fire engine." Looking closer, she exclaimed, "You've even got a bell round your neck!"

125

Tommy glanced fondly at his niece. She did look a mess but he wasn't about to tell her that.

"Marie's never been one to run with the pack, have you, love?"

The sound of his voice brought May's attention back to him. "Well, that makes a pair of you," she snapped angrily. She looked with despair at her son and added more quietly, "You'll come to a bad end running round with those brothers. They're a pair of crooks and nothing you can say will make me change my mind."

Marie could see that this was no ordinary argument; Nan was really upset. She went to put her arms around her. Tommy, seizing his chance to escape, quickly bent over and kissed May on the cheek before turning to run down the stairs. He'd had enough for one evening.

"Get yourself a decent job, any job, and find some new friends," May shouted after him, her voice changing to a pleading note. "For God's sake, Tommy, *please*."

Her words were cut off by the sound of the front door banging behind him. Wearily she sank back against the wall. She was wasting her breath and she knew it, but she had to try and keep trying until she got through to him before something terrible happened. Turning round, she saw Marie standing by the wall, a scared look on her face.

Forcing herself to smile, May said, "Well, to what do I owe this honour?"

"I couldn't stay away. I was missing you", Marie replied trying to copy May's mood, but she was frightened. There was something here she didn't understand. She knew Tommy was a friend of the brothers and she also knew they were no good – she wasn't that stupid – but she couldn't associate Tommy with being bad, he'd always been so good to her.

Walking towards the kitchen, May said over her shoulder, "Missing me? You were only here three days ago. Does your mum know you're here? And," she added, "speaking of your mother, why hasn't she been round to see me?"

"Shall I make a cup of tea, Nan?" Marie said quickly, avoiding the question.

"Never mind the tea." Taking hold of Marie's arm, May asked again, "Well, why hasn't she been round? Is anything the matter?"

Marie stood silent, gnawing the bottom of her lip. When her mum had returned from her weekly visit two weeks ago she had been very upset. She had overheard Peggy tell her dad what had happened. Apparently one of May's light bulbs had fused. Her Aunt Teresa, who had also been visiting, had fetched a chair and was about to reach up to remove the bulb when May had stopped her, saying, "What do you think you're doing, you could get electrocuted. Let Peggy do it."

Marie had laughed about it at the time but thinking about it later she realised it was a terrible thing to have said to anyone.

"She's not been very well," she mumbled under her breath, to which May tutted and promptly dropped the subject.

When Marie returned home that night she didn't tell her mum about the argument with Tommy but she thought she'd better tell her about May asking after her just in case she came round to find out if her mum was really ill.

Lying in bed her thoughts returned to her uncle. When he had still been, living at her nan's house she used to see a lot of him but since he'd been married she'd only seen him whenever he dropped in to make sure May was all right, and of course when he came round to visit her mum. But on those occasions she had never had the chance to speak to him as she used to do.

A smile came to her lips as she recalled last Christmas, when Tommy had come round a few days before Christmas Eve and asked Peggy if she wanted a turkey. Peggy had looked at him suspiciously and then asked straight out if it was stolen. Tommy had stepped back from her, a shocked look on his face, and with hand on heart he had promised faithfully that it wasn't. He had looked quite hurt that his own sister could think such a thing of him. Reluctantly Peggy had agreed to accept the turkey, knowing that it would save her money.

On Christmas Eve Tommy had arrived with the biggest turkey they'd ever seen in their lives. Peggy had hidden her pleasure at the sight of the welcome gift and had invited

Tommy to stay for tea. As she only had enough to go round she was relieved when he declined, saying that he had to go out. He'd stayed long enough to see Peggy prepare the turkey and put it in the oven, a procedure she always followed on Christmas Eve, and as he was leaving he'd wished them all a merry Christmas. Then, putting his head round the kitchen door, he'd added, "By the way, Peg, it *was* nicked."

Marie laughed out loud as she recalled the scene. He'd bolted for it with her mum in hot pursuit, and although they'd all enjoyed the stolen turkey her mum had refused to eat any of it. Turning over, she drifted off to sleep, unaware that some miles away in houses all over London a group of specially trained policemen were breaking down doors and arresting all known members of the brothers' organisation.

The news was splashed over every London newspaper. Looking down at the *Daily Mirror*, Peggy tried to read the story below the screaming headlines but the tears that streamed down her face prevented her from doing so. Marie stood nervously to one side. She couldn't take it in. The first she'd heard of it was when Tommy's wife had phoned that morning. She had been crying, so much so that at first Peggy hadn't been able to understand what she was saying, then when realisation had set in, she'd dropped the telephone back in its cradle. Bobby had been sent to buy the morning paper where the news was in black and white.

With a shaking voice Marie said, "Maybe he's been arrested by mistake."

Peggy looked up at her daughter, who had stayed home today, unable to face going to work. Silently she pushed the paper across to Marie who took hold of it gingerly. Skipping over the main story, she scanned the list of names of the men that had been arrested. There amongst the long list was Tommy's name. Her legs buckling, she reached out to grab the support of the nearest chair and sat down.

The sound of the telephone ringing brought Peggy to her feet. Walking unsteadily over to the phone, she picked it up, looking at the instrument as if it were something loathsome. Marie watched her mother's face change to relief as she spoke to the person on the other end of the line. After a short conversation she replaced the receiver and then took the phone off the hook, resting it on the table. "That was Teresa," she said, answering Marie's unspoken question. "She's on her way to fetch your nan and take her home with her for a few days. I only hope to God she hasn't found out yet." Marie looked at her mother in surprise, her eyes wide.

"But, Mum," she stammered, "she'll have to find out, she's not stupid."

"I know she's not stupid," Peggy shouted, fear making her angry, "but it won't hurt to keep it from her for a few days at least. God knows how she's going to react when she does find out."

Peggy thought back to the other occasions when Tommy had been held at Her Majesty's pleasure. It had been easy enough then to keep the knowledge from her mother, as he had never before had to do a long sentence. And as he would frequently disappear for a few months then turn up again out of the blue, May was used to not seeing him for months on end.

But not this time, Peggy thought with despair. This time he was going away for a long time and, as Marie had pointed out, May was no fool, she more than likely knew about the times he'd spent in prison although the subject had never been spoken of.

The day passed slowly. Peggy had replaced the phone and since then it had hardly stopped ringing, with relatives and friends wanting to know the latest news. Peggy got tired of telling them all that she only knew what she'd read in the papers, the same as they had.

The younger children were puzzled by their mum's behaviour. With the intuition of the young they knew something was wrong. Bobby at seventeen was well aware of the situation – he, like Marie, had taken the day off work but for different reasons – he wanted to be near his mother in case she needed him. He'd read the paper on the way home, and although he was upset, he wasn't greatly surprised. He was genuinely fond of his uncle, but he had sense enough to know that if you ran with a wild pack, sooner or later you would be caught.

Peggy was trying to hurry the smaller children up as they were eating their tea. She wanted to see the news.

"Patti's got three fish fingers, and I've only got two," complained seven-year-old Jimmy. As Peggy walked over to the table to rectify the oversight, Patti hurriedly stuffed the remainder of her tea into her mouth before her mum could cut the extra fish finger in half.

"Oh, you greedy pig," Jimmy cried out, "I hope you choke."

As if in answer to his prayer, Patti began coughing, the bits of fish falling from her crammed mouth.

"Get up, come on, up out of there," Peggy shouted, grabbing her small daughter by the neck and slapping her on the back while Jimmy watched with glee. "And you," Peggy's free hand shot out and clipped him on the side of his head, "eat the rest of your tea."

With the danger of Patti choking over, Peggy left them to finish their tea while she washed up the plates from the previous sitting.

Spooning a mouthful of beans into her mouth, Patti looked at her mother's back then, seeing that she wasn't watching, she stuck a very large tongue out at Jimmy who in return kicked out from under the table, catching her on the shins.

Patti let out a shrill cry which brought Peggy running back to the table. Ignoring their cries of protest and accusations, she grabbed them both by the scruff of the neck and marched them out of the kitchen. Shutting the door on them, she sat down and waited for John to finish his tea. He hadn't said a word throughout the argument, so used was he to hearing his brother and sister fighting. He'd hardly laid his knife and fork down before the plate was whisked away from him. Clambering down from the table, he looked at his mother and asked plaintively, "Why did I only get one fish finger, Mum?"

Peggy hadn't thought she would laugh this day but now she did so.

Wrapping her arms around his small plump body, she said, "I'm sorry, love, Mummy's not very well today." When this statement didn't bring forth any sign of sympathy she decided to appeal to his stomach.

130

"You can have an extra one next time."

"One more than Jimmy and Patti?" he asked hopefully.

"Yes, one more than Jimmy and Patti," Peggy agreed, anticipating the arguments this would cause the next time fish fingers were on the menu. Patting him on the bottom, she watched him run to inform his brother and sister of his good fortune before returning to the washing up, glancing at the clock as she did so.

"Has she guessed yet?" Peggy asked anxiously as she spoke on the phone to Teresa. The television news had been bad and she wondered how Teresa had stopped May from watching it. The news was one of May's favourite programmes and Peggy knew from past experience that May would create a fuss if she was prevented from seeking it.

"Vic told her the set was broken, now she's making a fuss about going back home. You know how much she likes her television. But never mind that," Teresa said quickly, "we didn't see the news either. What did they say?"

Peggy went on to tell her sister what the news had revealed. The main news had been about the brothers, but Tommy's name had appeared on the screen under the heading, 'detained for questioning'. When she finally got off the phone, Peggy wandered aimlessly around the house.

Everyone was in bed except her and Bill. She normally looked forward to this time of day when the house was quiet, but now she longed for some noise to distract her thoughts from her brother.

"What did Teresa have to say?" Bill asked, coming from the sitting room.

Peggy told him briefly what had transpired, then added, "I'm more worried about Mum than Tommy at this moment. He can look after himself, he's had enough practice," she ended on a shaky laugh.

"Let's go to bed," Bill said gently. "Things may look better in the morning."

Peggy allowed herself to be led upstairs, not believing for a moment that it would be any better tomorrow.

*

"Was that your uncle on the news last night?"

Marie looked at the girl from the filing department with contempt. The vultures were gathering already. Without bothering to answer, Marie gave the girl a last withering look before sitting down at her machine. The punch room was now in an open plan building with neck high hardboard partitions sectioning off the different departments; the only time all the staff got together was at the two fifteen-minute tea-breaks they were allowed each day.

As Marie packed a stack of cards into her hopper she thought back on the girl's remark and admitted to herself it was partly her own fault. Never able to keep her mouth shut at the best of times, she had determined to impress the new members of staff, and what better way than to regale them with tales about her red-headed uncle. The tales had been harmless enough, usually bragging about the money or presents he'd given her, but now they took on a more sinister tone. All day long she had to endure the looks and whispered speculation that went on in the office, and for the first time since she'd handed in her notice she was now glad she would be leaving soon.

She was thankful when five o'clock came round and she could escape from the office and the prying stares. Her real friends had refrained from asking any questions and for this she was grateful. The journey home was without respite. Conversation on the bus was all centred on the outcome of the trial.

"It shouldn't take long to convict them," she heard one man say, "they're both as guilty as hell."

"And the rest of them, murdering bunch of scum," his friend answered back.

Unable to bear any more, Marie rang the bell and got off the bus four stops before her own. She walked miserably home. She hoped fervently that what the first man had said about the trial being a short one would turn out to be true.

The trial dragged on. Tommy had been arrested in May and it was now early December with no sign of it coming to an end. Witnesses had been hard to trace, and when they had

132

been found, many of them had refused to testify for fear of reprisals. Some had volunteered and then suddenly changed their minds. The one surprising thing that had come out of the episode was May's reaction to the news. Teresa had told her a week after the arrests.

May had simply shrugged and said, "I warned him, time and again I warned him; maybe something good will come out of it. Maybe once that evil pair are locked up, Tommy might have a chance to start a new life."

Teresa had phoned Peggy with the news. Peggy was relieved that there was no longer any need for secrecy but she couldn't agree with May's hope of redemption for her brother. She tried to picture him in a nine-to-five job. Silently she shook her head. She didn't know what the future had in store for him. But now her worries about her brother would have to be put aside for the moment. Christmas was fast approaching. There were presents to be bought, food to be got in. Christmas was always a busy time for her, and this year she was grateful for the extra work it entailed. It would keep her mind occupied.

# Chapter Ten

1968.

By the end of December there was still no news as to whether or not Tommy would be released. It was Bobby who first suggested that they go and visit Tommy in prison. Peggy was reluctant to let them go, but Marie had joined her voice with Bobby's and so, on a cold January morning, they set off, not knowing what to expect when they got there. Armed with a bottle of whisky they had bought as a birthday present for their uncle, they arrived at the prison gates. With great surprise they saw at once that in order to gain entrance they had to ring a bell that was attached to the huge wooden door.

As Bobby stuck his thumb firmly into the bell he said, "Shall I ask if Tommy's in?"

The smile was wiped off their faces as the small door within the larger one was suddenly opened and they came face to face with a prison officer. Both of them were unable to speak for a moment, then Bobby took charge. Clearing his throat and trying to appear older than his seventeen years, he addressed the officer.

"We've come to visit our uncle," he said in a firm voice.

"Name," demanded the officer.

"Bobby and Marie Cowley," replied Bobby, his courage deserting him when faced with the voice of authority.

"Not your name," the officer said tersely, "the name of the prisoner you wish to visit."

"Oh, um, Tommy Flannagan," Bobby stammered nervously, fidgeting with the collar of his shirt. Marie looked with affection at her brother. It should have been her place to take charge, but he had insisted that it was a man's job.

The guard looked down at a large sheet of paper attached to a clip-board, then ushered them inside the gates. The sound of the wooden gate closing after them made them both jump. Waving them towards a small room, the guard told them to wait until they were called and left them. Bobby opened the door gingerly, and they were surprised at the sight that greeted them. The room looked just like their doctor's waiting-room. People, mainly women and children, were sitting on long wooden benches, some chattering away quite happily as if it was quite normal to be in prison waiting to visit someone who had been banged up.

Then again, thought Marie wryly, I suppose for some of them it *is* normal.

When their turn came a police officer called their names and beckoned them to follow him. Still clutching the bottle of whisky, they made to leave the room. The officer, seeing the whisky, immediately asked Bobby to hand it over.

Taken aback, Bobby held onto the bottle saying, "It's a birthday present for my uncle." When the officer continued to hold his hand out, Bobby reluctantly handed it over saying again, "It's a birthday present."

"Only half litres allowed, son," the officer replied. Walking over to a side room, he disappeared for a moment before reappearing empty-handed.

"You can pick it up on your way out."

"Bobby was about to suggest that they drank half and took the other half to take with them, then changed his mind. He looked at Marie and shrugged. The officer had already started off and they had to run to catch up with him. A large iron gate loomed up in front of them. Taking a key from the huge bunch he had around his waist, the officer opened the gate and beckoned them through, to an enormous empty yard. Marie clutched hold of Bobby's hand. With wide eyes they both looked at the police guards patrolling the empty yard, accompanied by the biggest alsatian** dogs they'd ever seen in their lives. When they had set out that morning it had seemed to them like a big adventure. Although they were both genuinely fond of their uncle, they had both felt excited at the thought of being inside a prison. Now they had seen the reality, the adventure had turned into a nightmare. Subdued now, they walked across the courtyard in silence, keeping a wary eye on the dogs as if expecting them to break free any moment and pounce on them.

Jesus, thought Bobby wildly, how do some men escape from a place like this? More to the point, how do they stand it? It was enough to turn a person's mind, and Tommy had been in places like this four times. Tightening his hold on Marie's hand, they made their way towards one of the huge buildings that flanked the equally huge courtyard. With relief they found themselves outside another large door and waited impatiently for the guard to go through the same ritual with the keys, anxious to be out of the yard where they felt so vulnerable. Once inside, they were in for another shock. Men walked around dressed in blue shirts and navy dungarees, calling out to each other cheerfully as if they were at work instead of inside a prison.

"Are they prisoners?" whispered Marie, looking fearfully around her.

"I don't know," Bobby shrugged, at the same time casting an anxious glance over his shoulder. They were led to a small furnished room with a wooden bench and four chairs. Where, they wondered, were the barbed wire grills that were portrayed on television and in films? The visit was turning out to be nothing like what they expected. The sound of footsteps made them look up eagerly, but their faces fell when they saw that the guard was alone.

"*Mr*" – he emphasised the word – "Flannagan isn't seeing any visitors. I'm afraid you'll have to leave." They could only stare at him, open-mouthed.

"Did you tell him it was his niece and nephew?" enquired Bobby, wondering what they had done to upset their uncle. By the look on the guard's face it was obvious that he hadn't informed Tommy as to who his visitors were. Without a word he departed once more. Ten minutes passed in anxious silence. It was with relief that they heard the unmistakable sound of two men's footsteps approaching, and there Tommy was.

Coming quickly into the room, his face alight with pleasure at seeing them, he said, "Sorry about the mix up, I thought it might be reporters again."

"Are they allowed to come in here?" asked Bobby in surprise.

"They sometimes pretend they're relatives. I've never had so many relations in my life."

"But what do they want?" asked Marie, unable to keep her eyes off her uncle. She had expected him to be subdued, but he hadn't changed at all.

"A story of course," and, leaning forward he added, "There's been talk about making a film but I've told them, I'll only tell the story if they get Frank Sinatra to play my part."

As they all laughed, Marie was uncomfortably aware of the guard standing silent in a corner of the room.

"We brought you a bottle of whisky for your birthday, but one of the guards took it away."

"That's all right, son, just make sure you pick it up on the way out; there's a lot of thieves in here." Turning to Marie, he smiled, "It's your birthday soon, isn't it?"

Marie nodded; "My twenty-first, but it isn't till April. I wish you could be there, Tommy."

A huge grin split Tommy's face as he answered, "I'll be there, don't you worry. That's a promise."

"Mum says that a promise from you has as much chance of happening as a snowflake surviving in hell, which is where you'll end up, she says."

"Bobby," Marie hissed, angry at her brother for saying such a thing. It was true though; Tommy always meant what he promised at the time of saying it, but all too often when the time came to keep his word, he forgot.

"Time's up," said the guard, coming forward to take charge of his prisoner.

"But we've only been here a little while," said Marie disappointedly.

Tommy stood up to leave. "You're used to hospital visiting times, love; it's not like that in here."

Suddenly remembering the letter her mum had given her to pass on to Tommy, Marie opened her handbag and was about to take the letter out when the bag was snatched from her hand.

"Sorry, love," the guard said, handing the bag back to her, "if you want to give anything to the prisoner, it has to be shown to me first."

Shaking, Marie handed him the letter which he put in his breast pocket.

"What did he think it was?" she asked Tommy as they walked to the door. "A gun?"

"It has been known to happen, love." As he went to put his arm around her the guard stepped forward again.

"Time's up," he repeated.

"Is there anything we can get for you?" asked Bobby, not knowing what to say.

"A rope ladder would come in handy," Tommy said with a laugh.

Marie and Bobby stood awkwardly for a moment then Bobby put out his hand. For a moment the boy and the man stood appraising each other. Tommy looked at the youth he hadn't seen for over a year. Bobby had grown, he was nearly as tall as Tommy; his face flushed with the awkwardness of youth, topped with the same dark curly hair he'd had since he was a baby. Taking the offered hand, Tommy was surprised at the strength of the grip in one so young. Turning to Marie, he kissed her on the forehead before walking out of the room. They watched him walking down the long corridor flanked with identical rooms to the one they had just come out of. When he had passed through the iron gate at the bottom of the hall he was lost to them for a moment as other prisoners mingled about him, the only visible reminder of him was his red hair; and then he was gone.

The journey back to the front gate passed unnoticed, for both of them were deep in their own thoughts.

When at last they were out in the driveway Bobby turned to look at the tall building before exclaiming in a voice filled with emotion, "I'll never do anything that would put me behind those walls. *Never*."

The bottle of whisky stood on the sideboard. Marie had insisted that it remain there until Tommy was home. The preparations for her twenty-first party were well in hand.

Even though she had left Bush's, she still kept in touch with everyone there. Her new job was only ten minutes walk away and she often popped in to see her old friends in her dinner hour. She had invited everyone she could think of, including the firm's nurse and the milkman. Peggy had gone spare when she'd seen the list. "It'll cost a fortune!" she'd cried in alarm. "Why didn't you invite the paper boy as well?"

"I did," replied Marie seriously, "but he didn't want to come."

Peggy had thrown her hands up in despair and left her to get on with it.

There would be a hundred and fifty guests in all. She had hired a local hall, and as Peggy had predicted, it had cost a fortune.

Marie was looking forward to the big day when, for once, she would be the centre of attraction. The white trouser suit she'd bought for the occasion was hanging in her wardrobe. She had tried it on earlier together with her latest fad, a wig. Peggy, coming into her room, had taken one look and had tactfully talked her out of wearing the latter.

The day she'd been waiting for for months finally dawned, and for once she was up early, too excited to sleep. There was the party to look forward to and next week Bobby was taking her to The Talk of the Ton to see Frankie Vaughn. A frown crossed her face. Bobby didn't know it was Frankie Vaughn they were going to see, he thought Stevie Wonder would be appearing that night and was looking forward to it. Shrugging her shoulders, Marie began to get dressed. Maybe he wouldn't notice, she thought with a grin. The day dragged on but finally it was seven o'clock, time to leave. Bobby had agreed to accompany her and stand at the door to greet her guests as they arrived. Not for the first time, Marie wondered what she would do without her brother.

Although there was a four-year difference in their ages, it seemed at times as if the age difference were reversed and he was the elder. He had what her mum called a good head on his shoulders. Marie knew that he was Mum's favourite, but far from being jealous she was of the same opinion, she was as proud of him as her mother was. Marie often wished that her mum would be proud of her, but then she had never done anything to make her mother proud, she thought sadly.

"Marie, hurry up, we'll be late!" Bobby shouted up the stairs. She took one last, swift look in the mirror, wished she hadn't bothered, and ran down the stairs.

The party was a great success, Marie had never had such a wonderful time before. She forgot her illness, her lack of boyfriends; she forgot everything except Tommy. The trial had finally ended on the eighth of March, over three weeks ago. Tommy had been sentenced to twelve months, but because he'd already spent that much time in prison awaiting trial, he had been released as soon as the trial had ended. She hadn't really expected him to come tonight, but it would have put the perfect final touch to her evening. She was dancing with some friends when Bobby came over and pulled her to one side.

"Look who's just turned up," he said, pointing over to the far end of the hall. And there he was, standing between her aunts Teresa and Pauline, who had travelled all the way from Northampton with her husband and children for the celebrations.

Walking quickly over to him, Marie threw her arms around his neck, her face split wide with happiness.

"I didn't think you'd come," she cried.

Gently untangling her arms, Tommy looked down at her, his blue eyes smiling.

"Have I ever told you a lie?" he asked, his face deadpan.

"Yes," she answered, laughing, "more times than I can remember."

Leading him over to the bar, where his birthday bottle of whisky had been put under the counter, she looked up into his face. He was a villain; he'd probably done things that would have horrified her if she'd known about them, but she *didn't* know, and she would never make it her business to find out. He was her uncle, that was all that mattered.

# Chapter Eleven

Jimmy watched his bedroom door close behind his mum and pulled a face. It wasn't fair, he thought rebelliously, just because he had been caught in the girls' toilets at school on Friday he had to stay in all the weekend. Why he had been in the girls' toilets he couldn't remember, it must have been a dare. Jimmy could never refuse a dare. Unfortunately for him he had been caught by one of the prefects and reported to the headmaster. Flouncing over in his bed, he drummed on the eiderdown with his fingers. He was bored; he hadn't been allowed out of the house since Friday dinner-time when his mum had dragged him out of school by his collar after receiving a phone call informing her of his latest escapade. Mrs Willis from upstairs, whose phone was used for such emergencies, had relayed the news to Peggy with barely suppressed glee. Not having any children herself, she always felt a wave of satisfaction when one of the Cowley.

Peggy was wrestling with the problem of finding the money to buy John a bed of his own. At present he shared with Jimmy, but Jimmy was such a fidget there was hardly a night went by that he didn't end up on the floor.

Marie was deep in thought about her new job. She had only been there a few months but already there was talk of redundancy. Also she missed her friends.

"Mum," she started to speak, cutting in on Peggy's thoughts, "did I tell you that Mr Johnson had heard rumours about the punch room having to close down?"

Peggy looked at Marie in surprise; it wasn't often that her daughter confided in her. Pushing the worry of the bed from her mind, she concentrated on what Marie was saying.

141

Seeing that she had her mum's full attention, Marie hurried on. "We may be made redundant, I'm a bit worried."

Peggy waited for her to continue, but when no further information was volunteered she ventured to speak: "I don't know why you left Bush's in the first place," she said quickly. "You were happy there. Why cut off your nose to spite your face?"

Marie sighed deeply: her mum would never understand. She hadn't been able to stay on after the amalgamation; she hadn't felt children got into trouble, which, in Jimmy's case, was quite often.

Hearing the front door close after his mum, Jimmy ventured out of bed to the window where he watched his mum and sister on their way to church. He himself had been that morning with his dad, but he didn't class that as going out. As he was about to turn away from the window he glimpsed his friend Paul coming along on the other side of the road.

Banging on the window to attract his friend's attention, he put a finger to his lips and with the other hand beckoned him over. When his friend was standing directly beneath his window Jimmy carefully pulled open the window and leaned out.

"Where're you going, Paul?" he asked in a stage whisper.

"Up the flats to play on the swings. You coming?"

"Can't," Jimmy whispered, looking fearfully over his shoulders and expecting to see his father come into the room.

"Come on," wheedled Paul. "Tony's got some new marbles; we're going to have a game later."

Jimmy wrestled with himself – the temptation to get out of his room drawing him like a magnet. He threw caution to the wind. He'd get a wallop from his mum when he got back, but it would be worth it to get out for a while.

"Wait there," he said, keeping his voice low, his fingers still held to his lips, "I'm coming down."

Tip-toeing down the stairs, he edged his way across the wall, then with one quick bound he had the front door open and was out of the house, running excitedly along with his friends. For the next half-hour Jimmy forgot that he would have to face his mum when he got back home.

"Who's coming up the slide?" said a red-faced boy, his eyes alight with excitement. The other boys stood silent, not answering.

The slide in question was out of bounds to all of them. With one accord they all looked towards the large contraption. To their small eyes it seemed to reach to the sky. No one moved forward. "Scardey, scardey cats," chanted Dave, who had issued the challenge. Jimmy pushed his way towards the boy. Nose to nose they glared at each other. It was Dave who spoke first.

Pushing his finger into Jimmy's chest, he chanted again, "Jimmy Cowley is a coward, na na nana."

Jimmy, his fists clenched at his sides, felt a wave of fear hit his stomach but he wasn't going to back down.

Quickly, before his courage deserted him, he strode over to the slide, his feet beating out a tattoo on the hard ground. Pausing only to glance back at the now silent group, he put his foot on the first rung of the ladder. His eyes firmly in front of him, he made his way up the steps, not daring to look down.

One of his friends shouted after him, "Come down, Jimmy; you'll get into trouble," but Jimmy took no notice. He was halfway up now and the fear was being replaced by exhilaration. Up and up he went, not stopping for breath until he reached the top. Stepping out onto the small platform, he looked down for the first time. He couldn't see his friend's faces, they were just blurs. The fear came rushing back as he looked down at the vast expanse of space between him and the safety of the ground. His lips started to tremble as he felt the unfamiliar tears spring to his eyes.

"Mum", he whispered, his voice crackling with fright, "Mum, help me."

As the tears started to fall down his face he held tightly to the iron bars at the sides of the slide. Down below the small boys watched in terror at their friend's predicament, not knowing what to do. They didn't hear the caretaker coming up behind them until he was by their side.

"Here," the old man shouted at them, "what's going on? You know you're not allowed in this part of the playground."

No one answered him. Instead they all looked upwards towards where Jimmy was hanging onto the safety rails, his eyes closed in terror. Following their gaze, the old man looked up towards the slide, shading his eyes with his hand.

His first reaction on seeing the small boy trapped up on the slide was one of pure panic. He was on duty to prevent this sort of thing from happening. He'd only been gone a few minutes but that had been time enough. Stepping forwards, he shouted up to the small figure.

"You," he bellowed, "come down from there!"

When Jimmy heard the man shouting he started forward in fright. Forgetting where he was, he attempted to run. His hands let go of the iron bars, he stumbled, reached out to grab the safety of the rail, missed and felt himself floating into space. His eyes, wide now with terror, saw the ground coming up to meet him. The old man and the small boys looked in horror at the sight of the tiny body hurtling towards the ground, Jimmy's screams filling their ears, and then the sickening thud as he hit the ground.

Peggie and Marie were on their way back from Church when they were suddenly interrupted by a shriek of, "Mum, Mum, come quickly!"

Startled, they both looked up to see Andy running towards them, his face red from exertion. He reached Peggy and grabbed hold of her arm, his breath coming in small gasps as he tried to speak,

"Jimmy fell," he gulped hard, "Jimmy fell off the slide, he's hurt bad."

A ball of fear hit Peggy in the stomach and, grabbing Andy roughly by the arm, she shook him.

"Where?" she demanded, fear making her tighten her hold on his arm so that he winced with pain. "He's supposed to be in bed. Where's your father, why didn't he stop him from going out?" They were hurrying along now, Marie running to keep up with her mother and Andy who was still being held by the arm. As they sped along the pavement Peggy ignored Andy's whimpering. She was oblivious to everything but the picture conjured up in her mind of Jimmy lying on the ground, not moving. Thrusting the picture from her mind, she ran on, her face set in a grim line. As they rounded the corner into their street they came to a dead stop at the sight of the ambulance standing outside their door. Pushing through the knot of people that had gathered, she reached the door of the waiting ambulance. Without a word she climbed up the iron steps and sat down beside Bill. Not trusting herself to speak to him, she cast her eyes over the stretcher where Jimmy was. Her hand flew up to her mouth to stop the cry that threatened to burst from her lips. Jimmy lay there, his small face, usually so full of life, deathly white, his dark hair matted with blood.

As she reached out to touch him Bill caught her hand.

"Don't touch him, love," he said brokenly, "the ambulance man said not to disturb him."

Peggy looked up at her husband to see the fear she felt mirrored in his eyes. Wordlessly she sank back on the hard seat, her hand still held tightly in Bill's.

On the pavement Marie stood and watched as the doors were shut firmly in her face. She remained standing there helplessly long after the ambulance had gone.

"How did it happen? He was supposed to be in bed."

Bill watched as his wife walked around the hospital corridor. He wanted to comfort her but didn't know how. He would never forget the sight of Jimmy being dragged along the pavement by his friends as they struggled to get him home. Alerted by the frantic hammering on his door, he had opened it to be confronted by a small boy hysterically shouting something about Jimmy having fallen and to come quick.

Bill had run in the direction of the shaking boy's finger, and had stopped dead when he saw the trio coming towards him. Two of the boys had held Jimmy's feet with the third one frantically hanging onto his head. Their faces red with exertion, their small legs buckling under Jimmy's weight, they had progressed towards him. As if a giant hand had shoved him in the back, Bill had bounded forwards to take his son in his arms.

Relieved of their burden the young boys had sunk to the

hard ground, tears swelling in all their eyes at the enormity of what had happened.

Taking no heed of their abject misery, Bill had run towards home holding the precious bundle close to his chest. As if by some kind of miracle he had seen the ambulance coming along the road. He wasn't to know the ambulance had been summoned by the caretaker who had returned from the phone to find the playground empty. He didn't know that even now the poor old man was running round the streets trying to find Jimmy and his friends – all he knew was help was at hand.

Sending up a silent prayer of thanks, he had carefully removed one of his arms that was supporting the small body and run waving wildly to make the ambulance stop. He had been afraid to look at his son as he lay on the stretcher, heedless of the gentle reassurance the ambulance men had been trying to give him, and then Peggy had appeared, her face white and pinched, her hands pulling at the plaid scarf she always wore to church; afraid to speak, afraid to know the worst.

The sound of feet coming towards him brought him back to the present. Standing up, he turned to face the doctor coming towards him, Peggy appearing at his side. Silently they waited, fearful of what they might be about to hear.

The doctor stood in front of them, feeling Peggy's and Bill's eyes set firmly on his face. Just for a moment he wished he had chosen another profession. How many times in his thirty years of practice had he seen that same look, the same anxious faces? He had just come from the Cowley child.

Almost imperceptibly he shook his head; the prognosis wasn't good.

Peggy caught the slight movement and darted forwards. "How is he, Doctor?" In her distress she had clutched hold of his white coat. Gently disentangling himself, the doctor led her over to the long bench reserved for visitors.

"It's all right," he said almost mechanically, repeating the words often chosen in situations like this. The woman who sat next to him was searching his face, desperately trying to find some sign of hope, willing him to smile and say Jimmy would be all right.

"He's still unconscious I'm afraid," the doctor replied

quietly, wondering if the parents could take the stark truth at this time.

Looking into the woman's clear, pain-filled blue eyes and then over her shoulder at the small man standing behind her, he decided to tell them the truth.

"He's in a coma."

As he spoke the words, Peggy's hands came up to her mouth. Behind her Bill faltered for a moment before regaining his composure. Moving forward, he placed a hand on her shoulder.

The doctor reached out and caught Peggy's hand firmly in his own.

"Mrs Cowley, I'm sorry I can't give you any definite news. It wouldn't be fair to either of you, but," he added quickly, "he's got a good chance, we'll just have to wait and see. Only time will tell," he ended lamely. After all these years he still found it difficult to soften the blow, there was no good way to break bad news.

"Would you like to see your son?" he asked gently.

Squeezing back the tears, Peggy nodded mutely. Standing up she tottered for a moment, her head swimming. With a quick movement Bill was by her side, his hand steadying her. Without a word they followed the doctor down the long corridor, their heels clicking loudly on the cold hospital floor. Pausing before the intensive care unit, the doctor made to say something then changed his mind. Silently he pushed open the door and moved aside to let them enter. Hand in hand, Peggy and Bill approached the bed where the outline of a small body lay quietly.

Looking down at Jimmy's head swathed in bandages, his face almost obscured, Peggy let the long awaited tears flow freely down her cheeks.

Taking hold of his tiny hand, she whispered, "Fight, Jimmy, fight, love. You can do it, it's a dare."

As the doctor made to leave her voice came to him softly. "He likes a dare. He'll be seven on Wednesday. It's his birthday." Her voice faltered as she turned back to look at her son.

Shaking his head, the doctor left the room; there was nothing he could do here.

Marie lay on her bed. She felt numb. She had been shocked at the overwhelming love and fear she'd felt as she'd watched the ambulance pull away with her scamp of a brother inside it. The realisation that she loved her brother had hit her like a bucket of cold water. Apart from Bobby, she had never felt close to any of her brothers and sisters, and it had taken a tragedy like this to make her realise that although she hadn't really taken any notice of them they were a part of her that couldn't be erased.

She spent most of her time round her nan's or her Aunt Teresa's, and when she was at home she stayed mainly in her room. But somehow their presence had taken root into her very soul and she started seeing them all clearly for the first time. She had never got on with Ellen. Because you're jealous of her, that's why, whispered a tiny voice in her head. Impatiently she pushed this thought from her mind. Then there was Andy, he was always making jokes, never taking anything seriously, Vicky a bit like a perfect schoolgirl, her socks always that bit whiter than any of her school friends, her hair always perfectly plaited into long braids that hung on either side of her freckly face. John, the baby of the family, was always wingeing and tutting.

Then there was Patti. At seven years of age she was the quiet one of the family. Always intent with whatever she was doing, her plump face always smiling, the back of her hair always matted, no matter how often her mum brushed it. Every morning without fail her voice could be heard all over the house crying, "My socks, where's my socks?" Patti's disappearing socks were a standing joke among the family. Every night she would lay them out at the bottom of her bed very carefully, and every morning they would be gone. Then she would run to her protector, Ellen, whom she idolised, to plead with her to help her find her precious socks.

Marie smiled to herself. She would bet any money that it was Jimmy who kept hiding them although he strongly denied it. A cloud settled over her face – Jimmy: noisy, cheeky, annoying, lovable little Jimmy.

I've never told him I love him, she thought sadly. As she lay down on her bed, hands to her face, the thought came to her: Until now I never knew I did.

The hospital corridor was empty and quiet as the woman walked down the long aisle peering shortsightedly at the dimly lit signs. Coming to a square plaque that bore the name Victoria Ward, she gave a satisfied nod to herself and proceeded to follow the direction of the large arrow.

The ward was in semi-darkness, the only light coming from the table lamp that stood on the corner of the night nurse's desk. Pushing open the ward door, Sadie walked over to where the nurse was studying a sheaf of papers in front of her.

"Excuse me," Sadie whispered, careful to keep her voice low, "I've come to see Jimmy Cowley."

The nurse looked up startled; she hadn't heard Sadie come onto the ward.

"I'm sorry," she answered, "but it's nine o'clock. Visiting times finished two hours ago."

Not bothering to hide her disappointment, Sadie appealed to the young nurse.

"Please, I only found out about the accident a short while ago, I came as quick as I could."

As she stared at the nurse, her eyes imploring her to relent, she thought back to the events of a few hours earlier. She had gone to her local off-licence for a bottle of stout and had bumped into Daisy Clark, an old neighbour of hers. Sadie had been delighted to see an old acquaintance and the two women had chatted amicably for a while until Daisy's husband, who was waiting out in the car, had tooted his horn impatiently. Daisy had moved towards the door, calling out to her husband to wait a minute. Paying for her bottle of stout, Sadie had left the off-licence, anxious now to get home in time for the evening film she was looking forward to seeing, and had been surprised to see Daisy and her husband still sitting in their car. Rolling down the window, Daisy had called out, "You know the Cowley family, don't you, Sadie?"

Her mouth suddenly dry, Sadie had nodded.

"Well," Daisy had continued, as if reluctant to be the bearer of bad news, "young Jimmy's had a bad accident. I don't know the full details. I only heard myself a little while ago, you know how fast bad news travels in the East End. Anyway, he's in the hospital, Victoria Ward, I think. If you see Peggy, give her my best wishes won't you? I hope the little 'un will be all right."

Sadie had walked home slowly. Letting herself into the small flat that she had moved into only a few weeks earlier, she had sat in her old armchair, her eyes brimming with tears, wondering what course of action to take. She knew she would be unable to sleep tonight until she had been to the hospital and satisfied herself that Jimmy was all right.

And so here she was, her feet planted firmly on the floor, determined not to leave until she had seen him.

"Are you a relative?" the nurse asked.

"Yes, I'm his aunt," Sadie replied, her voice steady, her glance unflinching.

The nurse was in a quandary. She looked up and saw the silent pleading in the black eyes and felt her resolve weakening.

"All right. Just five minutes, mind. If Sister comes back early from her break and finds you here, I'll get shot."

Leading Sadie to a side ward, she ushered her in, motioning to the small still body that lay beneath the covers.

"Don't forget, five minutes," said the nurse, closing the door gently behind her, giving Sadie no chance to ask any questions.

Moving nearer to the bed, her hand flew to her mouth in dismay at the sight of the bandages that swathed Jimmy's head. Reaching blindly behind her for a chair, she sat down. Gingerly, as if afraid of hurting him, she picked up his hand and placed it against her cheek. Then, gazing down on the white still face, she let the tears fall, crying quietly, "Oh, Jimmy. Oh, my poor darling boy."

# Chapter Twelve

1969.

The house seemed so quiet; even John and Patti were subdued though they didn't know why. The laughter that usually resounded around the walls was stilled. Marie sat at the kitchen table drinking her tea before setting off to work. Putting the cup carefully in the saucer to stop the tea dripping onto her new mini skirt, she opened the *Daily Mirror* and began to peruse the latest news.

Peggy and Bill had gone to the hospital early this morning to be with Jimmy in case he came round. They wanted to be there when it happened, if it happened, she prayed fervently. Going to the front door, Marie glanced down the street hoping to see Nan coming along. She was coming to look after John and Patti until Peggy and Bill returned home. Anxiously checking her watch again, she turned and walked back to the kitchen.

"Morning, Marie," Patti walked into the kitchen rubbing the sleep from her eyes, her battered old teddy bear held by his one remaining ear. Putting her free hand on the table, she hitched herself up onto the orange vinyl chair and looked expectantly at her big sister.

"You want some breakfast?" asked Marie impatiently, again looking at her watch. Where was Nan? She would be late for work if she didn't show up soon. As if in answer to her plea, May's head went past the window. Ignoring Patti's hungry look, Marie ran to open the door.

"You're late, Nan," she said, the relief showing plainly in her voice. "I've got to go, could you give Patti some breakfast please?"

Shrugging herself into her coat, she made for the door.

"Oh, and Nan," she added, coming back into the kitchen to get her handbag, "try and flatten the back of her hair down

151

before she goes to school, will you? It looks like a bird's nest at the back."

Planting a quick peck on May's cheek, she threw a wave in Patti's direction and was gone.

May looked after the retreating back of her granddaughter. If Marie had bothered to ask her why she was late, she could have told her the reason. May had been to church before coming round; she had been to church every morning since the accident had happened. It was hard to believe that only four days had passed; it seemed like a lifetime.

"I'm hungry, Nan."

"All right, darling." As May began preparing breakfast she added absently, "And take your thumb out of your mouth there's a good girl."

Marie sat gazing out of the window, her machine idle. She normally looked forward to her tea-break, but since Jimmy's fall she would have preferred to keep on working to prevent her mind from dwelling on his plight.

"Why don't you go home, Marie?" She jumped as her supervisor walked up to her desk.

"No, thanks," Marie protested quickly. "I'm all right, really."

"Go home," Mrs Willis repeated kindly. "There's not a lot of work and I'm sure you'd rather be at home."

Marie got to her feet slowly. She knew Mrs Willis was trying to be kind and she didn't want to hurt her feelings. She was a nice woman, but she really didn't want to go home. Putting her newspaper and uneaten sandwiches in her bag, she flashed what passed for a smile and walked quickly from the office.

The sound of her mother's sobs stopped her in her tracks. Marie stood outside the front door listening to Peggy's racking cries, her whole body shaking as if with ague. Panic-stricken, she stood rooted to the spot.

He was dead, Jimmy was dead; there could be no other reason for her mother's heartbreaking sobs. One part of her wanted to go in and get it over with, the other part wanted to run and hide. But where would she go? Sooner or later she would have to come back. On legs that threatened to give way any minute she pushed the open front door wide and stepped into the hall. Her mouth dry and her heart beating as if it was trying to escape from her chest, she went into the kitchen. The noise of Peggy's cries drowned her footsteps on the lino floor. Marie remained where she stood, staring transfixed at the scene before her. Her mother's head on her arms leaning over the kitchen table, her dad standing over her looking ten years older than the last time she'd seen him.

Marie's mind went blank but her body jumped forward and then she was shouting, "No, no, please God no! Don't let him be dead, please!"

She felt strong arms go round her and then she was being held in her dad's arms.

"It's all right, love," he was saying gently, his voice thick with tears, "he's all right, he's come round, he's going to be fine."

Leading her over to a chair, he helped her sit down, saying as he did so, "He came round about ten o'clock, just looked up at us and said 'Hello', as if nothing had happened. He doesn't remember anything about going up the slide; the doctor says it's the mind's way of blocking out unpleasant memories, but that's not important."

Lifting a tear-stained face towards her mother, she said in a shaky voice, "But why are you crying like that, Mum? When I heard you I was sure something terrible had happened."

Peggy looked at her daughter's frightened face, feeling a wave of compassion for her. She had been surprised at Marie's reaction to Jimmy's accident. She knew Marie was fond of her brother but it had always been in an absent-minded sort of way. Maybe if this dreadful experience could bring Marie closer into the family then something good would have come out of it.

Gently drawing Marie's hand into her own, she smiled at her. "It's the relief, love. I'm so relieved I feel sick."

There was so much Marie wanted to say, but her tongue seemed to be stuck to the roof of her mouth. Squeezing Peggy's hand, she too burst out crying. Bill looked at both of them and gave a shaky grin.

"By Jesus," he said happily, a slight tremor in his voice, "if this is how you both react to good news I'd hate to be around if ever you get any bad news."

Going over to the sink, he started to fill the kettle for the inevitable cup of tea while Peggy and Marie remained holding hands, drawn together by the bond of love they shared for the seven-year-old scrap who had nearly died. All of a sudden the bile rose in Marie's throat. As she let go of Peggy's hand in panic to stand up red lights flashed before her eyes. She felt herself stumbling as the red turned to black, blacker than the darkest night. As she heard her mother's cry of alarm she fought against the darkness for a moment then let herself slip into its welcoming warmth.


Marie arrived at the London Hospital out of breath. The bus had been half an hour later than usual. It was a chilly day for August and she pulled her old black and white check coat around her as she hurried into the courtyard. Ignoring the shouts of "Fancy a game of draughts, love?" from two workmen outside the gates, she ran up the stairs and into the foyer of the hospital.

Locating the ward was easy and soon she was approaching the bed where Jimmy lay. Hearing footsteps approaching his bed, Jimmy turned his head to see who it was.

"Hello, love," Marie said as she bent to kiss him.

"Have you brought me anything to eat?" he asked, grinning as he wiped her kiss off with the back of his hand.

"Well, I can see you're feeling better, and yes, I've brought you some sweets."

Sitting on the side of his bed, she watched happily as he tore the wrapper off the Mars bar she had given him. When he had finished he began talking about the nurses and doctors and how they had fussed over him, his small body swelling with importance. Watching him, Marie could only marvel at the resilience of youth. He had nearly died but, to him, it was just a game.

"You gave us a fright, you know that, don't you?" Marie said bending over him. "How did it happen? You weren't supposed to be out in the first place, were you?"

For a moment his blue eyes clouded over as if trying to remember, then he shrugged. "Don't know, somebody must have pushed me," he answered, his fingers plucking nervously at the bedclothes. Marie looked down at his bent head, resisting the impulse to take him in her arms, an action that would have been met with disdain. She rose to leave.

Jimmy looked up at her in alarm. "You're not going, are you?" he asked, his voice breaking for the first time.

"I've got to, love," she explained softly, "I'm on my dinner break. But look," she added quickly, seeing the distress in his eyes, "Mum and Dad are coming tonight, and tomorrow's Saturday so I can come and stay as long as you want."

"Can you ask Bobby to come as well?" he asked hopefully, the tears quickly vanishing. Seeing that he was in a good position to bargain, he pulled himself up in the bed and asked, "Will you bring me some comics and crisps?"

"Yes and yes," Marie answered happily. It was good to see him in such spirits. She had been afraid for a while that he was going to burst into tears and if he had done that she could never have left him.

He leaned forward and whispered, "When can I come home, Marie? I don't like it here any more."

She wanted to pick him up and carry him out of the ward. She better than most people knew what it was like in hospital. Surrounded by strangers, being pulled and mauled about, injections administered at the drop of a hat, the deathly quiet nights, the dark wards with only the light at the end of the ward showing where the night nurse sat watching over her charges. But then, she told herself, it was probably different on a children's ward; the staff would be more gentle with their small charges. Still, hospitals were a frightening place to be if you weren't used to it, especially for someone as young as Jimmy. Knowing words of comfort would be lost on him, she resorted to bribery.

"If I see your friend Paul, shall I tell him your head is covered in bandages?"

She was rewarded by the grin that lit up his face.

"Oh, yes please," he breathed excitedly. "Won't he be jealous?"

"Yes, I'm sure he will be. Now you be a good boy and I'll see you tomorrow with Bobby." Patting his hand, she turned to leave.

"You can kiss me goodbye if you want. I won't rub it off this time."

Not trusting herself to speak, Marie gathered him in her arms for a moment and then quickly left him before she let free the tears she felt building up inside her.

"And you're sure he's all right now?"

Marie was sitting in May's kitchen drinking her third cup of tea.

"Yes, honestly, Nan, he's fine, he thinks it's all a big adventure."

Carrying a cup of tea in her hand, May came to sit by Marie.

"Ah now, it's a miracle, that's what it is." Inclining her head towards Marie, she confided, "Did I tell you I'd had a Mass said for him and Father Bailey himself prayed with me when it was over?"

Marie didn't believe in miracles although she had said a few prayers herself. Still, she mused quietly, it would never do to tell her nan that. May was a great believer in the power of prayer.

Gulping down the last of her tea, Marie stood up to go. "I'd better be off, Nan. It's getting dark and I don't like crossing the common too late at night."

"Why don't you wait for Tommy? He phoned to say he'll be home tonight."

Laughing, Marie began to put on her coat. "Goodness, Nan, if I wait for Tommy to show up, I'll never get home."

Seeing the worried look on her nan's face, Marie bent down to kiss her. "I'll be all right, I always walk around the common until I get to the last bit, then I run the rest of the way."

"Look," she added, seeing Nan wasn't convinced, "I'll phone you as soon as I get in, I promise."

Reluctantly May let her go, standing on the doorstep until she was out of sight. Then, giving a slight shiver at the cold night air, she turned and went back inside the house.

*

Twenty minutes later Marie was standing outside her own front door. Thankful to be home and off the dark street, she inserted her key in the lock, but before she could turn it the sound of a girl's giggle stopped her. She'd know that laugh anywhere – it was Ellen. The sound had come from the alley down the side of the flats. Her fear of the night forgotten, Marie walked towards the sound.

Peering into the gloom, she called out, "Ellen, is that you?"

The sound of a boy's laugh brought a tightening feeling to her chest. Her lips set themselves into a grim line. Ellen was down the alley with one of her boyfriends. It wasn't fair, Marie thought wildly; her sister was only fourteen but she had started early. Not that she put herself about – she didn't have to, the boys flocked around her like bees round a jamjar.

The object of her thoughts suddenly appeared before her. Ellen stood head bowed, her blonde hair falling to her shoulders, her body shaking with suppressed laughter. Marie felt the familiar anger rise in her at the sight of her sister. Out of the corner of her eye she saw the disappearing figure of a youth running down the road.

"Can you sneak me in, Marie? Mum doesn't know I'm still out; I got out over the back fence."

Marie fought down the impulse to grab her by the hair and fling her to the ground. She's laughing at me, she thought wildly, laughing because I've spent the evening round at Nan's while she's been sneaking out with another of her boyfriends. No matter how innocent the encounters, and Marie knew deep down that was all they were, her sister was no slut, still a voice inside her cried out, It's not fair.

Raising her eyes slowly, Ellen glanced at her elder sister wondering what she would do. Ellen was well aware of the dislike that emanated from her sister and she didn't hold out much hope of any help from that source. As the silence lengthened between them, Ellen looked at Marie's thin pinched face and wondered, not for the first time, why she chose to spend her free time round at Nan's or Aunt Teresa's. If she were Marie's age, she'd be out every night, and not visiting relations either. Suddenly Marie whirled round and opened the street door.

Sighing, Ellen waited for her to call out to her mum, telling her what had happened. To her great surprise Marie reappeared and beckoned her in. Not needing any further encouragement, she bounded past her and up the stairs before she could change her mind. Safe in her bedroom she picked her way round the double bed, careful not to wake Vicky, who was lying flat on her back, softly snoring. Patti, on the small bed by the window, had thrown her covers off. As she gently put them back over her, Ellen wondered again about Marie. She could have got her into trouble but instead she had helped her. Shaking her head, Ellen got into bed; maybe Marie was changing her ways.

The next morning when Ellen tried to thank her for helping her out, Marie cut her dead.

# Chapter Thirteen

1969.

"A hundred and fifty pounds, you lucky cow. What are you going to do with it?"

They were in Carol's bedroom looking down at the cheque marked payable to Miss Marie Cowley. The redundancy threat had come true and the cheque was Marie's pay off.

"Well," breathed Carol, still eyeing the cheque with unconcealed envy as she twisted the new diamond engagement ring on her finger. Marie noticed the movement and was surprised to find she felt no jealousy. She had been expecting the news, and when Carol had come bursting down to her house last week and told her she was getting engaged, she had hugged her friend tightly, wishing her all the best and meaning every word. She didn't know when the wedding was to take place, but she was to be chief bridesmaid; she wondered vaguely if Carol would let her buy her own dress.

"Well," Carol repeated, "what are you going to do with the money?"

Marie got up off the bed sighing. It was a lot of money, there was no denying that, but she was out of a job again which meant the rounds of employment agencies, and she hated that prospect. The interviews, making new friends and having to learn new formats were all a trial to her. Marie liked life to run smoothly and if there was any variance in her routine, whether it be unpleasant or simply inconvenient, she could never cope. These were the times she turned to Peggy for help in making her life easier.

Conscious of Carol's rising blood pressure, she walked over to the full length mirror that dominated the room. Standing before it, she looked for the tenth time at the dress she had bought that morning down Roman Road market. Bright yellow with short puff sleeves, its skirt barely covered her backside. Moving her eyes down to the pipe cleaners that passed for her legs, she winced and quickly looked away. I look like a bleeding daffodil, she thought wryly.

"Marie!" Carol's voice rose to a screech, and Marie was beginning to wish she hadn't come in to show her the cheque. She had received it yesterday along with her cards. Her first thought on reaching home had been to run down to Carol's brandishing her windfall, but then she'd remembered that Carol always met Pete straight from work on Fridays, so she'd had to content herself with waving it under her brothers' and sisters' noses. None of them had been impressed.

"I might go to Malta for a couple of months," she said airily. She wasn't disappointed. Jumping up from her bed, Carol stood in front of her, mouth agape, her hands busily brushing her long fair hair off her face. Marie watched with glee at the conflicting emotions that crossed her friend's face, and then Carol laughed.

"You," she shouted, "you, go to Malta for a couple of months? Don't make me laugh; you even get frightened if some fellow sits next to you on a bus."

Watching her friend's amusement something happened to Marie; she felt her back stiffen and her head go back in anger. For one wild moment she wanted to throw herself upon Carol and hurt her – really hurt her. Instead she turned on her heel and left without a backward glance.

Ignoring Carol's cry of "Marie, come back, I won't laugh again, come on, don't be daft," she slammed the street door after her as hard as she could.

Alone in her room Marie thought about what Carol had said, tears coming readily to her eyes. It was true, she admitted to herself, but it still hurt. Kicking off her platform shoes, she sprawled across her bed, thinking back to the last week when the idea of going to Malta had first arisen.

One of the girls she'd worked with was Maltese and the first thing Georgia had said on hearing about the redundancy money she was about to receive was "I know what I'm going to do with this, go to Malta for as long as the money holds out." She had then gone on to regale the office with tales of her homeland. Of the sun and the Mediterranean, the cheap booze but, most important to her, the thousands of servicemen of all nationalities that were based there. Marie had sat enthralled at the picture she had conjured up. When Georgia had asked if anyone wanted to go with her and share a flat, thus cutting down on expenses, two of her friends had immediately shown interest. The conversation had come to an end with the appearance of the supervisor, but later on Georgia had stopped by her desk and asked her if she was interested in going.

Marie had jumped as if she'd been stung, her face flaming as it always did whenever she was made to feel awkward. She'd mumbled something about having to think about it and Georgia had gone away. Think about it she had, all afternoon and all night, lying staring into the darkness, wondering if she would be able to summon up the courage to take such a big step. Deep within herself she admitted that she hadn't had the strength of character to go off to a strange country with girls she hardly knew until now. Carol's scorn had dragged up the strength she'd always had which had been buried by her mother's protective care all of her life. Suddenly Marie sat up and nodded to herself, "Sod 'em, I'm going." She got up and hurried from her room down to the call box to phone Georgia.

The dry humid heat hit her as they stepped off the plane. Glad to be off the aircraft and on firm land again, Marie didn't take in any of her surroundings until she was in the battered taxi taking them to their flat. The Maltese have their own special highway code, she was soon to learn. The rules are simple: whoever gets there first has the right of way. Georgia was used to it, but Marie and Julie clung together in sheer terror as the taxi spun round corners, tyres screeching, worn suspension rattling every bone in their bodies as they drove over bumps and craters in the road. The taxi driver and Georgia chatted away merrily, as relaxed as if they were in a horse and cart.

The little part of Malta Marie had seen so far consisted of old brick buildings and barren land. It was nothing like she'd expected. When at last the taxi stopped, Marie and Julie left Georgia to pay the fare as they climbed out gratefully, surprised and relieved to have arrived at their destination safely. Georgia's uncle had left the key with the porter and, after tipping him, their luggage was dragged upstairs and deposited outside a large door.

"Well, what do you think?" asked Georgia, sitting on one of the single beds and looking round her.

Dropping exhausted onto the bed opposite, Marie looked with tired eyes at the large room with its white walls. What did she think? She'd never been so disappointed in all her life. Her stomach was cramped, she felt tired and hot, all she wanted to do was sleep.

Aware that Georgia was waiting for an answer, she made a remark about being unlucky in their choice of taxi driver, at which Georgia threw back her head and roared with laughter, stating that all Maltese drove the same way, adding that they'd soon get used to it.

Never, thought Marie as she wearily got into bed. With just a single sheet covering her body she closed her eyes and slept, her last thought being I wish I hadn't come!

"Where do you fancy going tonight?"

Julie was in the bathroom putting the finishing touches to her make-up. At twenty she was an attractive girl, just a year younger than Marie, and with her blonde hair lightened by the sun, her skin a golden tan, she looked a knock-out.

"I don't mind," Marie answered as she slipped into a white mini dress. Much to her surprise she was enjoying herself enormously. They had been there three weeks now, and after the initial shock at the barrenness of the small island, the warmth and friendliness of the people had grown on her and now she felt completely at home. On their first night out in Valetta, Georgia had met a Maltese waiter and they had been inseparable ever since.

Thank goodness I didn't come with her on my own, Marie thought and sent a silent plea that Julie wouldn't meet anyone special.

A few minutes later Julie emerged from the bathroom and went across to an old wicker chair in the corner of the bedroom. As she crossed one long, tanned leg over her knee Marie looked at her with envy. She'd tried to get a tan, but the sun made her feel sick if she sat out in it for more than an hour, so she spent her time on the beach under an umbrella, much to the amusement of her friends. As she pulled on her tights, she reflected that she must be the only woman on the island who wore them.

"How about the Whisper," suggested Marie as she slipped into her sandals.

"The Whisper?" Julie repeated then shrugged. "All right by me; as long as there's plenty of uniforms I don't care where we go," she said, flashing Marie a toothpaste ad smile.

As they had left the apartment, Marie wondered why she'd ever been afraid of men. After spending three weeks surrounded by them she had completely lost her fear of the opposite sex. Sitting in the taxi on the way to Mdina she wondered how much longer they would be able to stay. They all had an open air ticket, but their money was dwindling fast even though they never had to buy a drink.

Five minutes after leaving the flat, three Italian sailors started to follow them. Marie marvelled at the fact that this occurrence didn't set her legs trembling or her heart racing with fear as it would have done if it had happened at home.

Julie looked over her shoulder at them and giggled, then, putting her arm through Marie's, the two girls walked on, waiting for the sailors to catch up with them.

Marie sat in the small bedroom surrounded by her luggage, listening to the sounds of her friend's weeping in the other room. It was time to go home. Back to rainy England, back to the rounds of employment agencies and, much worse, back to the loneliness of her room. There would be no more nightclubs, no sandy beaches like Melliha or Golden Bay, no more dressing up every night to sit in a bar or restaurant surrounded by soldiers and sailors making her feel important, and definitely no smiling at strangers in the street and being smiled at in return. You didn't do that sort of thing in London, not if you wanted to get home safely.

Swallowing quickly, she got up and walked over to the balcony. Standing quietly, she looked out over Sliema Bay, while in the distance she could see the huge expanse of the Mediterranean sparkling in the sun, the water so blue. Tears stung her eyes at the thought of leaving the island. She had never been so happy in all her life. The sound of footsteps echoing along the parquet floor brought her head round.

"Taxi's here," Julie said in a tear-filled voice, her eyes red with weeping. Not trusting herself to speak, Marie nodded, then turned to take one last look at the view she'd woken to every morning for the last seven weeks.

"I'll be back," she whispered, "I'll be back."


"There's a vacancy at Horne Bros in Hackney. Would you like to go for an interview?"

The girl at the job agency looked enquiringly at Marie sitting opposite her, waiting for an answer.

"All right," Marie replied without much enthusiasm. For the past week she had trailed round the job centres looking for work. There were plenty of posts to choose from, but they were mainly in the city and she wanted something nearer home. She was tired of travelling to work.

Taking the slip of paper the clerk gave her, she set off for her interview and, two hours later, she was in employment once again.

Coming out into the street, Marie felt small raindrops beginning to fall. Not bothering to put her umbrella up, she stuck her hands in her pockets and began to walk home.


"Can I have my pocket money please, Marie?"

Jimmy stood in Marie's bedroom, hand outstretched, the familiar grin on his face, waiting expectantly. He had fully recovered from his ordeal, but the memory of what had actually happened had completely disappeared.

Pulling on her thigh length black suede boots, Marie snapped back at him, "No, you can't. It's only Wednesday, you know I don't get paid till Friday."

Pushing past him she made for the door, calling for him to come out of her bedroom. Undaunted, Jimmy sauntered after her, wondering who he could touch for the sixpence he needed to buy the water pistol he had seen down Well Street last Saturday.

Peggy looked up from her morning cup of tea as Marie came into the kitchen.

Good God, she thought, what does she look like?

Hot pants were the current fashion, and Marie, as usual, had gone over the top. The suit she was wearing consisted of a short black jacket with patch pockets and a zipper front, tiny black shorts and thigh length boots studded around the top with silver loops. From past experience, Peggy knew better than to comment; instead she could only marvel at her daughter's nerve.

Muttering the grunt that served for a good morning, Marie snatched up the sandwiches Peggy had prepared for her and rushed out of the house, slapping on a black beret as she did so.

Peggy shook her head after her. Marie seemed to enjoy shocking people as well as making them laugh – although in this case she would be able to do both at the same time. The sound of smothered laughter brought her attention to John and Patti who were lingering over their breakfast. Pretending not to know what they were laughing at, she gently cuffed them both then went upstairs to wake Andy and Vicky.

It was eight-thirty when Marie passed through the foyer of Hornes. She had deliberately got in early so she could be at her desk before the rest of the office arrived. Contrary to what Peggy thought, Marie wasn't quite as brave as she made out. She knew her outfit would cause comment and she wanted to be safely tucked in behind her desk to put her in a better position to deal with it. Hurrying through the lobby, she reflected on her new job. She had started here three weeks after arriving back from Malta in October; it was now early December and so far she was enjoying her work. More important, she had made a friend in Mary, a woman near in age to her mum who had taken Marie under her wing.

Mary had listened to Marie's tales of Malta, watching her animated face as she relived her magical holiday. Since returning, Marie had lost touch with Julie and Georgia and she had enough sense to know that although they had got on well on holiday, they didn't have enough in common to form a lasting friendship.

Deep in thought she didn't see the two black girls waiting by the lift. They worked in the factory and they never missed a chance to pass some comment whenever she crossed their path. Dressed as she was today, she provided them with plenty of ammunition. Their eyes lit up at the sight of Marie coming towards them, gleefully they nudged each other as they waited for her to reach them. Too late she saw the danger; the sight of them standing there, grins splitting their faces, sent a spasm of fear up her spine. Coming to a dead stop, she suddenly snapped her fingers, at the same time uttering a tutting noise that John would have been proud of. Making a great play of pretending she had forgotten something, she made her way back down the lobby trying to keep her legs from shaking. Trying desperately to ignore the stinging taunts that followed her retreating back, she stumbled out into the cold December air where she remained shivering until Mary arrived for work twenty minutes later. With anyone else she would have brazened it out, but to Mary she told the truth about why she was standing out in the street afraid to go into the warm building.

When she was safely behind her desk, she looked down at her shaking hands. It wasn't only the cold that was making them tremble, it was anger, anger at herself for being the spineless coward she was.

From her desk behind Marie, Mary watched in pity as the young girl struggled to regain some kind of composure. Her mind went back to the first time she'd met her. It had been a very cold day in November. She had been off work ill when Marie had started in the office so when she had seen the young girl in front of her in the street struggling to walk in the heavy, ankle-length black coat, only her head and feet visible, she had smiled to herself at the latest fashion. The girl was so thin it looked as if the coat was walking on its own. As Mary had passed her the girl had suddenly stopped and leaned against the wall as if for support, and it was then for the first time that Mary had noticed the pinched white face under the dyed auburn hair.

From that day she had become quite fond of the unusual young girl who now came to visit her every Wednesday evening where they would sit for hours poring over the *Weekend* crossword. Mary worried about Marie's social life. Apart from her one visit a week, she didn't seem to go out at all. As she turned on her machine she reflected it was none of her buisness but she was fond of Marie and at times like this when she made a spectacle of herself to hide her insecurity she could weep for her. She might fool the younger girls in the office with her jokes and outrageous behaviour, but Mary could see beneath it to the desperately lonely girl that lay under the surface.

Marie's fingers flew over the keyboard, willing her mind to blot out the humiliating event she had just experienced, wishing she was back in the warmth of Malta. Christmas was only a couple of weeks away and she dreaded it. Bobby would be going out with his friends, as would Ellen, and what would she do? Sit at home with her mum and dad watching television? Shaking her head violently, she fought back the tears and bent her head to her work.

Mary approached the group of girls sitting round the table in the canteen. Just for a moment she hesitated, wondering if she was doing the right thing, then taking a deep breath she spoke.

"Are you girls going out tonight?" she queried.

One of the girls looked up at her and laughed happily. "Why?" she grinned. "You fancy coming with us?"

Mary returned the smile, thinking, Here goes nothing.

"No," she said hesitantly, "I was wondering if you'd ask Marie if she'd like to go out with you tonight," and seeing the looks that passed between them, she hurried on. "Look, she doesn't know I'm asking you, but it is Christmas Eve and she hasn't got anyone to go out with. Please."

"What do you reckon?" one of the girls asked her companions.

"I don't mind, as long as she doesn't come dressed as a pirate," the office junior said, the smile on her face wiping out any trace of malice in her words.

"Thanks," breathed Mary in relief, "but, look, don't let on I asked, pretend it was your idea, okay?"

Peggy was already stuffing the giant turkey when Marie burst into the kitchen, a happy smile on her face.

"I'll be going out tonight, Mum," she announced importantly. "The girls at work asked me to go to the Royal with them." Without giving Peggy time to reply, she whirled round and dashed upstairs, eager to begin her preparations.

"Well," thought Peggy as she carried on with the business in hand, "thank goodness for that." She had been dreading the thought of Marie sitting around the house tonight, wearing the long face she usually donned when she was miserable. She put a damper on everyone when she was in that mood, which unfortunately was often.

Giving the turkey's backside one final push, Peggy sat down to indulge in her favourite pastime: thinking. The biggest shock of the last year had been when Marie had calmly announced that she was going to Malta, not just for a holiday, but to live there until her money ran out. Peggy had never believed that she would actually go, she still couldn't believe it now. She'd even been quite pleasant when she'd first returned but it hadn't lasted. After the night out with the girls she'd gone on holiday with she'd retreated to her room once more. But now, well, she was going out with new friends. God's good, she told herself as she rose from the table to put the turkey in the oven. The turkey wouldn't have agreed.

Carrying the gaily-wrapped present under her arm, Marie made her way down to Carol's house. Just as she was about to knock, the door opened.

"Hello, Carol, I've brought your present round before I go out."

"Where're you going, round your aunt's?"

"No, of course not, not on Christmas Eve," Marie replied indignantly, then went on to tell her about the girls at work.

"Perhaps you'll meet someone tonight," Carol said, twisting her engagement ring as she spoke. Marie shrugged off the remark. If Carol only knew that Marie, not wanting to risk being left on her own at the end of the evening, had asked her mum and dad to pick her up at twelve-thirty, she would have split her sides laughing.

In the large ballroom, metallic globes flashed and sparkled as hundreds of youngsters gyrated to the sounds of the Stones' *Jumping Jack Flash*. In the midst of the crowd Marie was twisting and shaking her head in a good impersonation of Mick Jagger. She was having such a good time she'd forgotten about her mum coming to pick her up, until one of her friends commented, "Here, look at this old girl coming over. Wonder what she's doing here." Marie froze with horror at the sight of her mum bearing down on her, her usually smiling face grim.

Without saying a word, Peggy grabbed hold of Marie's arm and dragged her off the dance floor. She was angry. She'd thought it a stupid idea to come and pick her daughter up in the first place; good God, she was twenty-one. Ignoring the struggling form, Peggy wondered if this girl of hers would ever grow up. Once outside the Royal, Peggy looked down at Marie about to give her a tongue-lashing. Together with Bill they had loitered for over half an hour in the cold waiting for her to come out but, looking down at the forlorn figure beside her, she decided she'd had enough punishment for one night.

On the short journey home, Marie stared miserably out of the window. How would she ever face the girls after the Christmas holidays? One thing was certain, the episode that had just occurred would be circulated round the office for some time to come. This was one occasion when the laughter that was sure to follow wouldn't be of her own instigation.

# Chapter Fourteen

1970.

Marie sat at her punch machine, her fingers flying furiously over the keyboard in an effort to drown the laughter coming from the front of the office where the rest of the girls were having their morning tea-break. She was certain that the laughter was directed at her. Ever since that disastrous night on Christmas Eve when she'd been humiliated by her mum coming to fetch her from the Tottenham Royal, the girls in the office had been getting in sly digs at her whenever they could. She felt her face redden as another loud raucous laugh rang out and wished that Mary was in today. The girls respected Mary and they never dared laugh at Marie when she was in the office.

But Mary's not here is she? she asked herself. Mary's on holiday for a week, so how about doing something really out of the ordinary and sticking up for yourself for a change?

The silent battle went on in her head until Marie could take no more. She switched off her machine and looked straight ahead of her. One of the girls stopped talking and turned round in her chair, looking at Marie as if daring her to say something before turning back to her friends. Marie flinched as if she'd been struck; she'd seen the flicker of contempt in the girl's eyes and knew that the reason they laughed at her so openly was because they all knew she was too cowardly to say anything, no matter how far they pushed her. As this knowledge of herself hit her she felt sick with shame. If she was ever to have any self-respect she must speak out, no matter what the cost.

Getting slowly to her feet, she walked down to the small gathering and before she could lose her nerve she asked in a shaky voice, "How about letting me in on the joke? Or am I the butt of it?" Her entire body was trembling but she was determined to stand her ground. One by one the girls turned to look at her, amazement etched on their faces. For a moment no one spoke then June, the girl who had asked her to the Christmas dance, said quietly, "Well, well, the worm has turned."

Hearing the scorn in June's voice, Marie's fear left her, a terrible anger taking its place. Without thinking she put out her hands and pushed and watched with a mixture of satisfaction and horror as the young girl went crashing back over the table, knocking cups of tea and coffee over the rest of her colleagues, watched as they jumped up frantically as the hot liquid ran down their clothes. What would have happened next she didn't know, for at that moment Mrs Sladen, the supervisor, came running from her office, aghast at what she had just witnessed.

After assuring herself that none of the girls had been burnt she turned to Marie. "A word, Marie, in my office, if you please."

Meekly now, Marie followed, not believing the havoc she had just wreaked.

"I'm shocked, Marie, I could hardly believe my eyes; what on earth had got into you to do a thing like that?" Mrs Sladen sat behind her desk, her normally placid face troubled. She would have to sack the girl, no two ways about it. She couldn't allow that sort of thing to happen in her office. If she were to let Marie off with a caution the other, stronger girls would see it as a weakness on her part. No, the girl had to go – but, Marie, of all people.

"I'd like to hand in my notice, Mrs Sladen," Marie said calmly. "I can't work with those girls any more, not after today."

Relieved that she was to be spared the unenviable task of sacking Marie, Mrs Sladen nodded her head in agreement. "Yes, I think that would be the best thing for all concerned, and I won't want you to work out any notice. In view of the unpleasantness you'd be better off if you left now. I'll send your cards and any pay that is owing to you, but I'm afraid I can't write you a reference. I'm sure you understand."

Marie turned without another word and walked from the small glass-panelled office. Keeping her eyes straight ahead, she kept on walking until she had reached her machine. Mrs Sladen had been about to sack her, she was certain. That's why she'd handed in her notice so quickly. That would have looked good on her work record down at the employment agency: sacked twice, once for farting and once for fighting. She preferred the latter description – at least it had some kind of kudos attached to it. Her personal things packed into the carrier bag she kept in her locker, Marie took a deep breath and prayed silently: "Please let me make a grand exit, just once in my life, let me feel good about myself."

Her prayers were answered as she sailed from the office, her head held high; ignoring the hostile looks directed at her exposed back she held the green office door open a fraction longer than necessary, then with a haughty sweep of her head she was gone.

Peggy was dismayed at learning that Marie was out of work once again.

"One of these days," she stormed at her, "you won't be able to just walk out of one job and pick up another one the next day like you do now."

Marie looked at her mother as she stood at the kitchen sink peeling the potatoes for dinner and felt a mixture of annoyance and affection for her. Her mum did exaggerate. She'd only had two jobs prior to Hornes, yet Peggy was behaving as if she changed jobs every month. Still, Marie shrugged to herself, she supposed it was the Irish in her; they were famous for telling a tale. She hadn't told Peggy the real reason as to why she'd left in such a hurry, much as she would have liked to. Her mum wouldn't have been impressed, and she probably wouldn't have believed Marie anyway, so she'd just said there had been an argument and she didn't want to work there any more.

Taking her cup of tea from the table, she left the kitchen and went to her room, wondering what course to take next. She wouldn't mind having a few weeks off work before she found another job.

She hadn't been feeling very well lately and she knew that when she went for her next appointment at the hospital Dr Lawson would probably admit her for a few weeks. She was glad she didn't have to pay for her lengthy stays.

She'd once asked Bobby what he thought would have happened to her if they'd been born in America and had had to pay enormous medical bills. Before he'd had the chance to answer, Ellen had cut into the conversation. Looking up from the book she was reading, she'd announced in a flat tone, "You'd have died years ago."

Against her will, Marie had started to laugh. She had expected Ellen to get annoyed, but much to her surprise, her sister's face had creased into a wide grin, and for the first time in their lives they had laughed together.

The knock at her door brought her back to the present. It was dark in her bedroom, she must have fallen asleep.

"What?" she yelled out, ever angry when her privacy was invaded.

Sticking his head round the door, Bobby looked at his sister. "In your usual happy mood I see," he said, smiling down at her. Before she could answer he rushed on, "Just popped in to tell you we're going to the Lyceum on Saturday if you want to come, all right?"

"Thanks, Bob," Marie answered happily, a smile lighting up her plain face. She looked after the retreating back fondly. She could never understand why her brother was so kind to her. True, he was kind to everyone, and at eighteen he showed a maturity that she would never achieve, whatever her age.

Over the years Marie had dyed her hair every colour that had been invented despite warnings from her mum that it would fall out one day, had bought outrageous clothes, and had even forked out a fortune on contact lenses, only to find that she couldn't wear them for more than an hour without her eyes streaming. She still didn't have a boyfriend. And then just over a month ago Bobby had come into her room thinking she was round at Nan's to borrow her hairdryer, and had found her crying in the darkened room. Whereas another boy of his age would have backed out quickly, Bobby had sat by her side and listened to her cries of despair. She had poured her heart out that night. Her great fear of being left behind as the rest of them gradually left home to be married, the humiliation she was already feeling over the Christmas incident. He had left her after a while and the next morning she'd felt such a sense of shame at letting her guard down, but that very night he had stopped her on the hallway stairs and asked her if she'd like to come along with him and his friends for a night out. His young face flushed with embarrassment, he had waited for her to answer, all the while wondering what on earth his friends were going to say when he turned up on a Saturday night with his big sister.

That had been the start of a new life for Marie. In this way she had the best of both worlds. She was surrounded by fellows, but was entirely safe since they were much too young for her and none of them fancied her anyway. Because there was no pressure on her to impress, she found herself enjoying herself as she'd never done before, not even in Malta.

Looking at her reflection in the oval mirror, she stared at the small round face. She was twenty-two, but could easily pass for sixteen or seventeen at the most. She thanked her stars that one side effect of Chron's disease was a slowing down of the ageing process, so at least she didn't look out of place when she went out with Bobby and his friends. Throwing down her hair brush, she returned to her bed, and, flopping down on it, she wondered how long it would last.

Not many boys of Bobby's age would put up with a sister following him about, but she knew he was genuinely fond of her, and luckily she got on well with all of his friends. When she was with them at a dance or queueing up for the pictures, she would often see a group of girls in their teens staring at her, sometimes in wonder, other times with unconcealed envy, and she gloried in it. For the first time in her life she felt important, really important. She was wise enough to know it couldn't last. One day soon Bobby would meet someone special, as would all the gang, and then she would have to bow out gracefully. But while it lasted she was determined to enjoy her make-believe life and store away the memories to give her comfort in the lonely days she knew would eventually come.

She was going back to Bush's to work. As she got off the bus on a warm June morning her legs felt rubbery and she could feel her heart racing wildly as she walked towards the familiar gates. She had never thought she would come back here to work, but after weeks of being offered jobs that were unsuitable she had finally relented and accepted the job the agency had kept offering her.

Deep down she was glad she was coming back to the place that had given her so much happiness – and of course she would see Matthew again. Ignoring the little voice that kept asking her where her pride was to return to a place she had walked out on so short a time ago, she hurried on, eager to get settled at her desk and begin work.

"Excuse me, are you Bobby Cowley's sister?"

Marie looked at the young blonde girl who appeared at her side. Fame at last, she thought wryly as she studied the girl's face.

Anne Bristow returned the look, her blue eyes wide and open.

"Yes, I'm one of them," replied Marie, walking on. She wanted to get into the office before the other girls arrived, not wanting to walk into a crowded room.

"Where do you work, I mean which department?" Anne was keeping pace with Marie, trying to keep the conversation going.

Looking up at the girl who towered over her by at least a foot, Marie answered tersely, "Punch room," her anxiety making her short-tempered. As she made to walk off she saw the hurt look appearing over the young girl's face and was immediately contrite.

"Look," she said, her hand going up to her hair nervously, "I didn't mean to be rude, but I worked here before and I'm a bit nervous about coming back."

An easy smile came to Anne's face, the hurt look disappearing from her eyes.

"That's all right, maybe I'll see you after work, I go your way."

Marie nodded quickly, anxious to be gone. Returning the wave, she turned back towards the small building where she would be working and, taking a deep breath, she marched on.

Her worries about the reception she would receive quickly vanished after the first hour. There was so much work that everyone was much too busy to wonder at the reason for her return and, if she was honest with herself, none of them cared. Although she was kept busy on her first morning back she managed to keep an eye on the door, hoping for a glimpse of Matthew. Two of the other programmers had been in but so far she hadn't seen him.

Matthew still worked here. She had kept in touch with Pam, Irene and Jenny and they had filled her in with what was happening at the firm. She had arranged to meet them for lunch and at one o'clock she was waiting outside the building that housed the computer, a happy smile on her face at the prospect of seeing her friends again. Hearing the sound of the door opening, she walked forward then stopped quickly as she saw Matthew coming down the stairs. Her mouth suddenly dry, she searched her mind frantically for something to say.

"Hello, Marie," Matthew said quietly, coming down to meet her.

Only managing to return a mumbled greeting, Marie stared into his familiar face. She noticed with surprise that his hair was now worn long, almost reaching his shoulders, as was the fashion with a lot of young men. They stood awkwardly, neither knowing what to say, and it was with much relief that they heard Pam's voice as she came out of the building.

Taking the opportunity to get away, Matthew raised his hand in a gesture of farewell but as he brought his hand down he reached out and gently touched Marie's face.

"Welcome back, Marie," he said softly before turning away from her.

Pam, coming down the steps, saw the action and the look on Marie's face as she stared after Matthew's retreating back and sighed. She knew Marie would read something into that gesture that hadn't been intentional and also that she would have to tell her the truth before she started her wild imaginings.

"Did he tell you?" Pam asked, her head nodding in the direction Matthew had taken.

"Tell me? Tell me what?" asked Marie, still thinking of Matthew's hand touching her face. He was glad to see her, he would have asked her out if Pam hadn't appeared. On and on her mind raced: Matthew waiting for her after work, Matthew taking her out, Matthew coming to her house, Matthew telling her he . . .

"He's getting married."

The look of pain that passed over Marie's face made Pam wince. She wouldn't have hurt her for the world, but she had seen the rapturous look on her face as Matthew had touched her cheek.

Stunned, Marie turned slowly to face Pam, her eyes filling with tears, then with a quick movement of her hand she wiped her hand across her eyes, remarking as she did so, "Yeah, well, I'm not bothered about that. It's this cold I've got coming, I hope I don't have to have time off work."

Pam fell readily into the pretence Marie had created, saying, "Jenny and Irene are meeting us over at the canteen; we'd better go and save a table."

They walked out of the main gate still talking, with Marie sniffing into the paper handkerchief that Pam had given her. It wasn't fair, she told herself, it just wasn't fair. In those few moments she had jumped forward to Carol's wedding, seeing herself being escorted by Matthew. Now she would have to go by herself as usual. She was the chief bridesmaid; it would be the third time she had been a bridesmaid and, unbidden, the old saying came to mind: three times a bridesmaid, never a bride.

Snap out of it, she told herself fiercely as Pam repeated what she had just said. Concentrating on her friend, she pushed all thoughts of Matthew from her mind. She would have plenty of time tonight when she was alone to daydream once again of what might have been. Giving Pam a watery smile, she linked arms and started to chatter.

Standing in front of the mirror, she surveyed the long blue dress that Carol had picked out for her. It was quite nice, she thought, and the long skirt had the advantage of hiding her legs. She'd had her hair set in curls piled on top of her head with small blue flowers interwoven through them. Her mum had said she looked lovely but that was stretching it a bit. Turning once more to see the back of her reflection in the mirror, she gave one last pat to her hair before picking up her white gloves and going downstairs.

Peggy was coming from the kitchen as Marie entered. Looking up at her eldest daughter, she felt a lump in her throat. She looked so lonely. Peggy knew she was feeling sad that Carol was getting married but she would never have admitted it. Putting out her hand, she helped Marie down the last few steps as Marie held up the dress to stop it trailing on the floor.

"You look lovely, dear," she said softly.

"Oh, yes, a real beauty," Marie retorted sarcastically.

"Oh, love, why do you always put yourself down?" Peggy said, a note of despair in her voice. "You're just as good as your friends and you're prettier than Carol; yes you are," she said loudly as if to ward off contradiction.

"Then why is it that she's getting married and I'm the bridesmaid?"

"Now look," Peggy grabbed hold of Marie's hands and held firm, "if you had the chance, would you marry Peter? Well, would you?" she demanded, her eyes never leaving Marie's face.

Unable to break away from her mother's grip, Marie pondered the question, then, raising her eyes to her mother's, she answered, "No, he's nice and I like him, but no – I couldn't think of him in that way."

"Well then, that just proves my point. You'll do better one day, you mark my words." Giving a last flick at a piece of imaginary dust on Marie's shoulder, Peggy ushered her out of the front door. "You have a good time and give my congratulations to Carol." Waving once more, Peggy closed the front door, leaving Marie standing in the small court-yard in all her finery. Aware she was attracting attention from passers-by, she self-consciously made her way down to Carol's house.

She found Carol sitting on her bed looking very forlorn.

"What's the matter with you?" asked Marie in surprise.

"What if he doesn't show up?"

To Marie's amazement, Carol suddenly burst into tears. Quickly Marie ran to her friend's side. Putting her arm around her, she rocked her back and forth. "Course he'll show up, he's mad about you," she said, hugging her tight.

Slowly Carol began to regain control. As the tears sub-sided she wiped her eyes with the back of her hand and smiled ruefully.

"Surprised to see me crying, aren't you?" she asked, her voice still shaky. "Well, I've got news for you, you're not the only one with worries. Oh, I know you don't go on about things but you do worry about silly things." Smiling fondly at Marie she added, "We're a lot alike in some ways; we both put a front on. Me being all loud and bouncy, pretending nothing bothers me and you pretending you don't care about anything and both of us scared to death half the time."

"Come on, Carol." Gently pulling Carol off the bed, Marie went over to where the long white dress hung on the back of the door. Lifting it down, she carried it over to the bed and began taking the plastic wrapper off.

Half an hour later Carol stood ready to leave the house she'd been born in.

"How do I look?" she asked timidly.

Marie stared at her friend in awe. The long white dress seemed to cover her totally, the tiny pearls reflecting the light as she twisted and turned for inspection. She had left her hair loose and it fell in soft blonde curls to her shoulders, showing plainly through the long lace veil.

Mr Fisher came into the room and stared at his only daughter.

179

"It's time to go, love," he said softly, his eyes fixed firmly on her face. Crossing over to her father, Carol laid her hand on his arm as he led her from the room with Marie following close behind. As they reached the front door they stopped for a moment; Carol looked behind her at Marie and the two friends smiled at each other. Moving past her, Marie squeezed Carol's hand before making her way slowly towards the bridesmaids' car. Carol's two small nieces sat demurely in the back of the Bentley. Carefully easing her dress up, Marie got into the car and sat down. As the car drove off, she cast one last look at Carol standing framed in her doorway and put up her hand for a final reassuring wave.

Later that night as she lay in the dark, hands folded behind her head, Marie thought back to the events of the day. She'd enjoyed herself but as always was glad to come back to her own room to lie and dream. As she'd watched Carol walk up the aisle, she'd suddenly realised that she was no longer jealous of her and, stranger still, she was no longer lonely. Stretching out her hand, she turned off her bedside lamp, her mind moving forward to next week when she would be going into hospital for her yearly M.O.T. Luckily she got paid so she didn't have to worry about her finances, and after the usual tests had been completed she could have a nice rest. When she came out, she would have to start looking for a new friend. Maybe Anne. She'd seen quite a lot of Bobby's young admirer during the last few weeks and she wasn't that young, just four years younger than herself, the same age as Bobby. She had a feeling they would get on well. Trying not to dislodge her curls, Marie settled down to sleep.

Marie stood by her window, her gaze directed at the corner house where up until six months ago Carol had lived. She hadn't realised how much she would miss her until now. Hearing footsteps coming up the stairs, she quickly moved towards her bed, settling down in an attitude of sleep. She heard the boys' bedroom door slam and let her body relax. She had thought it might have been her mum coming to try and dissuade her from going round to Carol's tonight. Thinking back to Peggy's earlier words, Marie felt her anger start to build again.

"You'll wear out your welcome, love," Peggy had said when Marie had told her of her plans for tonight. Turning onto her side, Marie punched at her pillow, trying to give vent to the feelings of rage and shame that threatened to engulf her.

All right, she conceded to herself, maybe she had overdone the visiting at first, turning up on their doorstep the day they had come back from their honeymoon, but they had seemed pleased to see her, hadn't they? Swinging her legs over the side of the bed, Marie sat for a moment wondering what to do.

She had gone round to see Carol last night, so she wouldn't be expected again so soon. Giving a deep sigh, Marie stared unseeing at the floor. She could always go round to see Anne, but if she did, Anne would probably want to go out for a drink, and she didn't fancy the idea of sitting or standing in a crowded pub. No. Getting to her feet, her face determined, she picked up her coat from the foot of the bed and quickly put it on. She didn't care what her mum said, Carol and Pete were her friends. Hadn't they both said to her at the wedding, "Pop round anytime"? Well, hadn't they? Pushing down the feelings of doubt that had begun to assail her, Marie marched down the stairs and out of the house.

Her resolution lasted until she turned the corner into the street where Carol now lived and her steps slowed as she approached the terraced house, her eyes lifting upwards to the top window and the three-roomed flat that Carol and Pete rented by the week. Was her mum right? Maybe she should cut back on her visits, come round just once a week, or wait to be invited, instead of popping round whenever the fancy took her. Biting down on her bottom lip, she thought back to last night. Pete had hardly spoken to her all evening. She hadn't taken much notice at the time but now, with her mother's words still ringing in her ears, she wondered. Just

181

as she'd almost decided to go back home the heavens opened up.

"Oh hell, that's all I need," she said aloud as the rain started to fall on her exposed head. Quickly she pushed open the gate and rang the white doorbell. She was aware of her heart beating and a sudden dryness in her mouth as she waited almost fearfully for Carol to open the door.

"Oh, hello, Marie. I wasn't expecting you tonight. Come in." Carol held the door open to allow Marie to pass by her into the hall.

"Who is it, Carol?" Pete called out from upstairs.

"Only Marie," Carol answered, a resigned note in her voice. Marie heard the unfamiliar tone and felt her heart begin to beat even faster.

She was halfway up the stairs when she heard Pete mutter loudly, "Shit, not again" then the sound of his footsteps as he came out onto the landing pulling on his raincoat.

"I'm off down the pub, I'll see you later."

"Pete, wait a minute," Carol called out as he brushed by them, his back stiff with anger. Marie watched, her face stricken, as he ran down the stairs ignoring Carol's plea. Not knowing what else to do, she made her way to the small, comfortable sitting room and sat down heavily in the dark red armchair. She could hear Carol and Pete arguing downstairs, their voices low and angry, and she huddled back further into the chair feeling miserable and uncomfortable, wishing she had the courage to dash down the stairs and out of the house and so escape from this awful situation she found herself in.

Raising her eyes slowly, she gazed around the familiar room noting at once that the furniture had been rearranged. The television had been pushed into a corner and in its place stood the oblong kitchen table covered in a snowy white tablecloth, on which rested two silver-plated candle-sticks, large red candles burning brightly in the otherwise darkened room. Her eyes wide now, she took in the bottle of wine and the patterned napkins that lay beside the large empty dinner plates, and felt an overwhelming urge to weep. Hearing Carol come into the room, she turned to face her.

"I'm so sorry, Carol," she said, her voice breaking at the sight of her friend's tired face.

"No, it's all right, Marie. In a way, I'm glad you came round. I want to talk to you."

Marie nodded, knowing what Carol was going to say, and in all honesty she couldn't blame her. She had been shaken to the core by the open hostility in Pete's eyes and cursed herself for a fool for not taking her mum's advice.

She had to say something before Carol was forced to tell her some painful home truths. Looking towards the beautifully laid table, she said brightly, "Looks like I've put my foot in it again. It must be a special talent I have. What were you going to celebrate before I barged in?"

Carol looked at her friend knowing that what she was about to say would hurt her, but it couldn't be helped. Hints hadn't worked, she would have to tell her straight out. At least the news Pete had brought home tonight would make what she had to say a little easier.

"Marie, listen to me." She leant forward as if to touch her, then sat back again. Running a hand through her long hair she searched for the right words. "I found out today that I'm pregnant. That's what we were going to celebrate. I was just going to put the steak on when you arrived."

Pregnant: Carol was pregnant.

"Oh, Carol, that's wonderful," Marie said, her voice filled with excitement, and then, remembering what had happened, she added wistfully, "And I've ruined it for you, haven't I?"

Getting to her feet, she made to leave.

"I know what you wanted to tell me, but you're too kind, so I'll make it easy for you. It's the least I can do. From now on I won't come round again unless I'm invited, or perhaps we can arrange one day a week. Any day, I'm not fussy." She was tripping over her words in an attempt to make amends.

"Marie, sit down, please. There's something else I have to tell you." Taking a deep breath, Carol said quickly, "Pete's firm is moving to Southampton. If he goes with them we have

183

the chance to buy our own house. It's too good an opportunity to pass up, especially now," she finished, patting her still flat stomach.

"When are you going?" Marie felt the tears start again.

"Oh, not for a while yet," Carol laughed nervously. "I'll let you know before we leave."

*I'll let you know before we leave.* The words were dismissive, and for once Marie took the hint.

"Well, I'll be off then," she said, striving to keep her voice steady. When they reached the front door they stood for a long moment staring at each other, then Carol impulsively threw her arms around Marie.

"You've been a good friend, Marie. I won't forget you."

The finality of the words brought a tightness to Marie's throat.

Pulling away from Carol's embrace, she said, "Bye then, Carol," before walking away.

# Chapter Fifteen

1972.

As Anne came out of the office gates she saw Marie waiting for her and sighed. She knew what Marie would ask her and felt her stomach contract as she walked towards her, determined that this time she would say no.

"Fancy babysitting with me at Teresa's over the weekend?" Marie asked, expecting her friend to agree readily as she usually did.

"Sorry, not this weekend, I'm going out with Joyce." Seeing the look of disbelief on Marie's face, Anne hurried on. "You can come with us if you want."

The icy look on Marie's face stopped Anne from saying any more.

Glaring at her friend, Marie replied through clenched teeth, "Have a nice time. I'll tell Teresa you're busy." So saying, she turned quickly and walked off down the road, her back stiff with anger.

Anne watched her go with a mixture of relief and sadness. Their friendship had started when Anne had found out that Marie was in hospital and she'd gone to visit her a few times. After Marie had come home they had started going out together. At first Anne had enjoyed being with Bobby and his friends, and Marie, when she was in high spirits, was very good company. But last year Bobby had met a girl called Pauline and they had been going out together ever since. Fortunately for Marie, Pauline lived in Kent, so Bobby didn't see her much during the week and they still had their evenings out with him and his mates. But it was the weekends that were empty.

When Bobby had first started staying over at Pauline's for the weekend, Anne had hoped that she and Marie would start going out on their own, but instead Marie had preferred to spend the time at her aunt's place on the pretext of babysitting. Anne stared moodily ahead as she reached the bus stop but there was no sign of Marie. She must have decided to walk, Anne thought, relieved that she wouldn't have to suffer the injured look on her friend's face.

Thinking back to last weekend, Anne remembered the shopping trip she and Marie had taken with Teresa's three small children. They were lovely kids and it was clear that Marie adored them. Anne could still see the look on Marie's face when a woman had mistaken her for their mother. Marie hadn't corrected the woman; instead her face had lit up with a pleasure that had been painful to witness.

The sudden surge forward as the bus approached shook Anne out of her daydream as she battled valiantly to board the bus.

After a skirmish with a rather large woman she successfully acquired a seat. Ignoring the woman's baleful look, she settled down by the window and began to search in her handbag for her fare. Suddenly to her surprise she felt tears come to her eyes. She'd forgotten the cold reception Marie had just given her; instead she saw beneath the façade her friend had built around herself and recognised the deep sadness that lay beneath Marie's jokes and laughter. Anne knew also that Bobby was unhappy being caught between his sister and girlfriend but he was too good natured to tell Marie he didn't want her hanging round him any more.

As the bus swung into Well Street, Anne saw Marie walking along the side of the road, her hands in her pockets, her head hanging down dejectedly. For a moment Anne considered ringing the bell and getting off to join her friend, then decided against it. She would only be met with another rebuff. There was a battle raging inside Marie and Marie was the only one who could deal with it. She would have to realise that Bobby was a young man now with his own life to lead. Only then could Marie start to live her own life, because if she didn't, and it came to a choice between Marie and Pauline, Anne knew whom Bobby would choose.

*

Sitting alone in the small bedroom that she had acquired after Peggy had moved them to a larger house just a few streets away last year, Marie tried hard to swallow the lump in her throat.

"I'm not going to cry," she told herself fiercely. She was already beginning to feel ashamed about the way she had treated Anne. She was a good friend and didn't deserve to be taken for granted and Marie was truthful enough to admit that that was exactly what she had been doing to her. All right, she told herself, time for some home truths. Getting to her feet, she strode around the bedroom, all the while talking to herself.

"One," she began, ticking off her little finger, "you can't carry on putting Bobby in the role of make-believe boyfriend. If you don't let go and start to lead a normal life he'll end up hating you." As the dreadful thought struck her she sank down on the bed. Bobby hating her; she shook her head violently, she couldn't bear to contemplate that idea. But, a little voice told her, he will, you know he will if you don't change your ways. Putting her head in her hands, she leant onto her knees. If only she had hit it off with Pauline – but the two girls had taken an instant dislike to each other. To be fair, she supposed that if the boot had been on the other foot and she had a boyfriend with a sister that followed him everywhere she would probably feel the same way.

And what will happen when he gets married? the little voice said again. Are you going to latch onto Andy then work your way through your brothers right down to John? The thought so horrified her that she jumped to her feet, shaking her head against the awful prospect of what she might become. An old maid dressing up to look young, hanging round with boys twenty years younger than herself. Quickly she swung around and raced downstairs. Then before she could change her mind she rang Teresa to tell her she wouldn't be coming this weekend. Her aunt was only too pleased to hear that her niece would be going out with friends; she too worried about the way Marie seemed to be content to live her life through others, and she hoped this would be the start of a new way of life for her niece.

After hanging up the phone, Marie stuck her head round the kitchen door to inform Peggy that she didn't want any tea as she was going round to Anne's. Then she hurriedly put her coat on and made her way towards Well Street, hoping that it wasn't too late and she hadn't lost a good friend.

She needn't have worried: Anne wasn't the sort of person to hold a grudge, unlike herself. That night the three of them went up the White Hart. The night was nearly spoiled before it had begun by the landlord asking Marie how old she was, much to the delight of Anne and Joyce who were years younger than she was. Luckily his attention was diverted by the prospect of a fight breaking out. While he went to sort out the trouble they quickly deposited Marie in a dark corner and proceeded to shield her whenever the landlord came their way. The noise of the pub and the pressure of bodies round her made Marie feel slightly sick but she managed to keep a smile on her face, all the while keeping an eye on the clock hanging over the bar and wishing the hours away. After that night, going out became easier, mainly due to Anne's perseverance in not allowing Marie to slip back into her old ways. They all had a few one-night dates, but nothing serious until the night of the darts match.

She had been in the firm's darts team for only a few months when they held an away match with a rival firm. Marie was surprised to be asked to play but readily agreed, thinking it would be a quiet evening. Anne, not having anything better to do since Joyce had found herself a boyfriend, came along to keep Marie company. After an hour, Marie had been knocked out of the first three games and was making her way back to the table where Anne was sitting with Pam and Irene, when a tall, red-haired young man stepped in front of her. She apologised for treading on his toes and made to walk away when he spoke. "Hello," he quietly said, "can I buy you a drink?"

Marie hesitated for a minute, unsure of herself. "I'm with friends," she answered and started to walk on.

"Oh, sorry," he said, looking round him. "I've been watching you for a long time, I didn't see you with anyone."

She realised he meant a boyfriend and was pleased with the thought. Pointing to where Pam, Irene and Anne were sitting, she said, "My friends are over there."

Glancing at where she was pointing, he took in the three young women and laughed quickly, "That's all right then, I'll buy you all a drink."

Later, when it was time to leave, Stephen offered her a lift home. Marie hesitated; she had come on the mini-bus and, besides that, she was wary about going off with someone she had just met. Then there was the way Pam had kept looking at her all evening as if she was trying to tell her something. Her husband had picked her up a short while ago so she couldn't ask her what was wrong. Shrugging her shoulders, she decided to take a chance.

"All right then," she said, still nervous, "but only if you give my friend a lift too. She lives round the corner from me."

"Sure, no bother," he answered back easily.

Going over to where Anne was waiting, Marie told her about the offered lift home. Dubiously Anne looked over to where Stephen was waiting.

"I don't know, he looks a bit shifty to me," she said, at the same time smiling in his direction.

"Oh, come on, Anne; you're the one who's always on at me to be more adventurous," Marie replied, half hoping her friend would talk her out of accepting the lift. Before she could change her mind he strode over to where they were standing.

"Ready, girls?"

Picking up her bag, Anne followed Marie towards the door. Once she was safely deposited in the back of the battered old car she remained silent all the way home, keeping a wary eye on the stranger Marie had found. She still thought he looked a wrong 'un, and hoped for Marie's sake she was wrong.

They had dropped Anne off and were parked in a small side street adjacent to Marie's house. The moment Anne had stepped out of the car Marie had felt lost and frightened.

189

Visions of being suddenly driven off at high speed to some out-of-the-way spot and murdered flashed through her mind and it was with great relief she noticed he had parked within shouting distance of her home. As Stephen bent over to kiss her she felt the familiar lurch in her stomach.

"You're shaking," he said, surprise in his voice. "Anyone would think you'd never been out with a fellow before."

Little do you know, Marie thought silently. Trying to let herself relax, she reluctantly kissed him back. When she felt his hands start to fondle her, she shoved against his chest and began fumbling in panic for the door handle.

"All right, all right, no need to get hysterical," he laughed, pulling her back into the car. Putting his hands up in mock surrender, he laughed again, "I get the message; not on the first date, right?"

Nor any other time, mate, Marie thought wildly, but was afraid to make any comment aloud. She just wanted to get away from him to the safety of her home.

"When can I see you again?" he asked, his hands starting to wander again. Clutching at the offending limbs, she stuttered, "I'll send you a picture."

"Oh, very funny. I'm serious, I'd like to see you again."

After a moment's hesitation Marie agreed to meet him after work the following night. She didn't want to see Stephen again but lacked the courage to tell him so while sitting in his car. Formulating a plan in her mind, she refused to allow him to take her to the front door so he wouldn't know which number she lived at. Then tomorrow she would duck out of work early and avoid him.

Once out of the car, Marie fled to her front door, her hand shaking as she tried to find her key. Casting fearful looks over her shoulder in case he had followed her, she managed to get the door open. Inside the warm hallway she sagged against the heavy door and breathed a sigh of relief. Not feeling up to her mother's questions as to whether she had enjoyed herself, she shouted out a greeting to let her parents know she was home and ran quickly up the stairs. Letting herself into her room, she quickly divested herself of her clothes and within minutes she was tucked up in bed.

As she waited for the trembling to leave her body she suddenly saw herself running down the street as if her bum was on fire and started to laugh.

I'll never make a fortune selling my raunchy love stories to the *News of the World*, she thought, still laughing. Feeling the familiar cramps in her stomach, she sat up in bed. "Oh, blast," she cried out loud. Reluctantly she left her warm bed and made her way to the bathroom.

She found out the next day why Pam had been giving her funny looks last night.

"He's married, and he's got two little boys," Pam told her.

Marie greeted this news with heartfelt relief; now she had the perfect excuse not to see Stephen again. That night as she left work he was waiting for her. Before she could lose her nerve she told him that she knew he was married and also told him exactly what she thought of him. She managed to carry off the conversation with the right amount of indignation, but she wasn't prepared for his reaction.

"Look, let me explain; you've got it all wrong. I *was* married but I'm separated now," Stephen said, a pleading note in his voice. What excuse can I make now? Marie thought desperately. Not knowing how to cope with the situation, she got into the car without thinking. She didn't know him very well, but she had the impression he could turn nasty if provoked and that was the last thing she wanted.

As he weaved into the traffic she noticed a peculiar smell. Come to think of it, it had been present last night but she hadn't paid much attention then.

"What's that pong?" she asked, mainly for something to say.

"It's the chemicals I work with, they stick to my clothes," he explained, not looking in the least embarrassed.

"Pick you up at eight," he shouted as he deposited her in the main road outside her house and then shot off before she could refuse.

On the way home Marie had been silly enough to tell him her house number. There was no way she could get out of seeing him now. Cursing herself for her moral cowardice, she let herself into the house, banging the door loudly behind her.

When Stephen turned up that night he was half an hour early, giving Marie no chance of making a last attempt to get out of the house before he arrived. As Peggy showed him into the sitting room, smiling happily and winking behind his back, Patch, their Jack Russell, suddenly jumped up from the hearth and began barking furiously. Both Peggy and Marie shouted at him to stop, neither knowing why the normally happy dog was behaving this way. As Marie dragged him out of the room still barking she gestured vaguely towards a chair, but they were all occupied as the entire family was at home that night.

Once out of the room she grabbed the opportunity to delay being alone with him for as long as possible and stayed in her room fiddling with her hair and make-up. When she knew she couldn't put off the inevitable moment any longer, she reluctantly made her way downstairs. Upon entering the sitting room, she was surprised to find it empty except for Stephen who was sitting alone, his face like thunder. She was about to speak when she noticed the smell again. God, it was terrible, much worse than before. He had said it stuck to his clothes, but it smelled as if he'd bathed in it.

"Sorry I've kept you waiting," she said with a smile she didn't feel. Ushering him out of the room, she told him to go on ahead, pretending she had forgotten something. When he was safely out of the way she stormed into the kitchen where her entire family, including Patch, were huddled around the portable black and white television set.

"What's going on?" she demanded, already knowing the answer.

"Where did you pick him up, the rubbish tip?" asked Ellen, smirking.

"Quiet," Peggy admonished, trying to hide a smile. Marie bridled for a moment, trying to think of an answer, but Ellen was right for once. Shooting a withering look in her sister's direction, she flounced out of the kitchen, only to stop in the hall trying to smother a laugh.

She couldn't leave Stephen waiting any longer, so, trying to wipe the grin off her face, Marie went out into the street and got into the car.

Stephen started the engine without a word and shot off down the road causing her to fall backwards. Straightening up, she glanced timidly at his face, then wished she hadn't. He looked like thunder, but then if she'd walked into a room and everyone had got up and walked out, and was nearly savaged by the family dog as well, she'd be annoyed.

When finally he stopped the car outside a pub she breathed an audible sigh of relief. Still not speaking, she followed him into the saloon, all the while berating herself for being so spineless. "Tell him where to go," she told herself; "tell him you don't have to put up with this silent treatment. You've been looking for an excuse to get rid of him, now's your chance. Pretend you're annoyed with the way he's behaving, as if you don't know why, and storm off; make it convincing; tell him . . ."

"What you drinking?" he asked gruffly.

"Bacardi and coke, please," she replied meekly.

Sitting down next to a young couple, she waited for him to return with the drinks, hoping it might give her some dutch courage. A few minutes later he reappeared and deposited the drinks on the table with a bang. Five minutes later they were on their own, the couple having moved to another table. By this time Marie was trying desperately hard not to laugh, she could tell he wasn't the kind of person to take a joke at his own expense.

"Do your family always walk out of the room when a guest comes in?" The question was flung at her, making her jump.

Racking her brains for something to say, she muttered meekly, "They're shy."

"What, all of them? What about your dog, is he shy too? He nearly had my leg." Leaning forwards, Stephen stared into her startled face. "Is it because I'm married, is that why they all ignored me?" he demanded.

Jumping back from him, she said quickly, "No, I didn't tell them you were married." She could have added that if her mum had known it wouldn't have been just Patch going for his leg, her dad would have bounced him out of the door quicker than you could say knife. She wondered how he could be so ignorant of the smell that surrounded him – surely his wife must have mentioned it over the years? Maybe that was why she had left him? Marie's ever-active mind working, she tried to visualise them both living in the same house: what with his smell and her bowel trouble, she wondered which one of them would cry "uncle" first. Somehow they managed to get through the evening without referring to the incident again. When he dropped her off that night she found herself agreeing to another date.

Four months later she was still going out with Stephen and still trying to find a good excuse to end the relationship. Every time he came into the house Patch went for him.

Some nights one of the family, usually Andy, would suddenly jump up sniffing the air and say loudly, "I can hear Stephen coming."

Even her mum went round with the air freshener after he'd gone.

Marie could understand why he held onto her like grim death. Another fellow would have taken the hint by now and dropped her; she didn't exactly give him the impression she was glad to see him, and now that she was no longer frightened she often said things that would have provoked a row with anyone else, but he seemed to know she was trying to get rid of him and would quickly sidestep an argument.

Then came the opportunity she had been waiting for. Since that first night Pam hadn't said any more about him, but had remained tight-lipped whenever she saw them together. Taking the line of least resistance, Marie had skilfully avoided talking about Stephen while Pam was around, not wanting to risk any unpleasantness.

Looking up from her dinner, she could see Pam watching her. They were in the canteen and Stephen had just stopped by the table to remind her about their date that night – as if she could forget.

Unable to stand the atmosphere any longer, she burst out, "What is it, Pam, what's wrong?"

"You know what's wrong," Pam answered quietly. "I didn't think you'd see him again once you knew he was married, but that's your business; just don't expect me to approve."

"But he's separated, and I don't like him anyway. I just can't find the courage to tell him to get lost," Marie wailed.

Surprise showed clearly on Pam's face as she stared back at Marie. "He isn't separated. Surely you're not daft enough to believe that old chestnut?"

Stunned, Marie leaned back in her chair. She knew Pam was telling the truth and cursed herself for a fool. Surely she should have realised Pam wouldn't have given her the cold shoulder treatment unless there had been a very good reason? And that reason had just walked out the door.

Pushing back her chair, Marie ran from the canteen, ignoring the curious looks she received as she ran past the other diners, long chestnut curls bouncing on her shoulders.

Coming out of the building, she spotted Stephen walking towards the factory.

"Hey!" she shouted. She felt no fear of him now, only anger.

The look of pleasure on his face quickly faded as Marie tore into him. So surprised was he by the onslaught that he didn't utter a word. When at long last Marie ran out of names to call him, she settled for one of the icy looks for which she was famous; a look he'd never seen before. Turning on her heel, she walked away from him, and as she walked her back became straighter, her head higher.

You did it, she told herself proudly. You stood up for yourself. Well done, girl; well done.

# Chapter Sixteen

1973.

"What do you think of my new boots, Nan?" asked Marie proudly, tottering precariously on the four-inch – high platform soles.

May stared in dismay at the atrocious footwear her granddaughter was hovering on. "Holy Mary, if you fall off those, you'll break your neck," she answered in genuine fear. "That's if you don't trip over the hem on those trousers. God in heaven, I've never seen trousers like those before."

Marie walked unsteadily over to a chair, holding onto the kitchen table for support with one hand, while holding up the hem of her new bellbottom trousers with the other. It was a perilous journey and May breathed a sigh of relief when her granddaughter made it safely to a chair and sat down with a bump. Once seated, Marie looked up at her Nan and grinned.

"It's the fashion, Nan – don't you like them?"

"How did you manage to get across the common in those things?" May asked, indicating the boots with a nod of her head.

"Oh, I splashed out on a taxi."

Knowing from past experience that nothing she could say would make Marie change her taste in clothes, May walked over to the sink and began to fill the kettle. She could only hope the new fashion would die a quick death, before her granddaughter did.

"Teresa tells me you haven't been down for a while." Plugging the kettle in, she turned to face Marie. "Not that she's complaining, she just wondered how you were."

For a moment Marie felt a pang of guilt. She hadn't even phoned her aunt for some weeks.

"I'll phone her as soon as I get home," she promised. "Have you seen Tommy lately?"

For an answer May banged down the cups she had got out of the cupboard.

"That one," she sniffed. "No I haven't, begod; he comes and goes as he likes, with never a thought for his poor old mother."

"Now, Nan, you know that's not true," Marie protested, jumping to her uncle's defence. When she'd finished her tea, she heaved herself to her feet, still clutching the table for support.

"I'll see you next weekend," she said, bending over May to kiss her proferred cheek. "Take care, Nan."

May watched from the window as Marie wobbled off down the road and crossed herself.

"Please, God, don't let her come across any holes in the pavement."


"What do you fancy doing tonight?"

"I don't mind – where do you want to go?"

"Are you going out like that?" Anne asked innocently.

"Don't you start," Marie said a little crossly. "Everybody's wearing the same gear, why pick on me?"

Anne started to chuckle quietly and within seconds Marie had joined in the laughter.

"Anyway," Marie said, wiping her eyes, "I'm nearly as tall as you now." Ever since they had started going out together they had suffered taunts of "Wotcha, Mutt and Jeff" on account of the difference in their respective heights, Marie being just under five foot and Anne towering over her at five foot nine.

"Just as well I didn't get a pair of them then, I wouldn't be able to see where I was going for the clouds."

Once again the friends went off into gales of laughter.


"Hello, girls, fancy some company?"

Marie and Anne eyed the blond, curly haired young man suspiciously. They had been walking down Bethnal Green

Road when he had suddenly crossed over and accosted them, leaving his mates on the other side of the road. Unperturbed by the taunts of his friends, he continued to walk along beside them.

Marie left Anne to do the talking, just adding a few words now and then. She still felt a bit guilty about the way she had stopped seeing her while she'd been going out with Stephen. Just thinking of him made her shudder; she'd never get caught like that again.

They soon arrived in Wick Road and came to a halt when they reached the turning that Anne normally took to reach her home. As the three of them stood chatting Marie wondered idly which one of them he would go with when they went their separate ways.

"Goodnight then," Anne moved off, "I'll see you tomorrow."

"Yes, okay, about eight," Marie replied, keeping an eye on the young man. After a moment's hesitation he waved to Anne and started to walk alongside Marie. Bloody hell, she thought, two boyfriends in a year, things must be looking up. He became much quieter as they neared her home; he'd definitely had a few drinks and now it was obvious he had sobered up. Looking at him out of the corner of her eye, she wondered if he was now having second thoughts about leaving his mates and walking miles out of his way. He'd told them he lived in Bethnal Green.

"Well, this is where I live," she said lightly, coming to a stop in front of her door. "Would you like to come in for a cup of coffee?" she asked hopefully.

Shaking his head, he answered, "No, thanks, I'd better be making my way home."

"Well," thought Marie, "that one was short lived."

"To tell the truth, I feel a bit sick," he added. Marie looked at him again; he did look a bit white. She hoped he wasn't going to throw up outside her front door. With a great deal of willpower he smiled and said, "If I hadn't had so much to drink I wouldn't have had the nerve to chat you up. I wouldn't say boo to a goose normally. By the way my name's Stuart, what's yours?"

When he said goodnight to her a few minutes later she had a date with him for Sunday.

They continued seeing each other for the next three months and, unlike Stephen, there was no exodus when he walked into the room. The person he got on best with was Andy, for they shared a common interest: betting. Andy was now working at Hackney dog track, and he was forever giving Stuart tips, none of which unfortunately ever came up, but still Stuart kept putting money on the dogs and horses that Andy recommended. It was a happy time for Marie with just one worry at the back of her mind. She was going to Malta for a month in September with Anne and Vicky. She had been going with Anne, but Vicky, just out of school, had pleaded to go with them. Peggy had agreed to let her go, with misgivings because of her age, but she was such a good kid that Marie had had little trouble in persuading Peggy to let her go with them. They were all looking forward to their holiday, but Marie wasn't sure if Stuart would be here when she returned home.

They arrived back in England in mid-October to be greeted by torrential rain. Struggling with their luggage, they had found a taxi and made their way home, tired and weary after their journey. Peggy greeted them at the door, anxious to hear how they had enjoyed their holiday, but seeing the sombre faces before her, she made them all a cup of tea and packed them off to bed. Ellen was staying at a friend's house so Anne slept in her bed.

When Peggy passed their door before going to bed she wasn't surprised to hear sobbing coming from the other side. Obviously they weren't pleased to be back home, she thought, a wry smile twisting her lips. Shrugging her shoulders, she made her way to her own bedroom, thinking how different things were now to when she was a girl. To go off to a foreign country at their ages would have been unthinkable. Looking once more at the closed door, she thought, Lucky buggers.

*

Much to Marie's surprise Stuart turned up on the doorstep the very same night. Such was her nature she didn't let on how glad she was to see him, but deep down she sighed with relief. Although she hadn't wanted to lose him, the thought of giving up her holiday hadn't crossed her mind.

Two weeks later he didn't show up. They had arranged to go to the pictures and he was supposed to be at her house by seven. At eight-thirty Marie took her coat off and retreated to her bedroom without a word, ignoring the look of pity on her mother's face. Once inside her room she sat on her bed clenching and unclenching her fists. Blinking back the tears that threatened to flow, she stared sightlessly in front of her. Another girl with more confidence would have phoned him to find out if anything was wrong, but not Marie. She wouldn't take the chance of being fobbed off with some excuse by his mum, she couldn't stand the humiliation. She'd rather pretend she didn't care and let it go. Not able to face the inquisitive eyes downstairs, Marie slowly undressed and got into bed. She lay there for hours, not sleeping, hoping the phone would ring and her mum would come running up the stairs calling, "Marie, it's Stuart."

When it got to eleven she finally gave up all hope and turned her head into the pillow.

I don't care, she told herself fiercely. *I don't care.* Pulling the blankets up over her head, she sobbed herself to sleep.

The next few weeks Marie seemed to be going mad. Every night she went out she came home with a different fellow, hoping to forget Stuart, but it was no good. At first Anne had been sorry for her, until she found out that Marie hadn't even phoned him to find out if he was all right.

"What if he was genuinely ill?" she asked her. "He'll think you didn't care enough to find out."

Choking back the tears, Marie looked at Anne before answering, "I couldn't; at least this way I'll still have my pride."

Anne looked at her in amazement. "Pride; sod your pride. You haven't stopped crying since he left. Look," she added, putting her hand on Marie's arm, "I'll phone him shall I? I could pretend you'd been ill and that's why you haven't called to see what happened to him that night."

Pushing Anne's hand away gently, Marie shook her head. "No, leave it, Anne, if he'd thought anything of me, he'd have got in touch by now."

"But that works both ways, and if . . ." Anne broke off what she'd been about to say. Marie had turned away from her. The matter was closed.

It had been nearly a month now since Stuart had given her the push. Standing in the pub, she kept looking round nonchalantly, hoping for a glimpse of him. So preoccupied was she, she failed to notice the two lads making their way towards them.

"Hey up," Anne nudged her gently in the ribs.

"Fancy a drink, girls?"

As Anne accepted for both of them Marie couldn't help but be amazed. She'd been chatted up more times during the last few weeks than she'd ever been in her previous twenty-five years, maybe because she wasn't bothered. The evening over, the four of them stood on the pavement stamping their feet in the cold night air. In the distance Susy Quatro could be heard belting out "Can the Can."

"Someone's having a party," remarked the man standing next to her.

Marie looked at him properly for the first time. He was what her mum would have described as tall, dark and handsome. Well, he was in this light.

"Can I take you home?" he asked politely.

Resisting the impulse to enquire as to whether his mother would mind, she smiled and nodded with a willingness she didn't feel.

Her spirits were lifted, however, by his next words, "I'm afraid I can't offer you all a lift; my transport's very small, so I can only take one passenger."

Anne and her date walked off, chatting as if they'd known each other years. As Marie waited patiently for the sound of a revved-up sports car approaching, she heard her name being called. She looked over of where the voice was coming from. "Oh, no, I don't believe it," she whispered under her breath at the sight of the man she'd just met cycling towards her on a very battered pushbike.

"Come on," he shouted, "do you want a lift or not?"

Trying not to laugh, she crossed the road, planning to tell him there was no way she was getting on the handlebars of a pushbike.

As Marie opened her mouth to speak she looked into his face. It was deadpan, then she noticed his shoulders shaking with suppressed laughter.

"Your face," he spluttered, "I wish I had a camera."

Joining in with his laughter, she let him help her onto the handlebars, screeching with fear as they careered off down the road.

There followed a journey she would never forget. They were only doing three miles an hour, but she kept her eyes shut tight the whole time. She could feel the wind throwing them into the side of the road as cars and buses whizzed past them. When she felt him stop Marie breathed a sigh of relief. Then she heard the unmistakable laughter. It was Anne. Opening her eyes, she saw they were nowhere near her road. In fact, although Anne and her date had left the pub five minutes after them, they had made faster progress than the bike had.

"That's my lot," she declared, getting off the bike. "I'll walk the rest of the way; it'll be quicker."

Smiling, he pulled the bike onto the pavement and they began to walk the rest of the way. Marie found talking to John was easy.

"Come on, you two!" Anne shouted as she waited at the turnoff to her house. While the two men made arrangements to meet up later, Anne pulled her to one side.

"Thought he had a sports car, didn't you?" she demanded, a grin nearly splitting her face.

"No, I didn't," Marie protested.

"Yes you did, I saw the look on your face. Like a cat that got the cream."

Any further talk was stopped by the two men approaching. After the usual goodbyes, the couples parted, each going their different ways. The walk home was short and enjoyable as John kept her amused with jokes and anecdotes. Marie found she was disappointed when they reached her front door.

They had just settled themselves on the doorstep when the door was flung open.

"I want a word with you," Bill said, his usually placid face angry. Startled, Marie followed her dad into the hallway, casting a bewildered look over her shoulder at John.

"What's the matter, dad?" she asked, wondering what on earth could have happened to put her dad in such a mood.

"He's not coming in here," Bill started, "I've lost track of the men you've brought home these last weeks. Ah, darling," he continued softly now as he looked at his daughter's downcast face, "go and tell that fellow to go home. You don't want to be bringing home every Tom, Dick and Harry, you'll be getting yourself a bad name."

Marie couldn't believe her ears. Her dad thought she was turning into a tramp. Marie, of all people, it was laughable.

Turning away, she made her way back to the porch where John was waiting patiently. She had half hoped he'd be gone. The evening was ruined now, and she'd been having such a good time.

"Pick a bad night, did I?" he enquired, no sign of rancour on his face.

"You could say that," she answered miserably.

"Come on," he said, putting an arm round her shoulders, "let's go for a walk."

They walked the streets for over an hour, his humour making Marie laugh again. When they finally stopped at the end of her street he put his arms around her.

Drawing her close, he whispered, "Can I see you to-morrow?"

Happily Marie nodded her head in agreement. As he bent his head to kiss her he stopped and drew back. His face serious now, he said, "Did you notice I've got a glass eye?"

Clapping her hand over her mouth, Marie went off into peals of laughter. She didn't notice him backing away from her until moments later. As she straightened up her bent body wiping the tears of mirth from her eyes, she saw him striding away, his back stiff with fury. Unable to speak for a moment, she watched him climb onto his bike. He glared at her for what seemed an eternity then he pedalled furiously off down the road. Marie watched him go, her mouth opening and closing in surprise.

"Oh, hell," she exclaimed in horror as she realised what had happened. "He really *did* have a glass eye."

# Chapter Seventeen

Peggy looked at her watch for the fourth time in as many minutes.

"Where the bloody hell are they?" she muttered under her breath. She was waiting for a delivery of lino that she'd ordered weeks ago and if she had to wait much longer she would be late for work. Pulling back the net curtains, she looked out of the kitchen window, willing the delivery men to appear. The street was empty.

Sighing heavily, she once again looked at her watch, a present from Bill last Christmas. Not that he had bought it himself, he had probably given the money to one of the girls to buy it. Still, it was the thought that counted, as the saying went.

She could still remember the very first watch she had owned. As a young girl of nineteen, she had saved as much money out of her meagre wages as she could afford and after several months had purchased a cheap second-hand wristwatch.

When Marie had proudly shown the watch to her Aunt Bridie, her aunt had exclaimed, "Oh, Peggy, it's lovely. I've always wanted one myself." She'd then added, "And they're very handy for telling the time."

Peggy smiled at the memory. Just then the doorbell rang and she hurried to answer it, the smile slipping from her face. Opening the front door, she gestured to the two men to bring the roll of lino into the hall. With comparative ease the men dumped the lino on the floor then stood expectantly looking at her.

For a moment she was puzzled then realisation dawned and her temper flared. "If it's a tip you're waiting for, I'll give you one," she said, glowering at them. "Late Delivery in the two-thirty."

Slamming the door after them, Peggy took a quick glance at the lino as she hurriedly put on her coat. Walking into the kitchen, she checked that the note she had left for Bill was in a place where he couldn't miss it, then left the house and hurried down to the bus stop.

Waiting for the bus that would take her to the bank where she worked as a silver waitress, her mind switched from the matter of the lino to Marie. That child of hers was always in her mind one way or another, although she was no longer a child. Peggy had hoped she'd make a go of it with Stuart, but it had come to nothing and, after a few months of staying out till all hours and bringing home different chaps every week, she had suddenly stopped going out at all. She now spent the evenings huddled round the fire, only moving when it was time to go to bed.

Peggy knew that Marie was still hurting inside over Stuart but she would never admit it, and Peggy knew better than to try to talk to her about it. Marie never confided in her and, although Peggy had tried on many occasions to talk to her, Marie had always rebuffed her, sometimes cruelly.

Thinking back to the first time Marie had been waiting for Stuart to call, Peggy felt her eyes smarting at the memory. She had shown him into the sitting room and had called up the stairs to tell Marie he had arrived. Then on a sudden impulse she had run up the stairs smiling happily, intending to sit on Marie's bed while she finished getting ready, maybe have a chat and a laugh. Marie had been coming out of the bathroom, and when she'd seen Peggy coming up the stairs she'd walked to her room and deliberately shut the door, practically in her mother's face.

The woman behind her in the queue pushed against her, shaking her out of her thoughts. Blinking back the tears, Peggy walked forward to await the approaching bus. She'd been making excuses for Marie's behaviour all her life, telling herself that she behaved the way she did because she was unhappy and often in pain, but her daughter's cruelty towards her was getting her down and she didn't know how much more of it she could take.

*

Bill arrived home at one and read the note Peggy had left him. His only half day off in three months and she had found work for him. Woman must think I'm an idiot, he thought as he prepared himself some lunch. Two hours later he stood back and admired his handiwork. Walking across the newly laid lino, he filled the kettle then set out a cup and saucer for a much-needed cup of tea. Twenty minutes later he stood looking in dismay at the lino he had left over for the bathroom; there wasn't enough. Maybe she hadn't ordered enough, or maybe the shop had got the order wrong. Sighing deeply; he sat down on the kitchen chair. Whoever was at fault, he would get the blame; he always did. Lighting up a cigarette, he waited gloomily for his wife to come home.

"Now look, woman, don't start," Bill protested vainly.

Peggy was in full swing, her voice drowning out Bill's excuses. She had gone for him the moment she had discovered the shortage of lino, immediately blaming him for the discrepancy.

As she stopped for breath for a moment, Bill saw his chance and said quickly, "I've done the kitchen, you might at least give me credit for that."

Looking down at the newly laid lino, Peggy had to admit he'd done a good job. But why wasn't there enough to cover the bathroom? She'd ordered enough, she was sure of that.

"All right," she conceded grudgingly. "I'll have a look at what's left and get on to the firm in the morning." Bill heaved a sigh of relief; he'd thought she would go on all night.

"Where is the bit that's left over?" she asked as she set about preparing the dinner. "They're bound to want to measure it before admitting they didn't send enough."

"It's still upstairs in the bathroom," replied Bill, happily relieved the blame had been shifted from his back.

"All right, I'll see to it after dinner." Casting one more suspicious look in his direction, she continued to peel the potatoes.

"Bill, Bill!" Peggy's voice carried down into the sitting room. "You bloody idiot, come up here."

Sitting in his chair, Bill winced as he heard Peggy's strident voice. He'd had a sinking feeling that he had somehow made a mistake with the lino; he didn't know how, but by the sound of his wife's voice, he was about to find out. The sound of something heavy being dragged down the stairs brought him to his feet. As he ventured out into the hall he was followed by Bobby, Marie, Ellen and Vicky, all eager to see what was going on. Out in the passage Peggy stood red-faced with anger, holding up what was left of the lino.

"Look at it," she spluttered in his face, "I don't believe it, I just don't believe it!"

Bill couldn't see what she was caterwauling about, but apparently his children did, for they were falling about with laughter.

"Oh, Dad," Bobby said, laughing loudly.

Bill looked from his son's laughing face to his wife's angry one and started to get annoyed. Marie and Bobby were by now holding onto each other for support. They stared at the offending piece of lino their mother was holding onto grimly, and saw immediately what their dad had done. Instead of measuring out the amount for the kitchen, he had instead cut a large square from the middle, leaving only the edging remaining.

"It's all very well for you to laugh," Peggy shouted. "I try to make the place look nice and what thanks do I get for it? Well no more – that old lino can stay in the bathroom till hell freezes over. I'm not chucking good money after bad." Turning her back on her family, she marched into the kitchen, still dragging the mangled piece of lino behind her.

Half an hour later, thinking it was safe to go into the kitchen, Bill poked his head around the door and said tentatively, "Coronation Streets' on, love."

Casting a look upon him that should have turned him to stone, Peggy swept past him, her head held high, two small red spots on her cheeks telling him that the storm was by no means over.

For the next half-hour there was blissful silence as the family sat together watching *The Street*.

As soon as it finished, however, Peggy started again. "I don't know what to say," she began, "I'm speechless, words fail me."

And so it went on. The children needed no telling to get to bed that night; they were only too thankful to escape the sound of their mother's voice. Bill was not so fortunate. For a person who was lost for words, he reflected wryly, his wife was doing remarkably well. Upstairs Marie was getting ready to go round to Mary's for her weekly Wednesday visit. Tonight especially, she was glad to get out of the house.

Arguments in their house were very rare and never violent. They usually followed a pattern similar to the one being enacted out down below. Her mother went on and her dad listened in patient silence, getting a word in when he could.

Getting into the coat, pausing outside the sitting room door, she could hear her mum going on. Changing her mind about saying goodnight, she tiptoed quietly out of the house.

It was two weeks after the lino incident when another argument shattered the peace, and this time it did come to blows. Marie had met a fellow called Laurie at the Tottenham Royal a few days previously and he had taken her out on the following Saturday night. Tonight was Tuesday and she was waiting for him to come round; they were going to the pictures. As she looked in her wardrobe for something to wear she decided against the blue and black wrapover skirt and picked instead a pair of wide, bellbottomed beige trousers.

Ellen put her head round the sitting room door and was surprised to see the chair by the fire empty. This chair was normally occupied by Marie roasting her legs, thus preventing anyone else from getting any warmth.

When anyone complained Peggy would say, "Now you know your sister's not well, she needs the heat."

Never mind if the rest of them froze to death, as long as Marie was warm, Ellen thought, making a "humphh" sound to the empty room.

"Where's old corn beef legs?" she asked, wandering into the kitchen. Peggy looked up from the evening paper.

"Who?" she asked, a bewildered look on her face.

"Marie," Ellen explained. "She's not in her usual place by the fire. She's not crossed her legs too quick and set herself alight, has she?"

Trying to suppress a smile, Peggy turned on her daughter. "Why don't you try to get on with Marie?" she pleaded. "You are sisters, after all. I hate to hear you two always snapping at each other."

Shrugging her shoulders, Ellen decided to drop the subject. She couldn't answer her mum's question because she didn't know the answer. She and Marie had never got on and she couldn't see things changing at this late date. Hearing the object of her thoughts coming down the stairs, she walked over to the small formica table and sat down. Picking up the paper that Peggy had put down, she began to read.

Marie had just reached the bottom of the stairs when the front doorbell rang. She quickly opened the door with one hand while grabbing her coat off the banisters with the other, trying to leave the house before anyone came out to give him the once-over.

Her hopes were dashed by Peggy coming out of the kitchen.

"Come in, love," she said, eagerly drawing the young man into the hallway. Gritting her teeth, Marie struggled with her coat. Although Laurie was a nice enough bloke, she didn't intend to see him any more after tonight so she didn't see the point in introducing him to the family. He had barely got one foot into the house when she was pushing him out again, but not before Ellen had joined Peggy.

Ignoring her sister, Marie said a short, "See you later," to her mother, before following Laurie out into the street.

It was as she shut the door behind her that she heard Ellen remark, "Makes a change for her to bring someone decent home. Bet he doesn't last long." Peggy's answer was lost by the sound of the door slamming.

Marie walked alongside the bemused Laurie, her face like thunder at her sister's remark. But it wasn't only Ellen she was mad at. Marie knew that right now her mother would be on the phone to Teresa or one of the family to tell them Marie had a date as if it were a great occasion. She never acted like this when Ellen brought someone home, but then Ellen was young and pretty and – more important – healthy; she could take her pick of boyfriends. There was no danger of her being left on the shelf.

It was just as well she had decided not to see Laurie any more. After putting up with her miserable face all night, he had quickly seen her to the door and made a hasty retreat.

Letting herself in with her door key, Marie looked at her watch. It was only ten o'clock, it had hardly been worth while going out. Shouting out that she was home, she went into the kitchen to make herself a cup of tea and wait for Bobby to come home.

"You're home early." Vicky was standing in the doorway dressed for bed. "You making tea?" she asked, coming into the room.

Marie took a second cup from the cupboard, talking as she did so. She was glad Vicky had joined her, for she felt like company. A short time later Peggy came into the room.

Although she was dying to know why Marie was home so early she stopped herself from asking any questions, never quite sure how her daughter would react to probing. She was more than a little surprised when Marie volunteered the information without any prompting. Peggy was only too pleased to be included in the conversation, remembering the countless times Marie had stopped talking when she'd entered the room. Not for the first time, Peggy wondered why she was so soft with her eldest daughter. She wasn't a weak woman and of late she had felt her patience beginning to stretch, frequently just stopping herself from actually hitting Marie. She hoped it would never come to that.

Just at that moment Ellen walked into the room and strolled over to the teapot. Lifting it up to see if there was any left, she remarked casually, "Another one bitten the dust? Why don't you try Battersea?"

Peggy was about to make a sharp rebuke when Marie answered coolly, "I think Battersea would suit you better; you'd be at home with the other bitches."

Amazed at her daring, Marie tried to sidle past her sister before her words had sunk in, but she was too late.

As she passed her, Ellen grabbed hold of Marie's hair and pulled fiercely, screaming, "Take that back! You say sorry, or else!"

Desperately trying to free her hair from her sister's grip, Marie twisted round, grabbing hold of Ellen's neck.

"You asked for it, you cow!" she screamed back.

The shock at seeing her daughters fighting had frozen Peggy to the spot. Nothing like this had ever happened before. Then as if a hand had been shoved in her back she bounded out of her chair and tried to separate the two girls.

"Vicky, come and help me!" she cried, her voice near breaking. "Oh God, where's your father? Go and get him, quick!" she barked at the startled Vicky who had been enjoying the spectacle.

Running into the sitting room, Vicky shouted at Andy who was sitting sprawled in front of the television. "Quick, Andy, come and help Mum; Marie and Ellen are fighting."

A grin lighting up his face, Andy rushed past Vicky straight into the fracas. As Peggy pulled Ellen's hands free from Marie's hair, Andy easily pulled Marie's hands from Ellen's throat, where they hadn't been doing much damage anyway.

Summoning all her strength, Peggy managed to pull the still screaming Ellen from the room.

Marie watched with relief as Ellen was dragged out of the kitchen and down the hallway. Getting her breath back, she dashed after her shouting, "Think yourself lucky Mum saved you or you'd have got a good hiding". Ellen's answer was lost as Peggy bundled her upstairs.

Readjusting her jumper, Marie threw back her shoulders and walked unsteadily back into the kitchen. Her legs threatening to give way any moment, she sank down gratefully into the nearest chair. Aware of Andy's presence, she looked up into his grinning face. His eyes bright with excitement, he looked a younger version of Bobby.

"You didn't have to barge in to save Ellen, she deserved a hiding."

The laugh that erupted from Andy's throat made her jump. "She'd have killed you if me and Mum hadn't pulled her off you."

About to make a strong denial Marie looked up at him and laughed, "Yeah, I know."


It was Christmas Eve. Marie had risen early for work to get ready for the Christmas party. Peering into her wardrobe, she decided there was nothing there she wanted to wear and wondered if she dare ask Ellen for something of hers to borrow. The fight had long since been forgotten. A knock at her door caused her to grab her dressing gown to her partly-dressed body.

Vicky's head poked round the door, her freckly face smiling as always. "You got a party at your place?" she enquired, pushing her long hair out of her sleepy eyes.

"Yes, have you?" Marie went back to rummaging round in the wardrobe. Damn, there was nothing suitable at all. A thought suddenly struck her. Hopefully she turned to Vicky and, minutes later, she was dressed in a midi skirt with matching blue top that Vicky had bought the previous weekend. Brushing out her long chestnut hair, she quickly donned her new coat and made her way down the stairs. Peggy was getting the milk in from the doorstep as Marie passed her.

"Have a nice time, love," she said, smiling. Noticing the furtive way Marie slipped her left hand into her pocket, the smile slipped from Peggy's face.

A few years previously, Marie had gone through a phase of wearing cheap imitation wedding rings she'd bought from Woolworth's. She'd only worn them when she thought no one could see them, but Peggy had known. In the intervening years Marie had come out of her shell. Going to Malta had been the first step, since then she'd been going out regularly with Anne and, just lately, Vicky. The nights out with Bobby had gradually diminished as his relationship with Pauline had grown stronger.

As she watched Marie walk away from her Peggy sighed. She hoped the reappearance of the wedding ring didn't mean Marie was returning to her old ways. Going into the kitchen, Peggy set about preparing the children's breakfast, wondering if the "wedding ring" had anything to do with Ellen's forthcoming wedding. She reflected that it would be demoralising to any girl if her sister, who was eight years younger, should be getting married, while she herself didn't even have a steady boyfriend, but in Marie's case the effect of such a situation would be twice as hard to stomach. Then there was Bobby. He hadn't revealed any wedding plans yet, but Peggy guessed he was biding his time, waiting for Ellen's wedding to be over before announcing his news. He wouldn't want to steal his sister's thunder.

Setting the cereal bowls on the table, Peggy shook her head, her face worried. No, it wasn't Ellen's wedding Marie was bothered about, it was Bobby's she was dreading. If only she could have made friends with Pauline it would have softened the blow, but the two girls didn't get on, and it didn't seem as if they ever would.

Sitting on the bus on her way to work, Marie glanced at her "wedding ring". Tears stung her eyes. It was probably the only one she would ever get. And yet she didn't really want to get married, not even to Stuart whom she thought she'd loved. She had asked herself if she would want to spend the rest of her days with him, and after much soul-searching the answer had been no. She knew plenty of girls who had got married, rather than face the prospect of being left on the shelf, and were now paying the price of a loveless marriage. She would rather have her fake ring than be trapped in a marriage with someone she didn't love. Her friends were welcome to their real wedding rings; they hadn't brought them any happiness.

Twisting the ring around her finger, she wondered, not for the first time, why it gave her such a feeling of security. It was the same way she used to feel when she was out with Bobby and his friends, a feeling of belonging. But those days were gone now. He would be coming in any day now to tell them all he was getting married to Pauline, and then she knew she would hardly ever see him again. If only she and Pauline had become friends it wouldn't have mattered to her so much. She felt the tears prick her eyes again as her stop came into view. Before she got off the bus, she slipped the ring into her pocket and, as she looked at her naked finger, she silently said goodbye to her "pretend boyfriend".

# Chapter Eighteen

1974.

As Marie watched Vicky apply the thick black eyeliner she wondered, not for the first time, where the years were going. Vicky was now sixteen and at the moment she looked as if she'd just gone ten rounds with Henry Cooper and lost. Lucky Mum was out.

"You look like a panda," Marie remarked casually.

"It's none of your business," came the pert reply.

What a difference a year could make, Marie thought sadly. Vicky used to be such a quiet shy girl, but since her holiday in Malta she had changed beyond recognition. With her thick make-up and fashionable clothes she looked older than Marie herself did.

A minute later as they heard Peggy's voice in the hallway, Marie saw the child briefly reappear as Vicky cast a startled glance at the door, then quickly grabbed up the morning paper and ran out of the room holding it to her face before Peggy could see the plastered on make-up and drag her to the sink to wash it off.

"She was in a hurry," Peggy said coming into the kitchen carrying the usual heavy load of Saturday shopping.

Jimmy came in behind her, staggering under the weight of two full carrier bags. He was now coming up for fourteen and he hadn't changed one iota. In the intervening years since his fall from the slide when they'd thought they'd lost him, he had had many accidents. The worst had been last year when he'd fallen off a cliff while on holiday with the scouts. A helicopter had rescued him. The picture of him being lifted off the face of the mountain on a stretcher had been plastered on the front page of the *Hackney Gazette*. He had been very proud of that.

"Here you are, Mum," he said, still puffing. "Can I have my, pocket money now please?"

Holding out a dirty hand, he waited patiently as Peggy searched in her purse for some change, his face splitting into a huge grin as the five pence piece was deposited in his palm.

"Where've you been?" enquired Marie, noticing a shiny plastic bag among the bags of groceries.

"Down Walthamstow Market. Want to see what I've bought for the wedding?" Peggy asked, already lifting out a pale blue suit for Marie's inspection.

"It's lovely, Mum. I suppose I'd better start thinking about getting an outfit myself."

A startled look came into Peggy's eyes. "Do you want me to go with you?" she asked hopefully.

Marie saw the look on her mother's alarmed face and burst out laughing. "Don't worry, I shall buy something discreet," she said, her voice adopting a refined twang. Still laughing, she left the kitchen and made her way to her bedroom. Since Christmas Eve when she'd crept into bed with Ellen she had moved into the large bedroom on a permanent basis. Patti had jumped at the chance of a room to herself and so they had swapped over bedrooms. At the moment she shared the double bed with Vicky, but as soon as Ellen was married Peggy had promised to give them money towards buying separate beds. The double bed would be going into the boys' room. Everything was being changed round.

Lying down on the double bed, Marie put her hands behind her head and closed her eyes. She was surprised at how calm she felt. Gone was the jealousy surrounding Ellen's wedding. In fact she didn't think she'd ever been jealous, just a bit put out at all the attention Ellen had been receiving these last few months.

Even the prospect of Bobby getting married didn't seem to frighten her as much as it had done previously. Oh, she would undoubtedly miss him, there was no question of that, but a quiet kind of acceptance had crept over Marie of late. The pains that normally racked her body had been stilled for some time now with the aid of new drugs, she no longer feared going out, and she felt completely at ease in the company of men.

She didn't know when this transformation had come about, but she mourned the wasted years spent in fear and hiding from the outside world. She was twenty-six years of age, her teens long gone, the painful memory of them fading to a dim blur as if seen through the eyes of a stranger. She could never recapture what might have been, but she could start living now, go forward and try not to look back. She was lucky, she had a good friend in Anne, and a new friend in her young sister, Vicky. With their help she would build a new life for herself.

Ellen's wedding was now only a few weeks away and Marie and Vicky were in a boutique in Mare Street looking for new outfits.

"What do you think?" asked Marie, holding up a black trouser suit. Vicky carefully looked at the smart two piece suit, surprised and more than a little relieved that Marie had chosen something conservative. She'd half expected her to opt for a gold lamé dress with diamanté earrings.

"Yes, very smart. I might get a trouser suit myself," Vicky replied, giving the suit a closer look.

"I think I'll get a hat to go with it."

Vicky groaned. She thought it had been too good to be true. Watching her sister's dismayed face, Marie's face broke into a huge grin.

"Tell you what, I'll let you pick one out for me. Can't say fairer than that, can I?"

Not trusting Marie to be let loose in a milliner's by herself, Vicky weakly agreed.

An hour later they were sitting in the Wimpy bar having a much-needed cup of tea when a young man with black curly hair sat himself down uninvited beside Vicky.

"Hello, Vicky, remember me? I'm Sheila's brother," he said smiling, his hand outstretched.

The retort that had sprung to Vicky's lips vanished as she recognised her friend's brother. Introducing him to Marie, they all began to talk at once.

"Excuse me a minute," Vicky said, getting up from her chair, "I'm just going to the loo."

Aware of the sudden uncomfortable silence, Marie tried to put the young man at his ease.

"She won't be long. I'll make myself scarce when she comes back."

She watched with amusement as his face turned a dull red.

Feeling very much a woman of the world with her new-found confidence, she raised her cup to her lips only to be caught by a bout of coughing. Her tea slopped into the saucer as she tried to steady the cup in her hand. When she felt the sneeze coming she was unprepared for it and watched with horror at the huge bubble that appeared from her nostril. Mortified, she jumped to her feet, and with one last look at Paul's stunned face she ran out of the Wimpy bar. She didn't cease running until she was half way down Morning Lane, then she stopped and leaned against a wall, holding her stomach and trying to wipe away the tears of laughter that coursed down her face.

"Why me, God?" she asked herself. "Why is it always me?"

"What happened to you?" Vicky demanded, bursting into the bedroom.

"Didn't that fellow Paul tell you?" Marie asked, surprised.

"No, he just said you felt ill and you'd see me at home. Now, what really happened?" she repeated as she flopped down on the bed beside her sister.

As Marie recounted what had happened, Vicky sat staring at her, her mouth open in disbelief. Then her face crumpled, and they both fell about on the bed, laughing fit to burst. When they finally composed themselves they sat up, wiping their streaming eyes. Reaching down to the floor, Vicky picked up the carrier bags Marie had left behind in her mad flight.

"There's all your gear. Lucky Paul spotted them. I thought you'd taken them with you. I'll have to leave my outfit till next week now, I don't fancy going back up Mare Street today."

Feeling a bit sick with so much laughing, Marie stood up and took the trouser suit from the bag.

Then taking a cream silk blouse from another bag, she put the complete outfit on.

"What do you reckon?" she asked, turning this way and that, trying to get a better view. Privately Vicky thought it was the best outfit she'd ever seen Marie in. It was normal. She still had her reservations about the fawn Al Capone type hat but refrained from comment. Marie looked at herself in the mirror and for a change was pleased with what she saw. Noticing Vicky's eyes placed firmly on the hat, she turned to face her.

"Well, out with it. You don't like the hat, do you?"

The smirk that came to Vicky's lips was answer in itself.

"Listen, miss," Marie said, pulling the brim of the hat over her eyes, "it wasn't so long ago, you were going around with boot polish plastered over your eyes, so don't criticise my taste in clothes."

"That was just a phase I was going through, it didn't last long. Yours has been going on for twenty-odd years."

Pulling the fawn hat from her head, Marie lobbed it at her sister.

"You didn't tell me what that fellow wanted; apart from the obvious," Marie said taking off her new finery. She hoped Vicky wasn't going to see him again. After what had happened she wouldn't be able to face him. Vicky got up from the bed and walked to the door.

"He asked me to a party next Saturday. I said yes and told him I'd bring you along for his friend; all right?"

Before Marie could answer, Vicky had gone. Sinking down onto the bed, Marie's mind conjured up the scene in the Wimpy. She couldn't face him, not after what had happened. She just couldn't.

"God, I feel so humiliated," Marie groaned as she walked side by side with Vicky. She had tried to get out of going by asking Anne to take her place, but Anne was already going out with a friend from work, and Marie didn't want to let Vicky down. In no time at all they were standing outside the house where the party was taking place. By this time Marie was visibly shaking. If only she hadn't sneezed and coughed at the same time. It had never happened before. She could still see the huge bubble in front of her face and winced. Maybe they won't turn up, she thought hopefully, then she remembered the look on Paul's face as he'd stared at Vicky. He'd turn up. With shoulders slumped she followed Vicky into the house.

The party was already in full swing and after a quick look round to see if Paul and his friend had arrived the two girls headed for the makeshift bar. Quickly downing a double Bacardi and coke, Marie immediately felt better. As she was leaning over the bar to ask for a refill, Vicky's elbow nudged her sharply, almost causing her to drop her glass.

"Here they are."

As the two men made their way through the crowd towards them Marie thought wryly that her date wasn't exactly straining at the leash to get at her. In fact he looked downright miserable. It was obvious he had been roped into this date, as she had.

"Hello, girls," Paul said nervously. "This is Roy," he added, introducing a tall, well-built man with dark blond hair worn long in the latest fashion. Marie looked at him carefully, taking in the flared beige trousers and the dark green jacket, then she raised her gaze and found herself staring into a pair of light blue eyes – kind eyes that shifted away from her when he became aware that she was appraising him.

Then with a curt nod to her and Vicky he hurried away to the bar, calling over his shoulder, "I'll get the drinks in, Paul, you wait there."

Marie felt her stomach give a sharp kick at the obvious rejection, then she shrugged her shoulders. A few years ago such an occurrence would have demoralised her; now it just made her feel uncomfortable. Nothing a few more drinks couldn't rectify, she told herself, her spirits lifting. Turning to Vicky, she gave her the thumbs down, then they both started to giggle.

Roy Ellis stood waiting to be served. He felt awkward and angry with his friend. He had been watching television when Paul had knocked and practically demanded that he accompany him to this party. His first impression of his date had been of a small girl, about twenty with long chestnut hair, dressed in a white silky top with matching jacket and wide flared green trousers, and a pair of oversized glasses perched on her small nose. The girl beside her he recognised from Paul's description. Slightly taller than her sister with long curly fair hair and a pleasant smile. Acutely aware that his jacket needed cleaning, and his hair could have done with a wash, he cursed Paul for not giving him more warning. At the sound of the two girls giggling he felt his face burn and turned his attention to the bar, trying to attract the attention of the girl who was serving.

"You'll never get a drink like that. Move over and let me try."

Turning around he saw his date standing behind him, an empty glass in her hand. Pushing her way forward, she waved the glass in the air and shouted, "Excuse me, could I have some service, please?"

Almost immediately the girl detached herself from the two men she was talking to and came over to them.

"A Bacardi and coke, one vodka and lime and two pints of lager, please," Marie said confidently.

While the girl was getting the drinks she turned back to him and said, "It's no good being too polite, you'd die of thirst. My name's Marie. Hello."

Again Roy felt his face burn and wished he was back in front of the television and away from this pushy girl. Glad of the loud music that was drowning the awkward silence, they waited for their drinks. When the girl came back with their drinks on a tray he reached forward to take it from her hands then walked carefully through the dancing crowd towards where Vicky and Paul were standing.

Marie walked behind him, wondering whether he was just shy or simply wasn't interested in her. As Vicky picked her drink from the tray she looked at Marie, her face worried.

Sensing things weren't going exactly to plan, Paul put his drink on a nearby table and said cheerfully, "Come on, let's have a dance," and without waiting for an answer he grabbed Vicky's hand and led her onto the small square of floor that had been set aside for dancing. Marie stood undecided for a moment, then turning to Roy she said, "Would you like this dance?" her smile hiding the nervousness she suddenly felt.

Roy looked at her, not able to make up his mind whether she was laughing at him or not. Taking a chance, he smiled back.

"Sure, why not?" he said, feeling suddenly more confident. Then, taking her hand, he led her onto the dance floor.

The walk home was blurred by the effects of the alcohol Marie had drunk. She was silently wishing she hadn't made such a pig of herself and hoped she wouldn't be sick in the street. Somehow or other she found herself alone with Roy, sitting on the cold stone steps inside the block of flats opposite her house. Roy was talking quietly and she was having trouble keeping her eyes open. Vaguely she found herself hoping he wasn't a groper. She didn't have the strength for a wrestling match tonight.

As she listened to him talking, she found her senses returning and her head clearing. Feeling more at ease in his company she began to talk. What about she couldn't remember afterwards. It was with considerable shock that she saw it was two-thirty in the morning. Where had the time gone? Getting to her feet Marie nearly fell, so cold and cramped were her legs. They had been sitting and talking for hours. Hanging onto Roy's arm for support, she walked slowly to her front door. She was surprised and pleased when he asked if he could take her to the pictures the following night and she said yes happily.

Opening the door carefully so as not to wake anyone, she crept up the stairs and quietly let herself into her bedroom. Vicky was already in bed sound asleep, and she could see Ellen's outline against the lamplight shining through the window. Quickly undressing, she slipped into bed beside Vicky, not bothering to put her nightie on.

"Dirty stop out," came Vicky's voice in the darkness, making her jump. As she went to answer she realised that Vicky was talking in her sleep again, a habit that she vigorously denied she had.

Snuggling down in the warm bed, Marie was soon asleep.

# Chapter Nineteen

1974–76.

Ellen's wedding day was here at last, and the whole house looked as if a bomb had hit it. They had had months to prepare for this day and now everything seemed to have been left till the last minute. Peggy was run off her feet. In a moment's lull she managed to escape to the kitchen, which was mercifully empty, and make herself a cup of tea. Sitting down wearily, she closed her eyes for a brief moment. In her mind's eye she saw Eddie, her future son-in-law and nodded her head happily. Ellen and he would get on well enough, they seemed made for each other. She only hoped she would be a good mother-in-law.

Marie came into the kitchen, her eyes searching for and finding her mum. "Does my suit look all right?" she asked, turning around to give Peggy a better look.

Peggy nodded, she did look nice; shame about the hat.

"Is Roy coming round here? Or are you meeting him at the church?"

"I thought it best to meet at the church. There's not much room here, is there?"

Peggy was about to reply when she spied Ellen coming down the stairs. For a moment she stood as if uncertain in the hallway, then, lifting her head high, she walked towards them. Marie opened the door to allow Ellen and her voluminous dress to enter. Looking at the first of her daughters to be married, Peggy felt a lump in her throat.

She had borne ten children, eight were still living at home, until tonight. For a fleeting moment she remembered the two children she had lost – both of them daughters: Pamela, who had died at birth, and Barbara, still living in a home for spastic children where she would be until the day she died. Although they were no longer with her she had never

224

forgotten them. Coming once more back to the present, she thought of Bobby. He hadn't said anything yet but she knew he would be getting married soon, maybe next year, then there would only be six left at home. She had always assumed they would marry and leave in order. First Marie, then Bobby and so on – but life never worked out as you planned.

Casting a swift look at Marie as she adjusted Ellen's veil, she wondered if Roy would last the distance. Her eldest daughter had changed so much over the past two years; the shy, frightened girl who had longed to be married had been transformed into a young woman happy in her new- found independence, who felt only pity for her friends who had married young before they'd had a chance to live.

"Mum, do I look all right?" Ellen was standing before her, clad from head to toe in traditional white, her prettiness turned to beauty.

Turning her head to where Marie stood quietly, Peggy asked her, "What do you think of your sister?"

"She'll pass in the dark," came the reply, the smile on Marie's face taking the sting from her words. Marie wasn't comfortable in giving out compliments, maybe because she'd received so few. The next half-hour was spent in a frantic, last-minute dash to make sure everything was proceeding to plan.

Then came the performance of getting everyone into the cars, although the church was only a few minutes walk away.

Making sure May was put in the first car to leave, Peggy saw her mother off and left the rest of the relations and guests to sort out their own arrangements. The bridesmaids were sitting in the sitting room; two of Ellen's friends and Patti, the latter looking awkward and uncomfortable in her new finery.

Marie and Vicky saw the three bridesmaids off before starting their walk down to the church. There were only Peggy, Bill and Ellen left at home. Telling Marie and Vicky to wait for her, Peggy gave Ellen one last kiss before joining her other two daughters.

Ellen watched her father pacing the room and stifled a laugh. He was more nervous than she was. Suddenly he stopped still and, facing her, said quietly, "You don't have to go if you don't want to."

Again Ellen had to stop herself from laughing. He made it sound as if she were facing an unpleasant day at school. Then she realised what it must have cost him to speak out. He would be quite prepared to go to the church and tell everyone the wedding was off if that was what she wanted. But she didn't. Laying her hand on his arm, a feeling of tenderness and love for him running through her body, she said softly, "I'm ready, dad; let's go."

The look of happiness on his daughter's face stilled any misgivings that Bill might have had. Patting her hand, he led her out to the waiting car.

The wedding reception was a huge success. There had been none of the customary lull in the afternoon when most people usually left on the pretext of going home to change. This had been due to the non-stop music provided by the D.J. Ellen had hired for the day. There had been no awkward break in the afternoon. Peggy looked over to where Sadie sat talking to Joan and smiled, happy to see her two oldest friends getting on so well together.

Marie, who honestly hadn't been looking forward to the party, was having a wonderful time. It was turning out to be the best wedding she'd ever been to. Maybe it was because Roy was with her, but whatever the reason she was genuinely disappointed when the evening finally came to an end. Judging by the reaction of the other guests, she wasn't the only one. Who would have thought that the best wedding she had ever attended would turn out to be Ellen's?

Eddie stood by his new wife's side as they bid their guests goodnight. Her Uncle Tommy had turned up late and now he stood before them telling Eddie to look after his niece. The words were spoken with a smile, but Eddie had an uncomfortable feeling that he was being given a gentle warning. Well, he thought, looking down at Ellen, her uncle need have no worry on that score. Peggy and Bill came next, shaking hands and hugging Ellen goodbye as if she were moving to the other side of the world.

The last one to leave the hall was Marie. The two sisters looked at each other for a long moment, both feeling awkward. Then suddenly they had their arms about each other, crying. In all the years they had shared a home this was the first time they had ever hugged. Both were surprised at the depth of feeling they were discovering for each other. With a final hug Marie was gone, leaving Ellen staring after her. Aware of Eddie's presence by her side, she said, "Let's go home, love."

"One down, seven to go," yawned Vicky, her mouth agape. "Well," she added tiredly, "It's me for bed, I'm whacked. Shouldn't be surprised if Bobby got married next year, would you?"

Slowly Marie began to undress. "No, I wouldn't be at all surprised," she replied, her voice low. And suddenly she felt more hopeful for the future. She would make friends with Pauline. She didn't know how as yet, but she felt sure they could overcome this animosity they felt for each other. After all, they had one thing in common, they both loved Bobby. They would work something out.

Almost a year and a day later Peggy once more stood in front of her bedroom mirror inspecting herself in another new outfit. Today was her son's wedding day and she felt both happy and sad. Marie wasn't the only one who would miss him, they all would. Patting her newly bleached blonde hair, she stared back at her reflection, pleased with what she saw. Not bad for a fifty-year-old, she told herself, taking in the cream two piece suit that covered a still trim body. Moving closer to the mirror, a frown crossed her forehead. Should she have had her hair dyed at her, age? Everyone had said it looked nice and that it suited her; except May, but now she wasn't so sure. Still, not much point worrying about it now, she could always change it back to its original colour. The knock on the bedroom door brought her gaze away from the mirror.

"I'm off now, Mum. Now, does dad definitely know where the church is?" Bobby, dressed in a navy three piece suit, stood awkwardly in the doorway, his blue eyes twinkling in his handsome face. His dark curly hair, freshly washed, refused to lie down. Peggy stretched out a hand towards his face, pride and love for this son of hers nearly choking her. Fearing his mother was going to go "soppy" on him, Bobby quickly put his arm around her shoulders and gave her a shake. "Come on, old girl," he said laughing, "cheer up."

Managing a tremulous smile, Peggy stared up at him. "You'd better get off, love, and don't worry, I'll make sure we leave in plenty of time. Just in case we do get lost," she added as an afterthought. The wedding was being held in Kent, where Pauline lived, and Bobby had every reason to be worried as Bill was notorious at getting lost even on the shortest of journeys.

Marie watched Bobby dance his new bride round the floor. The smile she had plastered on her face at the start of the day had become fixed. By her side sat Roy, not knowing what to say to her. He had been overwhelmed when he'd first met her large family. Coming from a family of two – himself and an older sister – he hadn't been used to the continual comings and goings of people passing through the Cowley house. If it wasn't one of the immediate family, it was an aunt or uncle, or numerous friends. The house was never empty.

He had been wary of Andy af first, until he'd realised that the insults and jokes he hurled were nothing personal, and that he acted like that with everyone.

Then there was Patti. What a little cow she was. Only last week, she had thrown a bottle of milk over him. True, he had dared her to do it, but never in his wildest dreams had he thought that she would. He had been slightly mollified when Peggy had grabbed hold of her and given her a good shake, that was until she'd shouted, "That's all the milk we've got till the morning." Never mind him sitting there with milk running down his head and over his new jacket.

Then there was this business of Malta. Marie had gone for a month just a few weeks after they'd met, and he was pretty sure she intended going back again. He didn't know quite where he stood with her, but he knew better than to push it.

Much later after the D.J. had played the *Last Waltz*, against Bobby's protests, Roy stood behind Marie as she waited to say their goodbyes. Unlike Ellen's wedding, Marie had made sure she would be one of the first to leave, wanting to get the goodbyes over with. "All the best, Bob," she said, shaking his hand, unable to hide the tremble in her voice. For an answer Bobby put his arm around her, and pulling her close he kissed her tenderly on the cheek. Roy looked on in surprise. Although they were a close-knit family, they weren't very demonstrative, unlike his own, who always kissed each other hello and goodbye.

Pauline came to stand by Bobby's side. Facing her new sister-in-law, Marie put out her hand once again, this time warily as if unsure it would be taken.

"I'll get Bobby to give you a ring when we're straight," Pauline said, smiling. "Maybe you and Roy can come over for a visit."

Completely caught off guard, Marie could only mumble a reply. Once out in the street she turned to Roy, her face alight with happiness.

"Did you hear what she said?" she demanded. "I wonder if she meant it?"

"Of course she meant it," Roy answered, his mind praying this was so. He had always got on well with Pauline on the rare occasions they'd met at Marie's house; personally he thought she was very pleasant and not bad looking either, especially with that waist length, nearly jet black hair, but of course he had kept that opinion to himself.

Let them be friends, he thought, sending up a silent prayer. If only for Marie's sake, let them be friends.

The drive home had taken just under an hour. Roy and Marie had sat in the back of Bill's car, listening to Peggy chattering away happily about how well the day had gone one minute, and sobbing quietly the next, at the knowledge that Bobby had left the family home, leaving behind him a gap that nobody could fill.

It was after twelve when they all trooped tiredly into the house. Peggy and Bill made straight for the kitchen for a much needed cup of tea. It had been a long day.

Roy followed Marie into the sitting room and watched as she sank down onto the comfortable armchair, kicking off her shoes as she did so. He was about to follow her example when the doorbell rang, accompanied by frantic barking. The next moment Patch bounded into the room, his small sturdy body jumping from Marie to Roy then racing from them into the hall where Peggy was speaking to Mrs Dodds from next door.

"Thank you for looking after him, Sheila, I hope he wasn't too much bother."

"No, Peg, no bother, although he nearly went mad when he heard your front door close. I thought he was going to jump through the window. Anyway, how did it all go?"

While Peggy stood on the doorstep telling her neighbour about the day's events Bill came into the sitting room, a mug of tea in each hand.

"Get down, you little devil," he shouted as Patch, delirious with joy at seeing his human family after a day's absence, continued to jump and bark frantically as he tried to get into. Putting the tea down on the floor, he scooped the wriggling body up under his arm and carried him from the room, saying over his shoulder, "I'd best be taking him for a walk round the block, or else it's no peace we'll be getting tonight."

Alone once again Roy looked at Marie's forlorn face and wondered if this was the right moment to ask the question that had been on his mind all night. Soon the rest of the family would be home and the chance would be gone.

"You're quiet," Marie said suddenly, cutting into his thoughts. Picking up her mug of tea, she walked over to the settee and sat down beside him.

Roy was about to speak when he heard Vicky at the front door, then Peggy's voice as she called out goodnight and another thank you to her neighbour.

Instead of coming into the sitting room, both Vicky and Peggy walked into the kitchen. Roy could hear their soft voices but couldn't make out their conversation. Just as he was about to speak, the doorbell rang again.

Bloody hell, he thought wildly, doesn't anyone have a key in this house?

Turning to Marie, he said quickly "There's something I want to ask you." Looking at her tired face, he experienced a moment of panic. *What if she said no?* Then taking a deep breath, he blurted out, "How do you fancy getting engaged?" He saw a flicker of surprise pass over her face and held his breath.

Marie heard the question and felt her heart start to pound wildly. Once, long ago, she would have squealed with joy, been overcome with delight and rushed to tell anyone who would listen. But those kinds of emotion were for the young, and she had been through too much to ever feel that sort of elation. While Roy waited anxiously for her answer she examined her feelings, and suddenly realised she didn't have to.

Looking up into Roy's square face, his eyes clouded with apprehension, she felt her body relax. It felt so right, so comfortable, she couldn't imagine her life without Roy in it.

Putting out her hand, she held his tightly and said simply, "I thought you'd never ask."

Before they could move, the sitting room door was once again flung open and Andy, Jimmy and John burst into the room, while once again Peggy stood on the doorstep uttering thanks, this time to Joan's husband who had driven the three boys to Dartford and back again.

"Joan said to tell you she had a lovely time, Peg. She'll see you in the morning. Goodnight."

Peggy smiled wearily and closed the door. Passing through the hallway, she decided to forgo her late supper and go straight to bed. Opening the sitting room door she popped her head around and said with forced cheerfulness, "I'm off to bed. Goodnight Roy. I'll see the rest of you in the morning, so don't stay up too late, will you?"

"Just a minute, Mum." Marie jumped up, her arm out-stretched, her face smiling. Pulling Peggy to the nearby armchair, she gently pushed her onto the seat saying, "Wait there till I get Dad and Vicky."

Within seconds Bill was standing beside Peggy, a mug of tea in one hand and a half-eaten sandwich in the other, a bewildered look on his face, while Vicky peered over his shoulder.

"What's going on?" Vicky asked, her face alight with excitement, as she looked from Roy's face flushed with embarrassment to Marie who was perched on the arm of Peggy's chair.

"I don't want to make a song and dance about this, but Roy and I are getting engaged," Marie said, the awkwardness she was feeling showing plainly on her face and in her voice.

"Oh, love." Peggy's face lost its tiredness as she leant forward to clasp Marie's hands.

"All right, Mum, don't make a fuss, please," Marie said, wishing now she'd just left a note on the kitchen table.

Then the comments came fast and furious.

"I'm really pleased for you." Vicky came forward and hugged Marie, then bent over and kissed a still silent Roy.

"Well now, isn't that grand," said Bill as he wondered if it would be considered bad manners to finish his sandwich.

John, having had enough of soppy people in love for one day, sidled past his dad and headed for bed, while Jimmy, always expansive in his feelings, pumped Roy's hand vigorously, then swept Marie from the chair, swinging her round before planting a happy kiss on her cheek.

Only Andy remained silent. Then, shaking his head sorrowfully, he said, "Another blooming present to fork out for."

The house was quiet, everyone sound asleep except Marie. Turning over onto her side, she looked at the luminous hands of her alarm clock. Two-thirty, and still sleep eluded her. Lying back, she linked her hands behind her head and stared into the darkness. She was glad now she had told her family, at least it was out of the way. Now it only remained to tell Roy's parents, who were on holiday at the moment.

Roy had suggested they shop for the ring on Saturday, then go and tell his parents in the evening. Marie had protested, saying wouldn't it be better to let them unpack first, but he had been adamant. Maybe he was right – he told her they'd be pleased, and she hoped he was right. Finally the long, exciting day took its toll. Marie's eyelids drooped, and soon she was fast asleep.

"Are you sure your mum and dad will be pleased?" Marie asked anxiously, her feet dragging as they approached the block of flats where Roy lived with his parents. She had been coming to these flats once or twice a week for nearly a year and was pretty sure they liked her, but that was as a girlfriend. How would they view her as a future wife for their only son?

She waited as Roy inserted his key in the lock, then she was being shoved gently down the small hallway in the direction of the sitting room.

"Don't worry, they like you. They'll be over the moon, you'll see." On this optimistic remark Roy flung open the door to reveal his parents sitting in their respective chairs in front of the television.

Gladys Ellis rose from her chair at once, her face breaking into a welcoming smile. "Frank, turn that telly down. Roy and Marie are here," she shouted at her husband.

Frank Ellis turned slowly then, seeing them both framed in the doorway, he also rose to his feet. "Hello, we didn't expect you two tonight. You normally go out on a Saturday, don't you?"

Feeling a gentle dig in the small of her back, Marie walked into the room, careful to keep her left hand in her pocket. As she sat down she realised the irony of the situation. For years she had worn an imitation ring, displaying it proudly to strangers and hiding it from her family, and now, when she was entitled to show off her new diamond engagement ring, she suddenly felt awkward. She'd experienced the same

233

feelings when she'd shown it to Peggy and Vicky earlier that afternoon.

"Would you like a cup of tea?" her future mother-in-law asked.

"Yes please," Marie answered, for once stuck for something to say.

Roy was still standing, his whole being bursting with the news he was about to impart.

"Never mind the tea," he said, his face split into a wide grin, "we've got something to tell you both." Taking Marie's hand from her pocket, he proudly pointed to her third finger, "We got engaged this afternoon."

Marie looked quickly from Gladys' face to Frank's, searching for some sign of disappointment at the unexpected news.

She needn't have worried.

"Well, I can't say I'm surprised," said Gladys as she moved towards them, her arms coming around Marie in an affectionate hug. "I'm delighted. This is the best news we've heard in a long time, isn't it, Frank?"

"It is, Glad, it is. Now, would anyone like that cup of tea?"

An hour later the four of them sat talking: the conversation centred round the engagement and the holiday Gladys and Frank had just returned from.

After telling Roy and Marie about the holiday camp where they had spent the past week, Gladys asked, "Aren't you going to celebrate, go for a drink or something?"

Shaking his head, Roy answered, "No, we don't want a fuss, but we would like to take you and dad and Peggy and Bill out for a meal one night. It would be nice if the four of you got together before the wedding."

"That would be grand, wouldn't it, Frank?" his mother said, looking to her husband for confirmation.

Marie studied her future in-laws. Gladys was quite tall for a woman, her permed hair still retaining its natural auburn colour, a shade Marie for years had tried to imitate without success. Frank was slightly smaller than his wife, and like her own father still had a good head of hair. Of the two, Marie would say Roy took after his mum rather than his dad, although he did have his dad's large ears, a fact he tried to hide by wearing his hair long.

"Why don't you give Barbara a call, Roy?" Gladys was saying. "Or have you already told her?" The last question was couched in an accusing voice.

"No, no, I haven't told her yet, I was waiting to tell you first," Roy said quickly. "I'll give her a ring now."

Barbara, Roy's only sister, lived in Basingstoke, with her husband Jim and their three young daughters, Angela, Fay and the newest addition, two-month-old Claire. Marie hoped that she would be as pleased at Roy's announcement as Gladys and Frank had been. While Marie waited for Roy to call, the doorbell rang, causing a look of surprise all round. It was nearly eight-thirty, and though the ringing of the doorbell was a common occurrence in her own house, it was unusual for anyone to visit here unless they were expected. She heard Roy telling Barbara to hold on a minute as he went to see who it was. Curiosity overcoming her, she went out into the hallway.

"Hello, Paul, what brings you here?" she asked Roy's friend who was also Vicky's current boyfriend. "I thought you were going out with Vicky tonight."

"I am, but we wondered if you wanted to come for a drink."

Marie looked at him, horrified, "You haven't left her in a pub by herself, have you?" she asked.

Paul hesitated a moment as if thinking hard, then grinned. "No, leave off, of course I haven't. No, she met a couple of girls from work, so I said I'd come round and try and persuade you both to come and have a drink with us, you know, to celebrate."

Marie eyed him suspiciously. She didn't believe the story he'd just told; it was too pat, something was going on. She turned to Roy who was still talking to his sister on the telephone.

Putting his hand over the mouthpiece, he said, "What do you reckon, shall we go?"

Paul broke in quickly, "Yeah, come on, you don't want to sit in watching telly on your engagement night, do you?"

Again Marie looked at Roy, then at her watch.

"Okay, Barbara, yes I'll tell her, yes right yep I will, okay. I'll see you soon. Bye." Roy put the receiver down, his head on a level with the phone. "Just give me a minute to tell my mam and dad and we'll be off."

· Marie got her jacket from Roy's bedroom, folding it over her arm. She went to say goodnight to Gladys and Frank.

All the way to the pub Paul kept up a nonstop conversation with Roy, breaking off only to flash a smile and wink at Marie. When they reached the pub Paul jumped forward to open the door for them. Marie walked in first, with Roy and Paul behind her. She scanned the busy bar, her eyes searching for Vicky. Spotting the familiar, long blonde hair, she fought her way through the throng of the crowd to get to her sister, then stopped as she saw one familiar face after another,

"Surprise!" Paul shouted, his face split into a wide grin. Marie and Roy found themselves surrounded; all of their friends seemed to be here. The girls crowded around Marie as she held her left hand out for the customary inspection of the engagement ring. Then Paul and Vicky pulled a large, gaily wrapped parcel from under the table where their drinks rested, and handed it over to Roy.

Trying to make himself heard over the noise of the music, Paul shouted, "We all chipped in to buy you this, I hope you both like it."

Roy took the parcel, his fingers already eagerly pulling at the wrapping paper.

"Careful," Vicky called out cheerfully, "it took me ages to wrap that."

The paper finally came off and Roy and Marie looked down at the wooden presentation box. Balancing it awkwardly on his knee, Roy opened it to reveal a beautiful canteen of cutlery.

"Thank you, everyone," he said, his voice sounding shaky.

"Yes, thank you all. It's a lovely surprise," added Marie.

The box was carefully laid on the floor as two of Roy's friends placed a tray full of assorted drinks onto the table.

There was a moment's confusion as the drinks were dispensed to their rightful owners, then Paul, the spokesman, raised his pint of beer, held it in front of Roy and Marie and shouted, "All the best, to both of you."

The chorus was quickly taken up by the rest of their friends. "All the best," they all shouted in unison.

Marie and Roy sat in their chairs, idiotic grins on their faces as they received the homage being paid to them.

"So much for a quiet night," Roy shouted to Marie.

"What?" she shouted back.

"Never mind, let's enjoy ourselves."

"Yes – let's."

The following year Ellen gave birth to a son. Peggy looked down on her grandchild, the first of many she had no doubt. Pauline was pregnant, the baby being due early next year. So much seemed to be happening all at once. Marie appeared by her side.

Gazing down at her first nephew, Marie's face softened. It was strange, she thought. All the years she had fought with Ellen and vice versa, and now they had become the best of friends. They phoned each other every week, both of them finding plenty to talk about. Marriage has certainly changed Ellen for the better, Marie thought, or maybe it's me that's changed. Shaking her head, she concentrated on the small child who was looking bewildered by all the attention.

"Are you sure about this?" Roy asked nervously as they stood outside the large furniture warehouse. Marie's Uncle Tommy had told them to come down here and pick out a three piece suite, saying the owner was a friend of his and that he would pay for it as a wedding present.

When Andy had heard about Tommy's present he had gone off into gales of laughter.

"You'd better nail it to the floor," he'd laughed, nearly beside himself with glee. "As soon as his cheque bounces they'll be back for it."

Striding purposefully towards the entrance, Marie asked an assistant if she could speak to the manager. A man standing at the far side of the building heard the request and walked towards them smiling, a smile that quickly disappeared when Marie informed him who had sent them and why. Half an hour later they walked out of the warehouse with a receipt for a brand new suite, leaving a forlorn-looking manager behind them.

Peggy lay awake in her bed, sleep eluding her. This time tomorrow Marie would be Mrs Ellis and no longer her responsibility. No, that wasn't quite true. Parents never completely let go and she would always be there for all her children whatever their ages, whenever they needed her. Turning onto her side, she tried to get comfortable, her mind still churning. Three of them in as many years. She prayed as all mothers pray, that her children had chosen wisely. Slowly her mind wound down and she fell asleep.

"Hurry up in the bathroom."
"Has anyone seen my gloves?"
"There's somebody at the door."
"Ellen, Vicky, come and help me with my make-up."
Peggy walked from room to room organizing, helping and dishing out orders. At last everyone was ready and making their way from the house. The only thing left to do was to have one last word with Marie.

Marie stood before the full length bedroom mirror studying her reflection, amazed that a long white dress and net veil could bring about such a transformation. Turning around, she checked the long silk train that lay on the carpet then turned again to face the mirror. She was glad she had picked the square-necked design, the temperature was in the eighties today. If she'd worn her first choice with its high neck and yards of heavy silk she would have been suffocated. Pulling on her new white lacy gloves, she smoothed down the plain silk skirt, checked that all the tiny pearls on the bodice were intact and then adjusted her waist length veil. Stepping nearer to the mirror, she peered short sightedly at her face to make sure mascara hadn't run, then looked at her glasses lying on her dressing table, wondering if she should forget her vanity and wear them. Shaking her head, she decided against it. Hearing her door open, she turned to see her mum standing watching her and voiced the question all daughters ask on their wedding day.

"Do I look all right, Mum?"

Peggy came into the room looking resplendent in a beige and white coat and dress.

Looking at her eldest daughter, she felt a surge of pride. For a fleeting moment she thought back to that black time when she thought she would lose her, then, taking Marie's hands in hers, she held her at arm's length as if to see her better.

"You look beautiful, darling," she said, her voice thick with emotion. Then she asked the same question Bill had asked Ellen two years ago.

"Are you sure?"

Marie put down the cigarette she was holding alongside the large Bacardi and coke, then standing up she hugged her.

"I'll see you at the church," she said, smiling.

Feeling an absurd lump come to her throat, Peggy nodded and turned away quickly before Marie could see her tears.

Left alone with her dad, Marie's mind roved once more through the past. When she'd dreamed of getting married long ago, she'd never taken into consideration the headaches that went with it. Finding a place to live, choosing caterers, arranging a mortgage – and the biggest headache, bridesmaids. She'd chosen two of Teresa's children, two of Pauline's and two of Roy's nieces, all of whom were under nine years of age. Vicky was her chief bridesmaid and Marie hoped she'd be able to keep them in order. These problems had never cropped up in her make-believe world, where she'd lived for a large part of her life, in a world of fantasy and daydreams. Today was reality and all the tomorrows that would follow.

As the bell rang to announce the car that would take her to her wedding, she turned to her father.

"Ready, dad?" she asked.

"Whenever you are," he replied.

# Chapter Twenty

1977.

Sitting by the fire waiting for news of her second grand-child, Peggy looked at the clock anxiously. It had been hours since Bobby's last phone call. Shaking her head, she mentally chided herself for being worried. She, of all people, shouldn't be afraid of childbirth; look at all the wonderful drugs and equipment they had these days, unlike when she was knocking them out once a year. There were few comforts for expectant mothers then. She looked at the clock again. It was true medical science had come a long way since her day, but as clever as doctors today were, they weren't gods.

The sound of the phone catapulted her out of the arm-chair. Hurrying to the hall, she picked up the phone, a smile on her face. As she listened to Bobby talking quietly the smile slipped, her hand clutching the receiver so hard her knuckles turned white. Vicky, passing through the hall, stopped in her tracks, the sight of her mother's white drawn face sending her running to her side. She didn't have to be told it was Bobby on the other end of the line; she'd stayed in tonight especially, not wanting to be out when Bobby phoned with the news of the baby. She watched as Peggy slowly put down the phone. Unable to speak, Vicky waited for Peggy to break the news, but there was no need for words. As the tears sprang from her moth-er's eyes, Vicky ran to her and buried her head against her chest.

As he put the phone down, Bobby rested his head against the cool white wall of the waiting-room. He was frightened, he'd never been so frightened in all his life.

Sinking back against the wall, he heard again the doctor's words, "Your wife has lost a lot of blood. She's a bleeder,"

240

he'd added. At any other time Bobby would have laughed at the term, and would probably have made a joke. He'd been with her from the start and things had been going well until the blood had started pumping from her body. Pauline had been brave, hadn't made a fuss at first, but the fear had been plain on her face. Then all hell had broken loose, with Pauline screaming, doctors suddenly appearing as if from nowhere and himself pushed protesting from the delivery room.

Helplessly he paced up and down outside the green swing doors. God, he thought, I can't bear this. "Please don't let her die; I love her, please don't let her die." He knew he should phone Pauline's parents, but he waited a little longer hoping against hope that someone would come and tell him everything was all right. When he could no longer, put it off, he slowly walked towards the telephone all the while thinking, what am I going to tell them? Dear God. What am I going to say?

Roy listened to Marie's dry, racking sobs, powerless to give her words of comfort. He felt numb. Pauline had always seemed so healthy it was hard to believe that she could be dying. And poor Bobby, what must he be going through? Settling his big frame into the armchair, Roy thought back to the first time he had met Bobby. He had been prepared to dislike him on sight, mainly due to the fact that whenever Marie talked Bobby was mentioned, no matter what the conversation was at the time. It had been "Bobby said this", or "Bobby did that". Roy had been expecting to meet a cocky Jack-the-Lad type of bloke, but Bobby wasn't a bit like that. Within minutes of the two men meeting, Roy had hoped that he would become friends with him, and he had.

Looking upwards towards the ceiling, Roy pictured Marie lying on their bed and his heart went out to her and her brother. He had become enmeshed in their large happy family and now their pain was his pain also. Lying back in the chair, he prepared to keep vigil by the silent phone.

*

"Come on, Mrs Cowley, push, just one more, there's a good girl."

Pauline gritted her teeth, biting back the expletive she longed to shout at the nurse. God, it hurt, the pain was tearing her body apart. She knew something was badly wrong and at the back of her mind she hoped she wasn't going to die. A doctor was standing by her side. Picking up her wrist, he took her pulse, all the while talking to her, gently reassuring her that everything was fine. One more agonising push, her whole body crying out against this nightmare of pain, and then dimly she felt the child leaving her tortured body.

As the child cried out in protest at being expelled from its warm haven Bobby rushed into the room. Knocking nurses and doctors aside, he ran to Pauline's side. It was only after he'd seen her safely asleep in bed after receiving a blood transfusion that he went to see his daughter. Peering through the glass of the nursery, his face crinkled up into a watery smile as he watched her lying fast asleep, completely unaware of the drama she had evoked. Wiping the tears from his eyes, he gave a hiccup of a laugh and promptly fainted.

"For Christ's sake, come away from that window. They'll get here when they get here." Roy looked at Marie as she came reluctantly away from the window. She'd been up and down all night long looking out into the street, willing Bobby's car to come into view. The sound of a car pulling up outside the house brought her running back to the window once again.

"They're here, they're here!" she shouted, the excitement she felt spilling over into her voice.

"All right," Roy said gruffly, getting to his feet. "You'll have the street out in a minute."

Ignoring him, she ran to open the door. Ushering her guests in, she fussed round them, asking if they'd like a cup of tea or something to eat while her eyes kept straying to the Moses basket on the floor with the small pink bundle inside it.

"Sit down, Marie, you're making me nervous," Bobby said, grinning.

Mentally chiding herself as an idiot, Marie walked slowly past the wicker basket and sat down. There followed an awkward pause. Pauline hadn't said anything except hello when she'd first come in. She's probably come round under protest, Marie thought miserably.

Taking her courage in both hands, she spoke. "Could I have a look at her?" she asked, her voice cracking with nervousness.

"Yes, of course you can," Pauline answered, surprise registering on her face. "Pick her up if you want. She's due for a bottle if you want to feed her."

Quickly, as if fearing Pauline might change her mind, Marie bent over the small bundle and parted the pink blanket. The moment she pulled back the shawl covering the baby and saw its perfectly formed face, the blue eyes staring trustingly up at her, she immediately fell in love with her first-born niece. Gingerly she picked her up, aware of all eyes upon her. Walking slowly, her arms clutched protectively around the precious bundle, she lowered herself into the armchair. When Pauline handed her the bottle of milk, she directed it towards Kerry's tiny, waiting mouth and watched with happiness as the minute lips sucked greedily at the teat. Contentedly she sat there, her eyes fixed firmly on the small face in front of her. Lifting her eyes to where Pauline sat opposite her, she smiled timidly, and when she saw the smile returned, her happiness was complete.

"Phone, Marie."

Marking the invoice on her desk, Marie walked over to the supervisor's desk and picked up the receiver.

"Is it all right for you to talk?" Bobby's voice came over the wire.

"Yes, is anything wrong?" she asked, wondering why he was calling.

"No, just wanted to know if you'd like to be godmother to Kerry?"

She felt her body jerk as if she'd been stung. Godmother – she couldn't believe she'd heard right.

"Are you still there?" Bobby asked, fully aware of the shock he'd just given her.

Gulping loudly, Marie cleared her throat twice before she was able to answer. "I'd love to, but I don't want to cause any rows between you and Pauline."

"It was Pauline's idea, I didn't even think of you."

The blatant lie brought a smile to Marie's face.

"When's the christening?"

"Don't know for sure yet. I'll give you a ring later in the week." And then he was gone.

She didn't realise she was crying until one of her friends came over to her, an anxious look on her face.

"Bad news?" she asked expectantly.

"No," Marie answered tearfully, "I've just had wonderful news."

"Well, I wouldn't like to be around if you ever get any bad news," the girl replied, grinning, before returning to her machine. Marie sat down at her desk, a silly smile on her face. She was to be Kerry's godmother and Pauline had asked for her specially.

The war between them was finally over.


The christening took place in July, and it was while Marie was holding her niece that she decided the time had come to try for children of her own. She'd talked about the possibility of starting a family with Roy on numerous occasions. The problem that had held them back was her illness. For the most part she was well, but there were still times when she had to take to her bed and when you have a child to look after you have to be there for them one hundred per cent of the time.

The operation that could change all that had been discussed from time to time but had never been seriously considered – until now.

# Chapter Twenty-One

1978–79.

"Are you sure, Marie? It's not a step to be taken lightly."

She was sitting in Dr Lawson's office, listening to him explain the pitfalls and emotional effects of the ileostomy operation. When he realised that she had made up her mind he sighed deeply, knowing that it was useless to try and dissuade her. When Marie made her mind up, it stayed made up. Drawing a piece of paper towards him, he began writing out the necessary forms for tests to be performed before the operation could go ahead. When he handed them over to her Marie stood up, ready to leave. She wanted to get out quickly before she changed her mind. Looking down at the first piece of paper, she smiled thinly.

"Oh, goody," she said, trying to keep her voice light, "a barium meal followed by a barium enema. I can't quite decide which is my favourite."

She might have fooled another doctor with her "couldn't care less" attitude, but Dr Lawson knew her too well to be taken in.

Avoiding his concerned look, she shook his hand and quickly left his office. From there she went to the X-ray department and made an appointment. She had a plan of action worked out. First she would phone Ellen and ask her to come with her to the hospital and wait while she had the barium done. If she could keep herself surrounded by family and friends from now until the big day, she wouldn't have time to be afraid. After she'd phoned Ellen and made arrangements to meet outside Bart's at eleven o'clock on Wednesday morning she returned to work.

Arriving early, Marie decided to go to the X-ray department and book in. On arrival she was told there had been a cancellation and she would like to take an earlier appointment. Not wanting to have the test at all, but longing to get it over with, she agreed.

An hour later, feeling decidedly sick, she walked down to the front gate. Her heart sank as she saw the well-built figure of her sister pacing up and down, her long blonde hair flying from side to side as Ellen looked from one end of the street to the other searching for her errant sister.

Knowing a row was unavoidable, Marie decided to get it over with.

"At last." Ellen swung round on Marie, her face flushed with anger. "I've been waiting here for over an hour; where've you been?"

Nervously clearing her throat, Marie tried to explain what had happened but Ellen wasn't having any of it. Feeling thoroughly fed up, Marie walked alongside Ellen, listening to her going on about how difficult it had been for her to come at all. How she had had to get someone to look after Kevin, how she'd had to wait ages for a bus; on and on until Marie could take no more.

"For goodness sake, give it a rest, will you?" she exploded, stopping Ellen's tirade. "I've said I'm sorry, I can't do any more."

An uneasy silence sprang between them as they walked towards St Paul's station. As they passed a large stationer's opposite the Old Bailey, Ellen came to an abrupt stop.

Peering into the window, she exclaimed excitedly, "I must get that for Eddie. He's been wanting something like that for ages." Marie followed her sister's glance towards a large painting of Clint Eastwood, her brother-in-law's hero of the day. All differences forgotten, they entered the shop and while Ellen purchased the picture Marie browsed around and waited.

It was as she was bending down looking at a picture of an old sailing ship she thought Roy might like that the cramps hit her. Her face blanched, she straightened up and looked over to where Ellen was waiting patiently to be served.

"Can you hurry up, Ellen," she said, clutching her arm? "I want to go to the loo."

"So what's new? Can't you hang on for a minute?"

Nodding weakly, Marie moved away from Ellen's side and sat down on a nearby chair, ignoring an elderly woman who had been heading for it. Clenching her teeth, she waited, her face pale even though she was sweating. Finally, unable to wait any longer, she signalled frantically to Ellen and rushed from the shop. Tearing along St Paul's courtyard, she could hear Ellen shouting after her. As she neared the public toilets, Marie heaved a sigh of relief and ran into the building.

It was some time later before she emerged from the cubicle to find Ellen waiting for her. About to say something, she was stopped, puzzled by the look on her sister's face. Following Ellen's pointing finger, she looked down at herself and gasped. The front of her dress was covered in a white chalky substance.

"What on earth . . .?"

The loud strident voice of the cockney cleaner made them both jump. "Oi, what the 'ell's all this over me floor?"

Hardly daring to look, the two girls turned their eyes in the direction of the voice. What they saw caused them to stop dead in their tracks. A large luminous patch of white fluid was glowing ominously on the floor of the toilet Marie had just vacated.

As the cleaner turned her attention to the dumbstruck pair her eyes took in the condition of Marie's dress. Her face set in a grim line, she advanced towards them. The sight of the woman armed with a large broom bearing down on them galvanised Ellen into action. Grabbing hold of Marie's arm, she half pulled, half dragged her out of the building. As they ran with the cleaner's voice sounding in their ears, Ellen glanced back over her shoulder to see the woman leaning against a wall gasping for breath, her arm holding aloft her broom. Ellen was reminded of a film she'd once seen about Boadicea.

Clutching their sides, they ran on until they were sure they weren't being followed. Sinking down on the steps of

St Paul's, they held on to each other, laughing so much their eyes started watering.

"And there was me thinking I'd had a wasted journey," gasped Ellen, wiping the tears from her eyes. "I'll be able to dine out on this for months."

"How am I going to get home like this?" asked Marie, looking down at her dress in dismay.

"Come on," said Ellen, jumping up as their bus came into view.

"Stand in front of me, Ellen," said Marie.

And so with Ellen in front and Marie stuck close to her back, they boarded the bus, their giggles drawing glances from the other passengers.

She lay back in the hospital bed trying to get comfortable on the hard pillows and thought back to that day, the memory making her chuckle quietly to herself. She had spent some time with Dr Lawson that morning as he was still worried about the psychological effect such surgery might have on her. It was only when he'd felt she would be able to cope that he'd given her his full support. There had been many times over the long years when just the knowledge that he was here at the hospital had helped her through a rough patch. She hadn't even needed to see him, just knowing he was always within reach had comforted her. She had complete and utter faith in his ability to make her well again no matter how ill she might be.

Snuggling further down in the bed, she closed her eyes, her mind going over the events of that morning. Her mum and dad had been up to see her early on with Roy, the whole family having visited the night before. Just as she was dozing off she heard a childish laugh and then there she was, the light of her life, her goddaughter, Kerry. Barely eighteen months old, she toddled into the small side ward, held firmly by the reins Pauline was clutching in her hands.

"What a lovely surprise!" Marie cried, holding out her arms to the child. Ignoring her aunt's outstretched arms, Kerry pulled at the reins indicating the bowl of fruit and sweets that reposed on Marie's locker. They passed a wonderful hour. Marie sent up a silent prayer of thanks that the thing she'd wished for had finally come true. She had made friends with her sister-in-law at long last, the years before forgotton.

She lay in the dark thinking about tomorrow. In the quiet, darkened room completely alone with her thoughts Marie felt a stab of fear run through her belly. The time had finally come, and all the bravado she'd shown to the world was gone. In its place lay a lonely, frightened creature. Doubts assailed her as she tossed and turned, willing her mind to stop functioning and let her sleep. When at last sleep did overcome Marie the tears were still wet on her face.

Her stomach was on fire, she tried to move but couldn't. The pain was like nothing she had ever known before. Turning her head slightly, she could see the drips attached to her arm. There was a nurse sitting in a chair by her bed. Marie tried to call out but her lips seemed to be stuck together. As well as the burning pain she felt so dreadfully ill. So it was done. No going back now.

"Oh, God," she whispered to herself, "take the pain away, please, I don't think I can bear it."

The nurse stirred in her chair. Coming to Marie's side, she felt her pulse and then left. A few minutes later she was back with the sister.

"How do you feel, dear?"

Dear God, what stupid questions people ask when at a loss for something to say. Marie peered into the darkness, just making out the dim outline of the blue uniform. Again she tried to speak but could only mumble. Tears of pain and frustration stung at her eyes. Then she felt a sharp prick as the needle went into her arm and blissful oblivion came.

She was sitting on her bed when she heard the unmistakable clatter of doctor's footsteps. Looking up, her face broke into a huge smile as she saw Dr Lawson approaching her bed.

"Hello, my dear. How are you, apart from battered and bruised?"

"I'm a lot better than I was two weeks ago, Doctor."

As he sat beside her holding her hand, she noticed as if for the first time the grey hair that seemed to cover his whole head. She realised with a pang that he must be getting on for retirement age – what would she do when he was no longer there for her?

Being the person she was, she felt no qualms in voicing her fears. The question brought a smile to his face and those of the accompanying doctors.

"Don't you worry about that, my dear, I'll be around for a few more years yet."

Rising from the bed, he made to leave when she put out her hand, clutching at his arm. "Will I be able to have children now, Doctor?"

"Well, not just at the present. I'd give it a year before trying." He said the words with a smile then, his face changing slightly, he came back to sit on the bed.

"Marie, you've been ill for a long while. Your body has taken a severe battering. Take into account the enormous amount of drugs you've taken over the years, and . . ."

Marie felt a stab of fear deep in her belly as she listened to his words. What was he trying to say? That this had all been for nothing? That she would never be a mother? No, she wouldn't believe it. She'd been through a terrible ordeal for just one purpose, and she'd be damned if she gave up now.

"Are you trying to tell me, in the nicest possible way, that I won't be able to have children?" she demanded fiercely.

"No, no, my dear, I didn't say that. But you mustn't get your hopes up. I'm just trying to point out that many women who have never had a day's illness in their lives can't have children. I've never lied to you, Marie. No matter how unpleasant, I've always told you the truth. Just for the record I think you will attain your goal because you're a fighter. Wait a year before you attempt to become pregnant. Then if nothing happens after six months I'll refer you to a doctor friend of mine who deals in gynaecology." Rising from the bed once more, he squeezed her hand. "Is there anything else you're worried about?"

She thought for a moment, her forehead creased in concentration, then she spoke. "Just one thing."

"And what's that?"

"Where do I go to get shoes to match my bag?"

The explosion of laughter that followed her remark brought the smile back to her lips, a smile that faded as soon as the retreating figures left her bedside. Clenching her teeth firmly, she gave herself a mental shake. She'd do it. By God she would. Look at that Louise Brown, the first test tube baby born earlier in the year. If the normal way failed then she'd enquire into that avenue. But she wouldn't give up. *Never.*

As Marie packed her small suitcase one of the nurses stopped by her bed.

"Have you had any more records played on the radio?"

Marie smiled back at the young nurse. She knew instantly what the girl was referring to. Three days after her operation, this same nurse had come to her late at night saying that the night sister had received a phone call asking if Marie could listen to the night time radio as her sisters had asked that a record be played for her. After much difficulty in getting the right station she had waited for her name to be mentioned. The D.J. had read out her name and where she was and why, and had then played "Giving up, Giving in" by the Three Degrees. The nurse had been concerned when Marie had handed her the headphones so she could listen to the choice of record, but Marie had thought it was funny. It was typical of Vicky and Ellen to have picked such a record.

The heavy sound of footsteps brought her eyes to the ward entrance and there was Roy walking towards her. With much hand waving and goodbyes she left the ward and the hospital. The worst part was over, the easy part was still to come. She'd had her share of bad luck, from now on it would be good luck all the way.

A year after the operation, although Roy had given his all, Marie still wasn't pregnant. She had taken a week's holiday that was due to her and now as she wandered around the house from room to room she realised she was bored. For something to do she decided to phone Ellen for a chat. But as soon as her sister answered she gave vent to the misery she was feeling over her barren state.

"Are you sure you're doing it at the right time of the month?" asked Ellen on the other end of the phone.

"Right time? What do you mean?"

"Don't you know anything?" The question was asked with laughter as if Marie had said something funny. Feeling upset, Marie was just about to put the phone down when Ellen's voice caught her attention.

"I'm sorry, I didn't mean to laugh, but a woman only ovulates once a month, so you have to be very lucky, or very unlucky depending on what you want, to get pregnant straight away."

"I didn't know that – are you sure?"

"Course I'm sure, I thought you knew." Ellen went on to explain. When she'd finished Marie felt more depressed than before she'd phoned.

"All right, I guess I'll just have to keep my fingers crossed and hope for the best."

"As long as it's not your legs," Ellen laughed as she rang off.

There was more to getting pregnant than she'd first thought. She'd always been under the impression that you only had to "do it", and you got pregnant. Sighing, Marie turned on the television. Twenty-nine years old and she still didn't know the facts of life.

"Pauline's pregnant," Vicky's voice came down the phone, causing a wave of jealousy to hit Marie so violently she felt sick.

"Oh, good," she heard herself say lightly. "When's it due?"

"February, same as Kerry. Must be a special month for her."

After exchanging a few pleasantries, Marie made an excuse and hung up. February; that meant Pauline was already four months pregnant. Marie had seen her only last week and she hadn't said a word. When she realised why Pauline hadn't mentioned it, she felt even sicker. Pauline didn't want

252

to upset her, knowing how badly she wanted a child of her own. Things couldn't go on like this. Her whole world was dominated by her longing to become pregnant. She'd have to stop it. The first thing she must do was phone Pauline and offer her congratulations. Receiver in hand, she started to dial Bobby's number, but as she felt her lips begin to tremble she hurriedly put down the phone then sat down on the settee. She was still sitting there when Roy came home two hours later.

Ellen came away from the chemist's smiling happily. She was pregnant again. Due about July according to her calculations. She was putting Kevin into his pushchair and humming to herself when suddenly Marie's face floated before her eyes.

First Pauline, now her. How would Marie react to the news? Knowing Marie, she would put on a brave face and be happy for her but deep down she would be very upset. Well, Ellen decided, it wouldn't hurt to keep it a secret for a while, even though she was bursting to tell everyone. Maybe in that time Marie would find herself expecting and then there'd be no problem. Deeply troubled now, Ellen pushed Kevin home.

Ten days late. She'd never been that late before. She already had her pregnancy kit on standby. It had been sitting in the cupboard for over a year. She only hoped it would still work. With shaking hands she performed the intricate test, then, putting it in a darkened room and making sure it was on a firm surface, she went downstairs to wait.

She'd never known an hour to pass so slowly. The minutes on her watch seemed to creep by. When the hour was finally up she ran up the stairs only to come to a halt outside the bedroom door. Her heart pounding, she crept over to the mantelpiece. As she got nearer she closed her eyes, afraid of what she might see. Then, taking a deep breath she opened her eyes and looked.

The dark brown circle seemed to come up and hit her in the face. She took another look. Yes, it was definitely a solid circle. She was pregnant! Almost beside herself with joy, she ran back downstairs to phone Roy at work.

It took ages to get through the Post Office switchboard. Why, oh why, had this had to be his Saturday duty on, today of all days? Then his voice came down the line, concerned at first, fearing something wrong, then his voice changed to laughter. He couldn't speak for long but promised he would get home as quickly as he could. Marie had hardly put the receiver down before she picked it up again and dialled her mum's number. As usual Peggy wasn't at home, it being Saturday she was out shopping, but her dad promised to get her to ring as soon as she returned. Next she called Ellen, her fingers shakily picking out the long code for Witham where Ellen now lived. When she finally got through she was surprised and a little disappointed at her sister's reaction to her news.

After a moment's silence Ellen said, "Thank God for that."

# Chapter Twenty-Two

1980.

It was full as usual at the ante-natal clinic. Marie had already been for her scan and the nurse had given her a letter to give to the doctor. Idly glancing at the envelope, Marie wondered what was in it. Couldn't be anything serious – she had been attending the clinic for over seven weeks now and had had a scan only last week. She was five and a half months pregnant and had never been happier in her life. At last life was dealing her the good cards. Nearly six months gone. She looked down at her nearly flat stomach and wondered why she hadn't blown up like Ellen. Compared to her, Ellen looked like a barrage balloon.

A lot of people had laughingly asked her where she was hiding it, but she'd felt uneasy when they had asked. Her mum had been acting strangely as well, asking her lots of questions, but Marie wasn't worried, she was in the best hospital this side of London and Dr Lawson was never far away. He wouldn't let anything happen to her baby.

She took another look around the clinic. There must have been thirty women waiting for their appointments. Smiling to herself, she reflected that not everyone had found it difficult to get pregnant. Patting her stomach, she gave herself a mental hug. How often had she seen pregnant women in the street and envied them, and now she was one of them. Bored with waiting she let her mind turn to her new niece.

Pauline had had another girl in February, named Sarah. Marie hadn't seen her yet as she and Bobby had just moved to Kent. Still, she told herself, the baby had only been born two months ago and Bobby had promised to bring her round soon.

She did miss them though. Much to her surprise she had become very friendly with Pauline. It wasn't just a polite friendship brought about by circumstance. Once they'd got to know each other they had found that they had a lot in common. Life was funny, there was hardly a week went by that she didn't phone Ellen up. In the space of two short years, she had made two good friends in people she had started off disliking.

"Mrs Ellis?"

Marie jumped. There must be another Mrs Ellis, the nurse couldn't mean her, she'd only been here ten minutes.

"Mrs Marie Ellis please," the nurse called again.

With shaking legs, Marie rose from her chair and went towards the nurse. She noticed that she held the letter she'd handed in at reception just a short while ago. Following the nurse into the small cubicle, she began to take her clothes off when the nurse stopped her.

"Why not?" Marie demanded. "I always get undressed," she said, the fear in her voice showing plainly on her face.

"Not today, dear. The doctor just wants a word with you."

Although the nurse's lips were smiling, it didn't quite reach her eyes. When she saw Marie watching her she began checking a trolley that was standing by the wall. The tension was broken somewhat by the arrival of the doctor. When Marie saw that it was Mr Grant, the head gynaecologist, instead of the usual locum she felt fear rising in her throat, making her physically sick.

Mr Grant only saw his patients on their first visit, or if something. . .

"Hello, Mrs Ellis," he said, sitting down beside her on the narrow bed. That was something else that only happened if something. . .

Before he could say anything else, she started talking.

"It was my birthday last week. My husband took me out for a meal. And last week I went shopping with one of my sisters, we bought loads of baby clothes but I haven't bought the pram yet, people say it's unlucky. Don't want to tempt fate, do I?"

She was babbling now, not wanting to give him a chance to speak. And all the time she was talking, hearing her own voice laughing, her mind was screaming, "Don't tell me, I don't want to know, I don't want to know!"

Marie didn't know what she was saying. Anything would do. Anything to keep that moment when he would speak and kill her hopes at bay, just for a little while longer.

"I've got a carrycot though, and my in-laws are buying the big cot as soon as it's born." As she talked she kept her eyes firmly on her shoes. She felt the nurse move forward and take her hand, holding it tightly.

"I've even picked out names. Bobby for a boy and Vicki for a girl. And my baby's dead, isn't it?"

The silence in the room spoke volumes.

Raising her eyes to the doctor's, Marie was surprised to find genuine concern and even grief reflected there. She'd always assumed they were immune to occurrences like this. Apparently not.

"The nurse will take you to the maternity ward, Mrs Ellis. I'm truly sorry. We'll do everything in our power to make it as easy as possible for you."

Getting down from the bed, Marie stumbled and would have fallen if he hadn't put out his hand to steady her. Still dry-eyed, she walked from the clinic, refusing a wheel chair. She passed the waiting women, listening to them grumbling at the delay in being seen, and wanted to scream at them. To tell them to get down on their knees and thank God, or whoever was up there that their babies were still alive.

Passing the grounds, she stopped by a bench and sat down. Fumbling in her handbag, she picked out a packet of cigarettes. As she lit one with shaking hands she spoke to the nurse, who was looking as if she wished she were anywhere but here with her. "I cut down from twenty a day to seven. Didn't want to take any chances, but I don't suppose it matters now."

They sat in silence until she'd finished her cigarette. Stubbing it out with her foot, she stood up.

"I'm ready."


Roy let himself into the empty house, the eerie silence striking him forcibly. Walking into the large lounge, he sat down onto the gold-coloured settee that Tommy had bought them for a wedding present and wondered idly if he'd paid for it yet. Looking across the room, he stared at the blank television screen, then, rising from the settee, he walked over and switched it on. Immediately the set sprang to life, dispelling the unnatural silence in the room. Seated once more, Roy stared fixedly at the film that was being enacted before him, his eyes unseeing, but his mind grateful for the background noise.

He could understand now why many elderly people relied so much on the television for company. He could have company of course, all he had to do was pick up the phone, but Roy couldn't face anyone yet. He needed time to himself. Closing his eyes, he rested his head back on the cushions. This time yesterday, Marie had sat in the armchair by the fireplace knitting yet another matinée coat, cursing every time she dropped a stitch. She must have knitted half a dozen in the last couple of months, none of them coming even close to resembling the photo in the pattern book, but still she had preserved. "*Why?*" he whispered to the empty room, "Why us?"

He still couldn't believe his child was gone. When he'd received the telephone call at work asking him to go to the hospital he hadn't been unduly alarmed. There had been no sense of urgency about the request. He had been worried, yes, but the worst he had imagined was Marie being kept in because the doctor had decided she needed bed rest, or maybe she had become anaemic again and needed daily iron injections.

On reaching the hospital he had been directed to a small side room just off the maternity ward. Looking round the door, he had seen Marie, dressed in a hospital gown and sitting on the side of the bed. She had been surprised to see him walk towards her smiling, thinking that one of the hospital staff would surely have told him the bad news. But they had left the unpleasant task to her.

Roy had watched her face as she'd struggled to say the words, had felt a sick fear as she'd said over and over, "I'm sorry, I'm so sorry," and then she had uttered those devastating three words.

"The baby's dead."

Roy had stumbled blindly to a nearby chair, the tears already starting to fall, talking wildly, not understanding the unintelligible words that had poured from his mouth. He had wanted to be strong for her and had found himself being comforted, had wanted to stay by her side and help her through the ordeal that lay ahead, but she had insisted that she would be all right, that there was nothing he could do.

For a moment his mind shied away from the other reason he had come home, but soon he would have to pick up the phone and tell Peggy and Bill what had happened. After them he would have to go through the same painful procedure with his own parents, plus Marie's close friends. He couldn't do it; he just couldn't. Swinging his legs onto the settee, he lay back for a moment in an attitude of sleep, and as he reached out for a cushion to place under his head, his hand came into contact with something soft. Looking down, he saw the yellow matinée coat that Marie had finished last week.

Slowly he picked up the tiny garment, saw the unevenly matched front and odd arms, and remembered Marie's dismay when she'd sewn them in only to find that one sleeve was a good two inches longer than the other.

He hadn't think he could cry any more, didn't think he had any tears left, but as he held the soft woollen garment to his cheek he gave an anguished cry and pulled his body up into a tight ball. Still clutching the small garment, he rocked himself back and forth, repeating one word to himself. "Why? Why? Why?"

Peggy stood holding the receiver in her hand. Roy had hung up minutes ago but she seemed unable to move. She had known, dear God, she had known all along something was wrong. And she had been right. She pictured Marie lying alone, waiting to give birth to a dead child. Roy had wanted to stay, but she'd sent him away.

Slowly, as if in a dream, Peggy replaced the receiver and began to walk towards the sitting room. Going over to the television, she turned it off. Ignoring the protests, she waited until the family were quiet and then she told them. In the stunned silence, Patti burst into anguished tears and fled from the room. Jimmy, his face white stormed past her, heading for the nearest pub she guessed. Andy muttered, "Bloody hell," then remained silent, his face impassive. Only Vicky showed no immediate reaction. Reopening the book she held in her hand, she continued reading. Peggy looked round at them as if seeking help, then stumbled blindly from the room.

After her mother had left Vicky continued to stare at her book. The words were dancing before her eyes and she was having difficulty in swallowing. Closing the book gently, she rose from the settee and went to her room. Once there she sat down on the bed she used to share with Marie. The tight knot in her stomach had slowly climbed to her throat and stuck there. She felt the tears come, slowly at first, and then the dry racking sobs consumed her entire body.

Lying in the semi dark listening to the cries of the babies in the adjoining ward, Marie's brain seemed to have gone numb. She wouldn't wish the ordeal she'd just been through on her worst enemy. She didn't quite know what she'd expected, but never had she thought she would have to go into labour to deliver the child. She'd thought that she would be knocked out and the baby taken away. When the young doctor had arrived to place the drip in her arm which would induce labour she had come out of her stupor for a moment, long enough to clutch at his arm and ask if there was any chance at all that her baby was still alive. One look at his distressed face had made her sink back onto the pillows, all hope gone.

Seventeen hours, seventeen long, long hours, and then the feeling of something being expelled from her body. And just for a second, just a split second, she'd forgotten and had tried to sit up to see her baby. The nurse's hand gently pushing her back onto the pillow had brought reality crashing back.

Sensing a presence in the room, she turned her head tiredly, to the nurse standing at the foot of the bed. Tears were coursing down her face.

"Don't cry," Marie said, her voice devoid of all feeling. "My baby's dead, crying won't bring it back."

"You don't remember me, do you?"

Puzzled, Marie looked more closely at her then shook her head.

"I was on Elizabeth Ward when you had your operation. I brought you the headphones to listen to the request your sisters had sent in for you. Do you remember?"

Yes, she remembered now. There would be no radio requests this time.

As she prepared to leave, the nurse turned back to the bed. "You only had the operation done so you could have children. It isn't fair."

"Life is never fair, you should know that, nurse."

So many tears. Poor Roy, he had been heartbroken. She could still see his face when she'd broken the news to him. Now he faced the prospect of phoning round the family and then there would be more tears. Everyone crying except for her. She felt dead inside and was glad. She had willed her mind to blot out the last day and night, and so far it had worked. So far.

She lay waiting to be taken to the theatre for the scrape that was customary after an abortion. Abortion: such an ugly word. She winced slightly, then quickly turned her mind to other matters. Had Ellen heard yet? She'd asked Roy not to tell her in case the news brought on her labour. It would be tragic if both of them lost their babies. Then there was her nan. She was getting on and Marie knew she'd always been her favourite, God only knew why. She wasn't a very nice person, she'd always known that. She remembered clearly now the times she'd been nasty to her mum. She hadn't meant it, it was the anger inside her that had forced the cruel words, and deep inside she'd known that only her mum loved her enough to put up with it, and she loved her mum in return. She loved her very much. As she felt the hands lifting her from the bed onto the trolley she cried out silently, "I know what I am. I know I can be nasty and miserable and plain bad-tempered for no good reason, I know myself and I'm not proud of what I am, but dear God, I didn't deserve this. I didn't deserve this."

Roy sat by her bedside in silence. There didn't seem to be anything to say. She was so withdrawn. If only she'd cry, put her arms out to him, react somehow – anything but this calm acceptance. It was with relief that he saw Vicky and Patti coming down the ward towards them. They were both smiling. He knew how much they were hurting inside, but you would never know it to look at them. This knack of hiding your feelings must run in the family, he thought a little sadly. They only stayed a half-hour.

Marie was feeling tired and the drooping of her eyelids had served as an excuse to leave. He watched as they bent over to kiss her goodbye and was pleased to see the way both Vicky and Patti held tightly to Marie for a few seconds, their true feelings coming to the surface. Then it was his turn. Bending over her, he kissed her gently hoping for some response but there was none. Slowly he turned from her and followed Vicky and Patti from the ward.

"There's no reason why you shouldn't get pregnant again, Mrs Ellis," the doctor was saying. It was the same one she'd seen in out-patients. No Mr Grant for her today.

"Mrs Ellis, are you listening to me?"

Yes, she was listening. How could he stand there and say such a stupid thing? There was no way she'd take a risk of something like that ever happening again. And if anybody said that old cliché, "I know how you feel", she would go mad. *Nobody* knew how she felt, not unless they had gone through the same ordeal.

With an effort, she looked at the doctor, searching her mind for something to say, and then she saw his face. Like Mr Grant and the nurses who had attended her, this man was feeling some of her pain and she immediately felt ashamed at the way she had treated him. He was standing close to her now.

"You've had a pretty rough time of it, haven't you?"

"That's all right. If I didn't have bad luck, I'd have no luck at all."

His face took on a look of amazement at the sudden change in her. She too was surprised, she didn't think she'd ever crack a joke again. It was a sure sign she was getting better. Getting better? She seriously wondered if she'd ever be better again.

Roy arrived a little later carrying her overnight case. They had decided not to go straight home but to go round to her mum's for dinner. Peggy hadn't been up to see her and Marie knew it was because she'd never have been able to put on a brave face like Vicky and Patti had done. Besides, she'd only been in hospital two days. Only two days, and her world had been turned upside down. As she left the hospital she realised that the next few hours were going to be very difficult for her family. She must remember that.


"Hello, love!" Peggy cried, putting her arms around her, hugging her close. It felt good. Herself and the rest of the family weren't much for hugging and kissing, except for her mum. For a wild moment Marie felt like dragging Peggy into the nearest chair and cuddling up on her lap, feeling the security of her, as she'd done as a child. Then her dad came towards her. No hugs there, but she knew he was suffering just as much as her mother, he just wasn't very good with words.

There was an awkward silence in the sitting room. The boys, as she still thought of them, greeted her with a casual "Hello, Marie. All right?"

Only Jimmy came over and gave her a big hug. After that, the tension eased a little. She could tell they were relieved that she wasn't crying and throwing herself around. After a strained dinner Bobby turned up unexpectedly.

He too seemed ill at ease, not knowing what to say to her.

"Pauline couldn't come as Sarah has a bad cold. She thought it best to keep her at home," he told her, his eyes not meeting hers. She nodded, understanding at once why Pauline hadn't brought the baby round. But she wouldn't have minded, although if the positions had been reversed, she would have done exactly the same thing.

"It's all right, Bob, I understand. Maybe when Sarah's cold gets better you can visit one night."

They looked at each other, understanding passing between them. He didn't stop long, but he had cared enough to come, that's all that mattered.

She was having trouble staying awake. Her eyes felt heavy as if she'd been drugged. Maybe it was delayed shock.

"Do you mind if I have a lie down, Mum? I feel a bit whacked."

Immediately Peggy was on her feet, helping Marie up as if she were an invalid.

"Don't be silly, you don't have to ask." Fussing round her, she led her from the room. "Go up to Patti's room and have a good sleep."

Marie had been surprised to find both her sisters absent. Peggy had told her that Vicky was round at Stuart's and would be home later, and Patti was down at Ellen's for the day, as she was most weekends. Patti and Ellen were very close, they always had been.

"I can manage, Mum," she said as they stood at the bottom of the stairs.

"Have you cried yet?" Peggy asked, her face full of concern.

"What good will that do, Mum?" she answered tiredly. "It won't bring my baby back."

"Don't bottle it up, love, it's no good for you. Let it go, you'll feel better for it."

"I'll try, Mum."

Wearily Marie trudged upstairs, stopping halfway as her dad called after her.

"I've put a lock on Patti's door to keep Patch out. Be careful how you open it."

Nodding, she continued up the stairs. Turning the handle on Patti's door, she pushed against it but it wouldn't budge. She tried again but it still wouldn't open, it seemed to be stuck. Telling herself she'd try once more before calling for help, she put her shoulder to the door and pushed again, surprised at the strength in her body. The door opened slightly and she put her head around it to see what was making it stick. Probably some clothes left lying on the floor. Patti wasn't the tidiest of people. Halfway into the room she let go of the handle, whereby the door immediately swung back, nearly trapping her head.

The new "lock" her dad had fitted was a piece of elastic tied from the handle to a nail on the landing wall.

"Oh, Dad," Marie laughed weakly, sinking to her knees. "Oh, Dad."

# Chapter Twenty-Three

1980–81.

Marie reluctantly left the television to prepare Roy's dinner. She'd had all day to get it ready, but as usual she had left it to the last minute. The potatoes peeled and deposited in the oven along with a large pork chop, she returned to her favourite position by the fire.

It had been over a month since she'd lost the baby, but only a week since she'd become a lady of leisure. Since she'd lost the child she had suffered severe stomach and head aches brought on by shock. When one night she'd returned from her weekly visit to her old friend Mary, nearly out of her mind with pain, Roy had insisted that she give up work. Marie had been only too happy to agree. In the seventeen years since she'd left school, this was the first time, apart from her regular hospital stays, that she had been out of work and she didn't feel the least bit guilty. At the sound of a key being inserted in the front door she quickly jumped to her feet grabbing a duster she'd placed nearby, and began vigorously polishing the mantelpiece.

"Hello, love, I'm home."

Passing a hand over her forehead, she gave Roy a tired smile.

"Not been working too hard have you, love? You know what the doctor said."

"I can't sit about all day doing nothing; besides I like to keep busy."

Roy looked around the room, his eyes resting on the pile of ironing that had been languishing on the dining room chair for the past two days, then to the dry duster his wife held in her hand, and noted wryly that she'd forgotten to put the can of polish on view as she usually did. She'd once wondered aloud how she would die when her time came. Looking round the untidy sitting room, it was obvious it wouldn't be from hard work.

"What's for dinner, love? I'm starving."

"Oh, er – it's not quite ready yet,' Marie said, quickly going past him and into the kitchen. Opening the oven which hadn't yet got hot, she peered inside, her eyes resting gloomily on the still white potatoes and anaemic chop. Shutting the door quickly before he could see his raw dinner, she forced a bright smile on her face and began talking, hoping to take his mind off his food.

A sudden loud rumbling in her husband's stomach brought a guilty look to Marie's face. Nearly tripping over the vacuum cleaner which stood to attention by the kitchen door, she went back into the kitchen and put the kettle on, still talking.

"Nan phoned today, she's still a bit worried about me. Shall we go and see her tomorrow?"

As she spoke of her nan, Marie thought back to the day she'd gone round to see her, just a few days after the miscarriage. She would never call it an abortion. The visit had been a revelation to Marie. She'd fully expected her nan to be desperately worried and upset but she'd taken the news quite calmly once she knew that Marie was all right.

On the way home Roy had said it was probably because she'd lived a long time and had seen too much of life to let a miscarriage upset her. Losing babies in her day had been commonplace and as long as her darling granddaughter was safe that was all that mattered to her. After that visit Marie had gone to see Ellen, now enormous with her second child. She had expected to feel some kind of envy or sadness when her eyes had rested on the swell of Ellen's stomach, but she had felt nothing until last week at Vicky's engagement party.

She'd been coming down the stairs at her mother's house where the party was being held when Ellen had arrived. If possible her stomach had grown twice as large. It was then that she'd made some small talk then fled to Vicky's room trying hard not to cry. Patti had found her pretending to look under the bed for something she had lost so that no one would see the tears that rained down her face. Not fooled for a moment, Patti had fled from the room in search of her mum.

267

By the time Peggy had entered the bedroom, Marie was sitting on the bed composed once again.

The sound of Roy's rumbling stomach cut into her thoughts. Placing a biscuit on his saucer, she carried the cup of tea through to the sitting room, turning up the oven as she passed.

"Morning, love," Roy said cheerfully as he placed a cup of tea on the bedside cabinet.

Marie's eyes opened slowly; always reluctant to wake up, she could never understand how Roy could be so happy first thing in the morning.

"Morning," she answered, her voice thick with sleep.

"Are you doing anything today?" he asked, more out of politeness than real interest. As his words penetrated her still groggy mind she became suddenly alert. Trying to appear normal, she replied, "No, nothing important."

The moment she heard the front door close Marie jumped out of bed and headed for the bathroom. As she washed she wondered if she should have told Roy about the pregnancy test she had had at the local health centre last week. There had been so many false alarms since she'd lost the baby, it wasn't fair to raise his hopes unnecessarily. Going back to the bedroom, she dressed carefully then looked at the alarm clock. It had just gone seven-thirty and her appointment wasn't until ten o'clock. She had a long wait ahead of her. Picking up the now cold cup of tea, she made her way downstairs.

The waiting room was crowded as usual. Marie looked around at the miserable faces, her eyes searching for and finding an empty chair. Sitting down, she waited for her name to be called. Acutely aware of the reason for her being here, she remembered a night soon after she had left the hospital. She had been sitting watching the television and no matter how she'd tried she couldn't get comfortable. An ache she couldn't describe was tormenting her, and then she had realised what it was. Like many women before, her arms felt empty, even though she had never had the chance to hold her baby.

"Mrs Ellis? Dr Casey, room four."

"Yes, thank you." Getting to her feet, she walked down the hallway, painfully aware of her heart beating wildly. She could feel a weakness in her arms and legs and prayed she wouldn't faint. Knocking once on the surgery door, she waited a moment then pushed it open.

"Ah, Mrs Ellis, good morning." Dr Casey motioned her to the chair in front of his desk. She sat down and waited for him to tell her what she wanted to hear.

"Now then, what can I do for you?"

He was smiling kindly, unaware of the controlled effort she was making to remain calm.

"I've come for the result of my pregnancy test, Doctor. I had one done last week."

"Oh, did you? I'm sorry, I didn't know. Just a minute, I'll check your notes."

She watched as he searched through her folder. She thought how impersonal health centres were. There were so many doctors here, you rarely saw the same one twice unless you specifically asked. She wished now she had had the test done at Bart's. How comforting it would be if Dr Lawson was sitting in front of her. He wouldn't have to sort through notes to tell her what she wanted to hear, he would know.

"Yes, here it is. It came in yesterday."

Marie felt sick, her head was buzzing and her heart continued to beat at an alarming rate. Dr Casey was about to speak again when he looked up and caught the full impact of longing in the woman's eyes.

"Are you all right, Mrs Ellis?"

"Yes, I'm fine. Just tell me the result, please." She had given up the pretence of calmness; even her own ears could hear the desperation in her voice.

"The result is positive. I hope you're pleased."

He watched as her eyes filled with tears, and saw the tremulous smile come to her lips.

"Yes, I'm pleased, I'm so very pleased. Thank you, Doctor."

She was standing now, eager to get home so she could phone Roy. Pausing in the doorway, she gave him another smile and then she was walking quickly down the corridor and out into the street.

Roy hurried down the street, the ambiguous telephone conversation he'd had with Marie some hours earlier running through his mind. She had been excited, saying she had something to tell him, but when he'd pressed her for details she had simply laughed and told him he would have to wait until he got home. He was standing in front of his house now, the key already in his hand. Could it be what he thought it was? It must be surely. He hadn't heard her so happy since. . . . Brushing the still painful memory away, he inserted his key in the lock. She was waiting for him in the lounge. Looking at her face, alive with happiness, he asked tentatively, "Are you?"

Nodding her head wildly, Marie answered, "Yes."

With a great whoop of delight, Roy caught her up in his arms and swung her round in a circle.

"Careful," she cried, her voice holding a touch of fear, "nothing must go wrong this time."

Setting her down gently, he looked at her glowing face and said quietly now, "You're right, nothing must go wrong this time."

"Tabby, Tabby, where are you, you stupid cat?" On her hands and knees Marie peered under the car, the sixth one she had investigated in less than ten minutes.

"You shouldn't be doing that in your condition," a woman chided her as she walked past.

Feeling foolish, Marie straightened up with difficulty, gave the woman a watery smile, and began to walk home. Tabby had become a member of the family after Marie had seen a mouse run across the kitchen floor four months previously. She didn't really like cats, but given the choice between mice and a cat, there was no contest. She had got the cat from her old friend Anne who had three, all strays.

Reaching her terraced house, the first thing she saw was Tabby sitting on the window ledge calmly cleaning herself. Grabbing the startled cat under her arm, Marie opened the front door and flung it unceremoniously into the hallway. The cat stared up at its mistress, warily wondering whether the alsatian that had sent it into flight half an hour earlier was less dangerous than the woman standing before her. Looking down at the cat, Marie felt a twinge of guilt. Awkwardly bending yet again, she scooped it up into her arms, gently stroking its furry head.

"Next time a dog scares you, you can fend for yourself," she told Tabby, who continued to stare up at her with vacant eyes.

Still stroking the furry head, Marie felt her eyes begin to close and settled herself in the armchair for a sleep. She'd been asleep for only a short while when the first pain hit her.

"It doesn't sound as if you're in labour, love," Peggy's voice came reassuringly over the line.

"But the pain's so bad, Mum. Will you come round?"

"Now, don't go getting yourself worked up. It isn't due for another three weeks yet. It's probably wind. Look, if the pain isn't any better in an hour, call an ambulance just to be on the safe side."

Her hand shaking, Marie hung up the phone.

"What did your mum say?"

Suddenly the feeling of wanting to lash out at someone swept over her as she turned on Roy.

"She said not to worry and to call an ambulance if the pain gets any worse," she repeated sarcastically, the tears already starting to fall from her eyes. Frightened at the way she was behaving, Roy came over to her, his arms going round her shoulders. The anger that had made her hit out at her mum over the years was now directed at her husband. Flinging his arms from her, she sank down onto the settee, her hands beating the cushions.

"She doesn't care," she sobbed. "If she loved me, she would have come round."

Working herself up to fever pitch, she was stopped by Roy's arms about her again, but this time there was no pushing him away. The arms that held her were tight with anger now.

"Don't ever let me hear you talk about your mum like that again. Of course she loves you. You're getting hysterical, now calm down."

The shock of seeing him so angry quietened her. Roy was usually so placid.

Realising that he was shaking her, Roy dropped his arms. Not knowing what else to say, he left her sitting quietly and went to make some tea. Quietly now, Marie sat staring into space, thinking over what she had said. Did her mum love her? If she did then Marie didn't deserve it. What right had she to expect her mum to drop everything and come running? She hadn't exactly been a loving daughter. Many a night, when unable to sleep, she'd lain awake reliving the times she'd hurt her mum by some word or action, often deliberate. And each time the memories returned she would cry herself to sleep, all the while whispering, "I didn't mean it, Mum. I'm sorry."

If only you could go back in time. Take back the hurtful words. Undo deeds done in anger and frustration. If only . . . How many times had those words been uttered? Not just by her, but by the whole human race. Since she'd married, there had been no more occasions to regret. She knew, deep down, her mum bore her no malice and had long forgiven Marie for the way she'd treated her. If only she could forgive herself.

The sound of the doorbell brought her out of her reverie.

Roy swept by her, giving her a cautious look that spoke volumes, and a familiar voice made her rise to her feet. "Here, here, what's all this then?" Peggy laughed as she went into Marie's outstretched arms.

"Pain, Mum, terrible pain."

Quickly taking control of the situation, Peggy turned to Bill who was just about to sit down.

"Don't make yourself too comfortable, we're going out again," she said sharply. Within minutes Marie was being bundled up in the back seat of her dad's car and was on her way to hospital.

The young doctor stood at the front of the bed poring over her notes. He seemed more interested in her case history than in Marie.

She'd been lying here in the uncomfortable bed for hours. Raising her hand, Marie tried to attract his attention. When this failed she shouted, "Excuse me," the tone of her voice denying the politeness of her address, "would you mind telling me what's going on, if it's not too much trouble?"

The doctor looked at her as if surprised by her presence. Putting the folder down with some reluctance, he came to her side. "We're trying to stop the labour, it's too soon for the baby to be born."

Stop the labour, Marie thought in despair. God, no. She wanted it over with now, not to be sent home and go through all this again.

Desperately she clutched at his arm. "Can't I have the baby now?" she pleaded. "Please, let me have my baby now."

Disengaging her fingers, he walked slowly away from her, looking distressed at her plight. "It's not up to me, I'm afraid. But don't worry, we know what we're doing."

Don't worry, don't worry. What futile words. If anyone else said them to her she'd scream at them.

The injection she'd been given on arrival had made her groggy and the drip attached to her arm was paining her. One doctor had come in a few minutes ago and said she was going to have to have a Caesarean. The words had brought no fear to her; she'd greeted the news with relief. Then just a minute ago another doctor had told her they'd changed their minds and were going ahead with the first plan to stop the labour.

Thoroughly frightened now, Marie lay back on the pillow wishing they'd make up their minds one way or another. Her mum and dad had long gone and Roy had gone to phone his workplace to tell them what had happened, so for the moment she was alone.

When she heard the tramp of heavy footsteps approaching her bed she kept her eyes shut tightly. She'd been messed about so much since she'd arrived she didn't think she could take any more.

"Marie?" the voice said questioningly.

The sound of his voice brought her eyes wide open.

"Dr Lawson. Oh, Doctor, I'm so glad you're here. I've been so frightened."

273

She noted that the young doctor in attendance on her had seemed to spring to attention in the older man's presence, and for a moment she was tempted to show off and call Dr Lawson by his first name, Robert; but she didn't have the nerve. The next half-hour was a blur. After hurried consultation with several other doctors she heard Dr Lawson say in a firm voice, "Expel the uterus."

And suddenly she was on a trolley and being wheeled down to the theatre. "Anything good showing tonight?" she made a brave attempt at a joke as she was wheeled through the familiar green doors. The vain effort was wasted, she knew by the blank look in the nurse's eyes. The sudden pressure on her hand brought her attention back to Roy. He was walking alongside her, looking more frightened than she was, if that were possible. There followed hours of contractions, each one relayed to her by Roy who was watching the small monitor she was connected to.

"Whoops, that was a big one," he remarked, happily enthralled at the movements on the screen. Biting back the desire to ask him if he'd like to change places, she watched his face change. The smile was gone, a look of panic in its place.

"What is it?" she croaked fearfully, her mind crying out, Not again. Please God, not again.

Then she was being disconnected from the monitor, the doctor explaining that the baby was in distress and a Caesarean was now necessary. Just before the mask was placed over her face, she held tightly onto the hand holding the mask. Her eyes looking beseechingly into the young doctor's, she asked in a strong voice "Is my baby dead?"

"Go to sleep, Mrs Ellis. Go to sleep."

Roy sat outside the operating theatre his head in his hands. If anything goes wrong this time it'll turn her mind, he told himself, fear making him feel physically sick.

The doors of the theatre were suddenly flung open and a green-gowned man came out pushing a trolley on which rested a tiny glass cubicle.

"Are you the father?"

Dumbly Roy nodded his head as he stared down at the tiny bundle of life that was his child. The infant was naked except for a minute blue hat. A feeling of emotion such as he'd never experienced before swept through his body.

"What is it? Is it all right?" he asked in a husky voice, excitement and confusion making him ask the question in reverse order.

"It's a boy. Congratulations." As the man started to wheel his son away, Roy stopped him.

"What about my wife, is she all right?"

"The doctor's with her now," came the answer. The man was impatient to get his small charge to the safety of the special care unit. "She's had complications. We're waiting for another doctor to come down to perform some bowel surgery. It's probably going to be a long wait. You'd better get some rest." Before Roy could ask any more questions, the man was gone. Forgetting about his son for the moment, he sank back down on the hard wooden seat and stared at the closed doors behind which Marie lay. What had gone wrong? Was she all right? His thoughts went back to when he'd received the phone call from Bobby when Pauline was having Kerry. How sorry he had felt for his brother-in-law that night. Now he too was waiting for news of his wife. He knew now what Bobby had gone through, and putting his head down between his knees he uttered the same words Bobby had said all those years ago.

"Please God, let her be all right."

A hand on his shoulder brought his head up sharply, then he was on his feet looking into a strange face, not one belonging to the doctors he knew.

"Your wife's fine, Mr Ellis. Just a bit of twisted colon. I've put it back in place," he smiled, delivering the good news. "Now, if you'll excuse me I'm off to have my dinner, I'm starving."

Shaking Roy's hand and congratulating him on his son, the doctor strode away whistling. Roy stared after him in disbelief. Going to have some dinner, after what he'd just done. Roy knew he had a strong stomach, but nothing compared to the cast-iron insides surgeons possessed.

Shaking his head at such trivial thoughts, his attention was once again drawn to the theatre doors as they swung open and Marie was wheeled out. Looking down at her sleeping face, he sighed with relief. She didn't know yet that she had a son. He couldn't wait to see her face when she was told. He followed the trolley down to the maternity ward where the night sister offered him a bed in the side ward, warning him he would have to get out quickly should the bed be needed. The last thought he had as he laid his head on the pillow was, I'll never be able to sleep.

Her eyes opened slowly and for a moment she couldn't remember where she was. Then the burning sensation in her stomach brought her eyes wide open.

It was the same terrible pain she'd experienced after the first operation. But the pain in her stomach was nothing compared to the anguish of her mind.

Where was her baby, why didn't somebody come?

"How do you feel, Mrs Ellis?"

The nurse was standing by her bed, a small bundle in her arms. Running her tongue round her achingly dry mouth, Marie tried to speak. Then the bundle was being put into her arms. Painfully she tried to raise herself on the pillows.

"Is it all right?" she asked, hardly daring to voice the question.

"He's fine, dear. He's a little underweight so I'll have to take him back to the special care unit soon. You hold him for ten minutes and then I'll be back to take him off you. Believe me, you'll be glad of the rest."

Left alone with her child, Marie gently pulled back the blanket to reveal a small wrinkled red face, a blue woolly hat perched on its head. As if in a dream she stared down at her son, her finger stroking his soft cheek, the smile on her lips contrasting with the tears that were raining down her face.

"Hello, Bobby," she whispered proudly.

# Chapter Twenty-Four

1983–84.

It was New Year's Eve, 1983. In just a few hours time the long awaited and much-dreaded year – George Orwell's 1984 – would be here. Only time would tell if his predictions of gloom and destruction would come true. In the Cowley household, however, Peggy's children were determined that 1984 would bring only happy memories for their mother. The secret preparations had been going on for weeks and if everything went according to plan this New Year's Eve would be one Peggy would never forget.

Peggy sat in the kitchen idly glancing through the daily paper. But her mind wasn't on the news and with an impatient "tut" she pushed the paper away from her. Reaching out to the long velvet box, she picked it up for the tenth time that day.

Opening it, she looked down at the gold watch she had been presented with the day she'd retired, just before Christmas. The watch began to mist over as tears filled her eyes. How often in the past had she longed for this day when she would no longer have to go out to work? God knew there was more than enough to keep her busy at home, but now the day had finally come she felt trapped, as if her life had come to an end.

Raising her eyes to the mirror that hung over the fridge, she examined herself in the glass. She would be sixty next month, but everyone who knew her kept reassuring her that she didn't look her age and she had to admit that with the life she'd had and the children she'd borne she had worn well. Settling back in the chair, she reflected at how quiet the house was. There had been a time when the house had never been empty, now it seemed deathly quiet. Out of her large family there were only the three boys left, although the appellation "boys" could no longer be applied to them, and Jimmy would soon be leaving to live in the flat he'd recently bought.

She hadn't been surprised when he'd told her he was leaving home. He had always been independent even as a child. Andy at twenty-six and John at twenty showed no signs of wanting to leave. There would probably come the day when she would pray they'd meet some girl and get married, but for now she was glad of their company. She still had Bill of course and Patti, her youngest daughter and, over the last few years, her best friend and companion. Of them all Patti would be the one she would miss most when the time came for her to be married.

Come on now, she told herself, Patti wasn't even engaged yet. But at twenty-one, with a figure a model would envy and a face that made men turn their heads in the street, it wouldn't be long. She'd been going steady with her brother-in-law's brother for a few years now and if they did decide to make a go of it then there would be two Mrs Deeres and she and Ellen would become sisters-in-law. That would suit them both as they'd remained close over the years.

To give herself something to do she began to make a cup of tea, all the while thinking about tonight. Bobby had invited her and Bill over to their house to see the New Year in with them and Pauline's parents, but she didn't feel like going. She jumped to her feet as the front door slammed shut.

"I'm home, wench. Where's my dinner?"

Andy burst into the kitchen his face split into a wide grin. "Had a good day on the horses, dear?" Peggy asked him, smiling now. He had become manager of a betting shop two years ago and had never been happier. Although he liked a bet occasionally, he had never become a slave to it and for that she was thankful.

"Mind your business, woman," he answered in mock anger. "Fetch my dinner into the sitting room on a tray, and if I enjoy it I may give you a few extra bob in your wages." As he walked out of the room Peggy turned to the oven and began to ready his dinner, a smile on her face. There would only be him and John for dinner tonight, and Bill of course.

Patti was going round to a friend's house straight from work and wouldn't be home till later. Ellen was coming down with the boys later on in the evening to stay with Eddie's parents for the New Year, but she'd promised to look in on New Year's Day. Vicky too had arranged to spend the night with Stuart's parents but she also had said she would come around some time over the holidays. Marie had phoned up a few hours ago and wished her and Bill a happy New Year but had made no mention of coming over. Still, she had Roy's mum and dad for the New Year so she probably wouldn't have the time.

Just for a minute Peggy looked back down the years when the whole lot of them had driven her mad fighting for the bathroom as they'd run round the house getting ready to go out to parties and dances to see the New Year in, and recalled the relief she'd felt when the door had finally banged on the last one of them to leave. Those days were gone for good now. As she felt the tears begin to form again she gave herself a mental shake. Lifting the tray from the table, she carried dinner in to her son.

"That's all the sandwiches done. I've just got to wrap them in cling film and cook the sausage rolls," Marie said as she looked down at the mountain of sandwiches she had prepared.

"Leave it, love. I'll finish it off. You go and have a lie down. It's going to be a long night," her mother-in-law said, shooing Marie out of the kitchen.

Only too pleased to go and do as she was told, she made her way upstairs. Lying down on the bed, she found she couldn't sleep, and as often happens, the more she tried, the more awake she became. Giving up all hope of getting any sleep, Marie thought forward to the evening and smiled happily.

The whole family would be at Bobby's tonight. They had planned it for months. It hadn't been easy keeping the secret from her mum, but it had been Patti who, still living at home, had been under the most strain. They hadn't even told their dad; he would have only let something slip.

Yes, Marie reflected happily, it was going to be a good night. The only time nowadays the whole family were under one roof was at weddings and funerals. The last thought caused the smile to drop from her face as she thought of her nan.

May had died six weeks after Bobby was born. She had never seen him. She'd been ill for some time and her Aunt Teresa had taken her to stay with her and her family at their home in Essex. And it was there as she sat in her favourite chair watching the wedding of Charles and Diana that she had quietly died in her sleep. Marie felt the tears prick at her eyes as she once again cursed herself for not making the effort to get down to see her to show her her great-grandson.

But how could I have known she asked herself for the hundredth time.

Vicky had been married a week later; it had been much too late to cancel it. Two days after the funeral Vicky had put on her long white dress and smiled for the cameras, forcing back her sorrow.

Four months later Uncle Tommy had died from cancer as had his father before him. Although everyone had been deeply upset at May's death, Tommy's had come as a complete shock. He'd always been so alive. Marie had never known him to sit still for longer that two minutes. Even now, two years later, she still sometimes forgot he was dead, and expected to go round her mum's and find him in the kitchen telling some tall story. Getting up from the bed, she began to pace the room. 1981 hadn't been all sorrow; she had had Bobby, so named after her brother, but also because it was Dr Lawson's name. She'd been torn between naming her son after Bobby or the doctor, and had been delighted when she'd found out that his name was Robert too.

Then there had been Vicky's wedding. True, the sadness of Nan's death had cast a shadow over the first part of the day, but towards the evening everyone enjoyed themselves, knowing it was what she would have wanted.

Going to the window, Marie looked out onto the tree-lined avenue where she now lived. She and Roy had left Walthamstow and had lived in this lovely semi-detached house for two years, a far cry from the small terraced house they'd lived in in the early days of their marriage. When she'd told her mum she was moving to Kent, Peggy had assumed that it was to be near Bobby and Pauline who lived just ten minutes away. Marie had assured her that it was just a coincidence that she'd chosen a place in Kent so near to her brother.

Looking at her watch, she decided to forgo her rest and start to get ready. She didn't have young Bobby to worry about as he was already over at Bobby's house. How Pauline managed Marie didn't know. She had her own two to look after as well as Bobby, and he was a handful on his own. Then she had to get the house ready for the party. There were banners bearing her mum's name to be hung over the mantelpiece so that she would see them as soon as she walked into the room. Pauline had made them herself, as well as preparing most of the food, which included baking the cakes as well as the fancy vol-au-vents and savoury dips.

Then there were the children to get ready. Marie felt a momentary qualm, wondering if she'd taken a liberty in sending Bobby over to her, but Pauline had suggested it and Bobby had gone willingly; he adored his Auntie Pauline. Maybe one day she would be able to give him a brother or sister. She didn't believe in only children, but although they'd tried, she hadn't been able to get pregnant again.

Brushing out her long auburn hair, she started to giggle in memory of one occasion when, determined that this would be the month, she'd had Roy going in and out like a fiddler's elbow for three weeks but she still hadn't succeeded. After that they'd both gone off sex for quite some time.

"I thought you were asleep." Marie jumped as Roy appeared in the doorway. She hadn't heard him come up the stairs.

"I couldn't sleep, and anyway I don't feel tired now."

Sitting down on the bed beside her, Roy put his arms around her and held her close. "What are you thinking about?" he asked.

Turning to him, her eyes shining with excitement, Marie answered, "I was just thinking about Mum. I can't wait to see her face tonight when she walks into Bobby's and finds us all there."

"I don't think I'll go, Bill, I don't feel very well. Would you phone Bobby and tell him?"

Bill looked at his wife with concern. It wasn't like her to miss out on a party. He wasn't all that keen on social gatherings, he'd rather stay in and watch television, but Peggy . . .

"Ah, now, come on, me dear. What'll I say to him?"

Rubbing her hand across her forehead, Peggy was about to answer when the doorbell rang.

Bill went to open the door then there was a shout of "Surprise!" as his three daughters bounded into the hallway.

Hearing their voices, Peggy forced a smile to her lips as they came into the room.

"Hello, girls," she cried, putting her arms out to them. "I didn't expect to see you tonight."

"I met them coming down Cassland Road," explained Patti looking at her sisters. Then, saying she had to get ready, she almost ran from the room, leaving Vicky and Ellen with their mother.

Taking off her coat, Ellen sat down beside her mother. "Can't stop long. I've left the boys at Eddie's mum's. He's going to pick me up here in about half an hour."

"And me, Mum," Vicky joined in. "Stuart had to pop up his friend's house so I asked him to drop me off here first."

Peggy sat beaming at her daughters, little knowing that their husbands and Ellen's sons, Kevin and Liam, were at that very moment next door in her friend's house. Joan had been let in on the secret and readily fell in with their plans. She too would be a guest at Peggy's surprise party.

"Looking forward to tonight, Mum?" asked Vicky, trying not to smile too much.

Rubbing her hand once more against her forehead, Peggy answered, "Well now, love. I was just saying to your father, I don't think I'll go. I don't feel well enough."

Unprepared for her daughters' reactions she jumped as they both yelled at her.

"*What?*"

"Ah, now, don't shout at me, girls. I'm sure Bobby will understand."

Before she knew what was happening she found herself on her feet, Vicky and Ellen on either side of her.

"You go and have a lie down, Mum," Ellen was saying. "You'll feel much better after a nap, won't she, Vicky?" she asked desperately looking to her sister for confirmation.

Picking up the cue, Vicky answered quickly, "Course you will, and you know how upset Bobby and Pauline will be if you don't go. And what about Kerry and Sarah? They're looking forward to having both their nannies and granddads over for the night."

Gabbling now, they propelled their mother up the stairs, ignoring her protests.

Patti, hearing the commotion, came out of her room.

"Mum's having a lie down, she doesn't feel well."

Panic showed in Patti's eyes as she came forward to assist her sisters. Before she knew what was happening Peggy found herself on her bed.

"Now," Ellen admonished gently, "you rest a while. You've got another couple of hours before Bobby expects you, so try and sleep for a while."

Leaving her still stunned, they left the room.

Peggy lay back against the pillows, feeling the emotion rise in her chest. The way they'd fussed round her because she was ill. They really did love her; she was lucky to have such caring daughters.

Down in the sitting room the three girls looked at each other in alarm.

"Bloody hell, that was close. What if she won't go?"

"She'll go if we have to carry her there on a stretcher. Fancy getting ill tonight. She could have waited till tomorrow."

They all laughed, but it was an uneasy laugh. Crossing their fingers, Vicky and Ellen left the house to tell Joan what had happened, and also to tell them all to keep their voices down just in case Peggy heard them through the wall next door.

Left alone in the hallway, Patti sent an anxious look upstairs.

"God, we nearly died when she said she wasn't going to go."

Ellen was sitting at Joan's kitchen table relating to her what had happened. It had been an hour since they had left their mother lying in bed and Vicky was on the phone now talking to Patti.

"Don't worry," Joan said, seemingly unconcerned. "You've been telling me the same story for an hour now. She'll go. I know your mother, she won't miss out on a party."

Ellen was still looking unsure when Vicky burst into the kitchen. "It's all right. Patti said she's still moaning about not being well but she's dressed for the party."

Ellen let out a big sigh, the relief making her feel limp. In minutes they were all creeping out of Joan's house, keeping quiet just in case Peggy took it into her head to pop into her friend's house to wish her a happy New Year. Ellen, her hand clamped over three-year-old Liam's mouth to stop him asking once again why he couldn't go to Nanny's house, marshalled her two sons into their car and only breathed again once they were off down the road heading for Kent. Behind them followed Vicky and Stuart with Joan in the back seat. Patti and Chris would be leaving later, just before Peggy and Bill set out.

"I'm off now, Mum, see you tomorrow," Patti called upstairs.

Chris was waiting for her in the hall, Andy and John behind him.

"Just a minute, love," Peggy called back down.

Anxious to be gone, Patti hopped from one foot to the other.

"Oh, are you all going to the same party?" Peggy asked, seeing her two sons standing in the hall with Patti and Chris.

"No," Patti answered quickly, "we're just giving them a lift to the pub."

Before Peggy could ask any more questions they had all gone. A frown crossed her forehead. They had seemed anxious to get out of the house, and they hadn't even wished her a happy New Year. Feeling very upset, she wandered slowly into the kitchen, the hurt she was feeling showing plainly on her face.

An hour after her sisters had left Joan's, Marie, Roy and her in-laws arrived at Bobby's house. As Roy paid the cab driver Marie was praying that her mum and dad hadn't arrived yet. The cab had been over twenty minutes late, throwing them all into a panic. She could only hope that her mum would stick to her usual procedure of arriving late wherever she went. Throwing furtive glances left and right, the four of them hurried up the dark pathway. Before she could ring the bell the door was flung open and a disappointed voice said, "You can all go back in the kitchen, it's only Marie and Roy."

Walking through the L-shaped room, Marie turned into the dining room where her family were gathered. Amidst much laughter and cracking of jokes, Marie cast an anxious eye round for her son.

"I'm sorry," Pauline said, coming out from the small kitchen, "he fell asleep. I put him in Kerry's bed."

No sooner had she uttered the words than a loud wail came from upstairs. Roy ran up quickly and found his small son sitting on the edge of the bed, his eyes filled with tears, looking utterly bewildered. Upon seeing his father, his lips curled in a tremulous smile.

Cradling him in his arms, Roy made his way back down the stairs, only to stop halfway down as Vicky called out; "They're here! Quick, everyone, hide."

Nearly falling down the last few steps, Roy rushed into the sitting room and round into the alcove. Crushing himself and young Bobby into the mêlée, he cautioned his son to be quiet and waited.

Bobby took one last look around the assembled group, then, taking a deep breath, he went to answer the front door.

"Hello, son, I didn't think I'd get here tonight. I've not been very well." Peggy's voice carried through to where her family waited with bated breath.

"I must be getting old. Ellen and Vicky came round and they were very worried. I won't stay long, I'll just sit quietly until I feel bet . . ."

Unable to keep quiet any longer, Andy burst forward, crying, "You thought you were going for a quiet drink. But tonight, Peggy Cowley, mother of nine, friend to many, and a pain in the bum, tonight, *This is your Life*!"

Taking up the cue, everyone started humming the theme tune, halfway through changing the song to a rousing "Happy Birthday."

Peggy looked in stunned amazement at the sea of faces before her. And then they engulfed her. Crowding round, hugging her, kissing her on the cheek, all the while laughing.

She could neither move nor speak. She'd seen most of them leave her house not an hour before and now here they all were. Sons, daughters, grandchildren and even a few close friends she hadn't seen for months. And there was Joan, smiling broadly, delighted with her part in the surprise. Peggy didn't know she was crying until someone handed her a tissue.

"Where's dad?" Jimmy asked, his arm in plaster from a rugby injury.

As if hearing his name had conjured him up, Bill suddenly appeared.

Looking from one to the other, he said, "Hello, what are you all doing here?" Apart from that one question he showed no surprise at finding them all under one roof. But that was their dad.

Suddenly coming alive, Peggy moved from one person to the next talking all the while, still dazed but thoroughly enjoying herself. An hour later she was screaming for mercy as her sons and sons-in-law bumped her. After only twenty bumps, they gave up and left her in an untidy heap on the floor.

"Goodness, my heart's thumping," she gasped as Bobby helped her to a chair.

"I think my back's gone," Bobby winced, bending over in exaggeration. Laughing, Peggy swung her hand at him and missed.

Leaning back in the armchair, she looked round the room. She still couldn't believe this was happening. They must have all had a hand in the organising. Well, not Andy and John or Jimmy she thought, but they had turned up, hadn't they? How many mothers could boast that their single sons had given up their New Year's Eve to be with her on her birthday? Although it wasn't her birthday till next week, they had brought it forward a bit, that was all. Now she knew why Ellen and Vicky had been so concerned about her health.

Glancing to where the big birthday cake was laid out on a side table, she thought idly, "I bet that cost a few bob." And the food. The table in the dining room was groaning under the weight of it all. She felt the pride rising in her chest. They had done all this for her. The large red banner caught her eye.

Pauline had done her proud. They had all done her proud.

Watching their mother's face, each one of them felt a different emotion, but in all of them was a feeling of happiness, happiness brought about by making someone you loved happy. Marie watched as the children crowded round her mother, each one vying for attention. This wasn't a problem for Peggy. She had had a lot of practice in showing equal affection to all. At least, she hoped she had.

Shooing the children from Peggy's lap, Marie, Ellen and Vicky dragged Peggy up to dance. Wriggling her bottom, Peggy tried to emulate her daughters' movements, her efforts causing howls of laughter. Ignoring the girls' calls, she walked into the dining room where Bill was talking to Roy's parents. Gazing round the room, she studied the faces scattered through the lounge. All of them happy, all under one roof. Times like these came rarely; she would enjoy herself tonight, and she'd never forget this New Year's Eve as long as she lived.

"Come on everyone, in a circle," Bobby was ushering them together, waiting for the sound of Big Ben to come over the radio.

Into the quiet the pips sounded and they all began the countdown. "Five, Four, Three, Two, One – Happy New Year!"

Holding hands, everyone formed a circle, Peggy and Bill in the middle. "*May Auld Lang Syne be near and never more to part, may Auld Lang Syne hold dear for the sake of Auld Lang Syne.*"

Standing in the circle, tears filling her eyes, Peggy remembered the day she'd brought John home and vowed that her family was complete.

Looking round from one face to the other, she nodded.

Her family was indeed complete.